THE BONE GARDEN

Also by Simon Beckett

THE JONAH COLLEY SERIES
The Lost

THE DAVID HUNTER SERIES
The Scent of Death
The Restless Dead
The Calling of the Grave
Whispers of the Dead
Written in Bone
The Chemistry of Death

STANDALONE THRILLERS
Stone Bruises
Where There's Smoke

THE BONE GARDEN

SIMON BECKETT

ORION

First published in Great Britain in 2026 by Orion Fiction,
an imprint of The Orion Publishing Group Ltd.
Carmelite House, 50 Victoria Embankment
London EC4Y 0DZ

An Hachette UK Company

The authorised representative in the EEA is Hachette Ireland, 8 Castlecourt Centre,
Dublin 15, D15 XTP3, Ireland (email: info@hbgi.ie)

1 3 5 7 9 10 8 6 4 2

A CIP catalogue record for this book is
available from the British Library.

ISBN (Hardback) 9781 3987 0881 5
ISBN (Export Trade Paperback) 9781 4091 9281 7
ISBN (eBook) 9781 4091 9283 1
ISBN (Audio) 9781 4091 9284 8
Printed in Great Britain by Clays.

www.orionbooks.co.uk

For Hilary

Prologue

Bone survives.

Like the bricks and mortar of an old house, it outlasts the life that once animated it. Long after the rest of the body – skin, flesh and organs, cartilage and tendon – has succumbed to time, bone persists. The scaffold on which the soft tissues are built, it can outlast them by hundreds of years. Longer, in the right conditions. Acidic soil is more likely to preserve soft tissue but dissolve bone more quickly, for instance, while alkali soil has the opposite effect, slowing the degradation of bone almost indefinitely.

But nothing lasts forever. Bone will eventually disintegrate, returning to the lifeless minerals from which it was formed. Dust will, inevitably, return to dust. Until then, left to its own slow devices, the skeleton remains, a fossilised remnant of a life long ended.

Bone survives.

He felt the twig give under his boot as he started to put his weight onto it. Stopping dead, he eased off that leg, rocking back onto his other foot. The forest was full of natural snares at this time of year, the winter's freezing winds and rains stripping the trees bare. But the season had been unusually wet, turning the ground to mud under the carpet of spruce needles and giving the fallen twigs and branches a damp elasticity.

The twig creaked but didn't snap as his foot lifted clear.

Even so, it was a close thing. He chastised himself silently, dropping his gaze to examine the ground in front. The infra-red goggles turned the night-time forest into a monochrome green landscape, alien and strange. He held his breath as he scanned through the straight tree trunks up ahead. The rain had stopped, but icy water still dripped from the branches, pattering onto his hood and jacket. *Don't have heard. Still be there.*

She was.

Partly obscured by the trunk of a spruce, his quarry stood on the bank of a stream, relaxed and oblivious. He let his breath out again, silently. The air was cold, rich with a smell of loam and the resinous scent of the trees. More carefully this time, he took another slow step, planting his foot as though he was walking on ice. A few more metres and he'd be within range. *Careful now. Careful.*

In his dark jacket and overtrousers he was all but invisible. They would have made him hard enough to see in daylight: on a moonless night like this he was just another shadow.

Providing he didn't give himself away.

He was almost in range now. Keeping his breathing slow and steady, he eased forward another few paces, pausing to check where he was putting his feet. The ground was uneven, broken with rocks and snaking tree roots beneath the carpet of fallen needles. One misstep wouldn't only ruin everything he'd done so far, it could leave him out here with a broken ankle.

After a few more slow-motion steps he stopped. The cold wind chapped his face as he stood motionless, ignoring the silver drips of water as he watched the slender form through the trees. The distance was about thirty yards, just clear of the leaning tree's trunk. Not an easy shot, but as close as he dared.

It was up to him now.

Slowly, he nocked an arrow and raised the hunting bow. Steadily pulling against the bow's resistance, he could feel the thump of his heart as he drew. His concentration shrank until nothing existed except for his prey, and the tension in the bow. This was what he loved, the final moments of potential. *Easy, now. Easy does it.*

Her head came up. Looked right at him.

He released.

There was a thrum, more felt than heard, as the arrow sped away. A cry shattered the quiet, followed by the scrambling crash of a falling body. Then he was hurrying forwards, following the path his arrow had taken moments before. It had hit home, he knew that even before he reached her. The doe had taken a few steps and was lying on her side in the stream, brown eyes wide with pain and confusion, rasping breath misting the air. The arrow protruded from her chest, buried deep and quivering. He dropped down the bank by the leaning spruce, the triumph souring as it always did. He took out his knife – wickedly sharp and serrated – to finish the job. The doe took one more spasming breath and then lay still.

Not a thing of life and beauty anymore. Just cooling meat.

His night-vision goggles turned the blood a livid green as he washed his knife in the fast-flowing stream. Behind him, the muddy bank below the leaning spruce had been eroded over time by the stream, exposing its roots. They were thick and sinuous, like a nest of snakes. Or old bones.

The thought unsettled him. But then he always felt flat after a hunt. First the high, then the low. Suddenly weary of the whole business, he straightened and made to push up the goggles to rub his tired eyes. Before he could, a sliver of moon broke through a gap in the clouds, throwing the spruce's naked roots into sharper relief.

As the shadows changed, he saw a face staring down from them.

'*Fuck!*'

He stumbled backwards, tripping over the doe's carcass. Icy water seized hold of him as he landed in the stream. Splashing to his feet, he looked at the tree roots again in a panic.

The face had gone. There was only the tangle of exposed roots in the muddy bank. Soaking wet and freezing cold, he was already doubting that he'd seen anything at all.

Then, like a picture coming into focus, he made out the face again.

'Jesus Christ . . .'

Tearing his eyes away, he dragged the doe's still-steaming carcass from the stream. Moving quickly now, he took a sling harness from his pouch and trussed the small deer in it. With effort he hoisted it on his shoulders, stumbling in his rush to get away. Even so, he couldn't help but pause to take a last look behind him.

Then, stooping under the deer's weight, he hurried back the way he came.

Chapter 1

The sheep didn't have any legs.

That was my first impression, though lack of sleep and the sleeting rain might have had something to do with it. Caught in the beam of my headlights, the animal's eyes shone eerily in the darkness of the winter storm. I stared at it through the sweep of the windscreen wipers, trying to make sense of what I was seeing. Although its body was level with the ground the animal wasn't lying down, and I could see its legs weren't folded under it. But it was still alive and, apparently, unconcerned.

Blocking the narrow road.

The journey had been bad enough even before this. It had been late afternoon when I'd left London and set out for Carlisle to advise on a missing person search in Cumbria. I'd been a police forensic consultant for long enough to be used to travelling across the country at short notice, but this time the fault was all mine. The briefing for the search operation wasn't due to start until later the following day, so there had been no need for me to rush up there. I could have waited till first thing in the morning, made the drive in full daylight and better weather. Not start out on a three-hundred-odd-mile drive on a darkening winter afternoon, with an amber storm warning looming.

But I'd opted to set off straight away. Allow plenty of time for the unfamiliar route, check into my hotel a night early so I'd be well rested for what promised to be a gruelling few days' work. At least, that's what I'd told myself. The truth was the call about the police search had come at a bad time. I'd been upset and restless even before then, knocked off-kilter by the other news I'd received that day. When I answered the phone I'd grabbed at the excuse to get away.

It was possible I hadn't thought it through as well as I might.

The weather quickly deteriorated as the grey winter daylight died. According to the calendar we weren't far away from spring, but nature was working to its own schedule. Rain beat down, shattering on the road surface and throwing up a spray that turned the outside world into a collage of blurred headlights. Towards the top end of the Lake District National Park, traffic on the motorway slowed to a near-standstill. Through the smeared glass I saw flashing blue lights announcing an accident up ahead. Dragged from my thoughts by the prospect of tragedy and twisted metal, I'd waited until the crawling traffic allowed and then taken the first available exit.

It didn't take long to realise I'd made a mistake. I'd intended to rejoin the motorway after a few miles. Instead, after following the satnav, I found myself funnelled onto a series of narrow rural roads that seemed to grow steeper and more winding with every mile. Outside the car, blackness was unbroken by any lights. The satnav's screen had dimmed to the night-time view, showing the road as a meandering line. There were no land-marks, although judging by how the road climbed and dipped I was probably somewhere in the Cumbrian Mountains. But the mountainous landscape I was driving through was hidden by darkness and the storm.

By then the rain was coming down in earnest. It looked like silver wires in my headlights, thrumming on the car roof and smearing the windscreen like oil despite the efforts of the wipers. Even worse was the wind, buffeting the car like a toy and threating to tear the wheel from my hands. I sat hunched forward in my seat, straining to see through the downpour as the road twisted and turned. My world shrank to the headlights' tunnel, gusts of horizonal rain turning the night to static in their beam. Staring into it was dangerously hypnotic. It was easy to let your concentration wander, to give in to the illusion of falling . . .

I jerked my eyes open. *Snap out of it.* I sat up straighter, willing myself awake, but the strain of driving in those conditions was beginning to tell. Reluctantly, I was forced to accept what had been obvious for some time: there was no way I was going to make it to Carlisle that night. Not in a storm like this.

I needed to take a break but there was nowhere to pull over. The road was hemmed in by steep banks and wind-twisted trees. Resolving to stop at the first village or pub I came to, I glanced at the car's inbuilt satnav.

The display was blank.

No, don't do this . . . Trying to keep my eyes on the road, I stabbed one-handed at the satnav controls. Nothing happened. The screen was illuminated but apart from the arrow-shaped cursor of my car there was nothing on it. Not even the road. There was nothing to indicate where I might be.

I'd heard of a phenomenon called 'rain-fade', where atmospheric conditions were so bad they blocked satellite signals. Including the GPS used by navigation systems. But I'd never actually experienced it before.

Congratulations. Now you have.

My phone was in a handsfree cradle on the dashboard, but I knew before I looked that it wouldn't be any use. I was in a remote area celebrated for its mountains and wildness. It would be a miracle if there was mobile coverage, and a quick look at the screen confirmed the lack of signal bars. I felt an acid burn of frustration. I'd been meaning to upgrade my phone for a new model with a satellite capability for weeks, but not got around to it. *Too late now.* Even the road atlas I kept in the car boot wasn't much good until I had some idea of where I was. As I fought against another gust of wind, I couldn't deny it any longer.

I was lost.

The road had been climbing for some time, snaking along the side of either a steep hill or a mountain. Now it began to level out. In the rain-splintered beam of my headlights, I could see how the ground sloped above me to one side and fell vertiginously away on the other. There was nowhere to pull over, and the road was too narrow to stop without blocking it. I couldn't imagine anyone else being stupid enough to be out in this, but with visibility down to a few yards I daren't risk something driving into me. Not with a steep drop at one side.

The road had begun to descend, falling away in the headlights' beam. I'd slowed as they showed a torrent of muddy water running across the tarmac. It was coming down a gorge in the mountainside above, turning a broad stretch of road into a stream before tumbling off the other side. It looked as though a culvert under the road had either blocked or been overwhelmed by the sheer volume of water. I'd slowed even more. I'd got my car stuck in running water once before and was in no rush to repeat the experience.

But although the run-off covered a wide swathe of road, it didn't look very deep. Offering up a silent prayer, I'd rolled the car into it. There was a sideways shove as the water pushed against the wheels, and the car jolted as it bumped across stones and debris washed down from the hillside.

Then I was through. With a sigh of relief, I'd begun to relax. Dead ahead was a blind bend, where the road disappeared behind a rain-darkened shoulder of rock. I'd rounded it, and immediately stamped on the brakes as my headlights picked out something large and pale in the road. There was a weightless moment as the tyres aquaplaned, sliding frictionlessly towards the drop on one side. For a heart-stopping moment I thought I was going over, then the brakes bit and the car jerked to a halt.

I sat there, heart thumping, my hands still clenched on the steering wheel as the rain beat down on the car roof.

The legless sheep stared back at me.

It took me a second or two to realise what I was looking at. A laugh burst from me, part incredulous, part relief. *Oh, you're joking . . .* The sheep wasn't legless.

It was stuck in a cattle grid.

I knuckled my eyes, knowing what I was going to have to do. The sheep couldn't free itself, and I couldn't just leave it there. Even if I'd wanted to, there wasn't enough space to drive around. With another sigh, I unbuckled my seatbelt and reached for my waterproof coat from the back seat. As I did something slipped from the inside pocket into the footwell. I felt a gut-punch when I saw the pale rectangle of the envelope, my name neatly formed in familiar handwriting.

Retrieving it, I put it back in my pocket and climbed out of the car.

A frigid blast of rain hammered at me, threatening to pull the door from my grip. Slamming it shut, I pulled up my hood and hurried over to the cattle grid. In the headlights' twin beams, I saw that all four of the sheep's legs had slotted neatly through the gaps between the metal bars. I couldn't see any blood and the sheep didn't appear to be injured. Or especially bothered by its predicament, come to that.

Blinking against the rain, I looked around, hoping to see the lights of a nearby farm.

But the night remained dark and empty. Rain pounded against my back as I bent over the sheep, trying to ignore the smell as I wrapped my arms around it. Its fleece was matted and water-logged, making the animal even heavier as I started to lift. Who knew sheep were so heavy, I thought. Or pungent.

The animal didn't help itself or me, bucking and kicking as its legs came free. Staggering under its weight, I carried it clear of the grid before setting it down. The sheep shook itself, spraying water over me, then trotted off without a backwards glance. Massaging the muscles in the small of my back, I watched as it vanished into the blackness beyond the car's headlights.

You're welcome.

I was turning back to my car when suddenly the entire sky lit up, as though there'd been a soundless explosion beyond the horizon. As the sheet lightning flickered in eerie silence, I had my first glimpse of the sweeping, mountainous panorama I'd become lost in. The road was on the side of a steep hillside, or fell, part of a valley hemmed in by a range of blunt, hulking peaks. Snow-tipped and barren, they loomed over the skyline, their lower slopes covered with dense forest. The sight of them was startling, like a flashbulb revealing figures in a dark room.

Then the lightning died, and as though a curtain had dropped darkness fell again.

9

I hurried back to my car, grateful for its warmth as I shucked out of my wet coat. Almost straight away the moisture caused the windows to steam up, turning the cabin into a cocoon and making it even harder to see out. I turned up the aircon to clear it, the roar competing with the drumming of rain on the roof as the road continued to wind downhill. At first my headlights showed only barren, rocky slopes, but after a few minutes the landscape changed as the road entered a forest. Tall, straight conifers — probably fir or spruce, it was hard to tell in the dark — rose up on both sides like giant Christmas trees. They looked near identical, crammed so close together it was like driving through a tunnel. It was obviously a plantation rather than natural woodland, and a little further along I came to what looked like a lumber yard. The trees at one side were replaced by a high metal fence, behind which were shadowy portacabins and industrial-looking vehicles. Then I was past it and the forest closed in once more.

Still, the sight had raised my hopes. It was the first building I'd seen in miles, and where there was one there might be more. As though to confirm it, the forest abruptly ended and through the windscreen I saw a sprinkling of fireflies in the darkness ahead.

A village.

Thank you, God . . . The fireflies resolved into streetlights. Now there were stone-built cottages and bungalows as well, the glows from their curtained windows warm and reassuring. A little further along I came to a tiny village square. At one end was a lone, unlit shop, and at the other a larger, stone building with a sign swinging above its doorway.

A pub.

Pulling up outside, I switched off the engine and sat there, letting the tension ebb from my muscles as rain beat against the car. An overhead light shone on the pub sign, casting crazed shadows as it swung wildly in the wind. Its weathered paintwork showed a crossed lump hammer and chisel above stylised lettering.

The Perseverance.

The pub's doors were shut but light leaked out around the drawn curtains in the frosted glass windows, engraved with the names of long-forgotten beers. It looked open, so at the very least I could find out where I was. Even if the pub didn't have rooms, a village would be better to spend the night in my car than a mountain road. Finally, I thought, reaching for my coat and laptop from the back seat and hurrying from the car, finally my luck had changed.

Chapter 2

The pub sign squealed above me as it see-sawed back and forth on its chains. The heavy wooden door resisted when I tried to open it, then yielded. I half-stumbled inside, chased by a frigid blast of rain. After the cold night outside, the pub was almost cloying warm. A smell of stale beer overlaid the smoke of an open fire. As I forced the door shut against the wind, I was also aware of something else.

The silence.

Dripping water onto the stone-flagged floor, I put my hood back and turned around. Faces were turned towards me from the half-a-dozen occupied tables in the low-ceilinged room. A small group of teenagers sat at one, barely old enough to be legally in there by the look of them, while at another a pair of domino players had broken off their game. A big, heavily built man was playing a solo game of darts, gut straining his work shirt as he stood with one arm raised ready to throw. An open fire burnt in a hearth, crackling and giving off a resinous scent. On the wall above hung a pair of cracked leather boxing gloves and framed black-and-white boxing photographs.

Next to the fire, a gaunt old man sat at a large table with an elfin, sharp-faced woman and fraught-looking man in their forties who had the indefinable air of a married couple. A straight-stemmed pipe was clamped in the old man's mouth in defiance of no-smoking laws, and a handful of birthday cards cheerily proclaiming '90' were stood up on the table. He looked every day of it, the worn tweed jacket hanging loose on what must once have been an impressively large frame, and the harsh bones of his face jutting through the parchment-like skin. But despite his frailty, the lantern-jaw clenched on the pipe was uncompromising, and the eyes that glowered at me from under the bristling grey eyebrows were hard and unforgiving.

At the old man's feet, two large, bristly dogs lifted their heads to stare at me.

A comfortably blousy woman was serving behind the bar. She gave me a friendly enough smile, but there was a wariness about her as she took in the mud stains on my coat left by the sheep.

'You looked soaked, love. What can I get you?'

The big man playing darts smirked. 'A clean coat for a start.'

He looked somewhere in his fifties, unkempt and unshaven with a big, bulky frame running to fat. Conscious of the smell from my coat, I answered the woman.

'Coffee, please, if you have it.'

'Sorry, we don't do hot drinks.'

'Just an orange juice, then.' I'd have liked something stronger, but I didn't know yet how much further I'd be driving. 'Do you serve food?'

'Only snacks. Crisps, nuts or pork scratchings.' She took a carton of orange juice from a cooler and reached for a glass. 'You don't sound local. Come far?'

'London. I'm on my way to Carlisle.'

'*Carlisle*?' She stopped to stare at me. 'You're miles out of your way. Get lost, did you? You must have to end up here.'

'My satnav stopped working.' I hesitated. 'At the risk of sounding like an idiot, can you tell me whereabouts this is?'

The thump of a dart striking the board was followed by a barking laugh from the big darts player. 'Fuck me. They must have let him out for the day.'

'You're in Edendale,' the woman behind the bar told me, as though the interruption hadn't happened. 'We're at the top end of the Cumbrian Mountains, and I can tell you now you won't find us on your satnav. Stupid things, if you ask me.'

I'd strayed even further off course than I'd thought. 'How far is it to Carlisle?'

'Oh, thirty miles or so, back the way you came. But on a night like this—'

She broke off as the lights dimmed, then went out. A groan went up, becoming a muted, ironic cheer as they flickered back on.

'Bloody storms,' the woman muttered, then remembered herself and smiled. 'Don't worry, you get used to it out here. What was I saying?'

'Getting to Carlisle.'

'Right. Well, it's a bit of a palaver at the best of times. The road goes through the mountains, and it can be tricky if you don't know it. I wouldn't want to chance it in this weather, not unless I had to.'

Fantastic. 'Where does the road go to after this?'

'It doesn't.'

'Sorry?'

'It doesn't go anywhere. Carries on for a couple of miles and then stops.' She folded her arms. 'There's only one way in or out, and you've just come in on it.'

As that sank in, someone else came to the bar. It was the fraught-looking man who'd been sitting with the woman and old man.

'Another round, please, Stella. When you're ready,' he added with an apologetic smile.

Up close he looked older than I'd first thought, probably fifties rather than forties. He had a round, pleasant face, smooth and unlined except for a deeply corrugated forehead that gave him an anxious, harassed expression even when he was smiling.

'It's OK, I'm not in a rush,' I said. I'd still got to decide what I was going to do now.

'Thanks, that's very . . .' He managed to make eye contact for a second or two before ducking his head and turning back to the woman. 'Uh, pint of stout for Wynn, tonic for Evie and I'll have . . . oh, just a half, please. Thanks, Stella.'

A pint glass thumped down onto the bar as the big darts player came and joined us. He had a brash, domineering presence, with

15

a barrel-like gut and grey-stubbled jowls. He gave off a sharp tang of oil and old sweat.

'Another pint, Stella.'

'Wait your turn, I'm serving.'

He draped a beefy arm around the smaller man on his other side. 'That's all right, Eddie's buying. Aren't you Eddie?'

The smaller man managed a smile, but it seemed more like a defensive reflex. 'Oh . . . yeah, course. Pint for Vic as well, please.'

'Good lad.' The big darts player tightened the arm around his neck, almost pulling him off his feet before letting go. 'I'll have a bag of cheese and onion, as well, Stell.'

'Course you will,' she muttered, turning away. Across the room, the woman I took to be the smaller man's wife stared across at the bigger man, her mouth set in a hard line.

'Is there a hotel or something nearby? A B&B, anything?' I asked as the barmaid began to pull stout into a pint glass.

She turned down the corners of her mouth. 'Not round here. There used to be, but we're not exactly geared up for tourists anymore.'

'Stella's not married. She'll put you up if you ask nicely, won't you, Stell?' the big darts player leered. 'There's only one bed, though, so you'll have to share.'

He guffawed at his own joke. No one else laughed, except one of the teenagers sitting nearby.

'You watch your lip, Vic, or the next pint's going on your head.' The barmaid gave him a glare before turning to me. 'I'm not supposed to, but if you like I can rustle up a sandwich and pop the kettle on. You look as though you need it.'

'I wouldn't mind a sandwich myself,' the big man said, one hand rubbing his ponderous gut.

'I didn't ask you. And you're fat enough.' Setting the glass of stout down, she raised an eyebrow at me. 'Cheese all right? I hope so, because it's all we've got.'

'Thanks, that would be great,' I said. I indicated the stains on my coat. 'Do you have something I can wipe myself down with? I, uh, had to help a sheep out of a cattle grid.'

The big darts player smirked. 'That's your excuse is it?'

He elbowed the smaller man, whose smile now resembled a grimace. The barmaid sighed wearily.

'Oh, give it a rest, Vic.' She handed me a holed dishcloth from a sink behind the bar. 'There are paper towels in the gents. You can throw the cloth in the bin when you're done.'

The toilet was unheated and spartan, but scrupulously clean. I sponged off as much of the muck from my coat as I could, then dried myself on paper towels before going back out. Muted conversations had started up again, but the crackle of the fire was still the loudest sound in the room. The big man was back at the dartboard, front foot well over the line marked on the floor as he sighted for his throw. The sharp-faced woman who'd been sitting with the old man had gone over to the table of teenagers. She cut a slight, diminutive figure as she stood over the youth who'd laughed at the big man's joke. He wasn't laughing now. He sat hunched and resentful, his friends looking on uncomfortably as the woman berated him in a low but scathing voice.

'. . .with your granddad on his birthday, not sat over here with your mates—'

'But Aunt Evie—'

'Don't argue or I'll—'

She broke off as I went past. The teenager gave me a sullen stare. He shared the same sharp features as the woman, although by some trick of genetics what looked elfin on her seemed sly and feral on him. The woman waited until I'd gone past before continuing, dropping her voice so I couldn't hear what was being said. But it must have worked. The teenager's chair scraped back as he truculently stood up and went to the old man's table, flopping down into a chair with bad grace.

Going to an unoccupied table, I draped my wet coat over a chair to dry, then took my laptop from its case and opened it. I was intending to take another look at the file I'd been sent containing information about the police search operation in Carlisle, but I didn't get the chance. The laptop had barely

17

started up when the big darts player swaggered over and pulled out the chair opposite me.

My heart sank as he thumped down onto it, meaty legs splayed and beer gut thrust out in front of him. The pint glass looked small in his calloused hand.

'What's this for? Bit of secretarial work?' he asked, nodding down at the laptop with a wolfish grin. 'You won't get Wi-Fi in here, pal. No phone signal either.'

'That's OK.'

I wasn't planning on going online anyway. The work I did was too sensitive to trust to an open network. I waited with my laptop open, hoping the big man would take the hint. He settled further back in his seat.

'I was just kidding about the sheep. Got to have a laugh, haven't you?' His grin didn't reach the small eyes. 'I heard you say you're from London. Ever met the King?'

'Once or twice.' I felt a petty satisfaction as the smirk fell from his face. 'Just kidding.'

'Good one.' His smile was back but meaner now, and I regretted my jibe. He hitched his chair closer to me, so our legs were almost touching. 'So why're you going to Carlisle?'

Trying not to sigh, I closed my laptop. 'Work.'

'What d'you do? Let me guess. You're a poet. No, a vet. That's why you like sheep.'

'I'm a doctor.'

It was true, as far as it went. I'd originally trained as a medic and, during a dark period of my life, even worked as a GP. My new friend took another drink as he regarded me, rolling the beer around his mouth before swallowing noisily.

'A doctor.' He sounded disappointed, as though he'd hoped for better material. 'Bet you need a lot of qualifications for that.'

'A few.'

'Didn't stop you getting lost, though, did they?' His grin put me in mind of a dog wagging its tail while baring its teeth. 'Only qualification I've got is a driving licence. You see the spruce plantation when you came in? All them big pointy fucking trees?

18

That's where I work. Used to cut the bastards down, but now I get to drive them. Fucking tree taxi driver, that's me.'

He threw his head back and gave a laugh, spraying me with spittle and beer breath. The pub had fallen silent again. At the table by the fire, I saw the old man staring across at us stonily, the hard bones of his face as implacable as an Easter Island carving. Other people cast nervous glances at him, but the big man was too preoccupied to notice.

'You like trees?' he asked, leaning forwards. His face was flushed with alcohol, and there was a look about him that made me think it wouldn't matter what answer I gave.

'I suppose so.'

'You'll love it here, then. It might be the arse end of nowhere, but if there's one thing we've got plenty of, it's fucking trees. Want to hear a joke? You know why the road stops here? Because when God made Eden he—'

'*Don't blaspheme!*'

The old man's voice thundered out, a gravelly bellow that belied his frailty. It was as though an electric shock ran through the room. The big man's eyes widened, his mouth working as though he'd been slapped.

'Sorry, Wynn, I wasn't—'

'I'll not have God's name taken in vain! Not in my pub!'

Beside him, the elfin woman rested a hand on his arm. 'It's all right, Dad, don't get—'

'Don't tell me what to do!' he snarled, twitching his arm free.

His daughter's mouth compressed, but she moved her hand away. Beside her, the small man called Eddie, who I guessed was her husband, looked as though he were trying to make himself even smaller. No one said a word as the old man glared across at the big man.

'This is God's own country!' He levelled the pipestem, stabbing with it for emphasis. 'You hear me? God's own country!'

'I know, I wasn't . . .' The big man's jowls wobbled as he nodded. 'You're right, Wynn. God's own country.'

The room had fallen silent when I'd arrived, but there was a new tension to it now. Only the teenager who'd been summoned

19

to their table seemed immune. He sat, eyes glinting with manic glee as he tried to hide a smirk behind his glass.

Then the door behind the bar opened and the spell was broken.

A tall, shaven-headed man came out, wiping his hands on a dirty towel. Although he must have been in his late fifties he had the look of a boxer about him, with a raw, powerful build and a nose that had been broken and badly reset at some point, giving his face an asymmetrical tilt. The resemblance to the old man was unmistakable. They could have been cast from the same mould, wide-shouldered and strong-boned, with features that seemed naturally disposed to a dour scowl. They had to be father and son, yet despite the newcomer's imposing physical presence, he still lacked the older man's aura of authority. It was like looking at two renditions of the same person, one the original, the other an imperfect copy.

'I've stopped the worst of the leak, but water's still getting in through the grate,' he said, casting the towel down behind the bar. Even his voice was a less harsh version of the older man's growl. 'I'll have another look tomorrow, but . . .'

He broke off, picking up on the atmosphere. He looked around, his gaze resting on me for a moment, passing over Eddie as though he wasn't there before moving on.

'What's going on?'

'Vic was just telling us all a joke,' the old man's daughter told him. 'Weren't you, Vic?'

The big man's face was heavily flushed, though I didn't think it was just from alcohol anymore. 'Just messing about, Alun. You know me.'

The look the shaven-headed man gave him suggested he did. He turned to the barmaid, who was watching uneasily from behind the counter.

'Do you want me to take over?'

She gave him a smile. 'No, there's no need. You go and sit with your family.'

'You sure?' He didn't sound too thrilled at the prospect.

'Yeah, I was just about to make a sandwich for this gentleman.' She nodded towards me. 'I can make more if your dad fancies a snack.'

'Don't bother,' the old man rasped, clamping the pipe in his mouth again. 'I'm going up.'

Reaching for two walking sticks that were leaning against the table, he painfully began to lever himself from the chair. His daughter made as though to help him. 'Here, let me—'

'I can manage. I'm not an invalid.'

'I was only—'

'I said I can manage!'

Mouth tightening, she sat back, making no further attempt to help as the old man struggled to his feet. The two dogs got up as well, yawning and stretching. They were lurchers, hunting dogs that resembled bristly greyhounds. Their claws clicked on the stone slabs as they followed the old man out. There was a murmured chorus of respectful goodnights from the room as he left.

As the door closed behind him, his teenage grandson began to sing under his breath.

'*Happy birthday to you, Happy birthday to—*'

'Don't start,' the shaven-headed man snapped.

'Come on, Dad, I was only—'

'I won't tell you again.'

The teenager subsided but a sly grin remained on his face. As conversations resumed, the big man scraped back his chair and stood up. Giving me a last filthy look he went to a table where a group of men were playing dominoes. I thought about trying to work on my laptop but decided against it. Instead, I put it back in its case, ready to leave quickly if I needed to. No one else bothered me, but I was still relieved when the barmaid re-emerged, carrying a steaming mug of coffee and a plate of neatly cut sandwiches.

'Hope you like ploughman's pickle,' she said, setting them down.

The storm had grown worse by the time I went back outside. The rain had turned to sleet, while above me the pub sign was swinging so violently on its chains it threatened to tear loose. A flicker of sheet lightning brightened the sky above the streetlights as I ran to my car. I felt better for the sandwich and hot drink, but I wanted to put a little distance between myself and the pub before I found a place to park overnight. The big darts player had a mean look about him that wouldn't be helped by more beer. I'd sleep better once I'd found somewhere less public.

As I pressed the key fob to unlock the car, a shout came from behind me.

'Hold up!'

My stomach knotted when I recognised the burly figure hurrying towards me from the pub. The big man had pulled on a yellow high-vis jacket, his flushed face beaded with rain inside its hood.

'Pisser of a night, eh?' Wiping water from his face, he gave me an ingratiating grin. 'I was thinking about you needing somewhere to stay. There's a place not far away.'

I didn't trust his sudden concern. 'I didn't think there was anywhere round here?'

'Yeah, well, between you and me Stella's not a fan of the owners. That's probably why she didn't mention it. She can be a bit funny sometimes, you know how women get at that age. Probably going through the change.'

As though that were explanation enough, he turned to point down the road.

'Carry on out of the village, go straight on at the crossroads and then follow the road up the fell. It gets a bit narrow but after half-mile or so you'll come to a turn-off for a hotel. You can't miss it.'

I looked where he'd pointed. Beyond the last of the village lights there was only darkness. 'I thought the road didn't go anywhere?'

'It doesn't, except the hotel. That's as far as you can go. End of the line.' Water dripped from his stubble as he gave a wolfish smile. 'Be sure to tell them Vic sent you.'

He could barely keep a straight face as he hurried back to the pub. I watched him go, trying to decide if he really was as bad a liar as he seemed. It was obviously a trick of some sort. I didn't believe for a moment there was a hotel where he'd said, but I'd

22

been planning to find somewhere to park up anyway. Even if he was sending me on a wild goose chase, a quiet, dead-end road was as good a place to spend the night as any.

My wipers worked to clear the sleet from the windscreen as I drove through the village. There didn't seem much more to it. The streetlights ended a little further along, and after that I was driving through darkness again. I passed the warmly lit windows of a handful more houses, then I'd left the village behind. I came to a small crossroads and carried straight on as the road began to climb. Before long it had narrowed to an overgrown single track, twigs and dead stems of undergrowth whispering along the side of the car. I winced as something scraped along the paintwork with a noise like nails on a chalkboard. I got the joke now. I hadn't expected there to be any hotel up here, but the punchline was there wasn't anywhere to turn around either. And the single track road was much too narrow to reverse down in the dark, not without getting stuck.

I'd no choice but to keep going.

Angry with myself for falling for such a childish prank, I leant forward to peer into the driving sleet, expecting the overgrown road to end or become so choked I couldn't go any further. I was beginning to wonder if I should just stop and wait for daylight when my headlights fell on something up ahead.

Half-hidden by trees were two leaning stone gateposts. They stood either side of an unlit driveway that gaped between them like a dark mouth. Fixed to one of them was an old sign.

Hillside House Hotel & Spa.

I slowed the car to a stop. The big man hadn't been lying, not exactly. There was a hotel out here.

It just wasn't open.

Very funny. Hilarious. I swore softly, adding this to the long list of bad decisions I'd made that day. Still, it might provide a better place to park overnight than out on the road. If nothing else I might be able to turn the car around.

Edging the car forwards, I drove through the gates and onto the driveway. The headlights showed tall, dripping bushes with fat leathery leaves, either laurels or rhododendrons. They crowded

23

on either side, restricting my view as I drove down the steep driveway. It seemed to go on forever, winding through the bushes until they suddenly fell away, and my headlights showed a large building up ahead. No lights burnt in its windows and the huge timber door, set in an ornately carved portico, looked as though it had forgotten how to open. Turned black by the sleeting rain, the high stone walls were turreted and topped with spires, giving it the look of an imitation Scottish castle.

An empty one.

My tyres crunched on the broken tarmac as I pulled up outside. I'd been hoping for hot food and a warm bed. Instead, I was going to spend a cold night outside an abandoned hotel in the middle of nowhere. Not an ideal way to prepare for what promised to be a demanding day tomorrow. Switching off the engine, I sat in the dark after my headlights went out, trying to summon enough energy to reach into the back for my laptop.

Suddenly, a dazzling light shattered the darkness outside.

My first thought was that it was lightning, but it didn't flicker or die. It remained steady, bleaching out the shadows from the front of the hotel. Not lightning I realised.

Floodlights.

Something *banged* on the car window, and I jumped as I saw someone standing outside. It was a man, his approach masked by the storm. His face was hidden by the hood of a parka, but that wasn't why I froze.

Pointing at me through the car window was a shotgun.

Chapter 3

Water ran down the barrels and dripped from the twin black holes. The shotgun wasn't pointing directly at me, but it was being held in such a way that it soon could be. I looked from the barrels to the man holding it. Hidden by the hood of his black parka, all I could see of his face was a firm mouth set in a thick beard. He made a winding gesture for me to lower the car window. The sleet-smeared glass was scant protection from a shotgun, but I was still loath to open it.

I didn't have much choice, though. The window slid down with a whine, letting a shock of cold wind and rain into the warm cabin. I stopped it partway, still looking at the man standing outside. A pair of hostile eyes regarded me from inside the hood. They were strikingly pale above the dark beard, like a husky's.

'What are you doing here?'

I tried to sound as though this was a normal conversation. 'Looking for somewhere to stay. I was told there was a hotel here.'

'Bullshit. Who told you that?'

'Someone at the pub. Obviously their idea of a joke, so I'm sorry for disturbing you.'

I started to close the window, but he took a step forward.

'Hold on, I'm not done.'

The movement brought up the shotgun. It might have been unintentional but I stopped closing the window. I gave myself a moment, then looked from the gun barrels back to him.

'You need to point that somewhere else.'

I was surprised how calm my voice sounded. He glanced down at the shotgun as though he hadn't realised what he was doing. After a beat he lowered it.

'You still haven't told me—'

'Jon?'

A woman was hurrying across the broken tarmac towards us. She wore a parka as well, holding it closed in front of her against the driving sleet.

'What's going on?' she demanded.

Her voice had the flattened vowels of Lancashire. She was tall and dark skinned, her face set in hard, unforgiving planes as she confronted him.

'I'm trying to find out what he's doing here.' The man tried to sound assertive but there was a defensive undertone.

'Oh, for God's sake, Jon!' She gestured angrily at the shotgun. 'And what are you doing with that bloody thing?'

'It's not loaded,' he muttered, pointing it at the floor.

'*He* doesn't know that, does he?' She turned back to me. 'I am *so* sorry. You'll have to excuse my husband. We've been having trouble with poachers so we're a bit . . . security conscious.'

A bit? Whatever trouble they'd been having, I just wanted to end the conversation and get out of there.

'I'm sorry for disturbing you. I didn't realise the hotel was closed,' I told her. 'Someone at the pub said I could find a room for the night here.'

'Bullshit,' the man repeated.

'He was called Vic,' I went on, talking to his wife. 'A big man in his fifties. He said to tell you he'd sent me.'

The two of them exchanged a look.

'Fucking Hooley,' the man said. 'Jesus, one of these days—'

'Jon!'

His wife's tone silenced him, but his expression was still murderous. *OK* . . . I drew a breath as sleet peppered my face through the open window.

'Well, I better go. Sorry again for disturbing you.'

26

'No, wait,' the woman said quickly as I reached for the window control. Water dripped from her hood like a beaded curtain. 'Where are you heading?'

'Carlisle.'

'That's too far to be driving tonight.' She paused to push back a strand of black hair that the sleet had plastered to her cheek. 'Look, this isn't a hotel anymore, but there's plenty of spare rooms—'

'Whoa, hang on!' her husband interrupted.

'We can put you up for the night,' she went on, as though he hadn't spoken. 'It's no trouble.'

'Thanks, but I'll be OK.'

She frowned out at the sleet. 'I'd feel better if you did. It's really not safe to be driving in this.'

'You heard the man, he doesn't want to stay,' her husband said.

'Can you blame him?' she shot back, then turned to me again. 'Please. It's the least we can do.'

I started to decline. Her husband was right: storm or not, I'd rather take my chances on the road. But before I could get the words out lightning bloomed in the sky above us. It was forked rather than sheet, bright enough to cut through the floodlights. They dimmed and flickered as an ear-splitting *crack* split the night, loud enough to feel even in my car.

'That'll have woken Kiran,' the woman said anxiously, looking back towards the dark hotel. She turned to me again. 'Sorry, but we've got a baby asleep inside. If he wakes up and we're not there it'll be a horror show. Tell him he needs to stay, Jon.'

'What? Nisha, wait . . .'

But she was already running back towards the hotel, disappearing into the blackness beyond the floodlights. He stared after her, the shotgun dangling like a forgotten prop, then sighed.

'Look . . .' He seemed to struggle for words, then gave up. 'She's right, you should stay. It's not a fit night to drive.'

'Thanks, but it's OK.'

'Up to you.' He'd started walking away now himself. Hunched against the sleet, he shouted back over his shoulder. 'If you change your mind, just follow the path round the back.'

I wound the window up as he vanished into the darkness after his wife. *Well, that was different.* But whatever relief I felt was already dissipating, replaced by uncertainty. And a degree of incredulity, I admitted. If I'd heard about anyone else even considering the offer of a room from a stranger who'd just threatened them with a shotgun, I'd have thought they were mad. I'd witnessed first-hand what could happen when someone thought death and violence only happened to other people.

Yet oddly I didn't feel any threat. The shock of staring into the barrels of a shotgun seemed remote now, defused by a single sentence.

We've got a baby inside.

Irrationally or not, I found that reassuring. If the couple had wanted to do me harm they'd had ample opportunity. And when it came down to it, which was the most reckless? Accepting hospitality from strangers, or driving any further in these conditions, tired and lost?

The floodlights abruptly went out, plunging everything outside the car into blackness. The couple had either given up on me or else the lights were on a timer. Whichever it was, I couldn't sit there all night. As though to help me decide, the sky flashed again with lightning, followed a second later by another bellow of thunder. Sitting there, I thought about the crumpled letter that had fallen from my pocket, and suddenly the decision was made.

Grabbing my laptop case and coat from the passenger seat, I hurried out into the storm.

My office chair creaked as I leaned back, regarding the photographs on my laptop. A cooling mug of coffee stood on my desk, not so much forgotten as unwanted. The images on the screen were graphic. They showed decomposed human remains lying in a ditch, taken from different angles. The victim's identity was unknown, as was their age, gender and ancestry. The body was in a state of putrefaction, bloated by gases produced as bacteria and digestive fluids broke down its cells and tissues. The skin was darkened to a caramel colour that didn't necessarily signify its pigment when alive. It had begun to slough off like discarded wrapping paper, while blowfly pupae – maggots – seethed over openings both natural and unnatural like spilt rice.

I'd been sent the photographs, along with post-mortem and other results, by a former colleague. The physical evidence of the body's condition appeared to contradict the lab tests, leading to a dispute over how long the victim had been dead. Knowing I'd been involved in similar cases, I'd been approached for a second opinion.

It was the sort of problem that normally engaged my interest. As a forensic anthropologist, my main field of expertise was skeletal human remains. But early in my career that had broadened to trying to understand the larger metamorphoses that comes when life ends; the physical processes by which a once-breathing individual, capable of love and imagination, becomes a calcified relic. Ordinarily I'd have welcomed an opportunity to untangle such a convoluted case.

Not today.

The news I'd received the day before was still too fresh. It had been waiting for me when I'd arrived home from the university, lying among the junk mail and circulars on the tiled floor of my Camden flat. I'd smiled when I recognised the handwriting, even though I was puzzled why she'd send a letter rather than an email or phone call.

I'd understood when I'd read it.

I'd hardly slept that night. When I'd gone into the forensic department that morning I'd tried to put thoughts of the letter aside. But my mind kept pulling towards it, even as I tried to focus on the grisly images on my laptop screen.

When the phone rang the caller's number wasn't one I knew. Still, I was glad of the distraction as I snatched it up to answer.

'David Hunter.'

The voice at the other end was a woman's. 'Apologies for calling out of the blue, Dr Hunter. I'm Detective Sergeant Chaudry, Cumbria Police. This a good time for a chat?'

I said it was.

'We're carrying out a search for the body of a missing teenager,' Chaudry told me. 'Sixteen-year-old lad from Carlisle, been missing for six months. Run off a few times before so no one was unduly

worried. But we've received a tip-off that he died from an overdose, and the dealer buried the body on an abandoned industrial estate on the outskirts of Carlisle. We need a forensic anthropologist to assist with the op, and you came highly recommended.'

I almost said yes there and then, but practicality won. Cumbria was a long way from London. 'Isn't there someone nearer your neck of the woods who can do it?'

When I'd started out forensic anthropologists had still been something of a rarity. I'd been asked to work on enquiries from across the UK, but in recent years the influx of newcomers into my profession meant it was generally the nearest who got the call. Although reputation still helped.

'Not at this short notice,' Chaudry said. 'And DCI Perry, the SIO, has worked on an enquiry with you before. In the Grampian Mountains, before she transferred down here? She was only a DC back then, so she says you won't remember.'

I didn't. I could recall taking part in a search operation in the cold central mountains of Scotland, but not anyone called Perry. In fairness, though, it was a long time ago. A very long time if Chaudry's Senior Investigating Officer had risen from detective constable to a lofty detective chief inspector.

'When do you need me up there?' I asked, trying not to feel old.

'The SIO's briefing isn't till tomorrow afternoon, so you should have enough time. If you don't want to drive there are direct trains from London.'

It was a long journey, and one I hadn't done in years. Then I thought about sitting in a train carriage for hours, trapped with my thoughts.

'It's OK, I'll drive . . .'

My eyes jerked open. For a moment I'd no idea where I was. I was sitting upright, in an unfamiliar room instead of my office at the university. A kitchen, but not one I recognised. Then memory clicked into place, and I remembered.

I was at the hotel. Hillside House.

I massaged a crick in my neck as memory came back. The lamplit kitchen was head-swimmingly warm, filled with a rich scent of home-cooked casserole. It was a large room, doubling as a dining and living area. A well-worn sofa and armchairs were arranged around a silent TV in one half, with the kitchen and old dining table where I sat in the other. Around me was a mishmash of dated appliances, Formica cabinets from the 1970s and a woodburning Aga range that looked even older. In one corner, jarringly out of place in that setting, were two large computer monitors on what looked to be an old school desk repurposed as a home office. A straight-backed kitchen chair stood in front of them, an oversized cushion on its seat a token attempt at comfort.

Except for me, the kitchen was empty.

I'd made my way from my car in darkness. The floodlights didn't come back on, so shouldering the holdall packed for my stay in Carlisle, I'd used my phone's flashlight to guide me through the driving sleet. A muddy gravel path ran around to the back of the hotel. I had to squeeze past the shadowy bulk of a car parked at the side, but with the looming stone walls on one side and thrashing bushes on the other I couldn't see much of my surroundings. At the rear, the flashlight's beam showed part of what looked like a bedraggled kitchen garden, where the bare branches of fruit trees shook in the wind like skeletal arms. Beyond them was only a yawning blackness.

The path led to a single-storey extension. The glow from its curtained windows was a beacon in the darkness, but I hesitated when I reached the door. The wind tugged at my coat, sleet pattering on its hood as I stood by the frosted glass panel.

Are you sure you want to do this?

The answer was no, but none of the alternatives seemed any better. I knocked and after a few seconds the door opened. The man motioned with his head as he stood back.

'Come on in.'

He sounded as pleased to see me as he looked. But as I stepped inside and he closed the door behind me, his wife's smile seemed genuine enough.

'Hi, glad you decided to stay! I was just wondering where you were.'

She had a baby, not quite a toddler, in her arms, swaying with him gently from side to side. The child was awake, regarding me querulously with bleary, tearstained dark eyes. His mother soothed him, her thick black hair tied loosely back.

'It's all right, the nice gentleman's a guest.'

He buried his face against his mother, unimpressed.

'I hope I didn't wake him,' I said.

'Don't worry, it was the thunder, not you.' She smiled, again softening the severe lines of her face. 'I'm Nisha, by the way. And this is Kiran.'

'David. David Hunter.'

'Say hello to David, Kiran.' Nisha tried to coax her son into raising his head, but he was having none of it. 'He's a little grouchy when he doesn't get his sleep.'

'Aren't we all,' her husband muttered as he walked past.

'Have you introduced yourself yet, or were you too busy?' his wife asked, tartly.

He gave her a sour look before grudgingly lifting his chin at me in acknowledgement. 'Jon Reese.'

Without the parka he looked younger, perhaps mid- or late thirties. His skin was sallow, with the sort of pale complexion that always looked wind-burnt, while the cropped hair and unkempt beard were tinged with auburn. He had a muscular, raw-boned build, and a breadth of shoulder that made me think he wouldn't have needed a shotgun if he'd meant me any harm.

'Thanks for letting me stay,' I said, setting my bag down. 'I wasn't looking forward to sleeping in the car, so I'm more than happy to pay for a room.'

'No way! It's the least we can do after . . .' Nisha looked uncomfortable. 'Well. You know.'

After threatening me with a shotgun, she meant. She saw me looking at where it was propped against the wall by the door.

'Jon was just about to put it away,' she said quickly. 'Weren't you, Jon?'

'It needs drying first.'

'You can do that later.'

32

Silently, Jon put his coat and boots back on and picked up the gun. 'Happy now?' he asked, before heading out the door.

The door banged shut behind him.

His wife's smile failed to paper over the tension as she turned back to me, hitching her son into a better position.

'You'll have to wait while I make up a room, so you might as well sit down. Can I get you a tea or coffee, or something to eat? There's butter bean and root veg casserole, if you're hungry.'

'Thanks, but I had a sandwich and hot drink in the pub.'

I went to sit at the kitchen table, trying not to look at the two computer monitors in the corner. But I'd already seen that the same image was on both, a young man with a bare, chiselled torso working out on a gym machine. Rows of complicated graphics and text overlay both images.

'That's just work stuff, not anything dodgy,' Nisha said, going over and putting the monitors to sleep. 'I'm designing a new website for a health club. I said I'd get it to them tomorrow.'

'Don't let me interrupt . . .'

'It's fine, it's time I stopped working anyway. I can finish the rest in the morning.' She smiled as her son began patting a pudgy hand against her face. He gave an infectious chuckle as she pretended to bite it. 'I better put this little monster back to bed and then I'll make up your room. Make yourself comfortable.'

I had, more so than I'd intended. The huge old Aga was kicking out a serious amount of heat, and I'd lost the fight to stay awake in its soporific warmth. Sitting up, I checked my watch and saw I'd been asleep for over ten minutes. I rubbed my face, glad that at least no one had been there to see. Jon still hadn't reappeared from wherever he'd gone to put the gun away, but as I was wondering where he might have got to a door opened and Nisha came back into the kitchen.

'Jon not back yet?' she asked, looking around.

'I haven't seen him.'

Something that could have been worry or annoyance crossed her face, but she quickly covered it. 'He'll have found something to keep him busy in his workshop.'

She tried to sound relaxed, but there was still a tension about her. I wondered if she was having second thoughts herself about letting a stranger into their home. But her smile seemed warm enough as she held open the door she'd just come through.

'I'll show you to your room, shall I?'

Chapter 4

Nisha led me along a short hallway to a door at the far end. She went through first, leaving it open for me to follow. The extension's hallway had been cooler than the overheated kitchen, but the sudden drop in temperature now was like stepping into the chill of a mortuary. We'd emerged into the foyer of the old hotel. It had the dank, musty smell of somewhere long shuttered. Above us, a faux chandelier with plastic candles gave out a sickly yellow glow that barely lit the corners of the large, high-ceilinged space. The floor was a worn parquet, while the walls were panelled with dark, heavily varnished wood, creating the impression of being in a giant box. There were rectangular, discoloured marks on it where what looked like signs and cabinets had once been, and the scuffed reception desk bore the scars of drill holes that had been badly filled. Behind it were numbered pigeonholes, each with its own brass key hanging from a small hook.

It was like stepping back in time to an earlier age, preserved in aspic from decades ago. That wasn't what made me stare, though.

The foyer was full of dead animals.

Stuffed birds – owls and hawks down to robins and goldfinches – rubbed shoulders with badgers, foxes and even a deer. A stag's head complete with antlers was mounted above a granite fireplace, and next to it a bear reared up on hind legs, teeth bared in a snarl and front paws raised to display its claws.

No wonder they lived in the extension.

'Sorry about the state of the place, but we don't come in here much,' she said, looking around the cavernous foyer as though taking it in for the first time. Her expression wasn't fond. 'I didn't pick the décor, in case you're wondering. Lovely, aren't they?'

I looked at a nearby glass display case, where a field mouse lay pinioned in a kestrel's talons. 'I was going to say an acquired taste.'

'Very diplomatic. Jon keeps saying he's going to get them valued, but we've not got round to it. They're probably worth a fair bit, if you like that sort of thing.' Her expression made it clear she didn't. She seemed to shake herself. 'Your room's on the first floor.'

Our footsteps echoed as we started across the foyer's parquet floor. Heavy drapes were hung over the windows and main entrance, their crimson velvet faded and worn.

'How old is it?' I asked. By the look of the antiquated furniture and build-up of dust, the place clearly hadn't been open for years.

'Not as old as it looks. Some businessman built it in the 1920s. He bought most of the mountainside, with the bright idea of developing it into a sort of luxury spa. Log cabins, cold-water treatments. He even dammed off part of a stream up there to use as a swimming pool. A real "build it and they will come" sort of thing. Except they didn't, and he went bust.' She shrugged, without much sympathy. 'Nice idea, but we're too far from the Lakes and it turned out the rich and famous didn't fancy coming all this way to freeze their bums off on a mountainside. Can't say I blame them.'

Neither could I. And I couldn't understand why a couple with a young baby would choose to set up home there. It felt like living in a mausoleum.

Nisha seemed lost in her thoughts, perhaps thinking the same thing.

'Have you been here long?' I asked.

Her sigh was almost imperceptible. 'Nearly a year. That's when we moved back, anyway, but Jon grew up here.'

'That must have been . . . different.'

'One way of putting it.' She paused at the bottom of the stairs. 'His family bought it off the MOD back in the 1970s. The Army used it as a training base in the Second World War, with

36

the officers staying in the hotel and the poor squaddies stuck out on the mountainside in the cabins. When they decided to offload it, the lumber company bought most of the land but didn't want the hotel or woods that came with it. Too steep and rocky for logging, apparently. Jon's grandparents thought they were getting a bargain, but . . . Well, I won't bore you with the details.' She rubbed her arms, looking around at the time-capsule of a foyer. 'Long story short, we inherited it when Jon's mum died last year.'

She didn't sound happy about it, and I didn't blame her. Inheriting a crumbling old pile like this must be more a curse than a blessing. Even mothballed, the cost of maintaining it would be enormous. And renovating it would be a major project.

'So . . . are you planning to run it as a hotel again?' I asked.

Nisha's expression was unreadable. 'We don't know. Come on, I'll show you to your room.'

The stairs were wide, with a smooth, sweeping mahogany banister that must have been impressive in its day. Now it was thick with dust and ancient cobwebs were strung between the upright wooden spindles. The once-plush stairs' carpet was worn through to the hessian backing.

'I'd have put you on the ground floor but the rooms there are damp and the second floor's out of bounds because the roof leaks,' Nisha said as we made our way up. 'And yes, I do realise I'm not selling this very well.'

'It'll be better than sleeping in my car,' I said, and hoped I was right.

The stairs led to a galleried landing on the first floor. It was darker there, lit only by the glow from the foyer's chandelier. Nisha flicked on the lights, revealing a long corridor with wood-chipped walls and numbered doors. Odd numbers on one side, even the other. The only furniture was a cracked, marble-topped bureau, on which stood a stuffed fox. It looked in even worse condition than the ones downstairs, its fur faded to a dusty orange and glass eyes askew, so that it seemed to have a squint as it stared out from its plinth.

37

'That's Craig,' Nisha said, giving the stuffed head a pat as she went past.

'Craig?'

'Craig Fox. After a boy I had a crush on at school. He was red-haired too, but he wasn't cross-eyed. Right, this is you.'

She'd stopped by a door with *14* screwed onto it in paint-smeared brass numerals. I looked back and saw the door before it was *11* while the door opposite was *12*.

No number thirteen.

Seeing where I was looking, Nisha nodded.

'I know, it's a hotel thing. Silly isn't it? I mean, it's still the thirteenth room no matter what you call it.' She put her hand to her mouth. 'Oh, God, you're not superstitious, are you?'

'No, I'm not.' Even if I had been, I must have had all my bad luck for one night.

Nisha opened the door and went in. I'd steeled myself for a grim prison cell, but the room was surprisingly welcoming. The curtains were drawn and a bedside lamp cast a warm glow. The grate in the fireplace was empty, but a convector heater warmed the room with a smell of burning dust. There wasn't much in the way of furniture: an old oak wardrobe and chest of drawers, with a white sink fixed to the wall. Still, the room looked freshly cleaned, and in a nice touch the red coverlet on the bed had been turned down to display crisp white sheets.

'It's not exactly five-star luxury,' Nisha said. 'No en suite, and I'm afraid you'll have to make do without TV or internet. We've Wi-Fi in the extension you can use but it doesn't reach up here.'

'This is fine,' I said, setting down my bag. 'Really.'

I'd stayed in worse, and I could manage without email or internet for one night. Nisha looked critically around the small room.

'Well, it's dry and I've turned the heater up full so it shouldn't take long to warm. If you need spare blankets I've left some in the wardrobe. The bathroom's just down the hall, but the bad news is the tank's got to heat up so there's no hot water. There should be enough for a shower in the morning and you're welcome to a cold one tonight, although I wouldn't recommend it. The water here comes straight from the mountain and trust me, it's *really* cold.'

'In that case I'll wait.'

'Wise choice.' She took a last look around. 'Well, I think that's about it. You know where we are if you need anything.'

'I'm sure I won't.' Not if it meant going back down through the darkened hotel with its silent menagerie. 'I'd like to make an early start in the morning, so should I let myself out if you aren't up?'

She laughed. 'Oh, there's not much danger of that. Kiran makes a great alarm clock, so don't worry about disturbing us. And you're very welcome to have breakfast with us before you go.'

'If you're sure it's no trouble . . .'

'None at all. I've already told you, it's the least we can do. To be honest, it'll make a nice change having someone new to talk to.'

She paused, plucking at the edge of the coverlet before letting it fall. A nervousness had crept over her.

'Look, I'm sorry about what happened earlier. With the shotgun. But I *swear* Jon would never have used it. He really doesn't have any bullets or shells for the bloody thing, whatever they're called. It was his dad's, not his, but it was a *stupid* thing to do. Will you . . . will you be reporting it? To the police, I mean?'

I'd been wondering about that myself. Threatening someone with a firearm was a serious charge. I'd seen the terrible damage a close-quarter blast from a shotgun caused, and I'd only their word that it hadn't been loaded.

Yet, although the threat had been implied, Reese hadn't actually *pointed* the gun at me. I hadn't enjoyed the experience, but looking back I wasn't sure it was enough to warrant pressing charges. Or that the police could do anything if I did.

'Does he have a shotgun certificate?'

'Oh, yes! He'll show it to you if you like.'

I ran my hand over my face, but I knew I'd already decided. 'No, that's OK. Let's forget about it.'

Nisha visibly sagged, as though the tension had been holding her up. 'Thank you, that's . . . That's really good of you.'

'I've one question,' I said, and watched some of the tension reappear. 'You said you'd been having trouble with poachers. It wouldn't be anything to do with the same character who sent me up here, would it?'

Her expression hardened. 'That's Vic Hooley. He's a . . . Well, let's just say him and Jon don't get on.'

After meeting the man I could see why. Nisha turned to go, then hesitated.

'I've got a question myself. I know you're going up to Carlisle, so I'm guessing it's a work trip. If you don't mind me being nosy, what is it that you do?'

I could have given her the same answer as I had Hooley earlier. I didn't like to talk much about my work, and 'doctor' was usually enough to deflect casual questions. But if I was spending the night under their roof I owed them a straightforward answer.

'I'm a forensic anthropologist.'

Her eyebrows went up at that. 'Is that like a pathologist?'

'Not quite, but . . . similar.'

'So you work with the police?'

'Sometimes, yes.'

I thought she might be upset to find out who her husband had been waving his shotgun at. But her expression was more thoughtful than shocked.

'Right.' She nodded, distracted. 'Well, I'll let you get to bed. Goodnight.'

With a brief smile, she went out, closing the door behind her.

I heard her footsteps growing fainter as she went down the corridor, then there was quiet. Outside the wind moaned as it battered the house. The window rattled as sleet peppered the glass, the curtains shifting as draughts found their way through. But that only seemed to emphasise the room's quiet. All at once I was conscious of how empty the old hotel was, of the silent warren of rooms all around me. Nisha, Jon and Kiran were in the extension, a separate building.

I was the only living thing in there.

Suppressing a shiver, I went to get my overnight things from my bag.

Chapter 5

The storm had passed when I woke the next morning. The rattle of sleet on the window had stopped, as had the low moan of the wind. Except for the lonely piping of a bird outside, Hillside House was quiet and still. There was no background grumble of traffic, no subliminal hum of electrics. After the constant hubbub of a city, the silence seemed strange and unnerving.

Not London, then.

The room was cold and dark. I could feel the chill on the exposed skin of my face, of a weight of blankets pressing me into a sagging but comfortable mattress. I groped for my phone and saw it was still early. My alarm wasn't going to go off for another half-hour, but I knew I wouldn't be able to go back to sleep. Throwing back the blankets, I shivered in the freezing air, feeling the thin carpet's icy roughness underfoot as I went to draw the curtains.

They looked as though they'd first seen life in the 1970s. They were damp to the touch, the orange fabric speckled brown with mould. When I drew them the single-glazed window was running with condensation, the rot clearly visible under the flaking paintwork. A frigid draught fluted through the warped frame, but it was still too dark outside to see anything of the surrounding countryside. Still, at least the storm had passed. Yawning, I collected my things and padded out to the bathroom.

A musty smell of mildew greeted me when I went in. The shower was above the bath, screened by a nylon curtain hanging from metal hoops. The curtain and chequered linoleum underfoot had seen better days, but Nisha had left a fresh bar of soap and clean towels out the night before. Rubbing my goose-bumped arms, I turned on the shower and flinched back as a gout of icy water spattered my bare skin. It quickly warmed, though. Adjusting the temperature, I climbed under.

The water stung like hot needles, but I relished the heat. The cold bathroom soon filled with steam. I'd just soaped my head and face when the shower curtain wafted against me, cold and clammy. I pushed it away, and as I did I saw the steam beyond it eddy and swirl as though the bathroom door had opened.

'Hello?' I called.

Blinking soap from my eyes, I pulled back the shower curtain. The bathroom was empty, its door still closed. Must be a draught, I thought, and turned my face up to the stinging spray.

After I'd showered and dressed, I went out into the corridor and closed the door on my room. It was still dark outside, so I turned on the light to go downstairs. The old hotel hadn't improved overnight. There was no one about, and the foyer was empty except for the collection of stuffed animals. They hadn't improved either.

Nisha hadn't said where I'd be eating breakfast, but I guessed it would be in the extension rather than the hotel's dining room. My footsteps rang on the parquet floor as I crossed to the door we'd used the night before. It had been skilfully cut into the oak panelling, only the small iron ring inset into it giving away its presence. Going through, I went back down the small hallway and knocked on the kitchen door. Nisha called out from the other side.

'Come in.'

The warmth of the kitchen enveloped me when I stepped inside. A background murmur of voices came from a smart speaker and there was an enticing smell of coffee and toast. Nisha was working at the old school desk. The same gym photograph was on one of the two monitors, but the other screen was filled by complicated-looking code. Kiran was in a highchair, a bowl of something beige on the tray in front of him. He beamed at me and slapped his spoon into the mulch, spattering it on his front.

'No, Kiran,' Nisha told him without much conviction, getting up from the desk. 'Sorry. He's a messy eater so I'd give him a wide berth. Did you sleep well?'

'I did, thanks.' She didn't look to have got much rest herself. Her face looked drawn and there were dark shadows under her eyes. I gestured to the computer monitors. 'If you're busy . . .'

'No, it's OK, it's time I took a break anyway.' She put the monitors to sleep and came away from the desk. 'You don't mind eating in here, do you? You're welcome to use the hotel dining room if you like, but there's no heat on so it'll be freezing.'

I thought about the glassy stare of the stuffed animals. 'In here's fine.'

'Good call.' She made an attempt at being cheery. 'So, what would you like for breakfast? We're vegetarian so there's no sausage or bacon, but I can offer you fried bread, eggs and tomatoes if you're interested?'

'Toast'll be fine.'

'Really? Jon's the cook, but I can manage to fry or scramble a couple of eggs. It won't take long.'

'In that case I'll have scrambled. Thanks.'

'Scrambled it is. Can I get you tea or coffee?'

'Coffee, please.'

There was a brittleness about her this morning, as though the tension had built up in her again overnight. I didn't know if it was her work deadline, awkwardness because of my presence or something else, but I was beginning to wish I'd declined the offer of breakfast. I still might have, but then I saw that a place had already been set for me at the old pine table, cutlery neatly laid out with a dish of butter and jar of orange marmalade.

'Can I help?' I offered.

'No, you sit down. Just try and avoid any food Kiran throws at you.'

Her son beamed at me, as though enjoying the prospect. As I took a seat at the table the snarl of a chainsaw came from outside.

'Is that Jon?' I asked.

Nisha spoke over her shoulder, filling a kettle at the sink. 'Yeah, he's clearing up after the storm. The wind brought my favourite apple tree down, so he's cutting it up. A shame but it'll make good firewood. The Aga practically eats it.'

'Was there much other damage?'

'The outbuildings have lost a few tiles, but nothing Jon can't fix. He's really practical, which is just as well living here. Trying to keep on top of basic maintenance in a place like this is a full-time job.'

Outside, the chainsaw pitch went up a notch as it bit into something solid.

'Is that his job, building maintenance?' I asked.

'Oh, God, no. I just meant that's what takes up most of his time now. No, Jon's a trained chef. That's how we met. I was studying IT at Manchester Uni while Jon was doing his catering qualifications and working in an Italian restaurant to pay his course fees. I went in with friends one night and he dropped garlic bread on me.' There was a wistfulness to her lopsided smile. 'Very romantic.'

'So you've been together since you were students?'

'Pretty much. Over fifteen years now. A *lo-o-ng* time.' She was smiling but the sardonic edge to her tone made it hard to say how she felt about it. 'After we finished Uni we did the whole back-packing thing and then lived abroad for a while. New Zealand, Australia, North America. We'd spend a year, sometimes two in a place, get to know it, and then move on. It probably wouldn't suit most people, but we enjoyed the freedom. Jon would find restaurant work and I did freelance marketing and web design. Same as now, but with better broadband.'

She shook her head, her smile more relaxed.

'Anyway, we finally ended up living in Vancouver. God, what a fantastic place! We loved it there. We were seriously thinking about settling there permanently. Jon had been made sous chef at a really good restaurant – you know, like the second-in-charge in the kitchen – and when I got pregnant with Kiran, it just seemed like the right time. We were going to apply for residency but then Jon's mum fell ill and . . . yeah. Here we are.'

I don't think she was aware of the bitterness in her voice. 'It can't have been easy, coming back.'

44

'No,' Nisha agreed, and there was a weight of understatement behind the word. 'It was supposed to be temporary, but by then Jon's mum was struggling to cope and we couldn't leave her out here on her own.'

'She lived here *alone*?' I said, thinking about that huge, empty hotel.

'It was her choice,' Nisha sounded defensive, although I hadn't meant it as a criticism. 'It wasn't like Jon abandoned her or anything. He always kept in regular touch, no matter where we were. And he used to send money back to help out, as much as we could afford. Roz was always very independent, though. Right till the end. She had to be, bringing Jon up by herself.'

'What about Jon's father?' I asked without thinking.

Nisha turned away, taking a loaf from an enamelled bread bin. 'He hadn't been around for a long time.'

'Sorry, I didn't mean to pry.'

'You weren't, it's just . . . You know. Families.' She slotted two slices of bread into the toaster, ending that line of conversation. 'So, are you going to Carlisle for a "case", if that's the right word?'

'It's for work, yes,' I hedged.

'You must see some upsetting things. Don't worry, I'm not going to ask for details,' she added quickly. 'It's just . . . well, the thing is—'

There was a clatter as Kiran knocked his plastic bowl off the highchair's tray. He stared down at the spatter on the floor with comical dismay.

'Oh, nice one, genius,' Nisha sighed, hurrying over with a cloth. I picked up the bowl while she cleaned up the mess. 'None of it got you, did it?'

'No, his aim was off.'

'Makes a change, he doesn't usually miss. Here, I'll take that.' She took the bowl over to the sink. 'Do you have kids?'

The change of tack caught me off guard. 'No,' I said, after a moment.

'No? I thought you would have somehow. Are you married?'

'Not now.'

'Oh, God, now it's me who's prying. Sorry.'

'That's OK.' It was my turn to change the subject. 'What was it you were going to say?'

'I can't remember,' she said. She turned to open the fridge. 'It can't have been important.'

By the time I left the sky was lightening. Smears of high cloud skated across a pale grey sky, without any hint of the turbulence of the night before. This was the first chance I'd had to see where I'd spent the night, and as I fastened my coat I took a second to soak it in.

Hillside House was even less prepossessing by daylight. The hotel's stone walls had weathered almost black, while the Gothic roof spires and turrets could have come from an unusually dour fairy tale. Its age and abandonment was evident in the rusting cast-iron guttering, and the cracked and cobwebbed glass in its windows.

But what it lacked in architectural elegance it made up for in durability. The storm didn't seem to have caused the house any damage, although the same couldn't be said for its grounds. The kitchen garden I'd glimpsed in the dark the night before was strewn with garden canes and toppled climbing frames. Snapped-off branches from fruit trees littered the ground, while the cabbages, kale and winter greens growing in vegetable beds looked as though they'd been shredded. Even so, that wasn't what made me pause to stare.

The view from Hillside House was breathtaking.

The hotel was situated on the foothills of a mountain facing over a craggy valley, looking across to a sweeping range of hulking, grass-covered fells. Their lower slopes were thickly forested, rising to blunt, snow-capped summits that encircled the valley like a wall of clenched fists.

I'd known I was in mountain country, but the brief glimpse I'd had during the storm hadn't done these justice. Looking at them spread out all around, massive and elemental, I felt a sense of almost primordial awe.

Jesus Christ, how did I drive through that?

The snarl of a chainsaw started up again as I followed the path past a huge log store and around to the side of the hotel. Jon was outside a low, windowless stone building, cutting into a fallen tree trunk in a haze of sawdust. Despite the cold he'd taken off his parka, which was slung on a nearby pile of fresh-cut logs. The air was scented with applewood and petrol fumes, and in his safety goggles and ear protectors Jon didn't notice me until I was in front of him. The chainsaw grumbled into silence as he switched it off, pushing back the ear protectors and goggles as he straightened.

'Looks like you've got your work cut out for you,' I said, looking at the partly dismembered apple tree.

'Tell me about it.' His face was flushed and peppered with sawdust. 'You heading off?'

I nodded. 'Thanks again for the room.'

'Don't worry about it.'

There was a moment of awkwardness. Neither of us mentioned what had happened the night before, but it hung between us.

'Well, good luck with the clean-up,' I said. Jon gave a nod, already pulling his goggles back into place as I came away.

The chainsaw sputtered to life again behind me.

As I continued around the hotel to where I'd left my car, I thought about what Nisha had said. Giving up their life in Canada for Hillside House must have been a wrench, but it was understandable for Jon to want to come back when his mother was dying.

What I couldn't understand was why they were still here.

It was cold in my car, so I kept my coat on as I drove away. The darkness and sleet had disguised how badly run-down the hotel's grounds were. The long, steep driveway was crumbling and potholed, half-obscured by huge, leggy rhododendrons that grew on both sides. Their branches met overhead, turning the driveway into a dripping, evergreen tunnel, at the end of which the leaning gateposts stood like sleeping sentries.

But the road back to the village didn't seem either as narrow or winding as it had in the dark. By daylight, Edendale looked even smaller than I'd thought, barely more than a huddle of bungalows and stone-built terraces hunkered down in the valley between the mountains. The storm had left its scars here as well. Bins had been blown over, trees had shed branches and houses had lost guttering and slates. The street gutters were banked with twigs, leaves and stones washed down by the heavy rainfall, and the detritus had formed miniature dams, trapping and backing up the rivulets of water still running down from the hills.

Early as it was, the clean-up had already started. A few people were already outside, sweeping up and clearing away debris. As I drove past The Perseverance I saw that the pub's sign was now hanging from a single chain, in danger of falling off.

No one seemed in any hurry to do anything about it.

I drove out of Edendale without stopping. There was still no phone signal and the car's satnav was playing up, but now I knew whereabouts I was I wasn't worried about getting lost again. I'd studied the road atlas, and the route to Carlisle seemed straightforward enough. An hour and a half, perhaps two at the most on these roads, should see me there. I'd have time to check into my hotel and grab some lunch before the SIO's briefing. There was no need to even mention my unplanned detour.

The morning was still brightening when I reached the start of the spruce plantation, and then I was under the canopy of branches and the sky was cut off. In daylight it was obviously a man-made plantation, the tall, near-identical spruce trees planted so close together that everything under them was in permanent shadow. The gates to the lumber yard I'd passed on my way into the village were open now. A long flatbed lorry laden with giant logs was parked facing them. It looked to be getting ready to set off, and I was thankful I'd left when I had. A few minutes later and I might have been stuck behind it.

The road twisted and turned as it climbed through the spruce plantation. The high winds had left their mark here as well, littering the tarmac with broken branches. Most were small enough to either drive over or avoid, but at one point I had to stop and get out of the car to drag away a larger one. Evidently, I was the first person to have used the road since the storm, which said a lot about how isolated Edendale was.

The car thrummed as its wheels bumped over the same cattle grid the sheep had got stuck in. The bulging shoulder of rock was just ahead, and remembering the blocked culvert just beyond it I slowed as I approached the blind bend. As it straightened out I began to accelerate, only to immediately stamp on the brakes.

'*Shit!*'

There was a screech of rubber as the wheels locked. I braced, certain I wasn't going to stop in time. Then I was flung against my seatbelt as the car jerked to a halt.

I sat there, my heart pounding.

Christ . . .

My hands were unsteady as I switched off the engine. Shaky from adrenaline, I got out and went to the front of the car. Ahead of me was the section of road that had been flooded the night before. Water was still gushing down the mountainside now, but it wasn't streaming across the road anymore.

The road had gone.

Chapter 6

Where the road had been was now a deep gouge in the ground, three or four cars, length across, as though a giant scoop had been taken out of the earth. The water streaming down the mountainside above had carried away the culvert and road with it, scattering them on the rocky slopes below in a churn of mud, tarmac and broken stonework.

I stood at the edge, shaken by the narrow escape. Another few metres and my car would have gone over. If I'd been going any faster . . .

I looked past the deep muddy trench to where the road continued at the other side. It might as well have been a mile away for all the chance I had of getting to it. Even if I could have made it through the torrent gushing down from the upper slopes, the mountainside here was too steep and craggy to negotiate. There was no way anyone could cross over without ropes and climbing gear. Perhaps not even then, until the flow of water had eased.

But that was a problem for later. I needed to report this and make sure no one else came up here, but before anything else I had to move my car. This whole section of road was unsafe, the tarmac where I'd stopped had cracked and sagged.

Listening out for an approaching engine, I ran back along the road to make sure nothing was coming, then hurried back to my car and reversed down the hill. Once I'd cleared the blind bend I could see all the way back to where the road disappeared into the dark spruce plantation. More importantly, anything coming up from the village would be able to see me as well.

Pulling into a passing place a little further down, I got out and went to the boot. Taking out the reflective warning triangle from my car's emergency kit, I unfolded it and stood it in the middle of the road. I couldn't do anything about cars coming into the village, but the warning triangle would be enough to alert anyone approaching the blind bend this way.

I checked my phone as I went back to my car. There was still no signal, but I tried calling 999 anyway. Emergency calls would connect to any other available network even if mine wasn't working. But there was nothing. I swore, putting away my phone. I'd have to go back to the village for a landline to report what had happened. And let DS Chaudry know I wasn't going to make the SIO's briefing that afternoon. Probably not the search operation either. I swore as the reality of the situation began to sink in. Repairing the road would be a major engineering project. It could take years, and even rigging up a temporary bridge would take days. Perhaps weeks.

Unless I could find another way out of Edendale, I wasn't going anywhere.

Christ, what a mess. I opened the car door and was about to get in when I became aware of something. A new noise, barely audible above the splash and gush of water but growing louder, carrying on the cold air like the drone of an insect.

An engine.

I looked back down the hill. There was nothing in sight but the sound was more persistent now. It was too deep and throaty to be a car, and as I realised what it must be a lorry emerged from the edge of the forest. It was a flatbed, perhaps the same one I'd seen when I'd driven past the lumber yard. Laden with massive logs, it was barrelling up the hill, gears grating as it climbed the steep gradient.

I moved slightly away from my car, so I was in clear view. The lorry was already close enough now for me to make out the driver through the windscreen, an indistinct figure perched high up in the cab. Raising my arms, I started to flag him down.

The lorry didn't slow.

Come on, can't you see me? I waved my arms harder. In response there was another grind of gears and the engine pitch went up another notch. Christ, was he *accelerating*? I began signalling frantically, pointing at the warning triangle in the road. The lorry was almost on top of me now, close enough to see that the driver was grinning. I felt a twist in my gut as I recognised the heavily stubbled face behind the windscreen.

Vic Hooley, the loudmouth from the pub.

I knew then what was happening. He'd seen me standing on the roadside by my car, next to a warning triangle.

He thought I'd broken down.

'The road's gone!' I yelled, windmilling my arms. '*Stop*, the road's—'

The blare of an airhorn drowned me out. I had a last sight of Hooley grinning above me, one hand gesticulating with curled fingers and thumb. Then I was staggering backwards, buffeted by its wash as the lorry blasted past in a stink of exhaust and rubber. Daylight was blotted out as it roared by, towering above me with its huge cargo of logs, then it was gone.

Blinking grit from my eyes, I stared horrified as it approached the blind bend. There was a last crunch of gears, and then the lorry disappeared behind the buttress of rock. For a heartbeat everything seemed suspended. There was just time for me to think the lorry might have managed to stop, then I heard a pneumatic hiss of air brakes. The crash came an instant later, a rending of glass and metal merging with a rumble of ground-shaking, percussive thumps.

My breath rasped as I ran up the hill. Rounding the blind bend, I saw rubber tyre marks on the tarmac where the driver had tried to stop. But not in time. The lorry had jack-knifed and overturned as it went off the edge of the collapsed road, shedding its load of massive logs. They were strewn across the mountainside like giant toothpicks, while the flatbed and cab had come to rest on their sides in the muddy trench left by the washed-out culvert, their wheels idly turning.

The air was heavy with the stink of diesel and brake fluid as I scrambled down the rubble-strewn bank towards the cab. Its windscreen was crazed, preventing me from seeing in.

'Are you OK? Can you hear me?' I called. There was a moan. 'OK, stay where you are. I'm coming to get you out.'

That was easier said than done. The cab was lying on the driver's side, so I had to climb up to get to the passenger door. Through the broken window I could see Hooley slumped in his seat behind a deflated airbag.

'Hang on,' I panted, tugging at the door. It resisted, then opened in a series of creaking jerks. Pushing it as far back as it would go, I crouched to look inside. Hooley's face was streaked with blood and paler than ever, but he was conscious. He stared up at me, his pouched eyes unfocused.

'Wha . . .?'

'Don't try to move.' I couldn't see any obvious wounds except for the head injury, but that didn't mean there weren't any. 'Do you hurt anywhere?'

'What do you fucking think!' At least he was coming round now. He started to push himself upright. 'Ah, *shit!*'

'I said not to move,' I told him, without much sympathy. 'Does anything feel broken?'

This time he took a moment, gingerly flexing arms and legs. 'Don't think so . . .'

'Good. Can you unfasten your seatbelt?'

Ordinarily, I wouldn't have tried getting him out on my own. But the emergency services weren't going to be arriving any time soon, and I didn't want to leave him in the crashed cab on the cold mountainside while I went back to the village. Not unless I had to.

He groped for the seatbelt release and gave a gasp as it came loose. 'Jesus *fuck*! I-I think my ribs are busted.'

'Does it hurt to breathe?'

'Course it fucking does!' he snapped.

'Any sharp pain anywhere?'

'Yeah, my arse! Are you going to help, or what?'

I weighed the risk, then reached down into the cab. 'Give me your hand.'

Wincing, he grabbed hold and began to prise himself out of his seat. It wasn't easy because of his size. The man had some

54

serious weight to him, and the hand gripping mine was rough and calloused. I supported myself against the doorframe, taking as much of the strain as I could as he hauled himself out of the passenger door. I helped him down from the cab, letting him lean against me as we clambered back across the rubble to the road.

Both of us were labouring by the time we reached the top. Hooley sank to the ground, his ribs not bothering him too much as he sucked in rasping breaths. He had a cut on his forehead, and the area around it was swollen and already starting to bruise.

'How are you feeling?' I asked, handing him a clean tissue to staunch the blood.

'Fucking peachy.'

I held up three fingers. 'How many fingers am I holding up?'

'Three. How many am I?'

He stuck up a fat middle finger at me. Holding the tissue to his forehead, he seemed to take in the overturned flatbed and spilt tree trunks on the slope below for the first time.

'Oh fuck! Maud's going to kill me . . . '

I didn't know who Maud was, but I could sympathise. Now that he was safe, I felt my anger flare.

'What the hell were you *doing*? Didn't you see me?'

'Wasn't my fault,' he muttered.

'Are you *serious*? I tried to flag you down and you drove right past!'

He gave me a sullen glare. 'Give it a fucking rest. Can't you see I'm hurt?'

As though to prove the point he closed his eyes and let his head hang. I turned away, forcing myself to breathe slowly as I looked down the mountainside at the water tumbling over the wreckage. Now the lorry and lumber would have to be recovered as well as the road repaired. And that wasn't all. Lying just off the edge of the road was a symmetrical timber pole, its thick cables trailing in the mud.

When Hooley rolled his lorry he'd managed to take out the power line as well.

'I'll take you back to the lumber yard,' I told him. Recriminations would have to wait. As well as a first aid kit, the yard would have a landline. I could use to report the road's collapse. And call DS Chaudry. 'Do you think you can make it to my car?'

'Gimme a minute.' Hooley pressed the bloody tissue to his forehead before examining it. The cut had stopped bleeding and the tissue came away dry. He seemed disappointed, then started to push himself to his feet.

'Do you need a hand?'

'I'm not a fucking baby.'

After that, neither of us spoke as we set off back down the road. Hooley seemed to be brooding but none of his injuries appeared to be troubling him. He was lucky to be walking away from a crash like that with only a few cuts and bruises. Luckier than he deserved, I thought uncharitably, as we reached my car.

'That a hybrid?' Hooley asked.

'Yes.'

'Fuck's sake . . .'

Ignoring him, I went over to where the reflective warning triangle was lying in the road, knocked flat by the lorry. The red plastic was cracked and scuffed, and one of the supports had broken off, but it was still usable. Hooley watched sullenly as I stood it upright again.

'I didn't see you.'

'What?'

'I didn't see you,' he repeated, doggedly. 'No way I could have stopped in time.'

'Seriously?'

I shook my head, but I wasn't going to waste time arguing with him. As I walked past him to the driver's side he suddenly stumbled against me.

'Whoa, feeling a bit dizzy. . .'

He lay a beefy arm across my shoulders. I had to brace myself against the unexpected pressure. 'Are you OK?'

He didn't answer. His arm grew heavier, pressing down more. 'What you going to tell them?'

'Let's get you in the car and worry about that when we get there, shall we?'

I reached for the door handle, but Hooley didn't move. The arm tightened around my shoulders.

'I want to know what you're going to say.'

I looked round and found him staring at me. There was nothing unfocused about the jaundiced eyes now. They were sharp and mean. His arm tightened more, almost clamping my neck.

Then, from the road below, came the sound of a car engine.

Hooley didn't move his arm, but the tension in it was suddenly gone. I pushed it off my shoulders and stepped away as a car began to climb the hill towards us. He gave a grin, the clown again.

'Sorry, mate. Felt out of it there for a bit.'

The car was an old red Polo, small and well-suited to the winding mountain roads. Its driver was a woman in her sixties. Her expression was curious but wary as she pulled up and wound down the driver's window.

I opened my mouth to explain, but Hooley suddenly shoved past me. He'd developed a limp, and one arm was clamped to his ribs as he hobbled painfully over to the car. He held the bloodied tissue to his head even though the bleeding had stopped.

'Don't go any further, Carol! The bloody road's gone, the whole thing!'

His voice was strained, as though it hurt to speak.

'I need to get to a phone—' I began, but Hooley spoke over me.

'Can you give me a lift back down? I need to warn people!'

The woman blinked. 'Er, yes, I suppose . . .'

Hooley was already opening the passenger door, the car sinking down as he squeezed his bulk inside. As he slammed the door he said something to the woman I couldn't catch. I saw her expression change before she turned to glare at me through the glass.

What the hell . . . ? I stood in the road as the woman turned the car around, shunting it back and forth on the narrow road until it was facing downhill. As the Polo set off towards the village, I saw Hooley's face smirking at me through the window.

My car was bigger and took more manoeuvring to turn around, so it was several minutes before I was able follow the Polo. I was seething as I drove back down the road. The idea that Hooley might try to pin the blame for his crash on me seemed so outrageous part of me didn't want to believe it, yet I didn't doubt that was exactly what he planned to do.

What worried me even more was that people might believe him.

The gates to the lumberyard stood open. Ranks of tree trunks were stacked like a giant woodstore, while mud-spattered tree harvesters and other logging vehicles were parked nearby on a concrete apron. With their huge, tracked tyres and articulated arms they looked predatory and alien, like armoured insects. I couldn't see the red Polo but I noticed that no lights were showing in the two-storey timber building. That wasn't a good sign, I thought, remembering the downed electricity pole. A group of men were congregated by the gates, I guessed to stop any cars from trying to use the road. As I pulled up outside and got out, they broke off talking to stare at me.

That wasn't a good sign either.

'Can you tell me who's in charge?' I asked. For long seconds none of them spoke, then one of the men jerked his chin back towards the office building.

'In there.'

Conscious of their stares as I went into the yard, I pushed open the door and went inside.

58

Chapter 7

I paused to get my bearings as the door swung shut behind me. I was in a small reception area, untidy and decked out with well-used, utilitarian office furniture. Charts and plans were fixed to the veneered wood panelling, centred around a large-scale map of the spruce plantation. Two desks stood empty, but a door to one side was open. Through it came the murmur of voices.

'Hello?' I called.

The voices fell silent. A moment later a woman appeared. 'Can I help you?'

She was in her forties, with dyed dark-red hair and brutally plucked eyebrows. Pencil-thin lines had been drawn on to replace them, curved in arches that gave her a permanently startled expression.

There was nothing startled about her tone, though. And from the hard look on her face as she stared at me, I had the uncomfortable sense she knew who I was.

'Can I speak to whoever's in charge?'

She regarded me coldly before turning and going out. There was a murmur of voices, then she reappeared.

'Come through.'

The doorway led into a larger office, this one with more comfortable seating. A young brown labrador in a wicker basket lifted its head when I went in, cautiously wagging its tail. Sitting behind the desk in an old wooden Captain's chair was a large woman in her fifties I took to be the dog's owner. Her greying hair was cut short, and a pair of shrewd eyes regarded me coolly. Her hands looked chapped and raw as they rested on the desk, their bitten fingernails at odds with her chunky gold rings.

This would be Maud, then.

Hooley was perched uncomfortably on a chair in front of her desk, looking for all the world like an oversized guilty schoolboy in a headteacher's office. He scowled when he saw me, the bloodied tissue still held to his head.

'That's him! Stupid—'

'All right, that's enough,' the woman snapped, a slight Scottish burr to her voice. Hooley shut up but continued to scowl as she turned back to me. 'I'm Maud Kennedy, the plantation manager. And you are . . .?'

'David Hunter. I was up by the collapsed road when your lorry went past, but I expect you already know that.'

Hooley gave a derisive laugh. 'Talk about brass neck! I'm telling you, Maud—'

'When I want to hear from you again I'll tell you,' she said, without looking at him. The heavy rings looked like knuckle dusters as she folded her arms, leaning back in the chair. 'I want to hear what Mr Hunter has to say.'

'It's Dr,' I said automatically, and immediately regretted it. 'Have you contacted the police yet about the road? There's no mobile signal, so I haven't been able to report it.'

'No, *Dr* Hunter,' she said, stressing the title, 'I haven't reported it to the police yet, because there's sod-all mobile coverage out here and the bloody landlines are dead. They went off with the electricity and internet about half-an-hour ago, so my guess is either the landslip took out the line or my star employee did.'

'I didn't, Maud, honest—' Hooley began, but another glare from his employer silenced him.

I took a moment to absorb the news. I'd seen that Hooley had brought down the electricity pole, but I'd been too distracted to realise modern landlines needed power to work.

'Do you know anyone with an old phone, the type that plugs into the wall socket?'

The old copper cable network didn't rely on mains power, so they shouldn't be affected. But Maud's expression killed that hope before she spoke.

'Amazingly enough, we did think of that ourselves. The village store's got an old-fashioned payphone so I've sent one of the lads to see if it's working. But I wouldn't hold your breath. The phone and electricity lines come in on the same poles. If one's gone the chances are the other will have as well.'

Christ. 'We need to get word out somehow.'

It was frustration talking, but it was still a stupid thing to say. She cocked an eyebrow. 'Oh, do you think?'

Hooley gave a derisive snort. 'I told you Maud, he's—'

'Be quiet.' Her face was hard as she turned back to me. 'I'm fully aware how bad the situation is. I've got an overturned flatbed and a load of timber spread all over the fell, and no way to let head office know. And according to my driver, we've got you to thank for it. Is that right?'

I could feel my face burning. 'No. I don't know what you've been told, but—'

'What I've been *told* is that you stood back and let him drive past instead of warning him the bloody road had gone. I don't know what the police will have to say, but if that's true I hope you've got bloody good insurance! Because I promise you, you're going to need it!'

'It's true, Maud, God's honour!' Hooley declared. 'I had no chance, it's a miracle I wasn't killed!'

She gave him a flat look, then raised her eyebrows at me. 'Well?'

Before I could answer a door at the back of the office opened, and another face I recognised from the pub came in. It was the anxious-looking man Hooley had bullied into buying him a drink. He was holding a first aid box but hesitated when he saw me.

'Sorry, Maud, shall I . . .?'

'Oh, for goodness sake, come in. This is Eddie Drummond, my office manager,' she told me. 'Dr Hunter here was about to explain why he didn't warn my driver the road had gone.'

Eddie stood clutching the first aid box, looking as though he wanted to be somewhere else. Hooley was watching me now with a badly concealed smirk.

'I did warn him,' I said. 'I tried to wave him down, but he drove right past.'

'That's a fucking lie!' Hooley jumped up, forgetting his injuries.

'Sit down!' Maud told him.

'He's a fucking liar—!'

'I said sit *down!*'

Hooley did, still muttering. Maud considered me again, frowning.

'Nobody who knows that road would be stupid enough to ignore being flagged down. Are you saying he didn't see you?'

'No, but I was by my car so he must have thought I'd broken down. He knew who I was from the pub last night. I'd got lost and was looking for a place to stay, so he sent me up to Hillside House as a joke. He told me I could get a room there.' I turned to Hooley. 'I did, by the way, so thanks for that.'

Maud turned to stare at Hooley. 'Is that right?'

'Maud, this is bollocks . . .'

'I'll take that as a yes.' The Captain's chair creaked as she sat back. 'How do I know you didn't let him drive past to get your own back?'

I hesitated, but I couldn't afford to let Hooley's narrative gain traction. 'I'm a forensic consultant. I was on my way to Carlisle to help with a police investigation. I'm not about to cause a potentially fatal crash over a practical joke.'

'He's full of shit!' Hooley blustered. 'He said he was a doctor, Maud, you heard him!'

'There's more than one kind of doctor,' she said, dryly. 'Not that I don't believe you, Dr Hunter, but do you have any ID? We'll need it for the paperwork anyway.'

I reached in my pocket and passed across my driving licence and University staff card. Maud scrutinised them before handing them back.

'That doesn't prove anything,' Hooley glowered at me, folding his beefy arms. 'It's still his word against mine.'

He had a point. This had the potential to get ugly, but I'd one more card to play.

'Here,' I said, taking out my phone. Before I drove back down I'd taken photographs of the road where I'd left my car, just in case. I scrolled through to the one I wanted and offered it to Maud. 'I put out a warning triangle when I saw the road had collapsed. He drove straight over it.'

'That's bollocks!' Hooley said, craning his head to try and see the phone as Maud studied the photographs on it. 'He must've put it there afterwards!'

'Did he smash it up and put tyre marks on it as well? Jesus Christ . . .' Maud shook her head in disgust as she handed me back the phone. 'Go on, get out, Hooley. I'll decide what to do with you later.'

'But Maud——!'

'*Out!*' She gestured to the other man. He'd been so quiet I'd almost forgotten he was there. 'Go and patch him up, Eddie. And use something that stings!'

Giving me a venomous look, Hooley heaved himself to his feet. He spoke in a low voice as he went past.

'I'll fucking see you again.'

He seemed about to slam the door, but Eddie was right behind him. There was a moment of confusion in the doorway, then with a last 'Fuck's sake!' Hooley stormed out, leaving the smaller man to close the door behind them.

'Give me strength . . .' Shaking her head, Maud took a deep breath. 'On behalf of the company I'd like to apologise for our employee's behaviour. I promise you, as soon as circumstances allow he'll be dealt with appropriately. If it was up to me I'd skin the bastard alive, but HR are squeamish about things like that.'

Now I was no longer being blamed for the crash, I was more concerned with finding a working phone than an apology. 'At least no one was badly hurt.'

'In Hooley's case I'm not sure that qualifies as a positive. Half-a-day's overtime getting that shipment ready, pissed up the bloody wall.' She kneaded her eyes. 'Is there's anything else before you go? I don't want to be rude, but I need to try and sort this mess out.'

'Is there another way out of the village?' I asked.

'I wish there was, but none of us are going anywhere until they bring in a temporary bridge. And Christ knows how long that's going to take.'

'What about by foot?'

'Not short of hiking over the fells, and good luck with that in winter. Past them it's all open moors anyway. There are a few farms, but none within striking distance.'

Frustration boiled up in me. 'There must be some way to get word out? Does anyone have a satellite phone? Or one with a satellite SOS?'

That would at least allow us to report the road's collapse. But Maud gave a barking laugh.

'Shouldn't think so. I don't, anyway, and not many people round here are in a position to splash out on fancy new phones. The old landlines worked fine for emergencies, but then the bloody phone companies switched to digital. Now each time there's a power failure we end up cut off until everything's back up and running.'

I was racking my brain, unwilling to accept there was no way around this. 'What about your lorries? Do they have CB radios?'

'Not for years. And even if we did they're line of sight. We wouldn't get a signal past the mountains.' She sighed. 'Look, I don't like it either, but it is what it is. The winter before last we were cut off for five days after bad snow. It was a pain but everyone survived and the sky didn't fall in. You live somewhere like this, you learn to get used to it.'

I felt winded. 'What if there's an emergency? Doesn't the village have any contingency plans?'

'Like what? Most people in the village have open fires or wood burners and everyone knows to keep in torches and candles. If there's a problem neighbours rally round. That's what communities like this do.' She shrugged. 'Sorry, but the only thing we can do is wait till someone tries to get out to the village on Monday.'

Today was only Saturday, and the idea of being stuck in Edendale for the entire weekend, with no way of getting word out, seemed like a life sentence.

'What about the post? Or deliveries?'

'We haven't had a Saturday post in ages. Same with deliveries, everything gets bundled up and brought out in batches.' Maud gave a grim smile at my expression. 'Welcome to twenty-first-century rural Britain.'

'There are people I need to contact,' I said, uselessly.

'You and me both. You'll just have to be patient, same as the rest of us. Be thankful you're not trying to run a business out here.' Her labrador jumped up when she rose to her feet, thrashing its tail excitedly. 'Now, if you don't mind, I need to get on.'

I didn't see Hooley on my way out, but the stares of the woman in the office and the men in the lumberyard fairly scorched the back of my neck as I went back to my car. Maud might know the crash wasn't my fault, but no one else had got the word yet.

That was the least of my problems, though. Pulling away from the plantation yard, I went to try and find a way out of Edendale.

Chapter 8

There were more people out clearing up after the storm when I drove back into the village. Sweeping up, collecting debris or repairing damage. A stepladder stood underneath the hanging down pub sign, although there was no other evidence of anyone working on it.

The pub itself was closed, but the village's only store was open. It was a double-fronted shop whose windows were cluttered with pots, pans and a random assortment of tinned and dried food. Maud had said it had an old plug-in payphone that might still be working. If the phoneline to the village was still intact, whoever she'd sent would have reported the crash and collapsed road by now, so the emergency services would already be aware.

I hoped so, but I still needed to contact DS Chaudry to let her know I was going to miss the briefing. And probably the start of the search as well.

There was nowhere to park outside the store, so I left my car a little further down the main street. Someone emerged from the store as I approached, a bulging shopping bag in hand. It was Stella, the barmaid who'd made me the sandwich the night before in the pub. She looked more careworn by daylight, but then she saw me and her expression suddenly hardened. I felt the smile grow wooden on my face as she gave me a frosty stare before turning to walk away without speaking.

I could guess why.

A bell jangled loudly above the shop's door when I went in. There were no lights on, but enough daylight came through the windows to show an Aladdin's cave crammed with groceries, household items and hardware. A portable gas fire hissed at one end, adding its fumes to an already heady odour of mothballs, washing powder and matches. An elderly, birdlike woman was behind the varnished wooden counter, bundled up in a thick coat, while a customer stood on my side of it. When I recognised her my heart sank.

It was the driver of the red Polo who'd given Hooley a lift.

The two women had broken off their conversation to stare at me, every bit as coldly as Stella had. I gave a smile anyway as I went up to the counter.

'Morning. Is your payphone working?'

The owner of the red Polo gave a sniff, folding her arms in silent reproach. The birdlike woman inclined her head to a phone on the counter.

'There it is.'

I felt a surge of hope. The phone looked ancient, its coiled cord tangled and greasy, but I didn't care. Taking out my own phone, I found DS Chaudry's number and picked up the payphone receiver.

There was no dialling tone.

For a heartbeat I thought I might have to press something for an outside line, then I became aware of how the two women were watching me. I felt blood rush to my face.

'It's dead,' I said, replacing the receiver. The Polo driver's expression was venomous.

'And we know who to thank for that, don't we?'

I wanted to tell them they'd got it wrong, but I knew it wouldn't do any good. Hooley was from the village, one of their own, and his version of events had got here ahead of me. Even if Maud corrected it later, the damage was done.

By now half the village would think I was to blame for the phone and power lines being down.

I left the shop and headed back into my car. *Now what?* I'd no idea. The scale of my predicament was still sinking in. Not only was I stuck in a remote village, miles off the route I should have taken, I had no way of letting anyone know where I was. Not until the world outside realised that Edendale was cut off, and from what Maud had said that wouldn't be any time soon. Even if the disruptions to the phone and power lines were noticed, in the aftermath of the storm an engineer was unlikely to be sent out straight away. Sooner or later, someone would attempt to reach the village and discover there was no longer a road in or out. Until then, Edendale was on its own.

And so was I.

I'd parked on the other side of the street to the store. Still preoccupied, it wasn't until I crossed the road to my car that I saw there was someone standing by it. Not peering into it, exactly, but he seemed to be showing an interest. It was a youngish man in a green camouflage pattern jacket, a black beanie pulled down on his head against the cold. It made it hard to make out his face, but there was something familiar about him. As I drew closer I recognised the teenager from the pub. The one who'd seemed to find it funny when Hooley had been put in his place by the old man.

The sharp-featured face wore the same smirk again now when he saw me. 'This yours, then?'

I stopped by the car door. It didn't look as though it had been disturbed or broken into. 'Why?'

'Just asking.'

He made no attempt to leave, watching as I unlocked it and opened the door. I started to get in, then paused. 'Is there something you want?'

'Naw, you're all right.'

He was still grinning, as though at a private joke. He waited until I'd got into the car before he spoke.

'I heard about the crash.' His smirk widened. 'Vic's well pissed off with you. Looks like you're stuck here with the rest of us.'

I shut the car door without answering. As I pulled away I glanced in the mirror. The teenager stood where I'd left him, still grinning as he watched me drive off.

There was really only one place I could go after that.

Hillside House was waiting in all its decaying, crenelating glory when my car emerged from the dripping rhododendron tunnel. I felt a weight descend on me as I parked in the same place as before. *Get used to it. You might be here a while.*

Leaving my bags in the boot, I got out and followed the path past an old Renault parked at the side and around to the back of the hotel. The blown-down apple tree was now a stack of logs, with the chainsaw leaning against it. Next to it was an axe. There was no sign of Jon himself, but the heavy door to the low stone outbuilding was open. As I crunched down the path to the back garden he appeared, wiping his hands on a dirty cloth. He paused when he saw me, then closed the outbuilding's door. I caught a waft of something that seemed fleetingly familiar, then it was gone.

'Wasn't expecting to see you back.'

'The road's collapsed. About a mile from the village.'

That got his attention. 'Bad?'

'It's impassable.'

'Great.' He shook his head, but didn't seem either surprised or bothered. 'Nisha said the internet and power were off. What happened?'

I told him about the culvert, and Hooley's crash. He shook his head angrily, throwing the rag down on top of the logs.

'Hooley'll stitch anyone up given half a chance. Pity the crash didn't take him out as well as the power line.'

There was real venom behind the words. Hooley hadn't endeared himself to me either, but I wouldn't have gone that far.

'Is there another way out of the village? A track or trail, anything?'

Jon seemed reluctant to turn his thoughts away from Hooley. 'If it was summer and you'd got a good map and compass you could try going over the mountains. You wouldn't make it far at this time of year, though. Even if you didn't get lost you don't want to be wandering out there at night. Not in this weather.'

Maud had said much the same thing, but I'd wanted to make sure. I stood there, at a loss. Jon's jaw worked, as though he was chewing on something bad.

70

'I expect you're going to need somewhere to stay.'

That would have been my next question. 'I can pay for the room . . .'

An expression crossed Jon's face, but I couldn't have said if it was refusal or annoyance.

'You'll have to ask Nisha. She's inside. I'll warn you, she's not happy.'

Picking up the axe, he began sorting through the freshly sawn logs. The *chunk* of the axe blade on wood resumed as I went to the extension.

Jon was right. Nisha wasn't happy. As I neared the kitchen door I heard something slam and then her angry voice came from inside.

'Oh, come *on!* This isn't fucking happening!'

When I knocked on the door she swore again, not quite as loudly.

'For fuck's sake Jon, can't you—' she began, throwing it open. She broke off, her scowl replaced by surprise when she saw me. 'Oh. Hello . . .'

'Sorry, is this a bad time?'

'Yeah, you could say that.'

She strode back into the kitchen, leaving me to follow. Kiran was sitting in a playpen, engrossed in a plastic toy with flashing lights that made farmyard animal noises when he pressed buttons. It was still stiflingly warm in there, but the huge old Aga wouldn't be affected by the loss of power. It would carry on putting out heat for as long as there were logs to burn.

Nisha gestured angrily at the blank computer monitors in the corner.

'I thought my computers had crashed but the bloody power's off! Everything's dead! No lights, no internet, nothing. I checked the fuseboard, but nothing's tripped so it must be a power cut or something. God, talk about lousy timing!' Reining herself in with a visible effort, she attempted a smile. 'Anyway, what brings you back? Did you forget something?'

'Not exactly . . .'

Kiran's toy provided a background chorus of farmyard noises as I repeated what I'd told Jon. Nisha's face ran through incredulity to anger. By the time I'd finished she was thin-lipped with fury.

'Christ, bloody Hooley! I'm supposed to be going live with the client's website this morning, and now I can't even get in touch to let them know it's going to be late!' She pushed her hands through her hair. 'How long do you think it'll take to get the power back?'

'I don't know.' I decided against saying that Maud didn't think the road would be even reported for another couple of days.

'God, I don't *believe* this! I *said* we should have got a satellite phone for emergencies when we came here, I *told* Jon! Or even just get new ones like the rest of the world! This place is so remote, and what if Kiran's taken ill or something? But no one here bothers about anything like that, it's all, *oh, we'll get by, we always have*! This is so . . . !'

She threw up her hands, unable to find the words. I felt a stab of guilt, knowing it was because of me Nisha had been late getting her work finished.

'I'm sorry. If I hadn't interrupted everything you'd have made your deadline.'

She waved that away. 'If it's anybody's fault it's Hooley's. I'm just pissed off with myself for not sending the work sooner. And it's worse for you anyway. You can't even let anyone know you're stuck here, can you? What about that police thing in Carlise you're supposed to be going to?'

'I expect they'll have to make a start without me,' I said, with a breeziness I didn't feel.

The initial reaction would be annoyance at my no-show. There might be a few angry phone calls or emails to find out where I was, but no one would be sending out any search parties yet. And even if they did, I'd strayed miles off the main route. No one would come looking for me here.

'Won't anybody back home be worried?' Nisha continued. 'I know you said you weren't married, but won't people worry when they don't hear from you?'

72

No, was the honest answer. I was used to the solitary nature of my life, but I realised how sad that must sound. And from there it was only a heartbeat to thinking about the letter I'd tucked inside my bag. I pushed the memory away.

'Everyone knows I'm working away. They won't expect to hear from me for a few days.'

Nisha was tactful enough not to press. 'Well, you're welcome to stay here as long as you like. I haven't been up to your room yet, so it's still as you left it.'

'Thanks, that's good of you. I'll be out of your hair as soon as I can. And I'll pay for room and board, obviously.'

'There's no need . . .' she began, but half-heartedly.

'I'd feel better. Really.'

She didn't argue the point. 'So, what are you going to do now?'

Good question. I had my laptop with me and there was some work I could do offline. But more than anything, I needed to clear my head.

'I don't know. Take a walk, perhaps.' I said. 'See if I can find a phone signal somewhere.'

'I wouldn't bother. You'll be wasting your time.'

'It can't hurt to try.'

It wasn't as though I'd anything better to do. Nisha didn't answer. She seemed distracted, as though her thoughts were elsewhere. I'd got to the door when she spoke.

'Actually, there might be one place you could try.'

Chapter 9

The woods were ancient. Gnarled oaks, beech and larch that had been old before I was born extended over the hillside, their bare branches like black scribbles against the pale sky. The rocky slope under them was covered with thick moss, an emerald-green carpet against which the hibernating trees looked skeletal and lifeless. They were being slowly choked by the fleshy-leaved rhododendrons that had spread through the woodland in an ever-green invasion, and the storm had left its mark on the old woods as well. The wind had snapped off limbs and brought entire trees crashing down, centuries-old giants reduced to a wreckage of broken branches and uptorn roots in moments.

Yet that was part of the natural cycle. The decaying trunks provided essential nutrients and habitats for plants, insects and fungi. The woods were home to a vast assortment, from plate-like growths sprouting from rotting trees to ghostly white domes pushing through the woodland floor. Even in winter the woods were full of life. Birds called overhead while squirrels scratched and foraged in the undergrowth, and the dead-looking branches were beaded with the nubs of new buds, waiting only for spring's warmth and sunlight to unfurl. And then the cycle of death and regrowth would begin all over again.

My breath steamed in the crisp air as I stopped to rest. The lane that climbed through the woods was steep and rugged, and my leg muscles were feeling every inch of it. Taking out my phone, I checked again to see if there was any reception. There wasn't, although that didn't come as a surprise. Even Nisha hadn't seemed very confident when she'd given me directions.

'You might be able to find a signal in the spruce plantation higher up the fell,' she'd told me, turning away and beginning to chop vegetables. 'I can't promise anything, but Jon's mum said you could sometimes get one up there.'

Remembering the massive, blunt peaks and densely packed trees I'd driven through, that was hard to believe, but I'd kept my scepticism to myself.

'Whereabouts?'

She'd stood with her back to me as she'd answered. 'There's an old hiking trail in the woods behind the hotel. That's the most direct route but it's steep and muddy. If you don't fancy that there's a lane about a mile from here that comes out at the same place. It's further to go but you can drive as far as the lane and then walk the rest of the way, so it's probably faster.'

Faster sounded better. It was already nearly noon and I was conscious of how short the winter days were. The last thing I wanted was to end up stranded on a mountainside in the dark. Or break a leg on a muddy hiking trail.

'How do I get to the lane?' I'd asked.

Nisha had glanced around, startled. 'You really want to go up there?'

I'd shrugged. 'If there's a chance I might find a signal.'

'You need to drive back down as though you're going to the village' she said, her voice studiedly matter-of-fact as she resumed chopping the vegetables. 'When you get to the cross-road, instead of carrying straight on turn . . . left. No, right. The road runs alongside our woods. Keep going along there for, I don't know, a mile? Half a mile? Anyway, you'll come to a small lane on your right-hand side. It cuts up through the woods, and there's a gate set in a drystone wall at the bottom. It's overgrown so it's not easy to see, but if you miss it the road eventually loops back round to the village. If you end up there you've gone too far.'

'You said I can't take my car up the lane?' I asked, trying to memorise all this.

'No, no one uses it anymore. But you can park by the gate and then walk up to the top. That brings you out at a sort of clearing. The spruce plantation's dead ahead, and off to one side there's a ravine with a stream running through it. That's Foss Ghyll, where the old army base I told you about used to be. You need to go the *other* way, though, away from the ravine. Just keep walking along the edge of the plantation and eventually you'll come to a logging track that runs into it. Go up that and then just . . . Well, see if you get a signal, I suppose.'

I'd tried to hide my doubts. 'And Jon's mother actually found one up there?'

'I think so. Like I said, I can't promise anything.' Nisha put down the knife and turned to face me, her forehead creased worriedly. 'In fact, forget I said anything. It was a stupid idea. You'd probably be wasting your time.'

I thought so too. But even a slim chance of getting word out was better than none. Besides, I still felt bad that Nisha had put off finishing her work because of me. Long shot or not, if I could do something to make that right then it was the least I could do.

'It's worth a try,' I'd told her.

Now, though, I wasn't so sure. Time and disuse had turned the lane into little more than a rutted, weed-choked track. And Nisha had been right about the gate at its bottom being hard to see. Set in a crumbling drystone wall, its rusted metal bars were so snarled with dead grasses and weeds that I'd almost driven past before I noticed it hidden by the undergrowth. There was enough room to park in front of it, so I'd bumped off the road and cut the car's engine. In the aftermath of the night's storm the woods were quiet and still when I'd climbed out. I'd filled my lungs, enjoying the clean, loam-scented air. A crow cawed in the distance but nothing else disturbed the tranquillity.

I could have been the only man alive.

After changing into the waterproof hiking boots and cold weather gear I'd packed for the Carlisle search, I'd locked my car and gone to the gate. It was too overgrown to open, but jutting stones had been set into the drystone wall to serve as rudimentary steps. Climbing over, I started up the lane.

77

That had been half an hour ago. Uncapping the water bottle I'd filled back at Hillside House, I took a drink while I caught my breath. I hadn't held out much hope of finding a stray signal halfway up a steep fell to start with, and it was seeming less likely the further I went. Even so, I was glad I'd made the effort. These days the only time I got out into the countryside was for my work. It was hard to appreciate the scenery when you were exhuming a body from a shallow grave.

Fastening the top onto the water bottle, I put it back into my jacket's deep outer pocket and continued up the lane. At first glance, the wooded mountainside looked untouched, but a closer look revealed this wasn't an entirely natural landscape. The woods bore scars of quarrying, though not from this century or even the one before. Softened by shaggy growths of moss, angular, sharp-edged boulders lay tumbled against each other at the foot of sheer slate faces, themselves obscured by trees. There was evidence of later intervention here too. Even if Nisha hadn't told me there had been an army training camp up here during the Second World War, remnants of it were still all around. Rusted strands of barbed wire could be seen coiled in the undergrowth, while hidden among the trees and bushes were irregular lengths of brick walls. I'd been puzzled by them before realising they were meant to represent fortifications and bombed buildings for training exercises. Further off through the trees I could see a flat expanse of concrete wall set against the steep slope, all but engulfed by a gigantic clump of rhododendrons. It looked to be part of a larger structure built into the quarried mountainside, perhaps an old bunker or retaining wall. But whatever it was, or had once been, its purpose was long forgotten as nature inexorably reclaimed its territory.

The rippling chuckle of a stream was coming from some-where nearby. I couldn't see it but hoped it meant I was nearing the top of the lane. Not long after that I saw an opening in the treeline up ahead. It brightened as I drew closer, and then the lane levelled out as I reached the end of the woods.

Taking in deep breaths of cold air after the climb, I stopped to take in where I'd emerged.

Nisha had said the lane came out at a clearing, but she hadn't done it justice. Laid out ahead of me was a glade of almost Alpine purity. It was roughly the size of a football pitch, framed by trees on all sides and lushly carpeted with grass that still looked green even in the depths of winter. The stream I'd heard was about fifty metres off to my left, a fast-flowing ribbon of silver and black. It spilt over a vertiginous ravine of jumbled rocks, splitting off into small pools and waterfalls before disappearing down the mountainside.

This must be Foss Ghyll, I thought, remembering what Nisha had told me. The remains of the army training camp were still evident here as well, though only just. Rhododendrons had encroached into the glade, spilling out from the woods like a slow green tide. They'd completely overrun the old army encampment, until all that could be seen of the half-dozen abandoned huts were glimpses of moss-covered roofs hidden in the evergreen bushes. But neither the decaying huts nor the invasive rhododendrons could detract from the glade's beauty. The only jarring note was what stood at its far side. Nisha had been right.

The spruce plantation was impossible to miss.

A line of towering, pointed trees rose up in front of me like a barrier, their trunks as straight and bare as telegraph poles. Countless others pressed behind them, growing so near together that nothing grew between them. Even the storm didn't seem to have made any impression on the densely packed trees. The only foliage was towards their tops, where the needled branches had overlapped to form a canopy that blocked out the light. It cast a permanent twilight on everything below, making it impossible to see more than a few yards before the crowded trunks were swallowed by shadows.

It was a dark, dismal place. I'd driven through its lower reaches when I'd tried to leave the village, but from the road I hadn't appreciated how oppressive the plantation was. Up here, set against the natural backdrop of the fell, the brooding mass of near-identical trees looked regimented and artificial.

I looked back towards the stream splashing down the rocks of Foss Ghyll, tempted to linger here rather than spend any more time searching for a non-existent phone signal. But I'd come this far. Turning away from the ghyll, I headed along the edge of the plantation, hoping to find the logging trail Nisha had said was up here. After a short distance the glade ended, giving way to a strip of scrubland that climbed along the side of the mountain. Only a few yards wide, it separated the man-made wall of spruce trees from the old woodland that grew on the slope below it. There was no path or trail, and walking was difficult. I picked my way along, pausing from time to time to check my phone and asking myself how much longer I was going to waste on a fool's errand.

I was considering turning back when I saw a break in the spruce treeline up ahead. *Finally* . . . Overgrown with dead grass and bracken, the logging track was a narrow corridor running into the plantation, hemmed in between rows of dark spruce trees. They loomed over it, a hundred feet or more tall, so that when I looked up all I could see of the sky was a meagre grey ribbon trapped between them.

I stopped at its mouth, loath to go any further. The idea of finding a phone signal in that dark labyrinth seemed more far-fetched than ever. And now it belatedly occurred to me that perhaps I should have asked Maud before coming up here. There was no fencing or signs but the plantation was still private property.

As I debated whether to go on, the quiet was broken by the distant barking of a dog. Sound carried in the still mountain air, so it was hard to say how far away it was. It didn't sound too close, though, and the barking stopped almost as soon as it had begun. It wasn't repeated, and I reluctantly turned my thoughts back to what I was going to do. I knew I was looking for excuses because I didn't want to go into the plantation. But there was no good reason to turn back now. I'd be able to hear if there was any logging going on, and even though I might be technically trespassing, I was hardly going to cause any damage. Maud would have more important things on her mind right now. And, if by some miracle there was phone reception up here, I'd be doing her a favour anyway.

Giving a sigh, I started up the logging track.

The tall trees closed around me, pressing in on both sides. It was darker on the track, and the cold air was thick with the astringent, Christmas-tree scent of spruce. When I looked into the plantation on either side all I could see were countless bare trunks, disappearing into shadows. The ground beneath them was carpeted by fallen needles, as flat and featureless as coir matting. Nothing grew in there, no ferns or vegetation to break the monotony. The spruce trees had crowded out all other life.

My boots swished through the dead grass and bracken as I walked along the track. I had my phone out, but the signal bars didn't so much as flicker. I don't know how long I'd been walking for when I became aware of a vague sense of unease. At first I tried to ignore it, but eventually I gave in and halted. I looked round, but there was nothing to see except the dark trees. The narrow track was as featureless one way as it was the other, and it took me a moment to realise what was bothering me. I stood still, listening to make sure.

There wasn't a sound.

The old woods I'd walked through earlier had been a living ecosystem, alive with birds and animals. Here there was silence. No birdsong, no rustling. Only a faint, unsettling whispering as the wind stirred the pointed tops of the spruce.

Trying to shake off the disquiet I carried on, but my heart was no longer in it. My phone screen remained stubbornly devoid of signal bars, and I'd given up any hope of finding one. When I came to a point where the logging track forked, splitting into two, I stopped. Nisha hadn't mentioned this, and I'd no idea which way to go. Neither of the tracks looked very promising, and there was another consideration now as well. It would be easy to become disorientated in here, especially if whichever track I took continued to split off. There wasn't much daylight left, and I'd no desire to be wandering around this man-made forest in the dark.

Enough was enough.

I was about to turn round and head back when I became aware of a noise. It sat beneath the whispering from the treetops, a faint but unmistakable sound of a stream from somewhere in the trees. I went to the edge of the track, trying to see its source. Next to where I'd stopped was the fungi-covered stump of a dead spruce, victim of some long-ago storm. All I could see beyond were more spruces, vanishing into the plantation's gloom. The sound of water was clearer now, though, a fluid rippling that didn't sound very far away. I guessed then what it was, and after glancing back at the safety of the track to reassure myself I wasn't going to get lost, I headed further in.

The sound of running water grew louder. After a few more yards I could see through the trunks to where the plantation brightened as the trees thinned. A stream ran through them there, freshening the heavy spruce scent as it splashed down a stony gully. I knew then where I was. This must be the stream that fed Foss Ghyll, I realised as I reached its banks. If I followed it I'd come out at the glade, and the lane leading down to my car.

That was a lot more appealing than going back along the claustrophobic logging track. It was much brighter by the stream. The spruce here weren't quite as tall, so this part of the plantation had probably been planted later. They still towered high overhead, although none had been planted on the stream's rocky banks, leaving a gap in the dense canopy through which open sky could be seen. Grass, small saplings and other vegetation had seized on the extra light, turning the stream into a meandering oasis running through the dark plantation. Rhododendron had found a foothold here, too, but even the invasive bushes seemed natural by comparison, a welcome sign of life in the sterility of the spruce forest.

I had to watch my footing on the rocks, but there was enough room to walk alongside the stream. In places it had overflowed its banks, undercutting the nearest spruce trees to expose roots that looked like nests of brown snakes in the dark soil. The slope became steeper as the stream dropped towards the ghyll, the rocks larger and more difficult to bypass. More than once I had to scramble over them, and the open ground here had left the trees vulnerable to storm winds. At one point I was forced to detour around a huge tree throw, where a big spruce had been blown down across my path, taking down two smaller spruces along with it. As I skirted the huge tangle of uptorn roots, I was beginning to think that coming this way had been a mistake.

But the sound of the ghyll was getting louder. I couldn't be far away now, and not long after I'd passed the fallen spruce I reached the edge of the plantation and emerged from the trees. In front of me the ground fell away more sharply, dropping into a boulder-strewn ravine.

I was back at Foss Ghyll.

I'd come out at its head, looking out across the green swathe of glade. Below me the stream tumbled away through the rocky ghyll, filling the air with a fine spray as it cascaded through pools and falls on its way to the far woods.

I took a deep breath, enjoying the moment. It had been worth coming up here just to see this, phone signal or not. Bending down, I took off my glove and trailed my fingers in the stream. It was icy, burning to the touch. Perhaps being stuck here for a few days wouldn't be the end of the world, I thought. It was an idyllic spot, peaceful and unspoilt, so long as you could ignore the spruce plantation.

Cold, though. Too cold to be standing around. Getting back to my feet, I shook water from my numb fingers and began to look for a way down. Foss Ghyll was even steeper than I'd realised, I saw. Its jumble of rocks might be scenic but they were also slick and covered with moss. I might manage to scramble down them, but if I fell I'd almost certainly injure myself.

Reluctantly, I turned away and went back into the plantation, looking for a way to cut down through the trees to the glade. From the ghyll it looked deceptively close, but I knew how easy it would be to lose my bearings if I strayed too far into that timber maze. Intent on finding a route through the trees, I didn't pay any attention to the fallen spruce I'd walked past earlier. I'd already begun to pick my way around the crater left by its roots before some subliminal warning registered.

I looked up at the underside of the fallen tree.

Silhouetted against the sky, its roots rose above me. They were almost twice my height, a Medusa-like tangle clotted with soil and rocks. And something else, that I'd missed when I came past it heading the other way. Something that had no right to be there.

Entwined in the fallen tree's roots was a human skeleton.

Chapter 10

I stumbled backwards, almost overbalancing as my boot fetched up against a rock. Recovering, I looked around, half-expecting to see someone watching, as though this was a surprise that had been planned for me in advance. But I was alone. My heart thudded as I looked up at the knotted tree roots again.

The skeleton stared down at me.

'Christ . . .'

The sound of my voice was jarring in the forest's quiet, but it served to bring me out of my shock. My first impulse was to call the police, and I'd started to raise my phone before I remembered there was no signal. Even my phone's emergency SOS function wouldn't work without any service. *Idiot . . .*

Taking an unsteady breath, I took a long look at the macabre sight.

Embedded in the sodden mess of earth and roots, the skeleton was suspended above the crater like a tattered scarecrow. It was fully clothed, and the muddy rags of jeans, corduroy jacket and crew-necked sweater that remained ruled out any question of this being an archaeological find. The body was facing outwards, legs twisted to one side and bent at knee and hip. The left foot still wore a rotted leather work boot, held in place by a twist of roots, but the right foot was missing, probably detached when the skeleton had been wrenched from the ground. The outer clothing had ridden up to show that two lower ribs were missing as well, and so was the jawbone, or mandible. Its absence gave the impression that the skull was frozen in an endless, gaping scream.

But it was the tree roots that made the scene truly grotesque. The spruce must have blown down in the storm, because its roots hadn't had the chance to dry out or die off. Ranging from slender threads to stems several inches in diameter, they'd grown through and around the bones of the slowly decaying body, displacing some while also holding them in place. Hairlike shoots had grown through the eye sockets, drooping over the zygomatic bones of the cheeks like beached sea anemones. The overall effect was of something not human, a twisted hybrid of bone and root hoisted into the air for all to see.

I'd lost count of the number of dead bodies I'd encountered in my work. I'd examined victims of violence and accident, seen bodies burnt, mutilated and in all stages of decomposition. I'd thought I was beyond being surprised but this . . .

This was a first.

My mind was working again now, enough to start to think through what I needed to do. This was a crime scene, and the fact the victim had been buried almost certainly made it a homicide.

I needed to record the scene as I'd found it.

Keeping clear of the muddy crater left by the roots, where detached bones and other evidence might be buried, I began taking photographs on my phone. I took them from every angle, getting as close as I dared. As I did, I began to form a better understanding of what I was seeing.

This had been a physically imposing individual, tall and heavy-boned. Although stature alone wasn't enough to confirm biological gender – there were large women and small men – there were other indications that this skeleton was male. Male skulls are generally bigger than female, with a rougher, more robust appearance, and this one fit that template. Rain had washed enough soil from the skull for me to see that it was large with a pronounced 'rugosity' about it. The sloping frontal bone – or forehead – and pronounced brow ridges were typical of males as well.

Those heavy brow ridges also suggested a white ancestry, as did the high nasal bridge and angular eye orbits. And the victim had reached maturity before he'd died. His size alone was a strong indication of that, but there was other evidence too. The visible joints showed early signs of wear and tear, and so did the teeth in the upper jaw, all of which had erupted. The rags of clothing prevented me from seeing if the clavicles, or collarbones, had fused where they met the breastbone and shoulder blades, which would mean the victim had been in his mid-twenties or older.

But the skull made up for that. Although it had been hoisted above me, it was tilted forwards, so by reaching up with my phone I was able to photograph its top. Between the bones of the skull are flexible joints called cranial sutures. Over time these gradually fuse shut in a process known as ossification, until by old age they've completely disappeared.

Beneath the covering of dirt, I could see that while these sutures were fully closed, they hadn't yet started to fade. That fit with the overall picture I was starting to form of the victim. A white male, well-built and around six feet in height. Not a young man, but not an old one either. Probably between thirty and forty, as near as I could gauge it.

The prime of life.

I couldn't see any obvious injuries, but that didn't mean there weren't any. The back of the skeleton – including the rear of the skull – was embedded in the earth and the decayed rags of clothes covered some of the bones. Still, looking at the fibrous roots that had grown through the eye sockets, I was already starting to form a theory about how this individual could have died.

That still left the question of *when*. Once the remains were in a mortuary where I could carry out a full examination, I'd be able to estimate the time since death interval much more accurately. Assuming the police decided to use me rather than bring in another forensic anthropologist, that is. But even without access to lab equipment and testing, I could still narrow things down.

The spruce tree that had grown on top of the grave was the most obvious indicator. It was on a small hummock of rocky ground where only a few other trees had been planted, creating a small clearing within the plantation. It was hard to gauge its height now it had fallen, but it had to be close to a hundred feet tall. Perhaps even taller. Taller than the other trees growing around here, I saw. That might be due to the extra nutrients released into the soil by the decomposing remains, but there could be any number of other environmental factors. On a commercial plantation like this the trees would be a fast-growing variety. Even so, it would still have taken years for it to reach that height. And since the spruce had been planted on top of the grave, accidentally or otherwise, the body had to have been buried already for at least the lifespan of the tree.

The remains' own condition told a similar story. A buried body decomposes at a much slower rate than one left on the surface due to the lower temperature and lack of oxygen. This one had almost completely skeletonised except for a few scraps of connective tissue, and the bones had become stained and dark from prolonged exposure to soil. Soil that would be acidic thanks to the rotting spruce needles, which would have slowed the soft tissue's decomposition even more.

It all pointed to long years in the cold earth. Given the height of the tree, at least two decades would be my conservative guess. It was possible that the body had been buried long before the tree was planted, but looking at the rags of clothing hanging from the old bones I didn't think so. Fabrics deteriorate at different rates. While silk and some synthetics could survive being buried for decades, cotton – including denim – would only last ten years or so. The jeans and corduroy jacket had almost rotted away, so they'd been buried for at least that long. Probably longer, since the chemicals released by a decomposing body could help preserve clothing. The sweater had fared better but that was starting to rot as well. The grime and mud made it hard to be sure what it was made from, but I could see that the knitted fibres were pilled and matted. Possibly acrylic, but the look of it made me think it was more likely wool.

Which was useful. Wool could last up to thirty-five years underground, with severe decay kicking in after around fifteen. The sweater looked somewhere in between that range; holed and rotten but with a few years left before it disintegrated completely.

So, the remains had probably been buried for somewhere between twenty and thirty years, give or take. The plantation would have records of when these trees had been planted, which would narrow it down even more. But from what I could see, the age of the fallen spruce corresponded to that time-frame as well. Either it had been planted coincidentally not long after the remains had been buried.

Or someone had deliberately planted it on top of the grave.

I'd taken all the photographs I needed. As I put away my phone there was a streak of black and white, and I looked up to see a magpie swoop down and perch on a root by the skeleton's head. It hopped closer, cocking a speculative eye at the grisly relic before flying off, chattering in protest when I clapped my hands.

But it was a reminder of how vulnerable the remains were now they were out in the open. And not just to scavengers: wind, rain and freezing conditions could all damage the fragile remains. Ordinarily I wouldn't have even considered disturbing a crime scene, but this was different. The remains had already been disturbed when the tree blew down and ripped the skeleton from its grave. The priority now was to preserve them as best I could until the police and SOCOs got here.

Whenever that might be.

It was too late to do anything more today. Even if I could find a plastic sheet or something to cover the remains without arousing suspicion, the light was already starting to fade. It would be madness to attempt to come back up here in the dark.

I shivered, suddenly aware of how cold I'd become. The temperature was starting to drop as well as the light. I looked at my watch, surprised at how late it was, and as I was about to go I heard a noise behind me.

The next second I was bowled over as something slammed into my legs.

The breath exploded from me as I landed with a thump on my back. Winded, I struggled for breath as the silence was split by a piercing whistle.

'*Here!* Get here!'

Upside down, I saw someone emerge from the trees at the far side of the fallen spruce. The battered green camouflage parka and a black woollen hat pulled low over his eyes looked familiar, but it took me a few seconds to recognise the teenager who'd been loitering by my car. A delighted grin spread across his face as he stared past me at the skeletal remains.

'Fucking *hell!*'

Still winded, I pushed myself up. *So much for keeping this a secret.* As I climbed painfully to my feet two dogs bounded past, one grey, the other black. They were the lurchers I'd seen with the old man in the pub, the grey one older and more grizzled, the black one younger and excitable. Either they hadn't noticed what was in the tree roots or weren't interested. Even so, I didn't want them going any nearer.

'You need to get your dogs under control,' I told him angrily, brushing spruce needles and dirt off my jacket.

'Look at the *state* of it!' he said, not taking his eyes from the skeleton. 'Did it get blown down last night?'

He was carrying a small crossbow in the crook of one arm, I saw now. A dead crow and a limp, bloodied rabbit dangled from the canvas bag slung over his shoulder.

'It doesn't matter. You need to take your dogs away from here.'

'Fuck that, I want a proper look!'

He started to go past me. I stepped in front of him, blocking his way. The dogs turned their heads to stare over, suddenly alert.

'You need to go.'

He tore his eyes from the tree roots and gave me a truculent glare. 'Why? Who put you in charge?'

'Listen, this is—'

The lurcher's bark cut me off, shockingly loud in the quiet. Both dogs had gone to stand by the teenager. The hackles on the back of the older one's neck had risen. It stared at me, poised and intent as though waiting for the word.

The youth grinned. 'What's up? Scared?'

I ignored him, trying to pin down an elusive thought. Then I remembered. The distant barking I'd heard earlier, the feeling of being watched as I'd walked on the logging track. Something clicked into place.

'Were you *following* me?'

'No, why would I do that?' He said it too quickly, with a defensive edge. 'I was out with the dogs and heard you clapping. Can't blame me for that.'

'You know hunting with a crossbow's illegal?' I said, looking at the dead animals lolling from his shoulder bag.

'So what? You're not a cop, what's it to do with you?'

I let it go. It wouldn't do any good, and there were more important things at stake.

'Look, you need to leave,' I went on. 'This is a crime scene.'

'Didn't stop you from taking pictures, did it?' His face became sly. 'Tell you what, if you send them to me I won't tell anyone.'

My patience had worn thin. 'They're for the police. I work with them, I'm a forensic scientist.'

For someone who didn't like talking about his work, I was beginning to sound like a broken record. But it took the smile from his face.

'Fuck off, I don't believe you!'

He was sounding defensive now. 'What's your name?' I asked.

'Why? You going to ask me out?'

My patience was running thin. 'Look, I don't want to see you get into any trouble. The police will need everything here left undisturbed. We should both go now.'

He didn't answer. I felt my irritation rise as I saw him struggling to keep a smirk from his face. That was when I noticed there was only one dog, the grizzled lurcher, still next to him.

Where was the other?

I spun round to see the young black lurcher nosing in the crater made by the tree roots. There was something curved and pale in its mouth.

The skeleton's missing mandible.

'No!' I shouted, running towards it.

The dog bounded away with the mandible still gripped in its jaws. It jinked away as I tried to catch it, as though this was some kind of game. I made a grab for its collar, my thick gloves slipping on the thick leather. Then the animal had pulled free and was sprinting into the forest.

Within seconds I'd lost sight of it.

I stared into the shadowy maze of spruce trees, my breath ragged, then turned back to Drew. He was convulsed with laughter as he gripped the older dog's collar.

'Your face! Brilliant!'

'Call it back!'

He was still giggling, wiping tears from his eyes. 'Sorry, mate. Give a dog a bone . . .'

That set him off laughing again. I fought to control my temper.

'I told you, this is a crime scene, and those are human remains you've just let your dog run off with! You think the police will think it's funny?'

His laughter dried up. 'The police aren't here, are they?'

'They will be. And what do you think's going to happen then?'

'It's not my fault.' He sounded sulky. 'They're not my dogs anyway.'

'Whose are they, your grandfather's?' I said, remembering the old man from the pub. 'What do you think he's going to say?'

I'd wanted to rattle him, but I didn't expect the threat to have the effect it did. He blanched.

'Don't tell him. Please!'

'Then get your dog back here. Now.'

His bluster had evaporated. Hooking a finger and thumb into his mouth he gave a piercing whistle. *Fury! Here, boy! Here!*

The young lurcher appeared almost immediately, trotting out from a different area of spruce trees as though it had been waiting to be called. Its tongue lolled from its mouth in a happy grin as it rejoined them.

There was no sign of the jawbone.

I tried to keep the anger from my voice as I turned back to the teenager. 'You better help me find it.'

'No chance.' He was already hurrying away, clicking his fingers at the dogs to follow him. 'Come on, this way!'

'Wait, don't just—'

But I was talking to his back. He was almost running as he headed off into the trees, the dogs loping along with him.

Within moments they'd disappeared, leaving me alone in the darkening plantation.

Chapter 11

It took me half an hour to find the mandible. I'd wasted some of it staring into the murk between the close-packed spruce trunks, reluctant to venture too far into them. I tried to convince myself I should wait until the next day before searching for the jawbone. The dog could have dropped it anywhere, and my getting lost or trying to find my way down the mountain in the dark wasn't going to help anyone.

But I couldn't leave without at least making the attempt. The lurcher had come back quickly when it had been called, so I didn't think it could have gone far. Trying to retrace the dog's route, I left the clearing where the spruce had fallen and began to search among the trees. The silence and shadows seemed to deepen as they closed around me. If this had been a natural woodland, with an ecosystem of plants, shrubs and trees all competing for light, my chances of finding the mandible would have been slim. As it was, the plantation's monoculture worked in my favour. Nothing grew between the spruce trunks, and the mat of dead needles covering the ground between them was barren and empty.

Empty of any sign of the jawbone, too. Frustrated, after a while I glanced back at the clearing to get my bearings.

I couldn't see it.

I'd come further than I'd realised. Wherever I looked, all I could see were the featureless trees receding into the gathering dusk. I knew I couldn't be far from the glade, and once there I could find the lane back to the road easily enough. But without knowing where it was I might end up heading deeper into the plantation. Trying to suppress a rising alarm, I looked for some recognisable feature among the endless trunks. I couldn't see anything, but as I stood there I picked out the faint splashing of a stream through the trees. That meant Foss Ghyll had to be nearby. I cocked my head, trying to pinpoint the direction where it was coming from, then set off towards it. The sound of running water steadily grew louder, and after a few minutes I noticed a slightly brighter area of plantation. As I drew nearer I made out the horizontal line of the fallen spruce through the vertical trunks and felt my neck and shoulder muscles unlock with relief.

I really *had* wandered off course, I saw, walking faster. There was no question of staying to look for the mandible any longer. The plantation was too easy to become lost in, especially now the light was dropping. I didn't like giving up, but I'd pushed my luck enough already. It was time to go.

I was almost back at the clearing when something pale and angular caught my eye at the foot of a spruce. It was half-hidden in the fallen spruce needles, and as I went over I told myself it was probably just part of a root or branch.

It wasn't.

The jawbone was coated with the lurcher's saliva and spruce needles but otherwise didn't appear to be damaged. Wishing I'd brought an evidence bag with me, I carefully picked it up. I didn't make a habit of handling evidence, but the lurcher had changed the game when it ran off with the sickle-shaped bone. Although the rest of the skeleton needed to be left undisturbed, I couldn't leave the mandible out here where other scavengers might run off with it.

At least I was wearing gloves.

A murky haze was settling on the plantation as I returned to the clearing. I paused by the fallen spruce, taking a last look at the skeletal remains. I wondered again who it might be, and how they'd come to be here. But it was too cold to stand around speculating, and the light was fading faster than ever. With the splashing from Foss Ghyll to orientate me, I struck off through the plantation in what I hoped was the right direction.

This time I didn't wander off course, and within a few minutes I came out at the glade.

By now the day had given way to a grey twilight. It continued to darken as I crossed the glade and started down the lane through the woods, making me regret not bringing the torch from my car. Although my phone had a flashlight I wanted to conserve the battery, so I made my way down the steep and overgrown lane in near darkness. The character of the old woods had changed as the light failed, the peace and tranquillity I'd enjoyed earlier turning into something more sinister as the shadows deepened and the trees grew more indistinct.

But I'd plenty to occupy my mind. Any hope I'd had of keeping the skeletal remains a secret until the police arrived had ended as soon as the teenager walked into the clearing. By morning most of the village would have heard what was in the plantation. Ghoulish curiosity being what it was, there was a good chance at least some of them would want to see it for themselves. They needed to be persuaded to stay away, and I couldn't do that on my own.

Like it or not, I was going to need help.

The sound of my boots made a lonely soundtrack as I went down the darkening lane. An owl hooted mournfully nearby but other than that there was no sign of life. The lane seemed longer than I remembered, and it was a relief when I finally saw the drystone wall ahead of me in the dusk.

I was cold, tired and hungry as I climbed over the wall and unlocked my car. It gave an electronic squawk, flashing its lights, and in their brief glow I noticed that the car seemed oddly lopsided. With a sinking feeling I took the torch from the glovebox and shone it down at the tyres.

One of them was flat.

Oh, fantastic . . . My first thought was that I must have picked up a slow puncture on the drive there. Then I crouched down for a closer look and saw the hole in the tyre wall. In the torch beam it was small and round, about the same size as a pencil.

Or a crossbow bolt.

Night had fallen by the time I'd changed the tyre. Experience had taught me not to rely on recovery services in some of the more remote places my work took me to, so I had a full spare in the car boot, along with a jack and the necessary tools.

That didn't mean I was happy about it.

I'd no doubt about what had happened, or who was responsible. I shone the torch on the ground underneath and on the far side of the car, but there was no sign of the crossbow bolt. Either the teenager had stabbed it into the tyre like a knife or retrieved it afterwards.

My fingers were both numb and aching after I'd replaced the wheel and climbed back in the car. Turning up the heater, I offered a silent prayer that the new tyre would stay on as I pulled away. A thin gruel of sleet began to come down as I drove into the village. The main street was deserted, the streetlights standing in darkness. I'd forgotten until then that there was no power. The houses I passed were either dark or lit by the dimmer glow from candles or battery-powered lanterns. As I drove by The Perseverance a flickering light through the cracks in the drawn curtains suggested it was business as usual in the pub, if nowhere else.

The broken sign had been repaired, I noticed.

Changing the tyre had given me plenty of time to decide who I should approach for help to protect the remains. The obvious person was Maud. As the plantation manager her voice would carry more weight than mine, and she'd hear about the remains anyway. It was better if she heard it first from me.

I'd hoped to find her at the lumber yard, but as I approached it I could see the plantation office was dark. It looked as though I was too late and everyone had left for the night. Or not quite: my headlights picked out someone in a hooded coat locking up the big mesh gates. He turned as I pulled up and I saw it was Maud's office manager, Eddie.

The cocky teenager's uncle, judging by what I'd seen in the pub last night.

But I decided against mentioning that. Sleet peppered my face when I lowered the car window.

'I'm looking for Maud,' I said.

'Maud . . .?' He looked around, as though expecting to see her. 'She's gone home.'

'Can you tell me where she lives?'

His brow furrowed worriedly. 'Er, I don't know if . . .'

'It's important.'

'She'll be here in the morning,' he said, hopefully. 'You could come back then.'

'Sorry, this can't wait.'

He rubbed the back of his neck. 'I suppose if it's important . . . Head back down the road and it's the first road on your left, just before you get to the village. The house is about half a mile along. You can't miss it.'

I thanked him and closed the window on the sleet. Turning the car around, I drove back towards the village. I almost missed the turn. It was another single-lane, hard to see for the high banks and dead undergrowth on either side, but Eddie was right about the house being easy to find. There was only one house there, a square Edwardian villa with windows either side of the front door, giving it the basic symmetry of a child's drawing. Light leaked out from the drawn curtains, showing that someone was home.

Parking on the gravel drive, I put my hood up against the sleet and hurried past what in the darkness looked like a Volvo SUV to the front door. A dog barked inside when I rang the bell, and after a short pause the door was opened. Maud's brown labrador lunged through the gap, barking furiously before being hauled back by its collar.

'Behave, Max!' Still gripping the dog's collar, Maud frowned when she recognised me. 'Dr Hunter. Can I help you?'

'Sorry to disturb you, but we need to talk.'

Her expression said she doubted that. 'How did you know where I live?'

'Someone at the lumberyard told me.' I didn't want to get Eddie into trouble, though she could probably guess who it had been. 'I said it was important.'

'If this is about Hooley—'

'It isn't.'

Sleet beaded Maud's face as she considered me through the partly open door. 'No offense, but I don't know you from Adam, and I'm not about to let a total stranger into my home. What's so important it wouldn't wait till tomorrow?'

'I found human remains on the plantation.'

She stared at me, then stepped back with a sigh.

'You'd better come in.'

Chapter 12

After Maud's cluttered office at the lumber yard, her house was a surprise. The hallway was neat and modern, all neutral colours with pale oak furniture and clean lines. Light shone from an open doorway at its far end and the soothing piano of Beethoven's *Moonlight Sonata* drifted from the same room. I pushed my hood back, conscious of dripping water onto the coconut mat in the doorway.

'Hang your coat up and come on through,' Maud said.

Without waiting, she went into the room, the labrador bounding ahead of her. By the front door was a row of wall hooks, where a jumble of thick coats and waxed jackets hung over a selection of boots and Wellingtons.

Hanging up my jacket, I followed Maud. The classical piano grew louder as I went into an open plan living and dining room. Flames flickered behind the glass panel of a large log burner, but most of the light came from a powerful battery-powered lamp on top of the slate island that separated the kitchen from the rest of the room. An ancient-looking portable CD player stood there as well, while diced red pepper, onion and garlic scented the air from a chopping board. A large kitchen knife lay next to it, and a glass of red wine, now part-empty, stood next to an open bottle.

'I don't normally drink at this time, but this has been a sod of a day. And something tells me it isn't going to get any better,' Maud said, going over to the glass of wine. She started to raise it, then hesitated. 'Can I get you anything . . .?'

A hot drink would have been welcome after being on the freezing mountainside, but I got the impression I was intruding enough as it was.

'No, thanks.'

Maud took her glass to where two armchairs and a matching sofa were arranged around a low rosewood coffee table. Lowering herself into one of the chairs, with something partway between a grunt and a sigh, she waved at its twin.

'Take a pew,' she told me, then gave the dog a tap on its rump. 'Behave yourself, Max. Sit!'

The brown labrador reluctantly did as it was told, producing a low rumble in its throat that was more excitement than threat. Sitting back, Maud took a drink of wine, closing her eyes briefly to savour it before regarding me across the table.

'So whereabouts are these "remains" you reckon you've seen?'

She listened as I told her how I'd found the remains near the ghyll, though without giving away too many details of exactly where it was.

'Since the remains are on your land I thought I should let you know,' I said, when I'd finished. 'I'm assuming that *is* planta- tion land up there?'

'We don't own the woods or the land immediately around Foss Ghyll, but if there's spruce trees growing on it then yes, it's probably ours.'

'How old are the trees up there?'

'I can't say without checking the records. But if it's where I think it is, that area would have been planted about eighteen or nineteen years ago.'

That was less than I'd expected, both from the condition of the remains and the size of the fallen tree. 'This is near Foss Ghyll? The trees looked pretty mature.'

She gave a wry smile. 'They're Sitka spruce. Grow up to four feet a year for the first two or three decades, that's why they're so popular in plantations. They're usually ready for felling after thirty-five years or so, so the ones up there will be seventy or eighty feet tall by now.'

That sounded about right, but I'd have said the one that had blown down was bigger. It had been hard to gauge how tall the still standing trees had been, though, especially with them growing so close together. And I wasn't about to contradict Maud.

She was frowning, her mouth pursed in disapproval. 'Leaving aside the fact that you were trespassing, did I hear right that you went up there to make a *phone* call?'

It wasn't the question I'd expected her to lead with. 'I thought there might be a signal,' I said, deciding to leave out Nisha's involvement.

'On the *fell*?' The look she gave me said what she thought to that. 'And these bones you found. Are you certain they aren't just a deer or sheep's?'

'It wasn't an animal. The remains are human.'

'Are you sure? With all due respect, Dr Hunter, we do get a lot of animal carcasses around here, so——'

'These were wearing clothes.'

'Right. Well, that does sound . . . conclusive. Lord, what a time for the bloody phones to pack in.' She shook her head, then gave me a shrewd look. 'I presume you aren't just here out of courtesy. What is it you want?'

'Until the police can get out to us we need to keep everyone away from there. I thought you could put word out that the plantation's off limits?'

'Didn't stop you, did it?' Maud said, raising an eyebrow. 'Sorry, but I'd be wasting my breath. Apart from anything else, the plantation covers ten square miles, so there's no way you're going to keep people out. I wouldn't worry, though. I can make sure none of my lot go anywhere near, and I can't see many people bothering to wander all that way out. Provided we don't say anything there's no reason anyone else needs to know about it.'

'They already do,' I said, and told her about the teenager.

Maud puffed out her cheeks. 'Wonderful. I don't suppose you've any idea who this lad was, do you?'

'I think he might be related to your office manager. They were both at a family gathering in the pub last night.' I would have gone on, but I could see from her face there was no need.

103

'Christ on a bike, today just keeps getting better and better,' she said, sourly. 'That'll be Drew Beddoes. He's Eddie's nephew. By marriage, anyway. Lives in the pub with his dad and grandfather. If you've met him there's no need for me to tell you what he's like.'

There wasn't, but I'd hoped I might be wrong. 'Can you ask Eddie to have a word with him? See if they can persuade him not to tell anyone about it for a day or two?'

Maud was shaking her head before I'd finished.

'Wouldn't do any good. Eddie's a decent sort, and so is his wife, Evie. But her family are . . . Well, let's just say they aren't going to listen to anything Eddie says. The old man, Wynn Beddoes, is a nasty piece of work. The story is he made the money to buy the pub from illegal bare-knuckle fighting after he was banned from boxing. Used to run a gym from the back room of the pub until he had a stroke and found God. His brand of religion's more Old Testament than turn-the-other-cheek, and the old sod's still hard as nails even now. Everyone round here tiptoes round him, even his family.'

That sounded like the old man I'd seen in the pub. 'Will you come with me to talk to him? He's more likely to listen to you than he is me.'

Maud gave a sour laugh. 'Wynn Beddoes doesn't listen to anybody. Sorry, but I don't see how I can help.'

'What about Drew's father? Is it worth talking to him?'

'Doubt it. Alun jumps to the old man's tune, and he's a dour bugger himself. He had to bring up Drew on his own after his wife left him. Might explain why the lad's turned out as he has, with just the three of . . . Oh lord!' Her face suddenly changed. 'This skeleton you found, is it a man or a woman?'

'It's hard to say,' I hedged, unwilling to give away that sort of information. 'Why?'

'Something I've just remembered. It was before my time, but Wynn Beddoes had another son who went missing years ago. God, what was his name? Begins with a J . . . Jeff, no. Jed, that's it. The story is he was killed in a fight with another local over a woman. Some New Age hippy traveller or something who'd been staying in the village. The other man did a runner afterwards

104

and the son's body was never found. I think it was after that Beddoes had his stroke.' Maud looked as though she couldn't decide whether to be concerned or intrigued. 'You don't think this could be his *son*, do you?'

Christ. It was possible. It would need a familial DNA test to confirm it one way or the other, but the skeleton I'd seen had the same strong, heavy bone structure as the old man in the pub. And his son, the middle-aged man with the shaved head, come to that. That was far from conclusive, but it wasn't such a stretch to believe they could be the victim's father and brother.

'How long ago was this?' I asked.

'I'm not sure. Like I say, it was before I came here. But from what I've heard probably twenty, twenty-five years?'

That would fit my time since death estimate for the skeleton- ised remains, but it was several years before Maud had said the trees around Foss Ghyll had been planted. I tried to keep my expression neutral.

'Do you know how old Jed Beddoes was?'

'Lord, I've no idea.' Maud turned down her mouth. 'Twenties, perhaps, from what I've heard?'

I'd have said the individual in the tree roots had been younger than that when he died. But I could be wrong, about that as well as the time since death. The discrepancy wasn't so great as to rule anything out, and my estimate had only been based on a limited visual examination. The remains would have to be X-rayed, cleaned and carefully examined at the mortuary to get a more accurate picture, and by then DNA testing, dental records or some other factor should have confirmed the victim's identity anyway. Until then, regardless of how it looked, it was too soon to jump to any conclusions.

But I knew people here wouldn't see it that way. A local man had gone missing years before and now a buried skeleton had been found. Once word of the discovery spread, there would be no doubt in most minds whose it was.

I stood up. 'I need to talk to Jed Beddoes' family.'

'That's not a good idea.'

'If I don't they might want to go to see the remains for themselves.'

'Were you not listening to what I said? The family's going to take their cue from the old man, and if Wynn Beddoes thinks this is his son . . . Well, I don't know what he'll do, but you certainly don't want to get in the middle of it. And bear in mind that Vic Hooley's close to the Beddoes. He practically lives in that pub, and he'll have told them and anyone else who'll listen that it's *your* fault there's no phones or power. You're the last person they'll want to see.'

She was probably right. I was an outsider while Hooley was one of their own. And I'd already seen how quickly his story had taken root.

'I still have to try,' I said.

'Up to you. Just don't say I didn't warn you.' Maud scratched the labrador's ears, frowning. 'One other thing. Did I hear you say earlier that you stayed at Hillside House last night? The old Reese place?'

'That's right. They're letting me stay there for the time being.'

'Ah. Well, that complicates things.'

I couldn't see how the situation could be more complicated than it already was. 'How?'

'There's no love lost between the village and Hillside House, as you've probably gathered from your encounter with Vic Hooley,' she said. 'Have your hosts mentioned that?'

'Not really.' Nisha had said they'd been having trouble from poachers, and there was obviously bad blood between Reese and Hooley, but that was as much as I knew.

Maud gave a snort. 'Didn't think so. Well, next to the plantation, the Reeses are the biggest landowners around here, but I daresay they didn't mention that either. The woods and old army camp? That's all theirs. Acres of it, doing nothing.'

Nisha had already told me much the same thing, but I let it pass. It was a huge tract of land, and I could see why Maud might disapprove of it going unused. Still, I couldn't pretend I was sorry that the old woods and beautiful glade with its dramatic ghyll hadn't been swallowed up by the spruce plantation.

'OK, but I don't see why that complicate things,' I said, trying to be tactful.

'That's because you don't live here. All due respect, but you're probably thinking all that nice, chocolate box country-side should be left untouched rather than being used to grow something that, God forbid, people actually *need*. Like timber for furniture and construction, and pulp for paper and cardboard. Admittedly, biodiversity might not have been a priority when some of the trees here were planted. But things have moved on. We're a sustainable industry now, more ecologically aware.' She gave an airy wave of dismissal. 'OK, some of the land owned by Hillside House land is too steep for felling, but not all of it. And when there's a dearth of jobs and investment like there is around here, it rankles when local people see someone sitting on an asset that could bring in both.'

'I still don't see what this has to do with me or the remains,' I said. I had to go and see Wynn Beddoes, and I was conscious it was getting late.

Maud raised her hands.

'OK, fine. I apologise for riding off on my hobby horse. But the point is there's a lot of resentment towards the Reese family. Even the son — Jon, is it? He inherited Hillside House and moved in with his wife and baby about a year ago, when his mother died. Not my idea of a starter home, but never mind. She'd sold a small parcel of land years ago, and when she died my employers contacted her son with a *very* reasonable offer for several tracts of land, hoping he might be more reasonable. He never bothered to reply. And word gets out about that sort of thing.' Maud paused, giving me a meaningful look as she reached for her wine glass. 'Then you've got their history with the Beddoes.'

She sniffed and took a drink. I was clearly meant to ask, so I did.

'What sort of history?'

Maud set down her glass. Sitting back, she looked across at me with the satisfied air of someone who was finally getting to the point.

'You remember I told you Wynn Beddoes' son was supposed to have been killed by a local man? It was Jon Reese's father.'

Chapter 13

The sleet had grown heavier when I left Maud's. Whipped by the wind, the icy flecks stung my face as I hurried to my car. I turned on the wipers to clear the build-up of frozen slush from the windscreen and pulled out of the drive. When I reached the junction with the main street I stopped, watching the sleet in my headlights as I decided what to do.

Maud was right. The situation was even more complicated than I'd realised. Nisha had told me that Jon's father hadn't been around for a long time. She'd neglected to mention that he'd abandoned his family when he was suspected of murdering Wynn Beddoes' youngest son. Whose body I might well just have found. The sensible thing to do would be to go back to the hotel and leave it for the police to sort out. I'd done all I reasonably could for one night, and it wasn't my job to try and persuade a volatile and grieving family not to do anything rash.

Or to get involved in a blood feud.

The wipers ticked like a countdown. Swearing under my breath, I put the car into gear and headed into the village and The Perseverance.

Edendale was in darkness. The streets were empty and unlit, the streetlights reduced to shadowed poles as I pulled up outside The Perseverance. Cracks of muted light still seeped around the gaps in the pub's drawn curtains, but when I tried the doors they didn't open. I rattled the handle, leaning my weight against the cold wood before accepting they were locked.

That's it, then. You tried. The car was a seductive presence behind me. I allowed myself a moment to think about climbing back in and driving away, then I knocked on the door.

It shuddered under my hand. I waited, but no sound came from inside. I raised my hand to knock again when there was a sudden clack of bolts being shot back. The door was opened by the shaven-headed man Maud said was Drew's father, Alun.

His face looked hard as granite as he stared out at me. 'What do you want?'

'I'd like to talk to your father.'

'We're closed.'

He started to shut the door, but the deep rasp I recognised from the night before came from behind him.

'Let him in.'

He looked tempted to slam the door anyway. Then, with obvious reluctance, he stepped back and opened it.

I went in.

The room was dark. A fire crackled and spat in the hearth. The only other illumination came from candles and battery lanterns set out on the bar and tables, creating pockets of light that threw the corners of the room into deep shadow.

No one was serving behind the bar tonight, and only the large table by the fire was occupied. The Beddoes sat around it as before. They stared across at me in hostile silence, the firelight and flickering shadows giving the scene the *chiaroscuro* look of an old painting. I recognised everyone from my last time there. Hooley sat at the edge of the group, glaring daggers with a pint in his hand and a collection of empty glasses on the table in front of him. Drew was there as well, still looking as though he was trying to keep from grinning at some private joke. Eddie, Maud's office manager, looked more harassed than ever. He was sitting next to his wife Evie, Beddoes' daughter, who looked as though she'd been crying.

Wynn Beddoes sat at the head of the table, the two lurchers at his feet. He was slumped and wizened, parchment skin drawn tight over his sunken cheeks, yet there was nothing feeble about

110

his eyes. Hard and shrewd, they fairly burnt with venom as he glowered out from under bushy grey brows.

I jumped as the door bolts were rammed home behind me. As though that was his cue, Hooley spoke up.

'The fuck's he doing here?'

'Shut it, Vic,' Alun said, his limp more pronounced tonight as he brushed past me to stand beside his father.

Seeing them side by side the resemblance was unmistakable, yet for all his frailty it was still the older man who commanded attention. He remained silent as Alun jutted his chin at me.

'Go on, then.'

'I expect you've heard what I found in the plantation this afternoon, so you can probably guess why I'm here,' I said, with a glance at Drew. His smirk had widened. 'My name's David Hunter. I'm a forensic anthropologist and—'

'We don't give a shit!' Hooley spat. 'Who do you think—'

Wynn Beddoes' walking stick crashed down onto the table, making the glasses jump and rattle. The two lurchers bolted upright, ears pricked.

'Let him speak,' the old man grated.

Hooley subsided, glaring at me as he reached for his glass. Ignoring him, I addressed Wynn Beddoes.

'I realise how difficult this must be. I've heard that your son went missing and I know you're going to want answers. I wish I could give them to you. I can't, but I do have experience with this sort of situation.'

Hooley seemed about to say something else, then looked at Beddoes and thought better of it. The old man's gaze remained fixed on me, sharp and unwavering.

'And what sort of *situation* is that?'

'Of recovering human remains.' There was no point trying to sugar the pill. 'I know waiting is hard, but it's important that no one goes up there until the police get here. The fewer people who know about this the better, so . . .'

I trailed off as all eyes went to Drew. He had a shifty expression, and I could guess why.

111

'Who else have you told?' I asked.

'Go on, answer him,' Eddie's wife said sharply, when Drew didn't respond.

The teenager tried for a cocky shrug. 'I told a few mates on the way home. So what? Not a secret, is it?'

Not anymore. Any hope I'd had of keeping this contained to the immediate family disappeared. Even without phones, word would have spread through the village by now.

'It's important that everyone keeps away from the site,' I said, choosing my words carefully. 'The more people go there the more risk there is of evidence being destroyed or lost. That's going to make it harder to identify whoever this is and find out what happened.'

'"Whoever this is?"' Beddoes repeated, his mouth curled in contempt. 'I already *know* who it is! And what happened to him!'

'I wasn't trying to—'

'*That's my son up there!*' he thundered, extending an arthritic finger towards the mountain. 'My *son!* Twenty-six years I've been waiting, without so much as a grave to stand over! And you've got the audacity to come here, to my *home*, and lay down the law to *me*? Nobody tells a Beddoes what to do! Nobody!'

'That wasn't my intent,' I said, with a sick feeling at how quickly this had turned bad. 'If that's how it sounded, then I'm sorry. But we don't know enough yet to—'

'*I* do! *I* know!' Beddoes struck his fist against his chest with a hollow thud. 'That's my flesh and blood up there, murdered by that Godless bastard Owen Reese! I don't need some police lackey to tell me that!'

Owen Reese must be Jon's father, I realised. Maud hadn't known his name, but I wasn't given a chance to reflect on the information.

'Too fucking right!' Hooley chimed in. 'Who's this bastard to come here, saying what we can and can't do? He's staying with Reese's son so he's probably on their side! I say we throw the fucker out!'

112

'Oh, for Christ's sake, will you *shut up!*' Beddoes' daughter burst out. 'I'm sick of hearing you!'

Hooley blinked, looking hurt. 'I was only—'

'Well don't! This isn't anything to do with you, I don't even know why you're here!'

Her husband made a pacifying gesture with his hands, but his appeasing grin looked more like a rictus. 'Evie . . .'

'Oh, don't start!' She turned away, her expression harsh but her eyes brimming.

'I'm not on anybody's side,' I went on, before anyone else could interrupt. 'All I'm trying to do is protect the remains. They're fragile and we can't afford any more incidents like this afternoon.'

As soon as I'd said it I realised my mistake. The old man' eyes narrowed. 'What do you mean, *more incidents*? What happened this afternoon?'

Drew didn't give me chance to answer. 'Nothing! He meant the storm!'

A flush had darkened the teenager's cheeks, and his smirk had vanished. He couldn't have looked more guilty if he'd tried. Beddoes slowly turned to face him.

'Tell me what happened.'

'Nothing, Granddad, honest!'

'Don't lie, boy!'

'I'm not!' He looked around, but if he was searching for a sympathetic face he didn't find one. 'It was Fury anyway, not me! It wasn't my fault!'

The black lurcher looked up when it heard its name, tail thumping on the ground. Now all eyes were on Drew. Alun Beddoes didn't raise his voice, but the skin on his face seemed to have tightened as he spoke to his son.

'I'm only going to ask you once. What did you do?'

'Nothing! Fury ran off with, with some old bone, that's all! I-I tried to stop him . . .'

There was a stunned silence. Even Hooley seemed lost for words. Alun, Drew's father bowed his head, rubbing his hands over his shaven scalp.

'Jesus Christ . . .'

'It's OK, I found it. It wasn't badly damaged,' I said, hoping to calm things. I might as well not have bothered.

'It was just a bit of bone, that's all!' Drew insisted, looking from one of them to the other.

'A bit of *bone*?' Wynn Beddoes intoned. 'That's your uncle's *remains* you're talking about! And you let a *dog* slobber over them like something from a *BUTCHER'S SHOP!*'

The old man's voice rose to a roar. Drew had gone chalk-white. 'I-I'm sorry, Granddad . . .'

The old man lifted a gnarled, bony fist, half rising from his chair as though he were about to hit his grandson. But the effort seemed too much.

'Get out of my sight,' he said, sagging back onto his seat.

'You heard your Granddad! Get to your room!' Alun snapped, his face red.

Fighting back tears, the teenager stood up and hurried through a door next to the bar. No one spoke as it swung shut behind him. The fire spat and crackled in the silence as Beddoes bent down to stroke the younger lurcher's head. I saw Evie and Eddie exchange an uneasy look, then the old man gave a short gasp. His face was suddenly ashen.

'You all right, Dad?' Evie asked. 'Here, let me get your tablets.'

'I'm all right,' he grumbled, but didn't try to stop her as she took a small pill bottle from his jacket pocket. Shaking out a tablet, she quickly slipped it into his mouth. He swallowed it, his eyes closing as he put his head back.

'What medication is he on?' I asked, guessing it was probably glyceryl trinitrate or some other angina treatment. 'I used to be a GP, let me take a—'

Alun's face twisted. 'We don't want your fucking help! Just get out!'

'Yeah, fuck off! You've done enough damage!' Hooley jumped to his feet, a mean glint in his eyes. 'It's all right, Al, I'll sort this fucker out.'

He started towards me, but suddenly Eddie had interposed himself between us. Putting a hand on my arm he gently steered me towards the pub's door.

'You should go,' he said, apologetically.

I looked back at Wynn Beddoes. I didn't like to walk away and leave him like this, but it would only make things worse if I stayed. The old man still looked cadaverous, but his colour was better.

'He'll be all right now, but you need to leave,' Eddie said, then lowered his voice. 'Please.'

He followed me to the door, though less to usher me out than act as a buffer between me and Hooley. I didn't argue. The cold took my breath away when I stepped outside. The sleet was coming down heavier than ever, icy shards probing for gaps in my coat. The pub's door banged shut behind me, leaving me alone in the dark street.

As I went back to my car, I heard the door bolts being shot home.

Chapter 14

The pinnacles and turrets of Hillside House loomed above me, a block of deeper black in the dark as I pulled up outside. Its unlit windows gaped blindly, square black holes reflecting only the night. Switching off the engine, I sat in the darkness, listening to the soft patter of sleet against the car.

Going to The Perseverance had been a mistake. I should have known that trying to reason with a grieving family was asking for trouble, but I hadn't expected it to go as badly as it had. If anything, I'd only made things worse. And now I had to tell the man who'd taken me into his home that I might have found the body of his father's victim. Maud was right.

It had been a sod of a day.

Christ . . . I kneaded my eyes, wondering what the hell sort of mess I'd landed myself in. It didn't seem possible that I'd barely been in Edendale twenty-four hours, and I found myself wishing yet again there was some way to contact the police. But there wasn't, and sitting there feeling sorry for myself wasn't going to change anything.

Climbing out of the car, I went to get my things from the boot. Lighting my way with the torch, I went to the extension at the back of the hotel. The muted glow from its curtained windows looked almost welcoming, but there was a heaviness in my steps as I went to the door and knocked.

It was Reese who opened it, a tea-towel in his hands. 'You made it back, then.'

Without waiting for a response, he stood back to let me in. Closing the door behind me, I set down my holdall. Reese was alone in the kitchen. The sleeves of his thick sweater were pushed back on his powerful, dark-haired forearms. A battery-powered lantern stood on the pine dresser against one wall, dazzlingly white to look at though not bright enough to dispel the shadows. In the corner, the lifeless computer monitors stood dark and accusing, as though already forgotten.

But the old wood-fired Aga made the room cosy and warm, and the smell of something mouth-wateringly spicy reminded me I hadn't eaten anything since morning. Going to the sink, Reese resumed washing dishes.

'We were starting to think you'd found somewhere else to stay.'

'No, I—'

Before I could say more the hallway door opened and Nisha came in. She looked pensive, and her frown only partially cleared when she saw me.

'I thought I heard someone.' Her smile seemed forced. 'Hi, David. I was just putting Kiran to bed. Are you OK? When it got dark we thought something might have happened.'

'Did we?' Jon said, putting a dripping plate in the drainer.

It was only then I noticed how strained the atmosphere between them was. 'There were a few things I had to do in the village,' I said.

Nisha's eyebrows arched. 'Oh? Is everything all right?'

It was a perfect opening to tell them about the remains. But whether it was the tension in the kitchen or just its overpowering warmth, all at once the day's events seemed to catch up with me. After the encounter with the Beddoes, I needed to collect my thoughts before launching into any more explanations.

'It was just something I had to discuss with Maud,' I said, knowing they'd assume it had to do with Hooley's crash. 'Look, if you don't mind I'd like to clean up and drop my things in my room. Assuming it's still OK for me to stay . . .?'

'Of course it is!' Nisha said, turning away to go to the fridge. I wasn't sure but for a moment I'd thought I saw something like disappointment on her face. 'Have you eaten yet?'

'No, not yet.'

'OK, well, Jon's made a veggie tagine. I can bring a plate up to your room if you like, or you're welcome to eat with us?'

'I expect he'll want to have it in his room,' Jon said, without turning round from the sink. 'No point trailing back down here.'

It was an unsubtle hint, and I'd rather have eaten in my room anyway than brave the tension radiating off them both. But they needed to know what had happened, and the news wouldn't wait till the morning.

'If it's OK I'll come back down,' I said.

There was a clatter as Jon put a plate on the drainer. He didn't say anything but the stiffness of his back meant he didn't have to. Nisha gave a too-bright smile.

'Great! It'll be ready in about half-an-hour. You'll need a torch on the stairs because there's no lights. The heater in your room isn't working either, but I made a fire earlier. I've left you some logs and matches so you can get it going again.'

I thanked her and went out of the kitchen. It was a relief to get away from the fraught atmosphere, but as I walked down the chilly and unlit hallway there was something else bothering me. Nisha had been distraught at being cut off from the outside world, with no way to contact her client. It had been her idea to hike up the fell to the spruce plantation in the first place, on the off-chance that I might stumble across a phone signal.

Yet she'd never asked if I'd found one.

The cold hit me like a slap in the face when I opened the concealed door from the extension and stepped into the old hotel. The foyer was pitch black, utterly still and silent. I fumbled for the switch on my torch, conscious of the echoing silence. Then the torch beam lanced out, dozens of glass eyes glinting in its light like stars in a threadbare sky. I suppressed a shudder. The hotel had been eerie enough when the lights were working, but now . . .

Jesus . . .

Under the dead animals' silent gaze, I headed across the foyer to the staircase. My footsteps echoed in the cavernous space, and I tried not to notice how the darkness closed in behind me. The stairs creaked more loudly than I remembered, and the corridor where my room was — number fourteen, not thirteen — seemed twice as long as before. Even the stuffed fox Nisha had joked about seemed more threatening in the torchlight, the crossed eyes gleamingly manic as it crouched, ready to pounce.

After the corridor's dank chill, the warmth of the room was a welcome surprise. Embers glowed orange in the small fireplace and the air held the flavour of woodsmoke. A small mesh screen had been placed in front of the fire, and off to one side was a cardboard box of logs, kindling and matches. Left on the bedside cabinet, next to the non-working lamp, was a battery-powered child's nightlight, a blue globe with shaped cut-outs. I switched it on and smiled as the wall behind it was dappled with bright moons and stars.

I hoped Kiran didn't mind sharing it.

I put kindling on the embers, then added logs once the fire had caught. The chimney drew surprisingly well, even though it couldn't have been swept in years, and soon flames were driving back the shadows with a dancing yellow light.

Hanging up my coat and outer layers on the door hook, I switched on my laptop. While I waited for it to start I took the mandible from the forest out of my holdall. I'd tucked it in there before I'd changed the car tyre, after first sealing it in a spare evidence bag from the flight case of equipment I carried in my car. The jawbone might have been better protected in there with the rest of my equipment but I didn't want to leave it in the car boot, and Nisha and Reese might have wondered why I'd brought the battered aluminium case into the hotel.

Without removing the mandible from the thick plastic bag, I held it close to the light to examine it. The bone had survived the lurcher's attentions surprisingly well. It was large and heavy, with the wider breadth typical of males. The chin was pointed rather than blunt or rounded, again suggesting white ancestry rather than Black or Asian. Although the thick plastic bag prevented me from getting a proper look at the dentition, I could see that there were wisdom teeth on both sides. That confirmed that this was a mature adult, since wisdom teeth don't normally emerge until after adolescence. The teeth showed wear as well, especially to the rear molars. Not so much for me to think the victim was more than middle-aged, at most, but enough to confirm my initial impression that the jawbone belonged to someone in his thirties rather than twenties, as Maud had thought Jed Beddoes might be.

She'd only been guessing at his age, though. And it was possible that the condition of the teeth was deceptive anyway. Diet and lifestyle can affect how someone ages, and whoever this was he'd had a lot of dental work. More than half of the teeth in the mandible had silver amalgam fillings, and there was a stump of bone where a crown had once been. I couldn't rule out this being the jawbone of a twenty-something who'd ground his teeth and had poor dental hygiene. Or . . .

I stopped, my train of thought petering out. Or I might be tired and overthinking things.

A snap of popping resin from the burning logs made me jump. I'd been drifting off. Looking at my watch I saw it was almost time to go downstairs, but there was something I wanted to do first. My laptop was waiting patiently, its screen luminous in the dark room. Its battery was at almost ninety per cent, which should be enough. I had specialist software on it that could use the photographs I'd taken to create a virtual three-dimensional model of the remains, a process known as photogrammetry. But first I had to transfer them onto it.

My phone was still in my coat pocket. I took it out to unlock it and stopped dead when I saw the screen. There were still no signal bars showing but I'd got a text message.

It was from DS Chaudry.

Have emailed and left vmail. Search op cancelled. Victim found alive & well selling Class B drugs in Carlisle. Now in custody and not, repeat not, in shallow grave so forensic anthro no longer required. DCI Perry sends thanx & aplgs.

The bedsprings squeaked as I sank down onto its edge, staring dumbly at the text. I hadn't heard any notification, but the phone had been in my coat pocket, where I might not have noticed.

It was a moot point anyway, because it was obvious what had happened. Somewhere, sometime that afternoon I'd encountered a signal without realising.

Nisha had been right.

I tried to think when I'd last checked my phone. There had been no service on the logging trail Nisha had sent me to, I was sure of that. And I'd have seen straight away if I'd received a text while I was photographing the remains. But once Drew Beddoes turned up with the lurchers I'd had other things on my mind. I couldn't recall looking at my phone when I'd been searching for the mandible, or during the walk back down through the woods to my car. After that my phone had remained in my pocket while I'd changed the tyre, then driven first to Maud's house and later to The Perseverance to talk to the Beddoes. That was roughly a four-hour window.

The text could have popped up any time then.

Neither Chaudry's voicemail nor email had arrived, so wherever the stray signal had been, it had been too weak for anything larger than the text to make it through. I could go out again in the morning and try to find it again, but even if I managed to retrace my steps exactly there was no guarantee the signal would still be there. It had probably been a fluke, some freak of weather conditions and geography.

And I'd missed it.

As bad as things were, I'd taken some consolation from knowing that my absence in Carlisle would be noticed. I'd known it was only a matter of time before someone realised I was missing. Now even that small hope was gone. DS Chaudry would assume I'd got her message before I'd set off, and everyone I knew in London already thought I was working away. No one was going to wonder where I was, let alone come looking for me.

I was on my own.

I sat on the bed, staring at the crude stars and moons cast by the nightlight onto the wall while I absorbed this latest blow. The last thing I felt like doing was going back downstairs to break the news about the remains, but I couldn't put it off any longer. Pushing myself to my feet, I connected my phone to the laptop with a USB lead and copied the photographs I'd taken earlier onto it. There wasn't time to run the photogrammetry software now, but the way I was feeling perhaps that was no bad thing. Shutting down my laptop again, I washed myself in freezing cold water from the sputtering tap.

Then I went to break the news to Nisha and Reese.

Chapter 15

Nisha was on her own with her son when I went back into the kitchen. Kiran was in a highchair, and the table had been set with three places and a plate of flatbreads sat in its centre. A saucepan bubbled softly on the range, filling the room with a sweet, spicy smell.

'Perfect timing,' Nisha said. 'You might as well sit down, Jon won't be long. And Kiran decided he wanted to join us rather than go to bed. Didn't you, monster?'

He gave his mother a gummy smile. I went to the table as she began spooning a fragrant stew from the pan into three earthenware bowls. Nisha didn't look at me as she spoke.

'It's vegetable tagine with chickpeas and dried apricots, so hope you're OK with that,' she said, her words tumbling over each other. 'It's one of Jon's recipes. He normally does it with couscous, but we're out of that at the moment so he's made flatbread.'

'Sounds delicious.' It did, but my appetite had died at the thought of the conversation I was about to have. 'You said he was a chef. Did he only work in vegetarian restaurants?'

'Oh, no, he's not actually veggie himself. When we were in North America a couple of the restaurants he worked in were nose-to-tail. You know, where they make use of all of the animal? He had to skin and butcher them.' She grimaced and gave a shudder. 'I was brought up vegetarian – my family's Gujarati – so I wasn't too thrilled about that. But we respect that we've different values and he doesn't eat meat at home. He still does most of the cooking, though, thank God. His

125

vegetarian recipes are *really* good. I keep saying he should write a cookbook but . . . well, maybe one of these days. Anyway, I forgot to ask how you got on with your walk? Did you manage to make a phone call?'

Nisha's sudden change of tack caught me out. Her expression was politely curious as she carried two bowls to the table.

'No, I couldn't find a signal.' One had found me, but there was no point in mentioning that.

'Oh, that's a shame. So whereabouts did you—'

The kitchen door opened and Reese came in. He raised an eyebrow when he saw the two bowls on the table.

'This is cosy. Starting without me?'

Nisha turned away. 'I didn't know how long you were going to be. I was just going to put yours in the oven.'

'Don't bother, I'll get it,' he said, going over to the range.

If I'd hoped that the tension between them might have eased, now I knew better. Nisha picked up a heavy jug from the table as Reese joined us at the table.

'Would you like water, David? I'd offer you a beer, but Jon doesn't drink.'

'No, he doesn't. Not anymore,' Jon said, tartly. He gave me a terse smile. 'One of the joys of the restaurant business.'

'Water's fine,' I said.

An awkward silence descended as we began to eat, broken only by the chink of cutlery.

'This is really good,' I said, automatically.

'Have some flatbread,' Nisha urged. 'I love it, it's got sesame seeds in.'

I accepted a piece dutifully, nodding approval as I took a bite and washed it down with a drink of water.

'So how was your walk up the fell?' Jon asked. 'Nisha told me you were looking for a phone signal. Did you find one?'

The question wasn't quite sarcastic, but it was close. The barb seemed meant for Nisha rather than me, but it was as good an opening as I was going to get. I set down my cutlery.

'No, but one of the spruce trees on the plantation had blown down. There were human remains caught up in its roots.'

126

There was a silence. Nisha shot a worried look at her husband. He'd gone white.

'Blown down? No, that's . . .' Jon looked stunned. 'Are you sure?'

'Positive.' I hesitated. 'I thought you should know.'

'Yeah? And why's that?' Colour suddenly rushed back to his face. 'What have you heard?'

Nisha hurriedly shook her head. 'On Kiran's life, Jon, I didn't say anything. . .'

'It was Maud,' I told him. 'I went to see her because the remains are on plantation land. She told me that a local man went missing twenty-odd years ago. And that there was . . . a potential connection with your family.'

'Good old Maud.' Jon sat very still, but his fists had clenched on the table. Nisha reached out for him.

'Jon—'

'*Don't!*' He pulled away from her. 'Just . . . don't!'

'There's something else,' I continued, wanting to get all the bad news out there now. 'I went to see Wynn Beddoes afterwards—'

'*Beddoes?*' Jon's face had become even more flushed. 'Jesus Christ. Jesus fucking *Christ*! Why the *hell* would you do that?'

'Drew Beddoes followed me up to the plantation. He saw the remains.'

Jon rocked back in his seat as though he'd been punched. Nisha closed her eyes.

'Oh, God . . .' she breathed.

'That's why I was late getting back—' I began but didn't get any further.

Jon's chair screeched across the floor, almost toppling over as he stood up. For a second I thought he was going to take a swing at me, but then I saw his face. He looked winded and ashen.

'Where are you going?' Nisha asked, as he went to the front door.

'I need some air.' Grabbing his parka from the coat hook, he jammed his feet into mud-stained boots and wrenched open the front door before glaring at Nisha. 'Happy now?'

'Jon, please—'

But he was already slamming the door behind him. It shook the walls, the draught from it making the candles flutter. Nisha jumped up as well.

'I-I'm sorry, can you keep an eye on Kiran for a few minutes?'

Without waiting for an answer, she pulled on a pair of Wellingtons, snatching her parka from the coat hook as she went out. *Nice one, Hunter.* I sighed and looked across at Kiran. He was staring at the closed front door, his food-smeared face crestfallen.

'It's OK, they won't be long,' I told him, as reassuringly as I could.

He looked at me doubtfully, then his face began to pucker. I hesitated, then lifted him from the highchair as he began to howl. The warm weight in my arms triggered a familiar, bittersweet muscle memory. It had been a long time, I thought, hushing him in soothing tones and bouncing him gently.

By the time Nisha came back Kiran was dozing against my shoulder. He stirred at the sound of the door opening, then settled back down. Nisha gave a wan smile when she saw him.

'Sorry,' she said, keeping her voice down. 'Has he been showing off?'

'He was a little upset when you went out, that's all.'

'You did well to get him to settle. He doesn't always once he kicks off.' Her eyes were puffy and inflamed when she came over, as though she'd been crying. 'Here, I'll put him to bed.'

Kiran niggled as I passed him over, then snuggled into his mother's shoulder. The sudden lack of weight in my arms was more an absence than a relief.

'Did you find Jon?' I asked.

Nisha nodded, but didn't expand. 'I won't be long.'

Taking her sleeping son into the hallway, she carefully closed the door behind her with a click.

I took a long breath, trying to release some of the tension I hadn't realised I'd been holding. I thought about going back up to my room, but that would have seemed too abrupt. And it didn't feel as though the conversation with Nisha was over just yet. Sitting back down, I picked at the cooling tagine, more out of politeness than hunger. Then the rich flavours hit my system and suddenly I was famished. I was just finishing the last of it when Nisha reappeared.

Shutting the door behind her she came over to the table and sat down.

'He went off straight away.' She looked drawn and exhausted. 'Thanks for babysitting. I shouldn't have dumped him on you like that.'

'It's OK, I didn't mind. How's Jon?'

'It's a lot for him to take in.' With a smile she changed the subject. 'Kiran likes you, anyway. I could see you've done that before. I thought you said you didn't have any kids?'

It was meant as a light comment, and another time I might have brushed it off. But it had been a long day, and the truth seemed easier than evasion.

'I used to have a daughter. Alice. She died.'

Nisha's eyes widened. 'Oh, God, I didn't . . . How? What happened?'

'It was a car accident.' I hesitated, but it would have felt more awkward not to tell her the rest. 'My wife was with her.'

'Your wife as *well*?' Nisha's hand had gone to her mouth. 'That's awful! I'm so sorry, I'd no idea!'

'I know. It's OK.'

'No, but I've been saying all these tactless things!' She looked mortified. 'How old was your daughter?'

'Six. She'd be in her teens by now.'

The idea of that still seemed too huge to comprehend. Over the years enough scar tissue had built up for me to be able to talk about Kara and Alice without feeling as though the ground had opened beneath me. The loss was still there, though, biding its time for something to trigger it. Like now.

'How's Jon?' I asked, steering us back to the present. Nisha took the hint.

'OK.' She shrugged. 'I think. He's in his workshop. It's where he always goes when he needs to clear his head. God knows, he's had to do enough of that since we came back to this place. This past year's been . . . Well, it's been pretty shitty, to be honest.'

'I'm sorry if I've complicated things.'

'Trust me, it's not your fault. It's just . . . *this* fucking place. I don't just mean the stuff with Jon's family, the whole thing. I don't exactly blend in here, you know? It's like half the people here haven't even *seen* anyone who's not white, not outside of TV. No one's been openly racist, I haven't had insults shouted at me or anything. But it's the way everyone treats you as *different*. Apart from Jon, you're the only person I've had a proper conversation with since I got here. Sometimes I could—' Abruptly, she stopped and got up. 'Sod it, I need a drink. Do you want one?'

'I thought Jon didn't drink?' I said, remembering the scene earlier.

'He doesn't. We don't buy it anymore but only Jon's actually given up,' she said, her voice hollow as she rummaged inside a kitchen cupboard. 'It wasn't exactly a problem for him, but it was getting there. And when Kiran was born we decided we'd better things to do with the money. It doesn't bother him if I have a drink, though. I don't very often but after today . . . OK, here it is.'

She emerged with a dusty, unlabelled bottle.

'Thought we'd still got some. Dandelion wine,' she said, taking a corkscrew from a drawer. 'Jon's mum used to make it. Not exactly *grand cru*, but what it lacks in subtlety it makes up for in strength.'

Opening the bottle, she brought it over to the table. Without asking, she poured the straw-coloured liquid into my empty water tumbler before filling her own. I took a hesitant sip. It was better than I expected. Nisha took a drink herself, shuddered and took another.

Then she told me what happened between Reese's father and Jed Beddoes.

The visitors came to Edendale at the beginning of summer. They arrived in an old VW Camper, its cream and orange paintwork rusty but distinctive, decorated with faded bumper stickers for Greenpeace and CND, and one in bloody red declaring, '*Meat*

130

is Murder'. The woman was in her early thirties, her daughter eleven or twelve. No one in the village was entirely sure, and no one thought to ask. But everyone agreed they appeared a few weeks before the start of the school holiday, which caused a few askance looks since the girl was clearly of school age. Still, they settled in easily enough. The woman, Megan, was friendly and attractive − though not *too* attractive − and her daughter Willow polite and well-behaved. They wore hand-made or second-hand clothes and carried with them a waft of patchouli. Megan cheerfully told everyone she was there for a working holiday. She was a keen forager, picking and drying her own herbs, fungi and berries, which she'd then sell. But her main source of income was from the jewellery and ornaments she'd craft from polished slate or wood, and naturally scented candles in salvaged teacups and jars. To begin with she and her daughter were disparagingly dismissed as tree huggers and vegans, while older inhabitants of the village turned down their mouths and called them 'hippies'.

But it was generally acknowledged that they were harmless enough. Pleasant, even. They shopped in the village store, greeted everyone with a smile, and did their best to fit in without imposing themselves. And while Megan was ostensibly there to build up her stock of goods to sell at craft fairs later in the year, she was happy to trade her work for food and supplies, and frequently gave smaller pieces away. Before long mother and daughter had become familiar faces, viewed warmly by most and even − whisper it − well-liked.

The pair were staying at Foss Ghyll, living out of their campervan at what used to be the old army training camp on the fell. The plumbing still worked in one or two of the ramshackle old huts, and Megan claimed the peaceful beauty of the spot, not to mention the negative ions from the ghyll, helped her work. She'd been granted permission to camp there by the new residents of Hillside House. Brought up in the old hotel by his grandparents after his under-age and unmarried mother abandoned him with them, Owen Reese had moved back there with his wife Roz and their nine-year-old son, Jon, from Brighton eighteen months before. A builder by trade, Owen planned to turn the site of the old army camp into an outdoor pursuits centre, offering corporate team-building courses to company managers and employees. The income from that would then go towards his longer-term plan to renovate and eventually reopen the old hotel, which had been mothballed following his grandfather's death several years earlier.

It was no surprise to anyone in Edendale that the work had got off to a slow start. Hillside House was a money pit that had defeated numerous owners before, including Owen Reese's own grandparents. Still, the arrival of their first guests was taken as a good omen, even if they weren't technically staying in the hotel. Plainly smitten with the newcomers, young Jon would go up to Foss Ghyll most days, going on foraging expeditions with Megan and Willow and learning what flora growing on his doorstep was edible and what wasn't. As the long days and warm nights of August wore on, it had seemed like the perfect summer.

But the stormclouds were already gathering. Wynn Beddoes' youngest son, Jed, began spreading stories about Megan, claiming to have bought magic mushrooms and other natural hallucinogens from her, and bragging that natural highs weren't the only thing he'd got at the old VW Camper.

Few people took much notice. A wannabe boxer but without his father's fearsome temperament or reputation, Jed Beddoes was considered a loudmouth and a troublemaker, more often found in the pub than the gym in its back room. No one wanted to believe his stories about the well-liked newcomer to the village. As Jed's boasts grew more lurid, mud began to stick. Even so, if events had continued along the same course, the entire thing might still have blown over.

Then Jed Beddoes had a fight with Owen Reese.

It took place one evening outside The Perseverance. Jed was still in his gym sweats after a training session with his father, cooling off over a beer with two of his drinking cronies when Owen confronted him. It wasn't much of a contest. Jed was boastful of his boxing skills and no stranger to pub fights. By contrast, Owen Reese was a family man who kept himself to himself. So it shocked everyone when it was Jed who ended up, dazed and bloodied, on the pavement outside The Perseverance. When one of his mates tried to jump Owen from behind, a single punch put him on the ground as well. By the time people rushed out of the pub, it was to the sight of Owen Reese standing over Jed, fists balled as he delivered a final message.

'Go near her again and I'll fucking kill you!'

The village was righteously outraged. Not so much about the fight: most people quietly agreed it was high time someone put Jed Beddoes on his arse. But there was no doubt in anyone's mind that the fight was over Megan, which as good as confirmed all of Jed's stories about her. Worse, it now seemed she'd been sleeping with Owen Reese as well.

Of the two men it was Owen who was judged more harshly. No one expected any better of Jed, but Owen had a family. He should have known better. Even so, everyone agreed that the blame lay with Megan. A fling with a single man could be overlooked, even one as dubious as Jed Beddoes. But for an outsider to take up with *two* local men at the same time, one of them married with a young son? And she a mother herself?

That was unforgivable.

Overnight, Megan became the village pariah. It came as no surprise to anyone when, late one night, the cream and orange VW Camper was seen rattling down the main street in a defiant crunch of gears, headlights blazing inconsiderately through the closed curtains of the sleeping village. *Good riddance* was the consensus, and with a collective sniff Edendale prepared to put the whole messy affair behind it.

Until Jed Beddoes went missing.

His car was found abandoned, close to the lane that led through the old woods to Foss Ghyll. But there was no trace of Jed himself. Naturally, suspicion fell on Owen Reese. It was obvious to everyone that he must have acted on his threat, and that a second confrontation between the two men had ended even more badly for Jed. Owen denied it, first to Wynn Beddoes and then, repeatedly, to the police.

No one believed him.

The woods near where the car was found were searched, as was the area around the old army camp at Foss Ghyll, and even Hillside House itself. On the night the police ended their search, Wynn Beddoes had driven up there with his eldest son, Alun, along with Vic Hooley and several other pub regulars. Owen had confronted them outside with a shotgun, stone-faced and silent as they hurled accusations and threats. It was heading towards violence until Owen ended the debate by discharging one of the shotgun's twin barrels over their heads.

Watching from his bedroom window, young Jon saw the whole thing. After the Beddoes and their posse had retreated, he'd lain in his bed and listened while his parents had a screaming row, their worst yet. Two days later, Owen Reese had hugged his son, told him to look after his mother and left the hotel.

He never came back.

The wine bottle wavered in Nisha's hand as she poured herself another glass. It was her third. I still had most of my second and shook my head when she offered a refill. She'd been right about the homemade wine being strong, and I wanted to keep a clear head.

Nisha took a long drink.

'The police searched all round here and up at the campsite, but they never found a body. Everybody thought Jon's dad must have buried Beddoes' son in the woods or somewhere on the plantation.' She paused as she realised what she'd said, then shrugged. 'Looks like they were right.'

'How old was Jed Beddoes when he disappeared?' I asked. It was hardly a question I could put to his family, not after that evening, and so far I'd only Maud's rough idea to go on. Nisha reached for her wine glass.

'God, I've no idea. Twenties or thirties, I expect. Why?'

'I'm just curious. You said the Beddoes threatened Jon's father,' I went on, not wanting to make too much of the missing man's age. Nisha's guess was closer to my own estimate based on what I'd seen of the remains, though. 'Could they have done something to him?'

'Jon's mum always said so, because she didn't like to think he'd just walked out. But Jon doesn't believe that. There's no love lost between him and the Beddoes, but there were sightings of his dad heading towards Newcastle after Jed went missing. The theory is he could have got a boat from there to Holland or somewhere, so who knows?'

It wasn't so easy to sneak out of the UK undetected nowadays. Isometric passports, more widespread CCTV and facial recognition had seen to that. But over two decades ago it was a different story. With the right contacts or knowhow it would have been much simpler for Jon's father to have skipped the country.

'What about the woman in the campervan? Megan. Did the police interview her?' I asked.

Nisha looked down at her glass. 'They tried. They thought at one point that Jon's dad might have hooked up with her and her daughter, but they couldn't find them. Nothing sinister, it just turned out no one in the village knew their second name or where they were from. Everyone just assumed they were travellers or something, so they didn't bother to ask. And they left before Jed Beddoes disappeared, so it wasn't like they were suspects or anything.'

She was talking quickly, as though she'd been bottling all this up for a long time. Now the words were gushing out of her, as though a tap had been opened she couldn't shut off.

'The worst thing is everybody treated Jon and his mum like it was their fault,' she went on, pouring the last of the wine into her glass. 'People wanted someone to blame, and with Jon's dad gone they were the next best thing. Easy targets. That's why they had floodlights installed, because their 'neighbours' kept coming out here at night and smashing things up. It was obviously either the Beddoes or their mates, but the police said they couldn't do anything because they couldn't prove it. Jon doesn't talk about it much even now, but it was hard for them. I think he got into a lot of fights when he was younger.'

I wasn't surprised. No wonder Jon seemed so intense. 'Why did they stay?'

'I used to wonder the same thing. But Roz, Jon's mum, didn't have any money or family to help her out. And you can't just walk away from a place like this, I've found that out myself.'

A bitter edge had crept into her voice. 'Couldn't she have sold it? Or some of its land, at least?' I asked, remembering what Maud had told me.

Nisha's face clouded. 'Amazingly, there's not a lot of demand for Gothic monstrosities in the middle of nowhere. And most of the land's heavily wooded and on a steep fellside. You can't farm on it, and it's too rugged and remote for any developers. The plantation offered to buy some of the land, but they wanted to cherry-pick which parts and weren't interested in the hotel. And they were only offering peanuts anyway, nowhere near enough for her to have made a fresh start. In the end Jon's mum had to sell a portion of land up by the ghyll, because she needed money to live on. They dug up everything there and covered it with more of their bloody spruce trees, so Roz refused to sell them anything else after that.'

It was a slightly different take to Maud's, but the broad points were the same. Even so, twenty-six years was a long time for Jon's mother to have remained at Hillside House, especially in the face of Edendale's hostility. It was hard to believe that she and her young son couldn't have managed to leave somehow. After everything that had happened, staying in that echoing mausoleum seemed downright perverse.

And now Nisha and Jon were living there. Nisha gave a sour smile.

'I know what you're thinking, but it's not that simple. Roz was desperate for Jon to get away. She nagged him into getting the grades to go to Uni, and after that she didn't even want him coming to visit. Not even Christmas or holidays. I used to think she was this cranky old woman, pushing away her own son and living on her own out in this . . . this *dump*. But I can see now she was doing it for Jon. And now we've inherited it, and we're stuck in the same fucking . . .'

She didn't finish. Taking a deep breath, she pushed away what was left in her wine glass.

'OK, I've officially had too much to drink.' She attempted a smile, 'Told you it was strong. And on that note, I better—'

She stopped as the front door opened, letting in a flurry of cold air and sleet. We both turned as Jon came in from the darkness, closing the door behind him.

Nisha rose to her feet, her expression a mix of relief and anxiety. 'Are you OK?'

'Never better.'

He took off his parka, water dripping from it onto the floor. He looked calmer now. Composed almost, as though he'd reached some decision. The outdoor cold radiated from him as he came over to the table. I saw him take in the empty bottle of home-made wine, but he didn't pass any comment. He turned to me.

'So what's next?'

'What do you mean?'

He made an irritated gesture. 'You can't tell the police what you've found, so where does that leave us? What needs to happen?'

Good question. 'The remains will need covering until the police can get here. Maud said there might be a tarpaulin at the yard I can use. I'll go there first thing and—'

'There's one here. It's got oil and sawdust on it, but it's big and its waterproof. I think there's some rope we can take to fasten it with.'

I didn't like the sound of that *we*. 'Thanks, but it's better if I go on my own.'

Jon's face could have been carved. 'I'm not asking. I'm coming with you.'

Chapter 16

The sleet had stopped by the next morning. The wind had dropped as well, but it felt colder than ever. The grey-white clouds gave the light a diffused quality, as though a sheet had been spread over the sky. Even the woods seemed unnaturally silent, the skeletal branches forming a lattice overhead as Jon and I made our way up the fell through the bare trees.

We walked in silence. Jon wasn't talkative at the best of times, and it took all my breath to negotiate the steep hiking trail leading through the woods up to Foss Ghyll. Nisha had warned me how steep and muddy it was, and she was right. But describing it as a 'trail' was doing it a favour. Every now and then we came to leaning timber marker posts that still retained the faded ghosts of painted arrows pointing uphill, while on the steeper stretches timber railway sidings had been hammered edgeways into the earth to make crude steps. But years of rain had rotted them away, and most of the ones that hadn't disintegrated had become dislodged. In places the trail had eroded away completely, so that little more than the suggestion of a route remained. It was marginally better than clambering up the steeply wooded fell unaided, but only just.

It had been Jon's idea to come this way rather than driving to the lane as I had the day before.

'It's a shorter route,' he'd said.

That might be true, but didn't mean it was quicker. Or easier. With the weight of Jon's rucksack on my back, I was soon out of breath and sweating, despite the cold. The rucksack was heavy, packed with old rope and tent pegs, but Jon had it worse. He was carrying a bundled-up tarpaulin, stiff and bulky.

The night before I'd told him repeatedly I didn't want him coming with me, that it was better if I went alone. It was like arguing with a wall. In the end I'd abandoned the attempt and gone to bed, telling myself I might have better luck in the morning.

I hadn't believed it even then.

Back in my room I'd been too restless for sleep, tired as I was. I'd loaded the photographs of the remains from earlier onto my laptop's photogrammetry software. The technology was still relatively new but it was a useful forensic tool, producing a virtual 3D model of an object that could be moved around and viewed from every angle.

In the darkness, the skeletal remains looked more lurid than ever on the laptop's illuminated screen. Before long I was lost in the macabre image, rotating it and zooming in on features I wanted to examine more closely. For the most part it only confirmed the impressions I'd formed at the scene that morning. The remains were those of a white male, somewhere between five feet ten and six feet two in height, with a solid, well-formed bone structure. Even after closer consideration of the cranial sutures and muck-encrusted teeth and joints, I would still have said the victim had been in the thirty- to forty- age range when he died. That was older than Maud had thought Jed Beddoes might be, although not too far off from Nisha's guess that he'd been in his twenties or thirties.

It was more of a discrepancy than I'd have liked, but I still didn't know for sure how old Jed Beddoes had been when he went missing. Determining age wasn't an exact science at the best of times, and my estimate was only based on a visual examination of a still-clothed skeleton entangled in soil and roots. I couldn't see most of the bone surfaces that changed the most over time and which more accurately indicated the age at death – parts of the pubic bone and pelvis, the ends of ribs where they meet the sternum. Cranial sutures could be good indicators of age as well, but they sometimes fused at different rates, and not all of this individual's were visible. Jed Beddoes had been a boxer, a high-impact sport that took its toll on the body. His joints would have been subjected to more punishment than most people's, which might explain why the remains appeared to belong to someone older than their twenties.

There could be another explanation as well. But I didn't know enough yet for that to be more than a troubling possibility.

Still, for now I'd keep my mind open.

It was clear from the 3D image that the skeleton hadn't been exposed to air for very long. There was no lichen or moss growth to suggest a more prolonged exposure, and no evidence of weathering from the elements. I'd already seen that the tree roots hadn't begun to die off, and a closer examination of the bones told the same story. Even in these rainy conditions, if they'd been out in the open for more than a few days I'd have expected there to be some evidence of them drying out, but there was nothing. Everything I saw said that the tree had only blown down recently. Very recently, judging by the absence of needles or leaf litter in the crater left by its roots. It seemed likely that the spruce had succumbed to the same storm I'd become lost in.

I'd been growing tired by then, my eyes strained from staring at the bright laptop screen in the dark bedroom. I didn't want to drain its battery and made a note to recharge it in the car next day.

Before I'd shut it down, though, I'd spent time studying the frond-like roots that had grown through the eye sockets. That wasn't too surprising. Tree roots will exploit even the smallest of gaps, probing into them with hair-like roots that over time can crack brickwork, drains, and even concrete as they thicken and grow. These had somehow found a way into the sealed chamber of the neurocranium – the braincase – of the face-down body and grown through the optic nerve channels until they emerged from the eye sockets themselves.

There could be a number of reasons for that. If the cranial sutures at the rear of the skull hadn't completely fused, or if there were what are known as Wormian bones – small bone pieces that sometimes grew in the sutures – then that could potentially provide a route for the roots to have found a way into the skull.

But I wasn't convinced. The number of roots that had emerged from the eye orbits suggested a larger opening than Wormian bones could account for. And since all the sutures I could see were fused together, it was reasonable to think the rest of them would be as well. Yet without a gap of some sort in the sutures, the spruce's roots would have been unable to penetrate the smooth, domed bone of the skull.

Not unless it was already damaged.

There were no fractures that I could see, but that didn't mean there weren't any. The rear of the skull was still embedded in the earth that had been ripped up along with the tree roots. I felt sure that when the skeleton was properly examined we'd find some trauma that had allowed entry for the roots to grow.

But for the time being that would have to remain a theory. I watched Jon's broad shoulders and uncompromising back as he walked ahead of me up the hiking trail. My attempts to dissuade him from coming hadn't been any more successful that morning than they had the night before.

'You're not listening,' I'd all but shouted.

'Neither are you,' he said.

I couldn't physically stop him, so in the end I'd been forced to accept it. I had to admit that it would be much easier for two of us to cover the remains than if I'd been on my own, and I couldn't pretend to be sorry Jon was there to help carry the ropes and heavy tarpaulin. It was what else he was carrying that I wasn't happy about.

Slung over his shoulder, in an old leather and canvas case, was the shotgun.

It had been propped up against the kitchen door before we set out. 'What are you doing with that?' I'd asked.

Jon had been bending down to tie his boots. He didn't look up but I could see sleepless shadows under his eyes that hadn't been there the day before.

'What do you think?'

'You're not taking a shotgun.'

142

'Aren't I?'

Oh, for God's sake . . . 'You said you didn't have any shells so what's the point?'

'It'll make me feel better.'

'What if the Beddoes show up?'

'Then they'll think twice about doing anything.' Moving past me he'd gone to the front door. 'Come on.'

We'd barely spoken since then. Even by Jon's taciturn standards he'd been unusually quiet, although that wasn't altogether surprising. If I'd been going to see the unearthed skeleton of the man my father was suspected of having murdered, I wouldn't feel like talking either.

But brooding in silence wouldn't help his nerves. 'Do you do much foraging?' I asked, seeing a cluster of distinctive oyster mushrooms growing near the fallen hulk of an old oak.

Jon paused to look round at me. 'What do you mean?'

'Only that it must be good having all this on your doorstep,' I said, taken aback. 'For a chef, I mean.'

'If you like that sort of thing,' he said, turning away.

I gave up on small talk after that.

Not that I had much breath for talking anyway. I was no stranger to walking on rough terrain, and liked to think I kept myself in reasonable shape. But the hiking trail had grown even steeper, the ground muddy and treacherous with mulch from rotted leaves. Above and ahead of us, the disintegrating steps went off to the left around a cluster of rocks from which an old oak was growing. But instead of following them, Jon left the trail and cut straight up the slope.

'What're you doing?' I panted, stopping.

He paused to glance back. 'It's a shortcut.'

I eyed the steep bank rising in front of us. 'Are you sure about that?'

'It brings us right to the logging trail. Go the other way if you want.'

With that he turned away and continued up the slope. I stared at his back, cursing under my breath. Then, hoisting the rucksack to a more comfortable position, I went after him.

It was hard work. If anything the slope became even steeper, and more than once I had to scramble over rocks using my hands to pull myself up. But after ten minutes or so I saw the edge of the woods ahead of us. Reese paused as the ground levelled out. He was breathing heavily as well, though not as much as I was. He'd been right, I saw, as I struggled up the last few yards. We'd come out lower down on the strip of no man's land that ran back to the glade. The spruce plantation rose up to face us on its other side, dark and forbidding.

The logging track was almost directly opposite us.

As we crossed the open ground to it, I checked my phone. There was no signal, and neither the email nor the text I'd written to Chaudry had been sent. I wasn't sure either would send automatically if the phone found a connection, but I hoped at least one might. I'd encountered a stray signal at some point the day before without realising it. Probably somewhere up here, according to what Nisha had told me. If that happened again today I didn't want to miss it.

But the email still sat stubbornly in my inbox, while the text was flagged with a red *Failed to send* message. Trying not to feel disappointed, I put away my phone as we started up the logging track.

'You're wasting your time,' Jon said irritably, without looking round.

'It can't hurt to try.' I didn't hold out much hope myself, though. As the tall spruces closed in on both sides, I looked up at the thin strip of sky visible above us, not liking the look of the dirty-white clouds. They seemed to sag overhead, heavy with threat. 'Do you think it'll snow?'

'How should I know?' he snapped.

I let it go, knowing it was tension speaking. After a moment he spoke again.

'These remains . . . you said the tree had blown down. They'd been pulled right out of the ground?'

I'd already told him as much. 'That's right.'

'So it must have blown down in the storm.'

144

'I expect so.' I glanced across at him, 'Are you OK? You don't have to do this. You can still go——'

'I'm fine, OK?'

That ended the conversation. We continued through the plantation without speaking, the silence broken by the whisper of our boots in the dead grass. But I could feel Jon's tension increasing. When I glanced at him again his mouth was compressed to a thin line, and his knuckles were clenched white where he gripped the shoulder strap of the shotgun case.

There was no point in trying to persuade him again, though. And we didn't have far to go now. We'd reached the fork in the track I remembered from yesterday. I paused by the broken stump of the dead spruce, looking around to make sure of my bearings.

'Down here,' I said, stepping off the track.

Reese had carried on walking towards one of the forks. He stopped and looked back at me.

'What?'

'It's this way.'

He looked into the plantation. 'Down there?'

'The stream's not far. I followed it yesterday to Foss Ghyll.'

'I know, but . . .' He looked round at where the track forked, then back into the spruce trees. 'Are you sure? It's easy to get lost in there.'

I know. 'This is the way I came yesterday. There might be a better way, but I know this brings us to it. Look, if you'd rather wait here . . .'

Jon's face grew closed. 'No. Show me.'

I went into the plantation, following the same route as before as much as I could. Jon was right to be worried, and I probably would have got lost if not for the murmur of the stream to guide me. The sound carried through the still air with crystal clarity, and it seemed to take even less time today before I saw where the trees thinned alongside its banks.

'We just need to follow this down to the ghyll,' I told Jon, setting off along its bank.

He didn't say anything, but his face looked paler than ever, and there was a look in his eyes that put me in mind of an animal about to run. Or attack. His edginess was contagious, so much that I found myself glancing at him worriedly as we walked by the stream.

Then, through the ranks of trunks, I saw the fallen spruce a short distance ahead. Jon slowed, staring at it.

'Is that it?'

'That's it, yes.'

Even if we hadn't been too far away to see anything, the remains were out of sight from this angle anyway. I'd managed to walk right past them the day before without realising, but I still heard a catch in Jon's breathing. Looking at him again I saw his face was pale and blotched behind the thick beard. He seemed rigid with tension, his chest rising and falling so rapidly I thought he might hyperventilate.

'No, this is . . .' He let the tarpaulin fall to the ground, shaking his head. 'I-I can't do this.'

'It's all right,' I said, but he was already hurrying away. 'Jon, wait!'

He'd started to run now, though, the shotgun case bouncing on his shoulder as he pounded off through the spruce trees. I called again, starting after him, but weighed down by the heavy rucksack I'd no chance of catching up. I stopped, watching helplessly as Reese disappeared into the murky forest.

In seconds he'd gone from sight.

I swore, angry at myself for not seeing this coming. I hoped to God Jon knew where he was going, but there wasn't anything I could do even if he didn't. If I tried to go after him I'd only get lost myself.

With a last look at where he'd disappeared, I went to retrieve the tarpaulin he'd dropped. It was cumbersome and heavy, smelling of old canvas and sawdust when I hugged it to me. Laden with the rucksack as well, I was badly out of breath by the time I reached the clearing where the spruce had blown down. Avoiding its broken branches, I walked the length of its prone trunk. Struggling under the weight of the tarpaulin and rucksack, I was almost at the bottom of the tree before I registered that something was wrong. I looked up at the clump of soil and uptorn roots in front of me, noticing for the first time how ragged and truncated were. As that sank in, a breeze blew against my face, carrying a pungent chemical taint.

The smell of petrol and burnt wood.

No, no, no . . . Dropping the tarpaulin, I ran to the underside of the tree and stumbled to a halt. It looked as though the base of the tree had exploded. Charred fragments of wood, cloth and bone were scattered all around. Where a human skeleton had been entwined in the tree's roots the day before was now a jagged mess of hacked-off stumps.

The remains had been destroyed.

The morning was getting old by the time I'd finished taking photographs. Checking again that there was still no service — there wasn't — I put away my phone. Still keeping my distance so as not to disturb what was now a very recent crime scene, I worked the stiffness from my neck as I took a last look at the debris of bone and timber.

It was no less shocking now than when I'd first seen it. Heavy-treaded footprints had churned up the crater and ground around it, while the remains themselves had been virtually pulverised. I recognised some of the bigger fragments as belonging to ribs, pelvis or femurs, while distinctive curved shards of skull lay scattered in the muddy crater like broken eggshells. I'd taken a lot of photographs of those, getting as close as I dared, but otherwise only a few smaller bones such as phalanges — finger and toe bones — had survived intact.

My first thought had been that an axe or maul must have been used, but I'd quickly discounted that idea. Even though I daren't go too close I could still see that the skeleton hadn't been bludgeoned or hacked. That would have caused the broken end of the bones to be crushed and splintered, whereas the ones I could see were clean-edged and flat. They'd been cut. No, not cut, I amended, seeing how the exposed surfaces were marked with fine, straight ridges. Sawn, by something sharp and powerful enough to carve through the skeleton like balsa, spraying everything nearby with a fine powdering of bone and sawdust. There was only one thing I could think of that would do that.

Someone had chopped up the skeleton with a chainsaw. Then, not content with that, they'd splashed petrol over what was left and tried to burn it.

Whoever it had been, they'd gone long before I'd arrived. There had been no heat coming off the scorched bones, so the fire must have burnt itself out hours ago. It hadn't been much of one to start with, I thought. Even the sodden rags of clothing were only charred, while unburnt accelerant had left oily, iridescent swirls on the mud and puddles. Petrol didn't burn at a high enough temperature to consume bone, and most of the charring was superficial. My guess was that the person or persons responsible – it was hard to tell how many there were from the muddy footprints – had simply splashed whatever fuel remained in the chainsaw's tank onto the fragmented remains, then thrown on a match and hoped for the best.

Starting a fire in a timber plantation didn't exactly shout of forethought, but then this whole thing seemed badly thought out. As catastrophic as the damage appeared, as an attempt to destroy the evidence it had been spectacularly botched. Even leaving aside the salvaged mandible and photographs I'd taken of the remains, enough DNA would have survived the fire to establish if the remains belonged to Jed Beddoes. And far from covering their tracks, whoever had done this had literally created even more, littering the scene with footprints that could potentially identify them.

More than that, though, they'd needlessly given themselves away. Until now there had been nothing to suggest this was anything other than a cold case. Everyone knew that Owen Reese must have murdered Jed Beddoes and now, twenty-six years later, here was the proof.

But Owen Reese couldn't be blamed for this. All it had achieved was to announce that someone in the village was desperate

148

enough to bring a chainsaw halfway up a Cumbrian fell in the dead of night to prevent the truth behind a decades-old murder from coming out.

That wasn't just clumsy, it was stupid.

I thought back to Jon's erratic behaviour. He owned a chainsaw, and it was conceivable that he might have brought it up here in the misguided hope that destroying the evidence would somehow protect his father's name. Except that Owen Reese was already guilty in most people's eyes. Destroying his supposed victim's remains wasn't going to change that. And, unless he was a gifted actor, his son hadn't known where the fallen spruce was before I'd taken him to it. Jon's surprise then, as well as his subsequent meltdown, had seemed genuine.

In any case, he wouldn't be the only person in Edendale to own a chainsaw. The plantation probably owned several, and it would be worth asking Maud to check if any were missing. I'd still like to take a look at Jon's, but thanks to Drew Beddoes shooting off his mouth the list of potential suspects could extend to half the village.

I stirred, taking a last look at the destruction. I was getting cold, toes and fingers aching from standing still. There was nothing more I could do up here. There was no longer any point trying to cover the shards of bone. They were too scattered, and if I tried I'd probably only disturb and damage them even more. It was time to go back down the mountain, yet for some reason I found myself thinking again about the grim family gathering in the pub the night before. A moment later, as though the thought had conjured it, I heard a distant noise carried on the still air.

Voices.

They weren't close enough to recognise but I already knew who it would be. I felt a tightening in my stomach. It was too late to leave now even if I'd wanted to do.

The Beddoes were here.

Chapter 17

I didn't have long to wait. Soon the voices were joined by the sound of branches snapping underfoot, and not long afterwards I glimpsed figures bundled in heavy parkas and insulated jackets, picking their way between the spruce trunks. Alun Beddoes led the way, his limp evident but not slowing him down. His son Drew hovered at his shoulder, while Vic Hooley followed a pace or two behind, his breathing loud and hoarse as he laboured on the steep gradient. Lagging further back was Eddie, radiating reluctance even at this distance. The older lurcher loped along with them, but there was no sign of the younger one that had run off with the mandible the day before.

None of the group were making any attempt to be quiet or hide their approach. I went to stand in front of the fallen spruce's roots, well clear of any bone fragments, and then waited. A moment or two later they all fell silent.

They'd seen me.

Alun reached the clearing first. He stopped a few metres away, fixing me with a cold stare as he caught his breath. I saw him frown as he saw what was behind me, then his face blanked with shock.

'What the fuck's this?'

'You know as much as I do,' I said. 'This was how I found it.'

Behind him Hooley looked hung-over, his eyes bloodshot under a greasy hunting cap. He was sweating and red-faced, his ragged breaths fogging the air. I could smell the alcohol on him even from where I stood. Eddie hung back further than the others, an anxious presence in an incongruous blue bobble hat. Only Drew seemed happy to be there, grinning as he took in the carnage.

'It wasn't like this yesterday, Dad.' Drew was fairly bubbling with excitement. 'There was a proper skeleton hanging in the roots. Somebody really fucked it up!'

'These are your uncle's remains, show some respect!' his father snapped, before turning back to me. There was pain in his eyes but also a deep anger. 'How do I know it wasn't you?'

I held back my exasperation, knowing how close to violence this was. 'Why would I do something like this? I came to cover the remains. I told you yesterday they needed protecting.'

As though drawn, his gaze went past me to the scorched mess of bone. He removed his black woollen hat, his bare skull shining with sweat as he rubbed a hand across it.

'So who the fuck did?'

'Could it have been lightning or something?' Eddie suggested tentatively.

Alun Beddoes didn't even bother to look at him. 'Don't talk stupid. Storm was the night before. Lightning doesn't stink of petrol, either. This was done with a chainsaw.'

'Got to be that fucker Reese,' Hooley chimed in.

'You don't know that,' I said, thankful Jon wasn't there. 'It could have been anyone.'

'Bullshit. Might have known this wanker'd stick up for him.' Hooley was glancing at Alun, as though gauging his response. 'It's fucking obvious, Al. That fucker Reese is trying to cover up for his old man. He needs sorting out once and for all.'

Alun wasn't listening. He started towards the scorched bone fragments, but halted when I moved to stand in front of him.

'You shouldn't go any closer.'

He stared at me. The angular face was set and hard, the pale eyes uncompromising. Behind him Drew grinned, Hooley's small eyes glinted with anticipation. Eddie didn't say anything but his worried frown deepened.

'That's my brother. Don't tell me what to do.'

'It's too early yet to say who it is. We won't know for sure until—*uf!*'

I staggered back as Alun straight-armed the heel of his gloved hand into my chest. It felt like being hit with a hammer. He stared at me, utterly still again but with a coiled tension that was poised to snap.

'Get the fuck out of my way.'

'Come on, Alun,' Eddie protested weakly. 'Perhaps we should—'

'Shut the fuck up, Eddie,' Hooley sneered. 'Piss off back home if you don't like it.'

'Go on, Dad, drop him,' Drew goaded, bouncing from foot to foot.

Alun Beddoes showed no sign of having heard. He didn't want me to move, I realised. He was hurt and angry and wanting someone – anyone – to take it out on.

I'd just volunteered.

'I can't say if this is your brother or not,' I said, rubbing my bruised chest. 'But whoever it is, someone's trying to cover up what happened to them. If you contaminate the scene you'll be helping them do that.'

Alun's pale eyes bored into me, but he didn't move. Or hit me again. I began to hope he was going to listen to reason, but then Hooley spoke up.

'Fuck this!' He strode towards me, jaundiced eyes small and mean above stubbled jowls. 'No southern wanker's going to tell us what to do! Let's see how he—'

The sound of the gunshot was deafening. I flinched along with everyone else, crows protesting raucously as they took wing from nearby treetops. As the reverberations died, all eyes went to the figure that had emerged from the trees.

Jon stood at the edge of the clearing, his shotgun pointing somewhere between Hooley and Alun Beddoes.

'Go on, Vic. Finish what you were saying.'

Hooley's eyes darted about. He took a shuffling step back towards Eddie, as though trying to hide behind him. Alun recovered first.

'Crawled out from under your stone, did you?'

Jon stared back at him. The two of them were the same height, and equally stony-faced. 'Heard the ruckus. Thought I'd better see what was going on.'

'You want to put your gun down?'

'Not really.'

'Big man with your shotgun, aren't you?'

Jon jerked his chin contemptuously towards the other three men. 'And you aren't, with your little helpers?'

Alun's glare promised violence. 'We've a right to be here. You haven't. It was your fucking dad who did this.'

'Don't make this any worse, Jon,' I said, seeing his face tighten.

'You think it could be?'

'Just think what you're doing. Lower the gun.'

'I will. Soon as they fuck off.'

'Come on, Alun, let's go,' Eddie said, nervously. His face had paled except for patches of colour on his cheeks. It gave him a cherubic look, like an ageing choirboy.

'Fucking coward,' Hooley muttered, but I noticed he'd managed to edge even further away.

But Alun hadn't moved. 'I'm going nowhere. Not until this fucker admits what he's done.'

Jon cocked his head. 'And what's that?'

'*Don't fucking pretend!*' Alun's shout sprayed spittle. He stabbed his hand at the charred wreckage of bone and roots. 'Fucking look! *That's my fucking brother!*'

Something shifted behind Jon's eyes, a shadow of uncertainty. Then he shrugged.

'I didn't do that.'

'You're a fucking liar!' Alun was breathing heavily but his voice had become ominously quiet. 'And a coward. Just like your old man.'

Jon levelled the shotgun at him. 'Say that again.'

'You heard.'

My legs felt heavy as I stepped in between Jon and Alun Beddoes. 'OK, everyone needs to take a breath.'

'Get out of the way,' Jon said.

I didn't, but my mouth was suddenly dry. 'You need to calm down.'

'Don't tell me what to do.'

He and Alun Beddoes were still glaring at each other. Off to one side, I saw Drew Beddoes slowly begin to raise his pistol-gripped crossbow. Jon saw as well. He gave a snort.

'Oh, yeah? What you going to do, shoot me with your toy bow?'

'Fuck off! It's not a toy!'

'Put it away,' his father said without turning round.

'But Dad—'

'*Put it down!*'

For several seconds the only sound was Hooley's adenoidal breathing. Then, eyeing the shotgun uneasily, Eddie went over to Alun Beddoes.

'We should go, Alun. Before someone gets hurt.'

'Too late for that,' Alun said, but there was no heat behind it. He considered Jon, then gave a nod. 'We're not done.'

'You know where to find me.'

With a last look at the charred bone fragments scattered around the tree base, Alun turned and left the clearing. The old lurcher went with him, along with Eddie and a sullen Hooley. Only Drew remained, glowering at Reese. He was gripping the pistol crossbow, though it was hard to say if he was trying to restrain himself or summon up the nerve to use it.

'It's not a fucking toy!'

He spat on the floor, then followed his family out of the clearing. I watched them disappear back among the closed ranks of spruce trunks, only allowing myself to relax when they were out of sight.

Jesus . . .

I turned to Jon. He hadn't moved. The shotgun was still aimed at where Alun Beddoes had been standing.

'I thought you said you didn't have any shells?'

'I found a couple, OK?' He broke open the shotgun with unnecessary force, ejecting a smoking casing from it. 'Don't you know any better than to stand in front of a fucking *shotgun*?'

'Don't you know any better than to point it at someone?' I was angry as well, shaky now as reaction set in. 'What the hell were you *thinking*?'

'I was thinking I had to stop them beating the shit out of you! You're welcome!'

I wanted to yell that I'd rather have taken my chances than risk someone being shot. Then I saw the tremor in his hands and the paleness of his face under the beard, and realised I didn't have to say anything. I took a deep breath and let it out, making an effort to release my tension along with it.

'Thanks for coming back,' I said, stiffly. 'I didn't think you would.'

'I don't like running away.'

He seemed calmer now, as though he'd either purged whatever demons had possessed him before or been exhausted by them. There was a strange look on his face as he considered the burnt scraps of bone and clothing littering the muddy ground.

'This is it, then. This is him.'

It wasn't a question, and I wasn't even sure if he was talking to me. I answered anyway.

'If you mean Jed Beddoes, it's too early to say.'

Jon didn't respond. He was staring at what was left of the remains as though he'd forgotten I was there.

'Are you OK?' I asked.

He nodded. 'I heard Beddoes say somebody must have used a chainsaw. I don't normally agree with the bastard, but I think he's right.'

'Perhaps.' I wasn't going to confirm anything either way. 'Do you have any idea who might have done it?'

'It wasn't me, if that's what you're thinking,' he said, giving me a sharp look.

'I'm not accusing anyone. I'm just trying to work out why anyone would go to so much trouble after all this time.'

'Yeah. That's the question, isn't it?' His expression was unreadable. 'I'll give you a hand with the tarpaulin.'

'It doesn't matter.'

He looked at me in surprise. 'Don't you want to cover . . . all this?'

'There's no point anymore. We'd only end up doing more harm than good.'

He considered the debris spread in and around the crater left by the spruce's roots. 'Doesn't seem right, just leaving it.'

'No, but there's nothing else we can do.' I told him. 'We should head back.'

Jon didn't like it but he didn't argue. While he put the shotgun back in its case and started to bundle up the heavy canvas, I went over to where I'd left the rucksack. As I hoisted it onto my shoulders, I felt something cold settle on my cheek.

Looking up, I saw the first white flakes drifting down through the branches.

Chapter 18

The snow continued to fall as Jon and I trudged back along the plantation logging track. We hardly spoke. I kept glancing up at the descending flakes, telling myself it might be only a brief flurry. They weren't coming down heavily, but neither was there any sign of them stopping. The snow fell slowly, drifting with a gentle persistence from an ominous white sky. It wasn't settling yet, but if it did I knew the chances of anyone driving to Edendale the next day and reporting that the road had collapsed would suddenly be much smaller.

When the logging track disgorged us onto the strip of scrubland separating the spruce plantation from the old woods, I stopped to rest. My breath swirled the snowflakes like a shaken snow globe as I manoeuvred the rucksack to a more comfortable position.

'You coming?'

Jon had paused at the edge of the woods, at the same spot where we'd emerged from his shortcut earlier. He seemed impatient to get back, not that I could blame him. The morning hadn't been a resounding success so far.

With a nod, I followed him into the woods.

Negotiating our way down the steep slope proved even harder than climbing up. Twice I lost my footing, clutching for handholds to keep from falling as my boots slithered on the slick and rocky ground. By the time we joined the hiking trail I was breathless and sore, my leg muscles aching from the strain. I was relieved when I saw the stile ahead of us that led to the crumbling but firm driveway of Hillside House.

Away from the bare woodland's meagre shelter, the snow was starting to settle more quickly. The hotel itself had been given a winter makeover, the white powdering on its minarets and turrets a stark contrast with the dark stone walls. Looking down, I saw that Jon's boots had left imprints in the snow as he walked in front of me. I didn't think it was the same pattern as the footprints by the fallen spruce, but it was hard to be sure.

I'd been intending to go up to my room and transfer the latest photographs onto my laptop, but when I reached my car I stopped. A thin coating of snow had settled on it, turning the windscreen white. I looked up at the sky, trying to gauge how long it might continue. The flakes drifted down from the white void, apparently endless. That decided it for me. I wanted to ask Maud about the plantation's chainsaws, and it was better to do that before the snow worsened.

Jon looked around when he heard the electronic beep of my car unlocking.

'Where you going?'

'I want to pick something up from the store,' I said, deciding at the last second not to tell him. 'Is there anything you need?'

He looked at me levelly. I couldn't have said if he believed me or not. 'If the snow gets much thicker you won't get your car back up here.'

'That's why I want to go while it's clear.'

'Up to you.' He held out his hand, still clutching the bundled-up tarpaulin to his chest with his other arm. 'Here, I'll take the rucksack.'

I hesitated, realising I might have missed a chance to see into Jon's workshop where he kept the chainsaw. But it was too late now. He stood waiting, his hand outstretched. Slipping off the rucksack, I handed it over. He took it without a word, hooking it over one shoulder as he turned and walked away.

I still wasn't entirely sure why I hadn't told him I was going to see Maud. There was probably no harm in him knowing, and if not for him Alun Beddoes might have bruised more than my pride. But if Jon had lied about his shotgun not being loaded he might be lying about other things as well. I didn't know how far I could trust him.

I didn't know how far I could trust anyone.

I pretended to be getting something from the car boot, waiting until Jon was out of sight. Then I took out my phone and snapped a quick photograph of the footprints he'd left in the snow.

It felt even colder in the car than it had been outside. Turning the heater on full to clear the misted windscreen, I compared the image I'd just taken with the footprints left in the mud around the fallen spruce.

They weren't the same.

Putting away my phone, I turned the car around and drove up the driveway into the village.

I didn't know if Maud would be at her home or spending her Sunday at the plantation office, trying to sort out the mess Hooley had left after wrecking his rig and losing a shipment of lumber. But her house was nearer so I tried there first.

I could see as I approached that she wasn't in. The light was already failing, and even though it was only mid-afternoon the Edwardian villa was in darkness. Her Volvo SUV wasn't in the driveway either, but since I was there now I got out and rang the doorbell anyway. Its muted chime sounded from inside, but this time there were no answering barks from Maud's labrador. I rang it once more to make sure, then went back to my car.

Only a few tyre tracks scarred the thin covering of snow on the main street, and in the gathering dusk the village looked deserted. A dim light from the store announced that it was still open, but the doors of The Perseverance were shut. Edendale seemed to be hunkering down as the weather closed in. As I headed out for the lumberyard I felt like I was the only living thing there.

The dying afternoon grew darker as the road climbed up through the plantation. Tall spruce trees closed in at either side, needled branches meeting overhead to turn the road into a tunnel. The car's automatic headlights flicked on, picking out the gentle fall of snowflakes in the tree-shrouded twilight as I reached the lumberyard's hurricane fencing. I slowed, intending to park outside the office, but the mesh gates were closed and padlocked. Frowning, I pulled up outside. The place looked empty. It was in darkness, its windows unlit even by the muted glow of battery lanterns, and no cars were parked outside. The harvesters and other logging vehicles were frosted with white, like prehistoric giants dug out of permafrost, but the snow that had fallen on the yard's concrete apron was pristine, untouched by tyre tracks or footprints.

I sat in the car with the engine running, trying to decide what to do. When Maud hadn't been home I'd been sure I'd find her at work, but it was obvious there was no one here either. For all I knew she might have gone into the village to see someone or stock up on supplies, yet I felt a vague disquiet.

I began to turn the car around. As I did its headlights swept over the office building, passing across something half-hidden behind it. I stopped. The rear end of a car was just visible jutting out from behind the building's wall. It was parked almost out of sight, so I couldn't see what make it was, only that it was a big car.

Big enough to be the SUV I'd seen parked outside Maud's the night before.

Snowflakes drifted down through the headlights as I stared through the mesh gates. The fact there was a car inside the plantation's locked yard didn't mean anything. It could have been a pool car, parked there all the time.

But if not . . .

Turning the car around, I drove back into the village and pulled up outside the village store. The door chimes tinkled when I opened the door. It was darker inside than out and the air was cloying with the fumes from the paraffin heater. The elderly shopkeeper was still bundled up in her coat behind the wooden counter, a small oasis of light in the gloomy shop. She stared at me coldly.

'I'm closing up.'

'I'm trying to find out where Eddie Drummond lives. He's the office manager at—'

'I know who he is.' The eyes behind the glasses were beady and calculating. 'This is a shop. Are you going to buy anything?'

I clenched my jaw. Near the counter was a shelf with a few dusty bottles of wine. I went over and selected one at random. Jon might not drink but Nisha evidently did, and it would replace the homemade dandelion wine she'd opened.

'So, can you tell me where Eddie Drummond lives?' I asked the shopkeeper as she rang it through the till.

'Why do you want to know?'

'There's something I need to ask him.'

She raised her eyebrows, waiting for more. I smiled but stayed silent, knowing that anything I told her would be common knowledge by morning. She gave a resentful sniff.

'He's at the end of the village. Last road on your left.'

'Is that the one at the crossroads?' That would make it the same road that the lane up to the old campsite was on.

'Last road on the left,' she repeated. Ringing through my bottle, she folded her arms. 'Cash only.'

Taking out my wallet, I gave her a twenty-pound note. She smiled for the first time.

'I don't have any change.'

Of course you don't. 'Keep it for the charity tin,' I told her.

The door chimes jingled merrily as I went back to my car.

The drive to Eddie's took barely ten minutes. The snow was still falling, but no more heavily than before. Perhaps even a little lighter, I thought, seeing the delicate flakes settle on the windscreen before vanishing in another pass from the wipers. But it seemed to be getting darker even earlier than usual under the thick cloud cover, and my headlights came on automatically before I'd reached the end of the road. When I got to the crossroads I turned off as the shopkeeper had said. There was no other road she could have meant, but there were no houses here either. As I drove past the rusting gate at the bottom of the lane I was beginning to think she'd sent me on a wild goose chase.

I was almost ready to turn back when my headlights fell on first a garden fence, then a white pebbledashed bungalow set back from the road. Dim lights glowed in some of the curtained windows and there was a snow-topped car in the driveway. I pulled up on the road outside but didn't switch off the engine. Now I was there this no longer seemed such a good idea. Eddie wasn't as bellicose as his in-laws, and he'd helped diffuse the confrontation in the plantation that morning before anyone got hurt.

But he was still married to Wynn Beddoes' daughter, and after what had happened that morning I didn't think either of them would be pleased to have me turn up on their doorstep. For all I knew Maud might be back at home by now, pouring herself a glass of wine after returning from whatever errand she'd been on. I could be disrupting everyone's evening for no good reason.

I hoped I was.

Turning off the engine, I climbed out of the car. Eddie's house backed onto the spruce plantation, I saw as I walked up the driveway. In the half-light, the tall, pointed trees were visible behind the bungalow, looming over its low roof. They'd have made an oppressive backdrop even in daylight. Now, as night fell, the dark spruces seemed primeval and menacing.

The front door was white uPVC, the upper half glazed with frosted glass. No light shone behind it as I rang the doorbell and waited. There was the thump of running footsteps from inside, then the door was opened.

A girl of eight or nine stared up at me through the gap. She had her grandfather's eyes and sharp features that were a smaller, undeveloped version of Eddie's wife's. She stared up at me, taken aback at the sight of an unfamiliar face.

I smiled. 'Hello. Is your dad in?'

She looked at me for a few seconds, then turned her head back and shouted over her shoulder.

'MOM!'

It was a loud noise from such a small frame. She continued to stare at me from the doorway as rapid footsteps approached. Eddie's wife Evie appeared in the hallway behind her, drying her hands on a towel. Her eyes were red and puffy, as though she'd been crying.

164

'All right, I can hear you, I'm not—'

She broke off when she saw me, her face hardening.

'Go inside,' she told her daughter, replacing her in the doorway. She waited until the girl had done as she was told. 'What do you want?'

'I need to see Eddie.'

'Why?'

'I wondered if he knew where Maud was.'

'Try the office in the morning.'

'I think something might have happened,' I said quickly, as she started to shut the door.

She frowned at me. 'What are you talking about?'

I was saved having to answer. 'Evie? What's going on?'

Grudgingly, she stepped back as Eddie appeared in the hall behind her. 'He wants to know where Maud is.'

'Why, what's—?'

'Ask him yourself.'

She went past him back down the hallway. Eddie looked after her uncertainly, even more harassed than usual, before turning back to me. He stepped partway outside so he could pull the door nearly shut behind him.

'Is everything all right?'

'I don't know. I hope so, but Maud wasn't at her house and the yard gates were locked. I couldn't see any lights on in the building.'

His forehead furrowed. 'The yard's closed today. Maud said she might go in first thing, but she wouldn't still be there this late. She might have gone somewhere after, though.'

'There was a car parked around the side of the building. I couldn't see much of it but it looked like an SUV.'

I'd hoped he'd brush it off, tell me it was always parked there. His frown deepened.

'That's where Maud parks. There shouldn't be anything else there, not if she's left. And you say you've been to her house?'

'I went there first.'

Eddie shook his head, his face pinched and anxious. 'Right. Well, I don't—'

165

There was a sudden commotion behind him, children's excited cries and laughter.

'*Dad, Fury's getting out!*'

Eddie turned around as a dark furry shape barged into him from behind. I recognised the young lurcher that had run off with the mandible, tongue flapping as it boisterously tried to force its way past Eddie. Behind it, their faces split in delighted grins, was the young girl who'd answered the door earlier and a boy of a similar age who could only be her brother.

Eddie caught hold of the dog's collar, showing surprising strength as he checked its run.

'I thought I told you two to keep him inside?' he said, making a token attempt at sternness as he struggled to restrain the lurcher.

'It was her fault!'

'No, it wasn't, you said—!'

'All right, just keep it down, you don't want to upset your mum,' he urged, lowering his voice as he glanced past them. 'Here, take him into the lounge.'

Neither his children or the lurcher seemed at all chastened. Eddie shook his head as he watched the three of them retreat down the hallway, but there was the ghost of a smile there as well.

'Evie thought we'd better look after him for a few days,' he explained. 'You know, after . . . what happened.'

I was pleased to see that the dog was alive and well. I'd thought the worst when only the older lurcher had accompanied Alun Beddoes into the plantation that morning, wondering if his father might have vented his anger on it. Evidently Evie had been worried about the same thing, which said a lot about her foresight and her father's temper.

But that wasn't the reason I was there. 'Does anyone apart from Maud have keys to the yard?'

Eddie blinked. 'Er . . . well, I have a set.'

'In that case, don't you think we should make sure everything's OK?'

He glanced back into the house again, then gave a resigned nod. 'Yeah. Yeah, I suppose we should.'

166

'I'll meet you there,' I told him.

My tyre tracks from before were still the only marks on the road when I drove back through the village and out to the plantation yard. They'd been nearly covered over by a smattering of fresh snow, but there was no question that the fall was easing. Only a few small flakes drifted down through the headlights' beams, and they grew even more sparse once I reached the start of the plantation and the spruce branches closed in overhead.

I pulled over in the same spot as before, leaving my headlights on while I waited for Eddie. I stayed in the warmth of the car, staring through the mesh gates at the darkened office building. Nothing had changed. The parked car was still there, hidden behind the wall of the office, only part of its boot and one wheel visible in my headlights.

As the minutes ticked by I began to wonder if Eddie was going to come. Perhaps I should have waited at the house, I thought, looking at the unrelieved darkness in my rear-view mirror. But then twin points of light appeared in the distance, quickly growing into two dazzling beams. Taking the torch from the glove compartment, I climbed out of my car and switched it on as Eddie pulled up in front of me. He got out as well, looking through the mesh gates in the light of his own torch.

'Is that Maud's car?' I asked.

'Hard to say,' he said, then gave a reluctant shrug. 'Might be.'

I waited while he unlocked the gates and swung them open. The yard was still and dark. Our boots left black imprints in the unmarked snow as we walked across it, shining our torches ahead of us. Neither of us spoke as more of the parked car came into view. Under the thin scurf of snow on its roof and bonnet I could see it was a Volvo SUV, like the one I'd seen outside Maud's house. We stopped by it, the car's yellow registration plate luminous in the torchlight. I glanced at Eddie, and saw the answer to the question I'd been about to ask written on his face.

'It's Maud's,' he said. He seemed at a loss.

'Can we take a look in the office?'

We went back around to the front of the building, Eddie talking nervously as he fumbled with a bunch of keys.

'There'd be lights on if she was still here. The emergency generator was playing up yesterday but we've got battery lighting. She wouldn't be working in the dark.'

It sounded as though he was trying to convince himself. Finally, he found the right key and let us in. The office building was in complete darkness. When I shone the torch around it showed only closed doors.

'Doesn't look like anyone's here,' Eddie said, hopefully.

'Let's try Maud's office.'

Maud wasn't in there, or any of the other places we looked. Neither was anyone else. Our footsteps echoed as we went from room to room, and then in a larger warehouse space at the rear of the building, but there was no obvious sign of a disturbance. Papers and files had been left on untidy desks and unwashed mugs were piled in the sink of a grubby rest area, but it was only the temporary abandonment of an empty workplace. Eddie's relief became more palpable with every room we checked.

'Well, she's not here,' he said as we returned to the main door. 'Maybe her car wouldn't start so she walked home?'

'She wasn't there when I went round,' I reminded him.

'No, but she might be now. She could have stopped off somewhere.'

I hoped he was right. It wasn't as though we could phone her to find out. 'We should still look around outside.'

He nodded glumly. Back outside, I shone my torch around while he locked the office door behind us. The plantation yard was huge, much bigger than it appeared from the road, extending well beyond the reach of my torch. Our footprints ran back to the gates, black dashes of Morse code in the snow. The heavy logging vehicles with their tractor tyres and caterpillar tracks were silent shadows, while the corrugated stack of sawn tree trunks extended into the darkness, black logs topped with white. It would take hours for the two of us to search the entire place.

'Is there anywhere else Maud might have gone? A friend's house in the village?' I asked.

'Not really, she doesn't . . .' He broke off, cocking his head. 'Did you hear that?'

I listened, then shook my head. 'No. What—?'

'Shh. There. Hear it?'

This time I did. Faint, but not distant.

The whining of a dog.

It was coming from past the office building, deeper in the yard. Without a word, Eddie and I hurried towards it, not quite running. The light from our torches revealed oily machine parts and rusty cutting blades as we went past more sawn tree trunks stacked in rows higher than our heads. The dog's whimpers grew louder, rising and falling but not stopping. Ahead of us our torch beams fell on a single-storey outbuilding, dirty brick walls dark against the white snow. In its centre was a recessed doorway in which was a solid-looking door. It was closed and the doorway looked empty until we shone our torches down.

Wet and shivering, Maud's brown labrador was huddled against the door.

'It's Maud's dog.' Eddie's voice was shocked and scared as he crouched down to stroke it. The dog cowered, giving another whimper as it feebly wagged its tail. 'It's OK, Max, it's only me.'

I shone my torch on the door. 'What's in there?'

'The tool room.' Standing up Eddie rattled the handle. The door stayed shut. 'It's locked.'

A chill was creeping through me that had nothing to do with the cold. *Tool room.* 'Do you have a key?'

'Yes, but she can't be in there. You can't lock it from the inside.'

His voice betrayed his own doubts. I looked down at the shivering dog. 'We still need to take a look.'

Eddie's hands shook as he brought out his keys and tried to pick one out. His smile was a travesty.

'Sorry, I-I can't . . .'

'Here, let me.'

He gave me the bunch and moved aside. There were only a half-dozen or so keys on the ring, and I found the right one on the third attempt. It turned with a heavy *snick*.

'Don't let Max in,' I said.

I waited until Eddie had a firm hold of the dog's collar and then opened the door.

It was heavy, thick timber under a riveted steel plate, with what looked suspiciously like a sheet of asbestos on the inside. It swung outwards on greased hinges, forcing me to step back. Beyond it was a pitch-black void.

The smell hit me straight away.

Death has many odours, but it's usually those that occur afterwards – days, weeks or longer – that I encounter most. Bloat and putrefaction, the spoilt meat-and-cheese stench of decomposition. Occasionally the dry, powdery odour of mummification.

The reek from the darkened plant room was none of those. It was the stink of recent, violent death. Blood, faeces and urine, blending with sweeter fumes of oil and petrol. Staying in the doorway, I shone the torch in a wide sweep. Gouts of something dark and viscous were splashed on the walls, spattered over the sledgehammers, mattocks, mauls and axes stored inside. At one side was a rack of bulky power tools.

Chainsaws.

An empty space yawned on the rack where one was absent, as obvious as a missing tooth in the torchlight. With a sense of unreality, I lowered the beam to the floor and felt my breath catch. Through the rushing in my ears I realised Eddie was saying something. He was still standing outside, his voice high and panicked.

' . . . is it? What can you see?'

I backed out of the room and gave a start as I bumped into him. It took me a moment to find words, and when I spoke I could still taste the stench of what lay inside.

'It's Maud.'

Chapter 19

I nearly crashed the car driving back to Hillside House. Although the snow wasn't deep, once past the crossroads the single-lane road became steep and winding, and the winter tyres struggled. I'd driven in far worse, and even when I felt the car start to slip in that loose, frictionless way, it shouldn't have been hard to recover. But I was slow and reacted too hard. The car lurched into a full-blown skid, and for a weightless second or two I was a passenger. If there'd been a ditch or drop I would have gone off, but the narrowness of the road saved me. As the car began to slew it thumped into the hedgerow at one side, checking the skid without any help from me.

I let the car sit there with the engine running, though the narrow escape barely registered. I felt numb and disconnected, my thoughts struggling for traction as much as the tyres. They slipped on the slick road again when I set off before finding purchase. I drove the short distance back to the hotel like an automaton and parked in the same spot as before. I switched off the engine and got out.

The snow had all but stopped, and it was only when I found myself standing in frigid darkness that it occurred to me I'd need my torch. Unlocking the car again, I retrieved it from the passenger seat and followed its beam along the path leading around the hotel.

When I reached Jon's workshop I stopped, my breathing loud in the cold, still air. That would be where he'd keep his chainsaw, and to my muddied mind it was suddenly important

171

to see it. Without thinking it through I went over and wrenched on the door handle.

Locked.

I tried it again, with the same result. It was only when I turned away and saw my footprints leading across the snow to the workshop door that I realised my mistake. They were mingled with the part-covered tracks Jon must have left earlier, but it was obvious they were two different sets. If he was innocent it wouldn't matter, and I didn't think he'd have gone to the trouble of stealing a chainsaw from the plantation yard when he already had one of his own. But if I was wrong, if he had killed Maud and found out I'd been prowling around outside his workshop . . .

Christ, you bloody idiot! I stared at the accusing footprints, trying to decide what to do. If I tried to get rid of them it would only make it more obvious I'd been there. All I could do was hope the snow had melted by next morning, and try to bluff it out if it hadn't. It was only for one more day, I told myself. There was a good chance a post van or some delivery driver would try to reach Edendale tomorrow and report the collapsed road. Once that happened it wouldn't be long before the police were on the scene, and I could hand this nightmare over to them.

Please, God.

Trying to put my blunder from my mind, I walked back to the path and carried on round to the extension. A dim glow showed through the drawn curtains, warm and inviting, but I felt a heavy reluctance at the thought of going in. I stopped outside the door, loath to knock.

A plaintive whine brought me back to myself. I looked down at the labrador. It gazed back up at me, anxious and miserable on the rope I'd fastened around its collar as a makeshift lead.

'Good boy, Max.'

I'd had no choice but to bring the dog with me. Even if his wife had allowed it, Eddie didn't have room for another dog in the small bungalow when they were already looking after Beddoes' lurcher. Maud didn't have any family, either in the village or anywhere else as far as Eddie knew, and had kept herself to herself outside of work. She had no friends there and he couldn't think of anyone else who might take the labrador at short notice. So, I'd said it could stay with me until something else could be arranged. I didn't know what Nisha and Jon would say, but having to look after a dog for one night was the least of my concerns.

Not after what had happened to Maud.

Eddie had been distraught at the yard. He'd tried to push into the tool room, letting go of the labrador in his desperation. I grabbed hold of the dog's collar as it tried to bolt past me, blocking the doorway with my body. I struggled to hold Eddie back as well but couldn't stop him shining his torch inside. I heard him gasp and suddenly the fight went out of him.

'Oh, God . . .'

'We need to come away,' I said.

'Oh, Jesus. Jesus Christ . . .'

He slumped against me, staring over my shoulder into the tool room. Awkwardly gripping the labrador's collar with one hand, I eased him back from the doorway.

'Eddie! *Eddie*, listen to me!' His eyes were wide, his face slack with shock. 'I need you to take Maud's dog while I lock up here. OK? Can you do that?'

He looked over my shoulder at the still-open doorway, then gave an uncertain nod.

'Sorry, I-I just . . .'

'I know. Here, take Max's collar.' I waited until I was sure he had a firm grip before I let go. 'Wait for me at the gate. I won't be long.'

I watched him go, bending to one side to pull the labrador along with him. The dog looked back, giving a plaintive whine as he led it away. When they were out of sight I turned back to the tool room. It was in darkness again, hiding what was inside. I started to shine my torch through the doorway again, then thought better of it.

I'd already seen more than I wanted to.

There was nothing I could do except secure the scene for when the police arrived. Touching as little as possible, I shut

173

the heavy door and made sure it was locked, then made my way back across the dark yard to where Eddie waited with Maud's dog. They made a forlorn pair. The labrador wagged its tail feebly when I joined them, looking past me expectantly. It whined when it saw no one was there.

Eddie looked down at it, shaking his head. 'I-I can't believe it. This doesn't seem real.'

'I'm sorry,' I said, knowing how empty the words sounded.

'Do you think it could have been an accident? If she accidentally started a chainsaw or something, it might have . . .'

He trailed off, unable to maintain the fantasy. We both knew what we'd seen inside the tool room was no accident. The mutilation was too severe to be self-inflicted, and there was no chainsaw lying near Maud.

Whoever had killed her had taken it with them.

'Is the tool room normally kept locked?' I asked Eddie.

'Yes. I mean, it's supposed to be, but I-I can't say for certain.' He ducked his head, uncomfortably. 'We don't get much theft or anything round here so . . . people don't always bother.'

'Is there another way in apart from these gates?'

'There's the main track we use for logging access at the back of the yard. There's no gate or anything but that just goes into the plantation. You can't get to it from the road.'

In other words, anyone who wanted to could just walk into the yard, completely unseen. *Great*.

'Who else apart from you has keys?'

'Wendy does, Maud's secretary. I-I think there are spare sets in the safe as well, but only Maud knows . . . *knew* the combination for that.' Eddie took a shuddering breath. 'Oh, Christ, I-I don't know what to do . . .'

'There's nothing we can do except lock the gates and let everyone know that the yard's closed. Can you do that? We need to make sure no one comes in here until the police arrive.' It was starting to feel like a mantra.

Eddie had nodded, looking close to tears. 'What do we say, though? About . . . about Maud. People are going to ask.'

'Tell them the truth,' I'd told him.

I was brought back from my thoughts by another whine from the labrador. He was looking up at me, miserable and confused, but still gave a tentative wag of his tail. Taking a breath, I raised my hand and knocked on the extension's door. A moment later Nisha called out.

'Come in.'

She was at the range, stirring a pan. Reese was on his hands and knees with his head under the sink. Both had their backs to me, but Kiran gave me a gummy grin from his playpen. A savoury smell of cooking filled the kitchen.

'Tea'll be half an hour,' Nisha said, turning around. 'If you want to—Oh!'

She broke off when she saw the labrador. Kiran laughed and clapped his hands delightedly. Pushing himself out from under the sink, Jon looked from the dog to me as he got to his feet.

'What the hell's this?'

The labrador wagged its tail nervously, glancing up at me for reassurance. 'He belongs to Maud, the plantation manager. His name's Max.'

'I don't care what its name is, why've you brought it here? We can't—'

'Maud's dead.'

There was a pause, then Nisha spoke.

'Oh, that's sad. I didn't really know her, but even so. Was it her heart or something? She was . . . well, quite big, wasn't she?'

'Someone killed her. At the yard.'

This time the pause was longer. A pan bubbled slowly on the range.

'Jesus.' Jon seemed shaken, but with him it was hard to tell. 'What happened?'

I shook my head, unwilling to say too much. 'It looks as though she disturbed someone who shouldn't have been there.'

175

Nisha had a quizzical expression, as though still struggling to take it in. 'Are you sure? That someone killed her, I mean? It couldn't have been an accident, or something?'

An image of the tool room suddenly flashed to mind, mangled flesh and splintered white stubs lying in a congealed black pool.

'I'm sure.'

'Do you know who did it?' Jon asked. I paused, looking for any sense of guilt or dissembling from him. If it was there I couldn't see it.

'No.'

'You said she'd suspended Vic Hooley after the crash. I wouldn't put anything past that bastard.'

Neither would I, and Hooley had been the first person I'd thought of too. He'd reason to hold a grudge against Maud, and he'd have known where the chainsaws were stored. But the same could be said of any of the plantation's employees, including Eddie. Everyone in the village would know there were chainsaws kept on site, come to that. If security in the yard was lax then anyone could have accessed the tool room, and making accusations without evidence wasn't going to help. Besides, I didn't think Maud had been murdered because she'd suspended an employee.

She'd just been in the wrong place at the wrong time.

'The police will question him, but I don't think it was anything to do with the crash,' I said.

Nisha went to the kitchen table and sat down, as though her legs wouldn't support her. Kiran beamed at her, a chubby finger pointing at Maud's dog, but his mother didn't notice.

'You don't think it had something to do with . . . with what you found in the plantation, do you?'

'I don't know.' It wasn't something I wanted to discuss, not with them and not now. 'Look, I'm sorry about bringing Maud's dog here, but there's nowhere else to take him. He can stay in my room, so he won't get in your way.'

'Don't worry about that,' Nisha said, before Jon could object. She gave a shiver and rubbed her arms, even though the kitchen was stiflingly warm. 'Seems the least we can do. God, this is awful.'

176

There was nothing more to say after that. Nisha asked if I wanted anything to eat, but I'd no appetite. Excusing myself, I went up to my room. The labrador's claws clicked on the parquet floor as we crossed the foyer. He came with me obediently enough, warily eyeing the stuffed animals caught in the torchlight. I had to coax him around the fox in the corridor upstairs, and by the time we reached my room I could feel him shaking.

Once inside I turned on the nightlight, switching off my torch as glowing stars and moons lit up the walls. The room was cold, but before I lit a fire I slipped off the rope I'd been using as a lead from the labrador's collar and set about feeding him. The village store had been closed and Maud's house was off limits now, but Eddie had let me have a few tins of Beddoes' dog's food, as well as the rope to use as a temporary lead. Filling one of the old bowls Nisha had given me with water, while Max lapped at it thirstily I opened one of the tins of dog food. The meaty smell turned my stomach, and I closed my mind to a sudden image of the bloody mess on the tool-room floor as the glistening chunks slid into the bowl.

But Max fell on it ravenously, and while the dog ate I busied myself lighting a fire. As the flames filled the room with a flickering light, I took off my coat and then transferred the latest photographs from my phone onto my laptop.

I'd intended to copy them onto the photogrammetry software as well, so I could compare a three-dimensional model of the destroyed remains with the older one of them still intact. Instead I found myself staring at the screen without seeing it, my hands resting motionless on the keys. The labrador came and flopped down in front of the fire. His tail thumped against the floor when I stroked him, but he kept glancing towards the doorway, giving a soft whimper as though expecting someone to come in.

'I know, Max. It's all right,' I said.

It wasn't though, and we both knew it. I felt restless and strange, haunted by the image of Maud's body, as well as older, darker thoughts I normally kept packed away. I'd lost count of the number of bodies I'd seen, many of them horrifically mutilated as well. Yet finding Maud like that had affected me in a way few of them had. It had swept aside my usual defences, slamming me with a visceral reminder of death's irrevocable nature. A living, conscious individual — someone I'd known — had become something lifeless and inanimate. An assembly of organic matter already starting to decay.

It had been like falling through an emotional trapdoor.

Without warning I'd been plunged back years, to that still-inconceivable moment when I'd walked into a chilled, antiseptic room and seen my wife and daughter laid out on mortuary tables, still and cold and dead. Of being confronted by the incomprehensible fact that Kara and Alice, the two people I loved more than anything, who gave my life meaning, had *stopped*.

Forever.

It came close to destroying me. I'd found it impossible to continue with my work, fled from everything I'd known. Friends, colleagues, home. I'd tried to start again, turned back to the medical training I'd abandoned. I'd found work as a GP, buried myself in a small village in Norfolk as far removed from my old life as possible. Then a friend had been savagely murdered, and my old life found me again anyway.

And now here I was.

I jumped as something wet and cold touched my hand. Looking down, I saw Max looking up at me with worried labrador eyes. When I stroked him he nosed at my hand, wagging his tail so hard he almost bent himself in two.

Despite myself, I smiled, and as I did I realised the crisis had passed. I still felt raw and brittle, but my thoughts were my own again.

'Good boy,' I said, and the labrador's wagging became even more frenzied.

One of the logs in the fireplace crumbled in a flurry of sparks. Pulling myself together, I turned my attention back to the laptop. The screen had gone dark, so I woke it and was about to open the photogrammetry programme when Max suddenly turned to the door, cocking his head as he stared at it. A moment later there was a quiet knock.

It was Nisha. She gave a tired smile, offering up a sandwich on a plate in one hand and a steaming mug of tea in the other.

'I know you said you didn't want anything but you might get hungry later. It's only cheese, so it'll save.'

'Thank you,' I said, taking the plate and mug. My appetite had returned, I realised, although I still was glad she'd brought a sandwich instead of the casserole.

She lingered in the doorway. 'How's Maud's dog doing?'

'He's behaving himself. Aren't you, Max?'

The dog took that as an invitation to come over. He sniffed cautiously at Nisha, then decided he'd found a new best friend when she rubbed his ears.

'He might need to go outside later,' I said. 'Is there another way out, so I don't have to disturb you?'

'The main door to the hotel's locked but I can leave the key in it. You'll have to undo the bolts as well, but we won't hear anything in the extension.' Nisha had been smiling as the dog fussed around her, but now it faded. 'I can't stop thinking about Maud. It doesn't seem possible that . . . that somebody here *killed* her.'

'No,' I said. It never did, but that didn't make it any less real.

I waited for Nisha to leave, but she showed no inclination to go. There was a nervousness about her now.

'Actually, I wanted a word,' she said, lowering her voice and glancing down the dark corridor. 'Can I come in?'

The last thing I wanted was more questions, but there was no polite way to refuse. Nisha stepped inside when I moved back, closing the door behind her. I switched on the battery-powered lantern, wanting to dispel the cosy intimacy of the log fire and moon and stars nightlight. I saw Nisha's eyes go to the laptop.

'Hope I'm not disturbing you?'

The laptop screen was angled away from her, but I closed it anyway. 'Just catching up on some work.'

Nisha took a deep breath, her fingers plucking at each other.

'I knew about the body.'

Chapter 20

The fire snapped and crackled in the grate as her words sank in. I recovered enough to ask the question.

'What do you mean, you "knew"?'

'When I told you Jon's mum had said there was a phone signal in the plantation. I-I made it up. I knew the body was there and I wanted you to find it. I didn't really think you *would*, it was . . . it was just a spur-of-the-moment thing!' She stared down at her hands. 'I'm sorry, I know it sounds bad. You've got every right to be upset.'

I couldn't have said exactly how I felt, but oddly I wasn't surprised. On some level I'd known there was something off, but I'd been too distracted for it to register.

'Why?' I asked.

'I was desperate, it was the only thing I could think of. Look, do you mind if I sit down?'

There was only the bed or the hard-backed chair I'd been using while I worked on the laptop. I took it over to her, then perched on the edge of the bed myself. Max came over and nudged my hand again. I patted him absently, my attention on the woman in front of me.

Nisha sat with her fingers knotted together on her knees.

'I had to do *something*. You don't know what this past year's been like. All the . . . the *bile* and resentment aimed at us. I'm sorry about whatever happened to Jed Beddoes, but it wasn't Jon's fault! He was just a kid, he didn't have anything to do with it! And I've got Kiran to think of as well. Being stuck out here with a baby, it feels like . . . like . . .'

'OK, take your time,' I told her. She paused, drawing in a shaky breath. I waited until she seemed calmer. 'Let's back up a little. How did you know the body was there?'

'I saw it.' She kept her eyes on her clenched hands. 'I needed to clear my head, so I went out for a walk and . . . there it was.'

I waited but she didn't look up. *OK . . .* 'How long ago was this?'

'I don't know. A few weeks?'

'Can you narrow it down? Was it two weeks, three . . .?'

'Longer than that, I think. Probably a month or two? I-I can't remember exactly, it was such a shock.'

I kept my face neutral. 'Can you describe what you saw?'

She glanced up at me, worriedly, then down again. 'There was a-a skeleton. All snarled up in the tree roots.'

'You mean the tree had fallen down?'

'Not . . . not all the way, no. It was more . . . at an angle? Like it had started to fall but only gone so far. You could see bones under it, in some of the roots. It must have blown down afterwards. By the time you saw it.'

I filed that away. 'Why didn't you report it to the police?'

'I *wanted* to, but I-I was too scared.'

'Of what?'

'What do you *think*?' she flashed, with sudden anger. 'I knew it must be Jed Beddoes, but can you imagine what'd happen if I said *I'd* found him? I know his family deserve closure. It must be horrible for them, not knowing what happened, but no one'd believe I'd found his body by accident. Everyone would think Jon must have told me, that he'd known all the time, and God knows what the Beddoes would do then! It'd just rake everything up all over again, except a thousand times worse! I couldn't do that to Jon.'

I rubbed my eyes, feeling very tired. 'So you sent me up there hoping I'd find the body and report it to the police.'

'Yes, but I didn't plan it, honestly!' Nisha leaned forward on her seat, staring at me earnestly. 'When you said you were a forensic expert I'd tried to think how I could let you know about the body without being obvious about it. But I couldn't think of how to do it, and then you left anyway so I-I thought that was it. It was only when you came back and said the road had collapsed that it seemed like, I don't know, *fate* or something! No one could blame us if somebody *else* found Jed Beddoes' body, especially a forensic scientist! I honestly never thought you would, not really. It just seemed too good a chance to miss.'

Looking back, the biggest surprise was that I'd fallen for it. What was even more incredible was that Nisha's scheme had worked. Somehow, despite the vagueness of her directions, in all those acres of identical trees I'd managed to stumble across the remains. The scientist in me baulked at the idea that it was anything other than a freak chance, more to do with the natural contours of the terrain channelling me towards it than some uncanny coincidence. Yet I couldn't begin to guess the odds of it happening. And the final irony was that there really *had* been a phone signal somewhere on the fell.

If it hadn't been so tragic I might have laughed.

'Does Jon know?' I asked.

'He does now. I didn't tell him at first, because I hoped he'd think you'd just found it. He . . . he's pretty upset about it.' She started crying, fumbling in her pocket for a tissue. 'I never expected anything like *this* to happen! I-I thought I was doing it for the best and now Maud's dead and . . . Oh, God, I am so, so sorry!'

'You didn't know what was going to happen.'

Nisha shook her head, wiping her eyes. 'No, but it just seems so *senseless!* Jon says it must have been the same person who trashed the skeleton. He thinks they were trying to frame him so it looked like he was trying to cover up for his dad, but who'd want to do that? What's the *point*?'

I couldn't answer that. I said nothing as she sniffed back the last of her tears.

'What will the police do to me?' she asked. Her fingers plucked at the tissue, shredding it. 'Am I in trouble?'

'Honestly, I don't know,' I said. A warning was probably more likely than charges for obstruction or concealing evidence, but I could be wrong. 'You need to tell them everything, though. And I *mean* everything.'

Nisha gave a subdued nod. 'I better go. Jon'll wonder where I am.'

We got to our feet. 'Thanks for the sandwich,' I said.

'You're welcome.' She paused to stroke Max, who'd stood up with us. 'I really am sorry . . .'

I waited until the door had closed behind her, then leaned back against it and let out my breath slowly.

Christ . . .

No wonder Maud had been so sceptical when I'd told her I'd gone up into the plantation to make a phone call, I thought, angry at my own gullibility. Yet although Nisha's confession rang true to some extent, something about it didn't seem right.

Opening my laptop, I went to the photogrammetry program. I still had to transfer the photographs of the destroyed crime scene from that morning onto it, but there was something I wanted to check first. I opened the virtual 3D model I'd made of the intact remains, and the macabre image of the skeleton suspended in the tree roots filled the screen.

Zooming in, I began examining it for any signs of weathering.

Nisha had been vague on details — again — yet according to her the spruce was partly uprooted but still standing when she'd discovered the remains a month or two before. It followed that the already unstable tree must have blown down in the storm of two nights ago. That would explain the lack of weathering I'd seen on the bones, since they'd only been out in the open for a matter of days.

Except they hadn't. Not all of them. At least some of the skeleton must have been exposed before the tree fell for Nisha to have seen it. Even if it had been sheltered from the worst of the weather underneath the tree, the uncovered bones would have still begun to dry out. And, skeletonised or not, I'd have expected at least a few curious scavengers to have shown an interest, like the magpie I'd had to scare off when I'd been there.

Yet the bones on the laptop screen showed no evidence of any of that. There was no indication of drying out or weathering, or any sign of gnawing or pitting from scavenging teeth and beaks. One or two months was probably too short a time for lichen or moss growth, but that was only how long it was since Nisha claimed to have discovered the remains. The tree could — and probably had — been leaning for longer than that. Perhaps for years, in which case the contrast between any sections of skeleton that had been exposed to air for all that time and those still buried until recently would be even more obvious.

But there was no differentiation. Even at full magnification I couldn't see anything to suggest that the entire skeleton hadn't been completely buried until two days ago, when the spruce had been blown down in the storm.

So why had Nisha lied?

My laptop battery was running low. I'd need to recharge it, as well as my phone, on the USB port in my car, but that would have to wait till morning. It meant I couldn't create a photogrammetry model of the destroyed remains as I'd planned, but there was still enough charge left to examine the photographs I'd taken that morning.

Lit by the blue light from the laptop screen, I ate the sandwich Nisha had brought as I worked. I didn't know if cheese agreed with dogs, and Max had already been fed, but eventually I succumbed to his mournful looks and gave him a couple of crusts. He seemed happy with that, and the labrador was a comforting presence by my side as I pored over the images.

Even on the reduced scale of the laptop screen, the devastation caused by the chainsaw was no less shocking. I spent some time examining the footprints in and around the crater left by the tree roots. They looked to have been made by a single individual, wearing large boots or Wellingtons — size ten or eleven at a guess — with heavy, zigzag patterned soles.

The muddy ground was so badly trampled that most of them were churned beyond recognition, although that seemed more by accident than design. Plenty of clear impressions remained, enough for the police to use to identify the person who'd destroyed the remains. Whoever it was didn't seem to have thought that far ahead.

Or didn't care.

I didn't want to run down what remained of the laptop's dwindling battery, but there was one last thing I wanted to check. I scrolled through the photographs until I came to the ones I'd taken of the bone fragments littering the muddy crater. I'd taken a lot of those and quickly went through them now, scanning for the pieces of skull I'd noticed earlier.

They weren't difficult to spot, recognisable by their thinness and curvature. Most were either too damaged or too small to be of use, but eventually I found what I'd been looking for.

It was lying at the very edge of the crater, half-hidden by a clump of earth. Larger than most of the other shards of skull, it might have been part of a porcelain bowl. Its broken edges were asymmetrical and jagged, except for one side that was still embedded in the fibrous tissue of a tree root.

I leaned closer to the screen, feeling a growing excitement.

The human cranium is made up of eight plate-like bones, each separated from its neighbour by a slowly fusing cranial suture. Two of these cranial bones, known as the parietals, extend from either side of the frontal, or forehead, to the back of the skull, where they meet the occipital bone that sits at its base.

I was looking at part of the right parietal, with a section of the occipital still attached. Its outer edge had been cut, and I'd no doubt under a microscope we'd be able to see the marks from the chainsaw blade etched on the bone. But its inner edge, where part of a tree root still clung, had a curved, uneven break. I tried zooming in to see more detail, but the image became too pixelated. The photogrammetry software was only as good as the photographs it had to work with, and I'd taken these from too far away to show the sort of detail I wanted.

Still, it was enough. I'd guessed that the rear of the skull must have suffered some sort of trauma, and here was the proof. It was hard to be sure from such a limited view, but from what I could see it looked as though something had punched a large hole in the parietal bone, allowing the tree's roots to grow through it and out of the eye sockets.

The damage *could* have been post-mortem, occurring at some point after death. But that was unlikely to have been after the body was buried, when it was protected by a cushioning layer of earth. Although I couldn't entirely rule that out, I didn't think this was a post-mortem injury.

I thought I was looking at the probable cause of death.

A scratching noise made me look around. Max was pawing on the door, which I took to mean he needed to go outside. I'd spent long enough on the laptop anyway; I saw the battery level was down to barely twenty per cent. Shutting it down, I put my coat on again, fastened the rope around Max's collar and took him downstairs. He bristled when we passed the stuffed fox in the corridor but didn't baulk this time, and he seemed indifferent to the silent menagerie in the dark foyer.

Nisha had left the key in the hotel's main door, as she'd said she would. I opened it as quietly as I could and took Max outside. All was still, dark and cold. It had stopped snowing, and the frozen white crystals crisped underfoot, glistening in the opalescent light from a sickle moon. The night sky was clear and black, unpolluted by city lights. I stared up at the vast sweep of stars while Max snuffled around the undergrowth, enjoying the cold and quiet. Now the snow had stopped someone was bound to try and reach the village in the morning and report the washed-out road. By this time tomorrow I'd be a cog in the machinery of a full-scale police murder inquiry, and whatever secrets Edendale was hiding would finally be brought to light.

Not before time, I thought, breathing the crisp air deep into my lungs.

Chapter 21

I woke the next morning to a white world.

It was the quiet that roused me. I lay in bed, slowly coming round as I tried to identify what was wrong. The air in the darkened hotel room was frigid, even colder than normal. Apart from the creaks and groans of its old structure, Hillside House was always silent, but there was something different about this. No breath of wind buffeted the loose window or rustled the trees outside, I realised. And there was something else missing.

There was no birdsong.

A diffuse white light came through the bedroom curtains. I got out of bed to open them and jumped when a dark shape rushed over. I'd forgotten about Max. He bounced around, wagging his tail feverishly, so I took time to fuss him before I went to draw the curtains. Ice had formed on the inside of the window, blurring the scene outside. It burnt my hand as I wiped it away, wafer-thin skims of it sliding down the glass as it melted.

Looking out I felt my heart sink.

A heavy fall of snow covered everything. Branches were bowed under its weight while bushes and plants had been transformed into unrecognisable humps and shapes. A few flakes of snow still drifted down, and low overhead a blank and colourless sky held the threat of more to come. But for the moment all was still.

I could have been looking out onto a photograph.

There was a glacial beauty to the scene, but I was blind to it. The steep road through the surrounding fells would be impassable. No one was going to attempt to reach Edendale today, not in this. Probably not tomorrow or the day after either.

No one would be coming out now until the snow melted.

I felt sick with frustration as I fed Max and went to the bathroom to get ready. The water that spluttered from the tap was like shards of ice, but I felt clearer headed after washing in it. By the time I got back to the room Max was desperate to go out. Taking him downstairs, I unlocked the hotel's heavy main door, dazzled by the sudden brightness after the foyer's gloom. The labrador bounded outside, ploughing a furrow through the chest-deep snow. He seemed to have recovered from his owner's death, and I envied his uncomplicated resilience. Even so, I couldn't help but smile as I watched him prance about in the snow, playfully snapping and biting at it.

Look on the bright side. At least you don't have to worry about Jon seeing your footprints outside his workshop.

Max came back happily enough when I called. I was brushing the snow from his legs and knocking it from my boots when Nisha appeared through the doorway in the panelling.

'Morning. Thought I heard you.' She looked drawn but gave a wan smile as she looked at Max. 'Glad someone's enjoying the weather.'

'I was just about to take him back to the room.'

She waved that away. 'Don't worry, he's not going to spoil anything. Come through when you're ready. I'll make a start on your breakfast.'

The smell of frying eggs greeted me when I went into the kitchen, making me realise how hungry I was. All I'd eaten the evening before was the cheese sandwich, and that seemed a long time ago now.

Nisha was opening a tin by the range, while Kiran was at the table in his highchair. He looked as though he'd been crying but grinned and held out a pudgy hand towards the labrador.

'We're running low of a few things, so it's just fried egg and tomatoes today,' his mother said.

'That sounds good. Thanks.'

Nisha emptied the tinned tomatoes into a saucepan. 'No one's going to try to get out to us in this, are they?'

'No,' I agreed.

'So what happens now?' She tried to keep her voice matter of fact, but I could hear the anxiety in it.

'I don't think there's anything we can do until the snow thaws.'

There was certainly nothing more I could do. Maud's body was as secure as I could make it inside the locked tool room. The cold temperature would slow down its decomposition, while the blanket of snow would help preserve what was left of the skeleton on the mountainside.

But I knew that wasn't what Nisha meant. She nudged the eggs around the pan with a spatula, her back to me as she spoke.

'I thought things here couldn't get any worse, but this . . .' She shook her head, still prodding at the frying pan as though she'd forgotten she was doing it. 'I can't stop thinking about Maud. I hardly knew her, but I still can't believe somebody would . . . would *do* that. I spent half the night trying to think who it could be. Jon's convinced it was Vic Hooley or one of the Beddoes, but it could be anyone, couldn't it? And Maud must have *known* them, that's what gets me. *I* probably know them, it could be someone I've spoken to! God, this is horrible!'

It was hard to know what to say to that. 'If it's any consolation I don't think it'll take the police long to catch them, whoever it is,' I said, uselessly.

'When they get here. But how long's that going to be?' She turned to me. 'Whoever did it's trapped here now. What do you think they're going to do?'

'If they've got any sense they won't do anything. They'll only make it worse for themselves if they do.'

'And what if they don't have any sense?' She glanced over at Kiran, her hands bunched and clenched. 'Do you think we're safe?'

The truth was I didn't know. The possibility that Jon had killed Maud seemed far less credible after a night's sleep. Everything pointed to her having been murdered when she'd disturbed someone stealing a chainsaw from the tool room, and while that didn't exclude Jon altogether, I couldn't see why he'd have taken such a stupid and unnecessary risk.

What worried me more was that the remains' destruction and Maud's murder both seemed like panicked, knee-jerk reactions. And whoever was responsible would be even more desperate now. I'd no idea what they might do next.

I doubted they had either.

'They're snowed in the same as everyone else. They'll probably just want to lie low,' I said, with more confidence than I felt, and changed the subject. 'Where's Jon?'

Nisha turned back to the frying pan. 'Out.'

'If he's clearing the snow I'll help him after breakfast.' I'd be glad of the exercise, and it would keep me from brooding.

'No, he, uh . . . he went for a walk.'

In this? I looked out of the window. Snow had gathered several inches deep on its sill, and beyond it was an unfamiliar white landscape.

'Did he say where?'

'No.'

She kept her back to me, but that failed to hide her tension. 'Is everything OK?'

'Fine.' Nisha picked up the saucepan, then set it down again. 'No, not really. We had a row last night. Jon was angry I'd told you about finding the body. He was still upset this morning. That's why he went out.'

'I expect he'll come back once he's calmed down,' I said, more to say something than because I believed it.

Nisha nodded, but she didn't seem convinced either. 'Yeah, I'm sure. Except . . . Never mind.'

The last thing I wanted was to get dragged into a domestic dispute, but Nisha seemed worried as well as miserable.

'Go on.'

'He . . . he found a half-full bottle of whisky in the hotel bar last night.' She swallowed, as though the words were hard to get out. 'He's lapsed a few times before, but not like this. He didn't come to bed and this morning he seemed . . . weird.

192

Not just drunk but *off*, somehow. I-I haven't seen him like that before. It frightened me.'

This wasn't sounding good. 'Did he threaten you? Or Kiran?'

'What?' Nisha looked shocked. 'God, no! *No*, Jon would never hurt us! I meant frightened for *him*. That he might . . . do something stupid.'

Next to her, the hot oil in the frying pan was starting to hiss and spit. She snatched it up, letting the pan clatter down off the heat.

'How long has he been gone?' I asked.

'I-I'm not sure. About an hour? Maybe more.'

'And he didn't give any idea where he was going?'

'No, but . . .' She hesitated, agonised. 'He said something about needing to make sure.'

'Make sure of what? Was he talking about the remains?'

'I don't *know*, he didn't—'

The distant clap of a shotgun cut her off. Nisha froze, staring at me with scared eyes as the echoes died away. I quickly went to the door, the crispness of the air a shock as I opened it and looked out. I squinted against the snow's glare, waiting for any further sound. But the gunshot wasn't repeated, and there was nothing to see.

'Did Jon take his shotgun with him?' I asked, coming back inside.

'I-I don't know, he might have. He keeps it in his workshop. Oh God, you don't think he's . . .'

She couldn't bring herself to finish.

'He's probably just hunting,' I said. 'It might not have been him anyway.'

But I didn't believe that any more than Nisha did. It was hard to imagine anyone else going up the fell, not in snow like this. And the fact there'd only been one shot seemed ominous after what Nisha had just been saying.

I took another look at the white wilderness, knowing what I was going to have to do.

'I'll go and look for him.'

The cold took away my breath when I went outside. Standing in the snow, I paused to adjust the rucksack straps. It was Jon's, the same one I'd used to carry the ropes in the day before. While I'd gone up to my room for my coat, Nisha had packed it with sandwiches and a Thermos flask of coffee she'd made, neither of us saying what we were both thinking.

It wasn't a good sign that Jon hadn't bothered to take it with him.

'Lock the door behind me and don't open it for anyone until we're back,' I'd told Nisha.

She'd looked scared even before then. She glanced at the door as though expecting to see someone there already.

'Why? Do you think we're in any danger?'

'There's no reason you should be,' I'd said, putting as much conviction as I could into it. 'It's just a precaution. Better not to take any chances.'

I hoped I was right.

When the rucksack was more comfortable, I set out into the white silence. I'd left Max behind with Nisha and Kiran. I would have welcomed the company but the snow was too deep for the labrador, and I didn't know how long I'd be.

Or what I might find.

The snow crumped underfoot, coming halfway up my shin as my boots sank into it. Walking in it was hard work but it made it easy to see where Jon had gone. He'd left a ragged trench in the snow, leading around the side of the hotel. I followed it but stopped when it veered off towards Jon's workshop.

The door was slightly open.

I could see that Jon had emerged from it and continued around the hotel towards the driveway and the woods behind Hillside House, but he must have been either too drunk or too distracted to remember to lock it. I hesitated, not wanting to waste time when Jon – or whoever he might have shot – could be injured or worse. But it wouldn't take long to see if his shotgun was still in his workshop.

And take a look at his chainsaw as well.

As I approached the workshop I caught the same smell I'd noticed before. Familiar, and not at all welcome in this context. It gave me a moment's pause, then I pushed open the wooden door.

'You in there, Jon?'

I wasn't expecting him to be, but I didn't want to risk surprising him when he might be armed. When there was no response I stepped inside.

The workshop was dank and cold. The only light came from the doorway and through a single window, so grimy and thick with cobwebs it might as well have had curtains. As my eyes adjusted I saw the workshop was long and low-ceilinged, with bare stone walls. A workbench and sink were fixed to the wall at one side, while in its centre stood a brick plinth topped with a waist-high marble slab. The smell was much stronger in here, overpoweringly so.

An abattoir reek of meat and old blood.

My heart was thudding as I looked around. A neat row of large, sharp-looking knives were laid out on the workbench, and I stepped back involuntarily when I saw the butcher's hooks hanging from a rail on the ceiling. But there was no body or blood splashes, no gore or body parts. A suspicion was starting to grow, confirmed when I saw the objects hung on the end wall. Grouped in pairs, they were elegantly curved and wickedly pointed.

Antlers.

Now I knew why Jon hadn't wanted me to see inside his workshop. He'd been hunting deer, hanging and butchering the carcasses in here. That would explain his secrecy, since it was illegal to hunt deer with a shotgun in the UK. It hardly fit with their lifestyle, but Nisha had told me that he wasn't vegetarian himself. I didn't think the meat would be for them anyway. Venison could fetch a good price, and I remembered Nisha saying Jon had learnt to skin and butcher animals working in restaurants in North America.

He was putting those skills to good use now.

A metal gun locker was fixed to one wall. It was unlocked when I tried it, its door opening with a squeal of dry hinges to release a sulphurous whiff of gunpowder. The only thing inside was an ancient cartridge box, lying open and empty. It confirmed that Jon had taken the shotgun with him, along with however many shells had been in the locker. It was even possible the shot we'd heard had been him shooting at a deer, and that Nisha was worrying needlessly.

Something told me she wasn't though. The more I thought about it, the less convinced I was that Jon was using his shotgun to hunt with. At least, not deer. The illegality might not have bothered him, but it was the wrong weapon for large game. A shotgun was far less accurate than the bolt action rifles normally used by deer hunters, with a much shorter range. Not only that, but any shotgun load big enough to a bring down a deer would cause a huge amount of tissue damage. That wasn't ideal for anyone wanting to sell the meat, and neither was selling illegal venison if it was full of pellets. I couldn't see a professional chef like Jon wanting to risk his reputation like that, no matter how badly he and Nisha needed the extra cash.

Looking round the workshop, I saw his chainsaw propped up in a corner. Going over, I crouched down to examine it. There were flecks of wood and sawdust on the casing and it looked to have been recently oiled. But I couldn't see any blood or bone, or evidence of the sort of forensic deep cleaning that would have been necessary to remove visible traces of Maud's murder.

That didn't necessary rule out Jon, but if he had killed her it wasn't with his own chainsaw.

I'd been in the workshop long enough. Straightening, I took a last look around and saw something I'd missed after coming in from the snow's glare.

A flat black carrying case, tucked away on a shelf in the shadows.

I needed to go after Jon, but the neat lines of the case looked out of place in the workshop. It was made from a tough-looking plastic composite, and the right sort of shape to hold a hunting rifle. There was no lock, just three sturdy catches. I hesitated, then flipped them open.

Lying inside was a hunting bow.

It was an intricate piece of engineering, a fibreglass and alloy scaffold strung with a complex system of cables and pulleys. Laid out in grooves next to it were a dozen slender metal arrows, each tipped with razor-sharp triangular heads. It was obviously a precision weapon, not a hobbyist's bow, and it wasn't hard to guess what Jon had been using it for. Bow hunting was illegal in the UK but not in the US or Canada, where he and Nisha had lived and worked for years.

Snapping the case shut, I went back out into the dazzling snow.

Reese's tracks led around to the front of the hotel. They headed up the driveway past my car, now an unrecognisable white mound from which the wing mirrors protruded like stubby antennae. I'd left without having any breakfast, so as I walked I ate one of the sandwiches Nisha had made. It was fried egg, cooling and greasy, but welcome all the same. Wading through the snow was hard work, and by the time I reached the stile bordering the old woods I was breathing heavily, my sinuses aching from the painfully cold air.

Jon had climbed the stile and taken the hiking trail that climbed through the old woods. If not for his ragged tracks I wouldn't have known where it was. The snow wasn't quite as thick under the bare trees but the earthen and timber steps cut into the steep slope were completely hidden. Even the surviving marker posts were hard to see, half-buried and frosted white by the snowfall. The normal sounds of the old woodland had been stilled. A lone blackbird called out nearby, its song clear and lonely.

Other than that, nothing disturbed the white silence.

He'd left the hiking trail again, his tracks cutting across the steeper slope we'd gone up the day before. It was even harder work in the snow. I kept stopping to rest and check my phone in the dwindling hope that there'd be a signal, or that either my email or text to DS Chaudry had been sent. Each time I'd put it away, disappointed, before carrying on up the slope.

When I emerged from the woods I paused to rest again, my breath fogging the still air. The strip of open ground separating the woods from the plantation was now a plain of pure white. Facing me across it, the spruce trees looked darker and more forbidding than ever. They reared up like a barrier, their regimented trunks marching into the distance like a giant barcode.

Jon had left a line of broken snow that ran across the no man's land towards the plantation, heading for the logging track that stood almost directly opposite. My breath swirled as I let out a sigh.

Hitching the rucksack into a better position, I set off after him.

I hoped the logging track might be easier going, but the dead weeds and grass under the snow snagged my boots as though wilfully trying to trip me. This was the same way Jon and I had come the previous morning, which seemed to confirm he was going out to the remains at Foss Ghyll again. He'd told Nisha he *wanted to make sure*, although for the life of me I couldn't see what he wanted to make sure *of*. He'd already seen that the skeleton had been hacked to pieces, and what was left would be buried under ten inches of snow.

But I couldn't think of anything else that might have brought him out here. I was expecting him to have left the logging track just before it split, cutting through the trees to Foss Ghyll as we had the day before. Instead, Jon's trail carried straight on past the broken spruce stump I'd used as a marker and continued along the lower fork of the track.

Now I'd no idea at all where he could be going, and I was beginning to think he hadn't either. His state of mind hadn't been good even before he'd stayed up all night drinking, so perhaps he was just wandering aimlessly. The trail he'd left in the snow didn't seem aimless, though. It ran unwavering up the logging track, as though Jon had some specific destination in mind.

Then, up ahead, I saw where he'd fallen.

His trail abruptly ended in an area of flattened snow. Something had clearly happened to him here. By the look of it he hadn't just fallen, he'd thrashed around in a frenzy. There were small patches of black in the snow I thought at first were deeper shadows, probably holes made when he fell. Then I drew closer and realised what they were.

Blood spatters.

They lay all around where he'd fallen, dark gouts that had melted into the snow before freezing over. There was a lot of it, although not enough to be arterial. Of Jon himself there was no sign, but a trail on churned snow showed where he'd scrambled away from where he'd fallen, making for the trees at one side of the logging track.

I rushed over but couldn't see him there either. The dusting of snow that had made it through the spruce canopy showed that he hadn't stopped when he'd reached the trees. Injured or not, he'd kept on going, heading deeper into the plantation.

'JON!' I shouted into the labyrinth of dark trunks.

There was no answer. I turned to look back at where he'd fallen, trying to understand what I was looking at. His tracks were unbroken to that point, so whatever had happened must have been sudden and unexpected. Despite Nisha's fears, I didn't think his injury was self-inflicted. I'd seen the damage caused by a close-quarters shotgun blast, and this wasn't it. If Jon's gun had discharged, accidentally or otherwise, I'd be looking at his body, not just splashes of blood. No, he hadn't done this to himself.

Someone had shot him.

First Maud had been murdered, now Jon had been attacked. The discovery of the remains had pushed someone over the edge. Perhaps more than one person. I quickly looked around, suddenly aware of how exposed I was. But there was still no one in sight, and it was almost an hour since Nisha and I had heard the gunshot. Whoever had attacked Jon would be long gone.

If not I might be lying bleeding myself by now.

There were no other footprints in the snow except mine and Jon's, so it didn't look as though his attacker had made any attempt to go after him. The shot had probably come from the trees at the other side of the logging track, since he would have headed away from his attacker. Why they'd let him escape I couldn't say, but that could wait till later. The more important question was where Jon was now.

And if he was still alive.

Turning away, I looked again at the scuffs of disturbed snow and spruce needles he'd left in his wake. It led into the dark forest like a line of treacherous breadcrumbs, so faint in places I could barely see it. I didn't want to have to follow it in there, with no idea who or where Maud's killer and Jon's attacker might be. But I didn't see that I'd got any choice.

Adjusting the straps of the rucksack again, I headed into the spruce plantation after Jon.

Chapter 22

I'd hoped the snowfall would have made it brighter under the spruce canopy, but instead it had made the plantation even darker. It had settled on the needled branches overhead, blocking out even more light than usual and casting the ground below into deep shadow.

The flakes that had filtered through formed a thin dusting under the trees, drifting into banks around the base of their trunks. Without it I wouldn't have been able to follow Jon at all, and as it was I had to cast around to locate his trail when he'd crossed a patch of ground that was clear of snow. It looked as though he'd managed to regain his feet once he'd made it into the plantation, but he was clearly injured. From the marks he'd left he looked to be dragging one leg, and his trail weaved around like a drunkard's. Every few yards I'd come across more dark splotches where he'd bled onto the snow.

There was something dreamlike about following his trail into the plantation. The light was eerie, while the silence in there seemed to have a physical weight. And no matter which way I looked, all around there was nothing to see but more spruce trees, a multitude of tall, bare trunks receding into the far shadows.

I tried not to think how far in I was going, or what I'd do when I found Jon. Despite the blood he was still mobile, which was a good sign. If he wasn't too badly injured then I might be able to get him back to Hillside House on my own. If not . . .

I'd cross that bridge when I came to it.

I'd been walking for about twenty minutes when I came to a spot where Jon had fallen again. A patch of ground had been churned into a dirty mulch of mud and spruce needles. There was more blood here, too. A lot of it, congealed and already skimmed over with ice where it had soaked into the ground. Jon's trail continued through the trees, so he'd managed to pick himself up again, but he was obviously bleeding more heavily now.

I was about to carry on after him when I noticed something lying in a thicker patch of gelatinous blood. It was about six inches long and no thicker than a pencil, almost concealed by a mess of clogged spruce needles. It was only when I saw the plastic fletching at one end that I recognised what it was. Jon had been shot all right, but not by a gun.

He'd been hit by a crossbow bolt.

The thing looked flimsy and cheap, too small to cause any real damage. But the headless tip was wickedly sharp, and the blood congealed on the thin metal shaft showed it was no less effective. Jon must have thought he was doing the right thing by pulling it out, but he'd only made the wound bleed more than ever. A lot more, I thought, looking again at the blood frozen on the ground.

He'd learnt the hard way that pistol crossbows weren't toys.

I couldn't leave the bolt out here. It was evidence of an assault, and once the snow thawed and Jon's trail disappeared I might not be able to find it again. I hadn't brought any evidence bags but Nisha had packed the sandwiches she'd made in a plastic freezer bag. She'd wrapped them in clingfilm first, so after removing the remaining sandwiches from the bag, I used it to pick up the crossbow bolt. Then, turning the bag inside out, I sealed the blood-smeared crossbow bolt inside. There'd be some contamination, but it was better than nothing.

Zipping the bolt into one of the rucksack's pockets, I hurried after Jon again.

His trail was easier to follow now, the blood splashes in the snow bigger and more frequent. I noticed that running alongside them were small, circular gouges in the ground. They had me puzzled until I realised they'd been made by the double barrels of Jon's shotgun. He was using it for support, leaning on the wooden stock as though it were a walking stick.

I hoped to God it wasn't loaded.

It said a lot for how badly hurt Jon must be to treat his father's gun that way. Yet still his trail continued, leading deeper and deeper into the plantation. He seemed to be wandering aimlessly, driven by a blind urge to escape even though his attacker hadn't pursued him. It was a testament to Jon's strength and endurance that he'd managed to come so far, but I was worried he was using up whatever physical reserves he had left. And the further he went, the longer and harder it would be to get him back to safety.

I heard the running water before I saw it. I had an idea then what it was but tried not to build up my hopes. But as the sound grew louder and Jon's trail continued to head towards it, I felt increasingly sure. After a few more minutes I could make out a brightening through the trees, and not long after that I came to the rocky banks of a beck. I knew then where I was.

Somehow Jon had managed to find his way to the stream that fed Foss Ghyll.

It was some distance from the ravine, though, further than I'd been the day before. But all I had to do was follow it and it would eventually take me to the ghyll. I could drop down into the glade from there, and then either go down the lane or even back down the hiking trail. From thinking I was hopelessly lost in the spruce maze, suddenly I could find my own way out of it.

All I had to do now was find Jon.

The stream was flowing too fast to have frozen. Jon's trail – now increasingly blood spattered – meandered alongside, occasionally veering away from it before going back again, as though his attention was wandering along with his body. At one point it looked as though he'd fallen, the snow trampled around a lopsided spruce as he'd struggled to regain his feet. His tracks carried on again after that, at times drifting dangerously close to the stream.

And then they vanished.

The trees were even closer together in this section of plantation. Snow had built up on their overlapping branches, blocking out the light so it was murkier than ever under them. It also meant enough snow hadn't filtered down to the ground for Jon to have left a trail.

I swore, searching in the half-light for some indication of which way he'd gone. There was nothing.

'JON?' I shouted. '*JON!*'

The only response was a soft thump as snow fell from branches overhead. *Now what do I do?* My breath clouded the air as I looked around. I could find my way back to Foss Ghyll easily enough just by continuing to follow the stream. But there was no way of knowing if Jon had gone that way, or if he'd blundered off deeper into the plantation. And while I stood there trying to decide, he could be bleeding out or freezing to death.

The tree canopy seemed a little lighter off to one side, so I struck off in that direction. It would mean heading away from the stream, but I was reasonably confident of finding my way back if I didn't go too far. With luck, I'd come across some sign of Reese before then.

I didn't want to think what I'd do if not.

After a few minutes the trees around me began to thin out. I walked in a wide sweep, first one way then the other, looking for anything to suggest Jon had come this way. There was nothing, even though there was more snow on the ground again here now the spruce canopy wasn't so thick. I tried to ignore the cold knot in my stomach, but as minutes passed I couldn't pretend any longer. It was obvious Jon hadn't come this way.

I'd lost him.

I couldn't bring myself to give up, even then. I carried on hunting round, scanning the ground beneath the trees for a while longer, but I knew it was futile. The only thing I could do was retrace my steps and continue to follow the stream down to Foss Ghyll, in case Jon had somehow found his way back to it.

When I straightened the first thing I realised was that I couldn't hear the stream anymore: I'd come further than I'd thought. The second thing that registered was the light was brighter off to one side, a white glare leaking through the trees. It grew brighter as I walked towards it, and then I found myself at the plantation's edge. Ahead of me was a broad clearing, a sweeping plain of unbroken snow. Higher up and off to one side, a stream cascaded down a ravine of snow-covered rocks in ribbons of silver and black.

I was back at Foss Ghyll.

I'd come out in the glade. The sprawl of rhododendrons that was slowly encroaching into it were now shapeless white humps, flattened so that the angular lines of the dilapidated army huts they'd swallowed were now visible. Rising behind them were the old woods, its oaks, beeches and larch stooped under the weight of snow. A gap in the white-rimed branches marked the overgrown lane that led back down through the woodland to the road.

Angling across the undulating snow towards it was a ragged line of tracks.

Relief surged through me. I'd assumed Jon must have found his way to the stream by accident, but I couldn't believe it was just chance that he'd come here. It was still a long way back to the hotel for an injured man, but getting him back to Hillside House would be a lot easier going down the lane to the road. And at least he wasn't lost.

Wounded or not, he'd known exactly where he was going.

An icy wind had picked up, blowing ghostly white streamers across the glade as I followed his tracks across it. The snow was deeper out here, my boots sinking into it almost to my knees. It was tiring even for anyone who wasn't wounded, and Jon's trail began to weave around as the effort of ploughing through took its toll. Halfway across the glade I came to where he'd fallen again, leaving dark Rorschach patterns of blood in the snow. He'd managed to drag himself up and continue, but his tracks changed direction after that. They angled away from the lane, cutting across the glade to the nearest rhododendron thicket. At first I thought he might have become disorientated, too weak to know where he was going. But his trail ran straight, and when I saw where it led to I realised there'd been method behind this as well. Reese must have finally reached the limit of his endurance. Knowing he couldn't make it all the way back home, he'd chosen the nearest shelter instead.

He'd headed for the old army camp.

There were around half-a-dozen of the old huts still standing among the snow-flattened thickets of rhododendrons. As I got nearer I could make out ruins of others in there as well, angular lines of collapsed roofs hidden among the bushes. I'd expected disintegrating prefabs, something military and utilitarian, but when I got closer I saw these were sturdy log cabins. They'd been constructed from whole tree trunks, giving their wet walls the look of black corduroy. I remembered Nisha saying the original owner of Hillside House had grand plans to develop Foss Ghyll into a sort of mountain spa, complete with swimming pool and cold-water therapies. That hadn't worked out, but it meant the cabins had provided a ready-made camp for the army to train from during the Second World War.

And shelter for Jon now.

He'd grown up here, I reminded myself as I waded through the snow to the nearest cabins buried within the rhododendrons. He'd probably explored the woods, played in the cabins and the ghyll. Things had changed since then, but I wondered if his childhood memories had drawn him here with some half-remembered promise of refuge.

Whatever shelter he'd thought they offered, it was mostly illusory. He'd gone into the nearest rhododendron thicket, snapping and trampling down branches to get to the overgrown log cabins. The first one I came to was little more than a pile of rotting logs under the covering of snow. Jon's tracks veered towards it, as though he'd wanted to make sure it was uninhabitable, then continued to the next. This one was more or less intact, its rough log walls and snow-covered roof still upright. The rhododendron branches in front of it were broken where Jon had blundered through them to get to the door. It was made from thick planks of timber, sagging and rotten as it hung from broken hinges.

His tracks led inside.

Something cold brushed my cheek as I stopped outside. I looked up to see miniscule white flecks drifting through the air. Hoping it was just spindrift blown from the branches, I pushed open the door. A dank stink of mildew and rot wafted out as it creaked open. It was too dark inside to see anything.

'Jon, are you in there?' I called.

My shout drifted away into silence. I stepped into the cabin, feeling the waterlogged floorboards sag under my boots. The door opened straight into a large room that seemed even colder than outside. A tree had grown through the single window, its invading branches all but blocking out the light. I paused in the doorway to let my eyes acclimatise to the gloom. Sodden fibreboard panels had fallen from the walls, exposing the bare logs underneath and littering the floor like rotting papier-mâché. In the centre of the wall was an empty fireplace, dappled with bird droppings. An empty noticeboard hung askew above it, while a broken metal office chair lay on its side in a corner, but there was little other evidence of the hut's former military occupation. In the shadows lay a doorless wooden cabinet, and as my eyes adjusted I made out the dim outlines of a figure on the floor behind it.

Jon was lying propped up against the wall, half-hidden by the cabinet. His head was slumped on his chest, his face obscured by the parka hood. A woollen scarf was tied around the top of his right leg, and both that and his jeans were caked with blood. He lay motionless, arms limp by his sides.

I couldn't see him breathing.

'Jon?'

As I hurried over he jerked awake, bringing up the shotgun that had been down by his side. I stopped, feeling a clammy déjà vu as the double barrels pointed at me, wavering unsteadily.

'Get back, you bastard . . .'

His voice was weak, and there was no recognition in the fevered eyes that glared out from the parka hood. I stayed very still, my hands held out where he could see them.

'It's all right, Jon. It's David Hunter. Nisha sent me to find you.'

Jon frowned, blinking as though waking from a deep sleep. 'Nisha . . .?'

'That's right. I'm staying with you, remember?'

'I thought . . .' His voice was weak, shaking from the cold. He dropped his arm letting the shotgun thump to the rotten floor. 'B-bastard shot me with a c-crossbow. . .'

I was already shrugging off my rucksack. 'Did you see who it was?'

He shook his head, closing his eyes as he rested it back against the wall. 'Got me from behind. But I kn-know who it was . . . Drew fucking Beddoes.'

I knelt down beside him. I could see now how pale his face was, and his lips were tinged blue. Blood loss and hypothermia were a bad combination, especially with shock from his wound added to the mix. It was a miracle he'd made it this far.

Now it was up to me to get him back alive.

His scarf had slowed the bleeding, enough that he wasn't in any imminent danger of bleeding out. I'd still have to take a look at it, but the immediate priority was to get him warmed up. I took out the Thermos and remaining sandwiches Nisha had packed and poured steaming coffee into the lid that doubled as a cup.

'Here,' I told him. 'Hold it in both hands and keep taking sips. Small ones, don't gulp.'

Jon raised it unsteadily to his mouth and took a sip, shuddering as the warmth hit his system. As he drank, I took off my weatherproof outer jacket. Even though I wore an insulated down jacket and had layered up underneath, I could feel the cold biting into me.

'Wha-what are you doing . . .?' he demanded as I wrapped the jacket over him.

'Trying to get you warm.'

He made a feeble attempt to sit up. 'I d-don't want your c-coat . . .'

'It's just until we go back out,' I told him. I would have let him keep it, but I'd need it myself if I was going to get him off the fell. 'You've probably got hypothermia on top of shock and blood loss, and we don't have time to argue.'

It was a sign of how weak he was that he meekly accepted it. As he nibbled half-heartedly at one of the sandwiches I turned my attention to the bloodstained scarf. It had been bound two or three times around his thigh before being tied off in a crude granny knot. It made it hard to tell where the bleeding was coming from.

'Where are you hit?' I asked, slipping off my gloves. The cold air hurt my bare hands as I gently worked at the knot.

Jon swallowed another mouthful of coffee. His colour was already a little better, and his voice sounded stronger.

'Back of my thigh, at the t-top. I pulled the bolt out.' He grimaced. 'Probably shouldn't have.'

It meant he'd lost more blood, but at least the scarf had slowed the bleeding. I didn't want to disturb the wound any more than I had to, but the scarf made a poor dressing at best. The rough wool was tacky with dried blood, and Jon gasped as it pulled loose.

'*Shit . . .!*'

'Sorry.'

Under the scarf his jeans were soaked through with blood. There was a ragged hole in the denim, under which the crossbow bolt had left a small but ugly puncture in the meat of Jon's upper thigh. From the position it must have come dangerously close to the femoral artery. He was lucky it hadn't nicked it.

If it had he'd be dead by now.

The area around the wound was swollen and bruised, and blood was already starting to ooze from it now the scarf had been removed. I'd used the freezer bag for the crossbow bolt, but Nisha had wrapped the sandwiches in clingfilm as well, splitting them into two packages. Giving the remaining sandwich from the one I'd already opened to Reese, I lay the clean side of clingfilm over the wound. It was far from sterile but neither was the bolt or scarf he'd tied around it. The main thing was that the plastic membrane would help stop the bleeding. Once that was in place, I bound the bloody scarf back around his leg, then threaded a short piece of rhododendron branch through the knot, turning it a few times to wind the scarf tighter. A 'windlass' was an effective way of keeping tension on a torniquet. I'd once seen the same technique utilised for a very different purpose, but used properly it could be a lifesaver.

I hoped.

I'd been running through my options as I'd bound his leg, and each time come to the same conclusion: I didn't have any. Leaving Jon here while I went for help was out of the question. Even assuming I could find anyone prepared to come back with me, it would take too long. Jon couldn't last much longer out here, not in these conditions.

I was going to have to get him down the fell on my own.

Even then it might not be enough. There were no medical facilities in the village, and no way of calling for outside help. Jon would need a blood transfusion and antibiotics, probably surgery as well. They were problems for the future, though. If I didn't get him somewhere warm and dry soon, none of that would matter.

He'd die anyway.

By now he'd finished the coffee and most of the sandwich. He was as ready as he'd ever be. Putting the Thermos back into the rucksack, I stood up.

'OK, let's get you home.'

Chapter 23

It hadn't been spindrift from the bushes I'd seen earlier. The snow had started falling again while I'd been inside the cabin. The wind was stronger as well, driving gusts and eddies of swirling white. Jon leaned against me, an arm across my shoulders while I had one of mine around his waist to take some of his weight as we waded through the shin-deep snow.

It was obvious he couldn't go any further under his own steam, so I'd searched for something he could use as a crutch. The shotgun he'd been using for support was where he'd dropped it, its barrels caked with snow, mud and spruce needles. Jon had watched from the floor as I broke it open to check.

'It's not loaded. I fired the last cartridge when I got shot. Don't worry, I didn't hit anyone,' he'd added sourly. 'More's the pity.'

I let that pass without comment. 'We'll have to leave it here. I'll find something better you can use as a crutch,' I said, snapping the shotgun shut.

'No, I'll take it with me.'

'We can't carry it.'

'It was my dad's. I'm not leaving it.'

'We don't have any choice.' I didn't like leaving it either, but the shotgun made a poor walking aid and it would be hard enough getting Jon back without the extra weight. 'I'll come back for it as soon as I can.'

He didn't have the energy to argue. In the end I'd hidden the shotgun out of sight inside the broken cabinet and searched around until I found a fallen branch sturdy enough to work as a crutch. It was a struggle getting Jon to his feet, but at last I got him upright. Giving him the branch to lean on at one side, I'd taken his weight on the other.

Then we'd set off.

The cold had hit me when we emerged from the hut. The wind felt like it was cutting through me, chilling me to my bones as we trudged across the glade to the lane. I'd briefly considered going down the hiking trail, but there was no way Jon could have managed that.

I wasn't even sure I could get him back to Hillside House whichever route we took. Just supporting him across the deep snow in the glade was bad enough, and the weather was getting worse. By the time we reached where the lane dropped down through the woods we were walking through a full-on blizzard. Sky and ground merged together, and the trees around us were almost lost in the white maelstrom.

I'd thought the going might be easier once we were on the lane itself, hoping we'd be out of the teeth of the wind. But I'd forgotten how steep it was. The snow had drifted almost knee-deep in places and the wind found us even here, peppering my eyes and face with icy shards. I could feel Jon shivering as he leaned against me, and after only a few minutes I knew we had to rest. Guiding him over to the shelter of a huge old oak, I propped him up against a low branch, careful not to catch his wound.

'You OK?' I panted, shrugging off the rucksack.

Jon nodded, dull-eyed. The tourniquet around his leg seemed to be holding, but even coming this far seemed to have sapped his strength. He stayed slumped against the tree as I poured a cup of hot coffee from the Thermos. The smell set my mouth watering, and the heat of the plastic mug on my gloved hands was like a cruel taunt when I gave it to Jon.

'Don't want it . . .' he muttered.

'Doesn't matter, you need it.'

I watched until he started taking small sips, then unwrapped the last of the sandwiches. Jon baulked at that, though, turning his head away like a child.

'Can't . . .'

I didn't press. He needed the calories, but it was more important for him to keep down what he'd already had. Putting one of the sandwiches away I ate the other myself. The bread was as cold as I was and the egg had congealed, but I savoured every mouthful as we rested. The wooded hillside around the lane was almost unrecognisable under the heavy snowfall. It took me a while to realise that the long, regular white humps dotted around the quarried slope were the remains of the army training camp's mock fortifications. Snow had flattened the rhododendron bushes that had overgrown the concrete structure I'd noticed before. Now more of it was visible, it looked to be some kind of retaining wall rather than a bunker, a vertical brown scab against the whiteness.

But I doubted even that would remain visible for long. Even in the few minutes we'd stopped the blizzard had grown worse. The snow was whipped by the wind as we set off again, joined by flurries blown from the overloaded branches. It was a complete white-out, dazzling and disorientating. The lane I'd hoped would be an easier route was completely buried, virtually indistinguishable from the rest of the snow-covered woods. Half-blinded by the swirling flakes, all I could do was keep us heading downhill and hope we reached the road soon.

Time seemed to stop. It felt like we'd been on the lane for hours, lost in a fragmented white wilderness. I didn't know how Jon was still on his feet but just keeping him upright was exhausting. Every now and then I'd take a rest, long enough to get more coffee into Jon and check his tourniquet. Then, leaning into the freezing wind, we'd struggle on again through the deepening snow.

The realisation came by degrees. I'd slipped into a fugue of chattering teeth and aching muscles, my mind empty of anything except the need to keep moving. I'd been vaguely aware that the terrain seemed more uneven, but it only slowly

213

dawned on me that something was wrong. Although the disused lane had been rutted and overgrown, I didn't recall it being as rugged as this. Under the thick snow, the ground still felt rocky and broken. And on the heels of that realisation came another, even worse thought. We'd been on the lane for a long time. Too long, even allowing for our agonisingly slow pace.

We should have reached the road by now.

I halted, causing Jon to stumble against me. He barely seemed to notice. Trying to quell a rising panic, I looked around, searching for some recognisable feature in the endless white. There was nothing. But through the driving snow I could see that the ground on either side was banked up higher than it should be.

Where the hell are we?

The chill I felt had nothing to do with the cold. I knew, with an awful certainty, what had happened. I'd stupidly assumed that the lane would follow the most direct route down to the road, that all I had to do was keep heading downhill. But the snow had blurred the ground's contours. At some point I'd strayed off the lane and into the woods without knowing.

We were lost.

I moved Jon into the relative shelter of one of the banks and gave him the last of the coffee while I tried to work out what to do. By the look of it we'd wandered off into a gully. It must have branched off from the lane and I'd blindly led us off into it. Behind us, we'd left a ragged furrow on the hillside, extending up the slope until it disappeared into billowing flurries of white. We could follow that back to where we'd wandered off the lane, and then carry on down it to the road.

But I didn't know how far we'd have to go, and it would mean going back uphill. Jon was in no condition to attempt that. He looked awful. Snowflakes frosted his eyebrows and beard, and his face had a deathly pallor inside the parka hood. He seemed barely conscious, oblivious to what was going on. I didn't know

214

how much longer he'd be able to go on even downhill. Going back up the mountain would finish him.

And perhaps me as well.

A wave of self-recrimination brought a fresh surge of panic. I fought it down, knowing I couldn't afford it. We needed to keep moving, and if we couldn't backtrack to the lane at least that simplified things.

We'd have to carry on.

Jon's weight was like a drag on me as we set off again. The gully's banks rose up for a while, affording some shelter from the wind. Then just as we'd grown used to that, they fell spitefully away again, exposing us to its full force. Not long after we came to the remains of a drystone wall, half-buried and the rest coated with white. The trees ended there, and once past that we were out on the open mountainside. I kept us heading down the slope, but I'd lost all sense of direction. For all I knew we might be heading towards the road or away from it. Our progress had reduced to a shuffle, the snow shackling our steps. I was shivering uncontrollably now, almost at the end of my own strength. At some point I realised with dull surprise that the wind had dropped. That was a mercy but along with it I noticed something else.

The light was fading.

My watch was under my glove, and with Jon slumped against me it was too much effort to check the time. It was probably still only mid-afternoon, but the heavy snowclouds were making darkness fall even earlier than usual. There was an hour of daylight left, perhaps less.

If we hadn't found the road by then we weren't going to.

Then I thought I saw something in front of us in the blizzard. I told myself I was imagining it, letting myself be hypnotised by the endless flakes. I stared into them, but it was still there, a line of darkness ahead of us. I slowed, not wanting to believe it. *No, no, no . . .*

We were back at the plantation.

The despair I felt in that moment almost made me give up. It seemed too cruel to have come all this way only to find our path blocked by yet more of the same spruce trees I hoped we'd left behind. It was only when I felt Jon sag against me that I realised I'd stopped. His weight was a reminder that this wasn't just about me.

Telling myself that at least the spruce trees would offer some shelter, I forced myself to go on.

Anything was better than staying out on the exposed mountainside.

We'd almost made it to the treeline when Jon collapsed. My own legs almost gave out as he sank into the snow, resisting my efforts to pull him up. His mouth was working, but his voice was so faint I struggled to catch what he was saying.

'I'm sorry, so sorry . . . All my fault . . .'

He wasn't talking to me, I realised. Didn't even seem aware I was there. I heaved desperately on his arm.

'Come on, Jon! *Jon!*'

' . . . so sorry . . .'

He was crying, a grown man reduced to a boy again. Whatever memory he was lost in, I couldn't rouse him from it. I let go of his arm, wondering if I had enough strength to drag him into the plantation's shelter and knowing it was beyond me. The cold seemed to tighten its grip, and as I looked across at the spruce trees I caught a faint smell on the freezing air.

Woodsmoke.

Fatigue and despair were swept away by a rush of adrenaline. Out here, at this time of year, woodsmoke could mean only one thing. I shook Jon by his shoulders.

'Jon, get up! *Jon!*'

He made a feeble attempt to push me away. 'Geddoff . . .'

'*Listen* to me, you need to get up! There's a house!'

He muttered something unintelligible. I tried to haul him to his feet but he was a dead weight.

'Get *up!* Think about Nisha and Kiran!'

' . . . better off without me . . .'

'Is that what you thought when you lost your father?'

It was a cruel thing to say, but I needed him on his feet. For a moment I thought he was too far gone to understand.

'Fuck you . . .'

It was barely a whisper, but he began trying to push himself up. Hooking my arm around his chest, I managed to haul him to his feet. I look around for the branch he'd been using as a crutch but I couldn't see it. I didn't care.

'That's it, you can do it,' I gasped, my legs trembling as we set off through the snow.

'Fuck off . . .'

But he didn't try to shrug me off, and he stayed upright as we stumbled and shuffled towards the plantation. It took all my strength to support him, but the promise offered by the woodsmoke kept me going. Its pungent scent grew stronger as we neared the trees.

Then, through the spruce trunks, I glimpsed a lighted window.

I could have wept with relief. 'Not much further,' I told Jon, my breath rasping.

I'm not sure he understood but he kept on his feet, and that was enough. I didn't take my eyes from the light as we entered the spruce plantation, praying it wouldn't wink out. The plantation wasn't deep here, and soon I could see that the light was coming from the window of a house, beyond the trees on the other side. I half-dragged Jon towards it. Walls and a low roof took form through the black silhouettes of the spruce trunks. I could make out lights in other windows now, shining like beacons as we emerged onto the edge of a large, snowy garden. The house was a bungalow, cloaked in snow yet vaguely familiar in the twilight.

But I was past caring who lived there. Bowed under Jon's weight, I staggered across the garden. As we neared the house he raised his head, then feebly tried to pull away.

'No . . .'

'It's OK, we're nearly there,' I managed to gasp. 'Just a little further.'

He was too weak to protest as we stumbled around to the front door. Wedging him upright against the wall, I banged on the frosted glass panel.

It seemed an age before a light showed behind the glass. A shadow appeared on the other side, taking on a human shape as it came nearer. I took Jon's weight again as the door opened and a wave of blissful warmth washed over us. I started to speak but the words caught in my throat.

Staring out at us was Wynn Beddoes' son-in-law, Eddie.

Chapter 24

Eddie stared at us, his mouth open in almost comic surprise.

'He's been injured, we need help,' I gasped, hunched under Jon's weight.

'What? No, hang on—' Eddie stammered.

But I was too exhausted to wait. Eddie hesitated, indecision playing across his face as I started through the doorway. Then, darting a look over his shoulder, he took hold of Jon's other side and together we half-carried him inside. The only light in the hallway was a battery-powered storm lantern, and I felt dizzy as the warmth of the house enveloped me. One wall was lined with framed photographs, and I stumbled against them as we staggered past, almost dislodging one.

'Evie! *Evie!*' Eddie shouted.

His wife emerged from a doorway further along the hall, from where the children's voices were coming from. 'All *right*, I'm not deaf. What's—Jesus!'

She stopped dead when she saw us. Her shock was instantly replaced with a tight-lipped fury as she glared at the semi-conscious Jon.

'What the hell's *he* doing here!'

'He's hurt,' Eddie said, more in apology than explanation.

'I don't care, I don't want him in my house!'

'Someone shot him with a crossbow,' I told her, struggling to keep Jon upright. 'He's lost a lot of blood, and he's got hypothermia. Please, we need to get him somewhere warm.'

I saw Eddie glance nervously at her at the mention of a crossbow, but I was too busy trying to keep Jon upright to think about it. Evie held out for a moment longer.

'*Christ*. All right, take him in the lounge! And mind the carpet!'

She hurried away, leaving the two of us to manhandle Jon into the living room. A log-burning stove stood in the hearth, giving off a stifling heat and the smell of woodsmoke. The young girl who'd answered the door the last time I'd been there lay on the carpet, bickering over a board game with her brother, who lay with Beddoes' young lurcher sprawled against his legs. A girl in her early teens sat alone at a small table where another lantern cast a bright light, schoolbooks and a laptop open in front of her, apparently oblivious to the racket.

They stared at us in surprise, then they all started talking at once. The lurcher jumped to its feet and began barking, adding to the commotion.

'Dad, who're—'

'What's he—'

'Is that *blood*—?'

We half-dragged Jon over to the sofa. 'Come on, scoot out of the way,' Eddie told the boy and girl playing the board game.

'But Dad—'

'You heard him!' Evie announced, storming in with a bundle of towels. 'All of you, out! Now! And take the dog with you!'

Her words had more effect than Eddie's. Still protesting, they headed for the hall. The teenage girl stopped in the doorway, books and laptop clutched to her.

'Where am I supposed to do my homework?'

'There's a lamp in the kitchen, you can work on the table.' her mother told her. 'I know, I'm not thrilled either, but go on.'

'I don't think they're going to be big enough to cover him,' I gasped, as she hurried over with the towels.

'They're for the settee, not him.' Pushing past us, she spread out the towels over the seat cushions. 'All right, you can put him down now.'

We eased Jon down onto the sofa, lying him canted onto one side to avoid the wound. He stirred, moaning as we moved his wounded leg. Evie looked at the wet tracks we'd left across the living room carpet. Her mouth tightened but she said nothing.

Pulling off my bulky gloves, I began to unfasten Jon's parka. 'Jon? Jon, wake up!'

''M 'wake . . .' he slurred. But although his eyes were open they were heavy and unfocused.

'We need to get him out of his clothes and into something warm,' I told Eddie, shucking out of my own wet coat. 'A quilt or blankets, if you have them. And do you have any way of making him a warm drink?'

'We've got a camping stove. We can do a hot water bottle, as well?' Eddie said, making it a question as he looked at his wife. She maintained a tight-lipped silence.

I thought for a moment, then nodded. We needed to raise his core body temperature, but not so quickly that it would do more harm than good. 'Only warm, though, not hot. And plenty of sugar in the drink.'

'Don't want much, do you?' Evie huffed, but turned to where her eldest daughter was still watching from the doorway. 'Come on, give me a hand.'

As they went out, Eddie help me to remove Jon's sodden parka. He peered round the room in bewilderment.

'Where . . .'

'We're at Evie and Eddie's house,' I told him, pulling the parka down over his arms.

He made a feeble effort to get up. 'I shouldn't be here . . .'

I pushed him back down. 'Don't worry, it's all right. But you need to help us get you out of these wet clothes.'

'What . . .? No . . .'

He began to struggle but didn't have any strength. With Eddie's help, I got Jon out of his thick sweater and long-sleeved t-shirt. His bare skin was icy and deathly pale, but he'd be warmer without the soaking wet clothes. The log burner made the room soporifically hot. I could feel the heat and fatigue tugging at me as I tried to organise my thoughts.

'Do you have a first aid kit?' I asked Eddie.

'Uh, I'm not . . .'

'Here, I've brought it,' Evie said, coming back into the room. She was carrying an old biscuit tin I assumed was the family first aid kit and had a floral quilt bundled under one arm. In her free hand were two mugs of what smelt like tea. One of them was a toddler's, bright blue plastic with a lid and drinking spout.

'It belonged to the kids. I don't want him spilling tea everywhere,' she said brusquely when she saw me looking at it. 'Here, I made a cup for you as well.'

I nodded thanks as I took both mugs. Jon stared uncomprehendingly at the plastic child's cup before taking it, his movements slow and uncoordinated. Evie had gone out and now returned carrying two hot water bottles with patterned fleecy covers. That was good: it would save having to wrap them in something.

My own hands throbbed with returning circulation as I covered his upper body with the quilt, then lay the warm rubber bottles against his chest before turning to Eddie. He was staring as though hypnotised by the sight of the injured man on his sofa.

'Can you help me get his boots off?'

'What?' He looked startled, as though he'd woken up himself. 'Right, sorry.'

'Oh, for God's sake, I'll do it,' Evie said, elbowing him aside. Kneeling, she began untying Jon's bootlaces with deft fingers. She spoke without looking up. 'Did he say who'd shot him?'

Even intent on unwinding the bloodied scarf from the top of Jon's thigh, I could still feel the sudden change in the room's atmosphere.

'No. He didn't see who it was,' I said.

I glanced up in time to see Evie and Eddie exchange another look. It seemed to confirm the suspicion I'd formed when I'd found the crossbow bolt, but this wasn't the time.

'Is there somewhere I can wash my hands?' I asked.

After I'd cleaned and dressed the puncture wound in Jon's thigh as best I could, Eddie helped me get Jon into a bedroom and lower him onto the bed. The bleeding had stopped, and the hot water bottles and quilt had gone a long way to countering his hypothermia. The main danger now was infection. I'd given him paracetamols, which would help bring down any fever as well as help with the pain. But other than making sure he drank plenty of fluids and ate as much as he could manage, there wasn't much else I could do.

The bed was barely big enough for Jon's large frame, and the superhero posters on the walls made his presence even more incongruous. He'd roused as I'd covered him with the quilt, looking at me without recognition.

'My fault . . . I didn't know . . .'

'It's OK,' I told him. 'You need to rest now.'

His eyes started to close, then flicked open again. 'It was looking right at me. Like it was crawling . . .'

'Don't talk. Get some sleep.'

But Jon's eyes had already closed, his breathing becoming deep and regular. Gently closing the door, I went back into the hall. The battery lamp had been moved but the light cast from the kitchen fell on the framed photographs on the walls. They were the usual collection of school photos and family snaps, a couple of them askew from where I'd brushed against them bringing Jon inside. As I straightened them, one of the others caught my attention. It had been taken in a gym and showed a young man, posing in a fighting stance next to a punchbag. He was stripped except for shorts that displayed a trim physique, well-defined but not heavily muscled, giving the camera a cocky grin that put me in mind of Drew.

Nisha had told me Beddoes' missing son had been a would-be boxer, and I felt the hairs of the nape of my neck rise as I realised I was looking at Jed Beddoes. He was in other photographs as well. In one of them a young and dark-haired Wynn Beddoes towered over a slight, slender woman I took to be his wife. Tall and well-built, he looked as stern as ever while his wife had a shy, nervous smile, hand raised to shield her face from the sun. In another a middle-aged Beddoes was on his own with his three adult children. Alun was as unsmiling as his father, while Jed had the same mocking grin as in the boxing photograph. The young Evie bore an unmistakable resemblance to her mother, slight and fine boned, with an almost identical strained smile on her face.

I stared at them a while longer, then carried on down the hallway to the kitchen.

Lost in thought, I'd started to go in before I noticed Evie and Eddie. They were by the sink, arms around each other. Her head was resting on his shoulder, and his expression as he stroked her hair was tender and sad.

Moving quietly away from the doorway, I paused in the hall for a few seconds and then went back into the kitchen, making sure they heard me this time. They stepped away from each other as though caught, Evie's face hardening into its usual mask as she turned to me.

'Thanks for helping,' I said.

'Not like I had much choice, is it? How is he?'

'He's sleeping. I don't think the hypothermia's going to be a problem now he's somewhere warm, but he needs to be in a hospital.'

'Yeah, well that's not happening, is it?' Evie folded her arms across her chest. 'You know he can't stay here, don't you?'

I kneaded my eyes, wondering how I'd become responsible for a man I hadn't even known a few days ago. 'He's not fit to go anywhere yet.'

'That's not my problem! We've got *kids* here!'

'We'll manage,' Eddie said. 'Ricky'll be fine on the settee—'

'Jesus Christ, do I have to spell it out? I don't want Owen Reese's son under my roof! Can you imagine what my *dad'll* say?' She glanced towards the hallway, lowering her voice. 'And for all we know he might have killed Maud.'

She was scared as well as angry, I realised. Eddie looked uncomfortable and uncertain.

'I don't think you need to worry about that—' I began but Evie didn't let me finish.

'That's easy for you to say, it's not your kids, is it? And how do you know anyway? We *live* here, you've only been here five minutes!'

It seemed like a lifetime. 'You're right. But I meant Jon isn't in any shape to hurt anyone, and if we try to move him now he could die. Whoever attacked him is already facing an assault charge at least. Do you really want to make that any worse?'

Eddie cast an anxious glance at his wife. Evie had gone very still.

'What's that got to do with us?'

'Jon was shot with a pistol crossbow,' I said, trying to choose my words carefully. 'Like the one your nephew threatened him with yesterday.'

I'd made the connection as soon as I'd found the bloodied bolt Jon had pulled from his leg. In a way it had been a relief, because while it didn't excuse what Drew had done, it meant the same person who'd murdered Maud hadn't tried to kill Jon as well. Drew might be cocky and stupid, but I couldn't see him attacking anyone with a chainsaw. And he hadn't even been born when the remains in the plantation had been buried.

Evie's chin jutted in a way that reminded me of her older brother, Alun.

'So? Doesn't mean Drew shot him, does it? Half the teenagers in the village probably have them. Anyone can pick them up on the internet for next to nothing.'

The flush on her cheeks showed she didn't believe that herself. But I wasn't there to prove Drew's guilt, or antagonise Evie. Not when Jon needed her help.

'Look, it's up to the police what they do about that,' I said. 'My main concern now is Jon. I give you my word I'll get him out of your way as soon as I can, but until the snow thaws there's not much I can do.'

Evie suddenly turned to Eddie. 'What about the snowplough?'

'There's a snowplough?' I asked.

'At the yard.' Evie arched an eyebrow at her husband. 'Well, isn't there?'

'Not a snowplough as such.' Eddie looked unhappy. 'It's just a plough blade that fits on one of the trucks. Maud always . . .

225

she always got one of the crew to clear the roads when there's snow. You know, a goodwill sort of thing. But with what's happened . . .'

'Will you need to go anywhere near the tool room?' I asked. Going in the yard was one thing: the living took precedence over the dead, even in a murder investigation. But the tool room where we'd found Maud's body needed to stay off limits.

Eddie looked upset at the reminder. 'Well, no. The plough blade's in a different part of the yard.'

'That's settled then,' Evie said, with finality. 'We'll clear the road tomorrow.'

'I still can't guarantee when Jon will be fit to travel,' I told her.

'We'll see once the road's clear.' Her tone suggested she'd already decided. 'You'll have to sleep on the floor of his room tonight, though. I'm not turning any more of the kids out of their beds.'

'I'm not staying. I need to get back to the hotel.'

I was bone weary, every muscle aching from slogging across the fell with Jon. But Nisha would be frantic with worry. I couldn't leave her wondering all night, not with a young child to look after in that cold, echoing place.

'And what are we supposed to do if he gets worse?' Evie demanded. 'Call for an ambulance?'

'I can come back after I've been to see Nisha,' I said. The thought of having to head out again seemed to sap my energy even more.

'Oh, forget it,' Evie said, impatiently. 'Look at you, you can hardly stand up. You won't be much good even if you do make it back. And I'm not looking after two invalids.'

I wasn't going to argue. 'I'll come back first thing in the morning.'

'Please yourself.' She started to go, then paused. 'There's a corned beef sandwich in the fridge if you want something to eat before you go.'

With that she went out. There was an awkward silence.

'She'll come round,' Eddie said. 'She's just upset. This is all a bit . . . a bit hard for her.'

226

I nodded. 'Thanks for helping out. And for yesterday, at the yard.'

His face fell at the reminder of Maud. 'It still doesn't feel real.'

It would when the police arrived. 'Did you let everyone know the yard's closed for the time being?'

'Enough to get the news round. There's no point going in anyway. Not until the company sends somebody to sort things out. I can't even think what that's going to be like.'

His voice had thickened. I didn't want to press but I had to ask. 'Do you know if anyone saw anything? Someone acting strangely, anything like that?'

'No, why would they?' He seemed upset at the idea. He cleared his throat, giving his eyes a quick wipe. 'Look, about Drew . . . He's not a bad lad. Not really, he's just a bit wild.'

It was as good an admission as I was going to get. 'He could have killed Jon.'

Eddie didn't try to deny it. 'I know, I'm not excusing what he did. But it was just a stupid stunt. He didn't even mean to hit him, just frighten him a bit. He was in tears when he got here.'

'So you saw him earlier?'

Eddie ducked his head in a guilty nod. 'He came here after . . . well, afterwards. He was in bits. Scared to death, he didn't know who else to go to. He always comes here if he's upset or in trouble. Evie's the only one he can talk to. She's got a temper, but she's got a good heart.'

I was starting to see that, even if she did her best to hide it. 'Where's Drew now?'

'At home. She made him promise to go straight back and not say anything to anyone, or she'd tell his dad and granddad.'

'And will he?'

'He wouldn't dare do anything else. Evie was livid.' He shook his head at the memory. 'Drew knows they're going to find out eventually. And she's made it clear he's going to have to own up to what he's done. But it's best left till the police are here. Her dad and Alun, they can be pretty . . . hot-headed.'

I could imagine. 'Why didn't she say something earlier?'

Eddie looked genuinely puzzled, as though I'd missed something obvious. 'Drew's her nephew. Family's family, isn't it?'

I supposed it was. I needed to get back to Hillside House, but there was still something I wanted to know. And Eddie had given me the opening I needed.

'Talking of family, is that Evie's brother in the photographs in the hallway? The boxer?'

'Yeah.' He sighed, looking down. 'Yeah, that's Jed.'

'He looked like Evie,' I said.

Eddie nodded. 'Him and Evie took after their mum. She passed away when they were kids, but her side of the family were all slightly built. Our four are the same. Don't take after their granddad at all.'

'Four?' I'd only seen the young girl and boy, and their teenage sister.

His face split in a smile. 'We've an older daughter. Louisa, she's at Nottingham University. She's doing a degree in art and design.'

He couldn't disguise his pride.

'You and Evie must have been together a long time,' I said.

'Twenty-five years. We got married the year after . . .' The pleasure went from his face. 'Well, after Jed.'

'Did you know him well?'

'We weren't really mates. But I was engaged to Evie, so . . .'

He shrugged, uncomfortable with the conversation. I was straying onto awkward territory, but there was one more thing I wanted to ask.

'He was only young, wasn't he?'

'Twenty-two. Four years older than Evie.' Eddie looked saddened. 'Not much older than our Louisa. No age, is it?'

No, I thought. No, it wasn't.

The snow had stopped by the time I left. The sky was black and clear, shreds of clouds obscuring the stars as I crunched down the covered-over driveway. A crude snowman had been built in the front garden, stones for eyes, nose and mouth, and branches for arms. The driveway and garden was churned up with small footprints and evidence of frenzied snowball fights, but once I reached the road they petered out, except for one set. Drew's, as he'd made his disconsolate way home.

I ate the corned beef sandwich Evie had made as I tramped through the snow, replaying the conversation with Eddie. It was the first I'd heard of how old Jed Beddoes was when he went missing. Twenty-two was more than a decade younger than my estimated age at death of the individual whose skeleton had been in the tree roots. There was always a margin of error, and it was possible I'd simply got it wrong – I wasn't egotistical enough to think I couldn't make mistakes – but on this occasion I didn't think so.

And there was another anomaly that was even harder to reconcile. The skeleton I'd seen in the plantation had belonged to a large man, heavily boned and approximately six feet tall. A similar height and build to Wynn and Alun Beddoes, so it hadn't been too much of a leap to think that the remains could belong to their missing son and brother.

But the young man in the photographs displayed in Evie and Eddie's hallway had been five feet eight or nine at most, smaller and less heavily built than his father and brother. Too small to be the skeleton I'd found in the plantation.

Whoever it was who'd been buried under the spruce tree, it wasn't Jed Beddoes.

Chapter 25

Walking back to Hillside House along the road was much easier than coming down the fell from Foss Ghyll had been. The snow was no less deep, blanketing the road nearly up to my knees, and it was a longer route. But the hedgerows and drystone walls on either side meant there was no danger of wandering off course, and now the blizzard had stopped it seemed almost tranquil. The snowfall gave the landscape an otherworldly quality, brightening the night as though there was a full moon, so much so that I didn't need my torch.

It gave me plenty of time to think, although that was a mixed blessing. I'd warned Wynn Beddoes against assuming the remains belonged to his son, but it had been a natural conclusion to make. A man had gone missing over two decades ago, and now a skeletonised body had been found. It seemed an easy equation.

Except I now knew the skeleton in the tree roots belonged to someone bigger and older than Jed Beddoes. I had a strong suspicion who that might be, but it meant everything I'd been told about the disappearance of Wynn Beddoes' youngest son was now open to doubt. Either Jed had faked his own death and then managed to fool everyone for over two decades, which from what I'd heard about the cocky young boxer seemed unlikely.

Or there was more than one victim.

Whichever it was, it explained why the remains had been destroyed. Someone was desperate to prevent the victim's real identity from becoming known, desperate enough to have killed Maud when she'd walked in on them taking the chainsaw.

They'd be even more dangerous now.

It was an unsettling thought, especially walking along the dark and empty road. I'd heard an owl call mournfully when I'd first set off, but after that the night was utterly silent and still. The only sound was my breathing and the muted crunch of my boots in the snow.

Yet I couldn't shake a feeling that I wasn't alone.

That I was being followed.

Get a grip, Hunter. Annoyed at myself, I stopped and looked back. The road behind me was empty, framed between white hedgerows until it curved out of sight, like a scene from a Christmas card. *See? Nothing. Now stop being—*

From beyond the bend in the road came the rhythmic whisper of someone walking through the snow.

The hairs on the back of my neck prickled. I stared at where the road disappeared behind the hedgerows. I couldn't see past that, but then I heard the noise again. A soft, shuffling sound, so faint it was hardly there. I held my breath, waiting for whoever it was to appear. No one did, but I could *feel* another presence.

Someone had stopped out of sight. Listening, just as I was.

My heart was thumping as I quietly slipped off the rucksack and took out my torch. I hadn't needed it to see, but I was glad of its metal heft now. Trying to make as little noise as possible, I carefully retraced my steps through the snow. Stopping just before the bend in the road, I took a deep breath.

Then I turned on the torch and stepped out.

Caught in the beam, the deer stood motionless in the middle of the road, eyes gleaming in the light. Before I could react it bolted towards me, slender legs kicking up white flurries as it shot past close enough to touch.

In an instant it was gone, vanishing along the dark road.

Relieved, I gave a shaky laugh. My night vision had been ruined by the torch, so I kept it on now as I turned and continued down the road. Its beam picked out the deer's dainty hoofprints in the snow, running in a straight line before disappearing through a gap in the hedgerow. A little further on the hedgerow gave way to a drystone wall, crusted with white, and behind it were the snow-stooped trees of the old woods. I recognised where I was now, but even though I was looking out for it I almost missed the rusted gate at the bottom of the overgrown lane. It was nearly buried under a drift, the gaps between its metal bars almost filled in with snow. I'd have had a hard time getting Jon over it, I thought, shining the torch beam onto the gate and wall. Or up the steep road from the crossroads, even if I'd managed it.

Perhaps getting lost had been no bad thing.

Something was scratching at my consciousness as I carried on past the lane. Something about the deer, or the deer's tracks in the snow, but it remained frustratingly out of reach. Eventually, I stopped grasping for it.

It would come to me in its own time.

It was a sign of how tired I was that the ugly spires and turrets of Hillside House were a welcome sight. By the time I'd reached the white hump that hid my car, I felt as though gravity was weighing me down more with every step. Ahead of me, the hotel reared up into the night sky, its walls bleak and unlovely even in the snow.

Around the back, a dim light shone through the drawn curtains in the kitchen window, a reminder that the hotel was still without power. Nisha must have heard when I paused to kick snow from my boots because she wrenched open the door before I could knock. She was holding Kiran and it was hard to say who looked worse, mother or son. Kiran had been crying, nose running and cheeks flushed and tearstained, although his tears had paused at the interruption. Nisha's face was etched with worry, and grew even more so when she saw I was alone.

'Where's Jon? Didn't you find him?' Her eyes widened as she saw the dried blood on my jacket. 'Oh, God, is that *his*?'

'It's OK, he's been injured but—'

'Injured how? You mean he's hurt?'

'Yes, but he's stable. He's at Evie and Eddie's house—'

'Beddoes' *daughter's*? Why the hell did you leave him there? Why didn't you bring him home?'

'We were caught in the blizzard. Look, can we talk about it inside?'

'What? Oh . . . right.'

Flustered, she stepped back to let me in. The kitchen was warm and fuggy with a smell of burnt food and overcooked vegetables. Saucepans were cooling at the side of the range, testament to Nisha's attempts to keep herself busy. As Max came over to say hello she tried to shush Kiran, her face anguished.

'Please, tell me what's happened?'

I did, my muscles aching as I took off my coat. Nisha looked dazed when I'd finished.

'He's going to be all right, though, isn't he? God, those *fucking* Beddoes!'

'He's out of any immediate danger,' I said, sidestepping the question.

'But it'll be *days* before any help gets here! I just wish I could *see* him!'

That wasn't an option. It was too far and too cold to take Kiran until the snow had started to thaw. And with Maud's killer still on the loose perhaps not even then.

But it didn't hurt to offer Nisha some hope. 'Eddie's going to arrange a snowplough tomorrow. We can see how things are once the road's clear.'

She didn't look reassured. 'Do you think he's going to be safe there? With them?'

'I think he's as safe there as anywhere.'

Safer, probably. Jon being at Evie and Eddie's was far from ideal, but I didn't think either Drew or anyone else would dare try anything while he was there.

Evie would kill them.

While Nisha put Kiran to bed I went up to my room. I wanted nothing more than to fall into bed and sleep, but I knew she would want to hear more details about what had happened. And I had questions of my own to ask. Shivering in the cold bathroom, I washed as best I could in the icy water that spattered from the washbasin tap and changed into dry clothes. I felt a

234

little better after that, and brightened even more when I remembered the bottle of wine I'd bought at the village store the day before. I'd put it down when I'd got back to my room and then forgotten all about it.

Taking it with me now, I went back downstairs. Nisha was on her own in the kitchen. The saucepans were simmering on the range and two places had been set at the table. My bloodstained jacket, which I'd left by the front door rather than take up to my room, had been cleaned and was hanging over a chair next to the range to dry.

'I thought I'd better wash your coat before it stains,' Nisha said. 'It's not perfect, but it'll do until it can go in the washer. We've got a waterproofing spray you can treat it with as well.'

'You didn't have to do that, but thanks.' I eased myself onto one of the chairs at the table, stroking Max who'd come over to say hello again.

'I was glad to do something.' She took plates from the warming rack above the range. 'Look, I'm sorry I lost it before. I don't want you to think I'm not grateful for what you did. Finding Jon and . . . and everything. It's just I've been going mad, stuck here all day not knowing anything. And after what happened to Maud, when it got dark and neither of you had come back I thought . . . I don't know what I thought.'

'It's OK.'

'No, it isn't, but thanks for saying so. God, I just wish he was somewhere else. *Anywhere!* I know you didn't have a choice, but of all the bloody places for him to be stuck it had to be with the Beddoes!' Her gaze fell on the bottle of wine I'd set down on the table. 'You're not saving that, are you?'

'It's to replace the one you opened. Don't feel you have to open it.'

But Nisha was already fetching glasses. I opened the bottle and poured us both a glass while she took something dark and crispy from the range oven.

'I thought you'd probably not eaten, so I warmed up a veggie shepherd's pie from the freezer,' she said, cutting into it with a

235

serving spoon. 'I wanted to use what's in there before it spoils, but I think I might have overdone it.'

'I'm sure it'll be delicious.'

It wasn't. It was burnt and dried out, the top layer of potatoes charred to shades of brown and black. I didn't even feel hungry anymore. I'd eaten the corned beef sandwich on the walk over from Evie and Eddie's and now felt too tired to eat anything. But I couldn't tell Nisha that after she'd gone to the trouble of cooking.

'That's plenty, thanks,' I said, as she was about to spoon yet more overcooked vegetables onto my plate. She served a meagre portion onto her own and then brought them over to the table. Sitting down, she took big drink of wine and gave a shudder.

'God, that's worse than Jon's mum's homebrew.' She grimaced, realising what she'd said. 'Sorry.'

'I won't take it personally,' I took a token sip myself, enough to confirm she was right, then tried a forkful of shepherd's pie. *God* . . . I forced myself to swallow. 'This is good.'

Nisha didn't seem to hear. She picked at the food on her own plate.

'I didn't thank you properly before. For going out after Jon, I mean. If not for you . . .'

'He's OK, that's the main thing,' I said, hoping it was true. I took another drink of wine, larger this time, and decided there was no point in waiting. 'Jon's workshop door was open earlier. I wanted to check if he'd taken his shotgun so I looked inside. I saw the hunting bow.'

'Oh?' Nisha took a sudden interest in her food, busily pushing it around her plate. 'He brought it back from the States. He did a bit of hunting over there.'

'Over here as well, by the look of it.'

She attempted a shrug. 'Yeah, he goes hunting occasionally. I don't like it but like I said, I'm the vegetarian. He isn't.'

'Bow hunting's illegal over here.'

She threw her fork down onto her uneaten food. 'Seriously? With all the other shit that's going on, you really think it matters if he kills deer with an arrow instead of a bullet? You think the *deer* care? It's a lot more humane than some . . . *dickhead* with a gun licence blasting chunks off them! Or buying meat reared in a factory farm!'

The argument sounded rehearsed, as though she was trying to convince herself. 'Does he sell the meat?'

'Why else would he do it? Fine, I know it's hypocritical. I *hate* it, but you'd be surprised how many pubs and restaurants turn a blind eye if the price is right. And God knows we can do with the extra money.'

'Does anyone else know?'

Her laugh was bitter. 'What do you think? That's another reason Jon uses a bow. It's quiet. He even bought night-vision goggles, so he can go out when it's dark and there's less chance of anyone seeing him. Rather him than me.'

'Does he go into the plantation to hunt?'

She took a hurried drink of wine. 'Sometimes, I expect.'

I watched her for a moment, debating. But I needed to know.

'It wasn't you who found the body, was it?'

'I don't know what you mean,' she said, not meeting my eyes.

'That's why your directions were so vague when you told me there was phone signal up there. You wanted me to find the remains, but you only had a rough idea where they were. You were just going on what Jon had told you.'

'No, that's . . .' She seemed to run out of steam. A sigh escaped her, then she nodded.

'What happened?' I asked, quietly. 'Did Jon make you promise not to say anything?'

'It wasn't like that. I mean, yes, but . . . He didn't know what to *do!* You don't know what it's been like for him. Living under a cloud all his life, because of . . . of what his dad did. And then for *him* to find Jed Beddoes' body . . . It was *killing* him, I-I had to do *something!*'

It wasn't Jed Beddoes' body that Jon had found. But Nisha didn't need to know that just yet. Neither did anyone else.

'Does he know you told me you'd found them?'

She gave another nod, wiping her eyes with the heel of her hand. 'He was furious I'd told you at all, but I thought he'd

237

calmed down. He seemed OK when he went up there with you yesterday morning, but when he came back he was more upset than I'd ever seen him, even when his mum died. He told me someone had smashed up the skeleton, but after that he hardly spoke. And after you'd told us about Maud he just went in the bar and got pissed. He stayed there all night, and then this morning he went out as soon as it was light.'

'But he didn't say where he was going?'

'No, he just mumbled something about "needing to make sure". I don't know what he meant, though.'

I thought about Jon's surprise when he'd realised the remains were near Foss Ghyll. And the way he'd broken down and run off before he'd even seen them. I'd have sworn his distress was genuine, but if Nisha was telling the truth he'd already known where they were. He'd been the first one to find them.

There was something I was missing here.

'How long ago did he find the remains?' I asked.

'God, I don't know . . . Like I said before, maybe five or six weeks? Perhaps two months. It seems like forever now. Why?'

'I just wondered,' I said.

We didn't talk much after that. There wasn't much left to say, and it had been a long day for both of us. I wanted to think over what I'd heard, while Nisha seemed subdued and distracted. She turned down my offer to help with the dishes, so I excused myself and went to collect my jacket from where it was drying on a chair by the range.

'Oh, I forgot, there was something in your inside pocket,' Nisha said. 'A letter or something. I took it out before I washed it. It's on the dresser.'

Looking over, I saw the handwritten envelope on top of the pine dresser. The envelope was creased and damp when I picked it up, the familiar handwriting slightly smudged from being wet.

'I hope that was all right?' Nisha said, uncertainly, perhaps seeing something in my face. 'I wasn't being nosy, I just felt it rustling. I didn't read it or anything.'

'That's OK. Thanks.'

All at once I needed to get out of the kitchen. I started to go before belatedly remembering Max. After prising him away from the warmth of the range, I took him into the foyer and unlocked the hotel's big main doors to let him out. The cold air was like a slap in my face, and I was thankful when the labrador didn't show any inclination to linger in the snow any longer than he had to.

Back in my freezing room, I lit a fire to burn down overnight, putting the mesh guard in front of it so Max couldn't get too close. I was sore and aching, spent emotionally as well as physically. But as tired as I was, if I went to bed I knew I wouldn't sleep. I could feel the thoughts I'd been avoiding, prowling around the edges of my mind. The moment I closed my eyes they'd have free rein.

Ordinarily, I'd have tried to distract myself with work, but both my phone and laptop were almost out of charge. I'd meant to recharge them from the USB port in my car, but then I'd had to go after Jon and after that everything else had been forgotten.

After lighting the fire, I sat on the edge of the bed, watching the flames take hold. I turned the envelope over in my hands, then gave in and took out the letter. The faint smell of perfume had almost faded, but the neat handwriting was still painfully familiar. Rachel and I had met two years before, when a case had taken me to the tidal waters of the Essex marshes. She was a marine biologist, drawn there after the disappearance of her sister, and over the course of the investigation we'd grown close. We'd even planned to marry.

Then a murderous individual from my past had crashed violently back into our lives.

After that, Rachel had said she needed time out. She'd gone to work on a research vessel in the Aegean Islands before returning to Australia's Barrier Reef, where she'd worked before I met her. We'd kept in touch by phone, text and email, but less so as time passed. Yet neither of us had ended the relationship, preferring to maintain the illusion that the break could be temporary.

When I'd got home from the university and seen the letter lying under the letterbox, I'd recognised her handwriting immediately. Rachel wasn't the letter writing sort, so I knew it had to be important news. I'd actually smiled as I'd opened the envelope, thinking she must be coming back to the UK.

Then I'd started to read, and my smile died.

Dear David,

I'm sorry if this seems a coward's way of telling you, but I've lost count of the number of times I've picked up the phone to call or started an email and then deleted it. I've been seeing someone . . .

I read a little further before lowering the letter, numb. Rachel had begun a relationship with Alain, one of her colleagues. French and almost clichédly good-looking, he'd been on the research vessel with her in the Greek islands. She'd mentioned that he'd joined the project in the Barrier Reef as well, but I'd convinced myself it was just a coincidence.

The letter shattered that, but once the initial shock had passed I'd realised I wasn't really surprised. On some level I'd known this was always going to happen. *Of course it was. What did you expect?*

Thinking I was over the worst, I'd carried on reading.

. . . I was going to tell you before, but there was something I needed to be sure of first. Now I am, so I wanted you to hear it from me. I'm pregnant . . .

The words swam on the page.

Pregnant.

I'd only scanned the rest of the letter before clumsily cramming it back into its envelope. I'd told myself that I'd no reason to feel hurt, that Rachel was a free agent. It didn't help. I'd felt shellshocked, emotionally blindsided. I told myself I'd think more clearly after a goodnight's sleep, that my perspective would be restored in the morning. Except I hadn't slept. I'd lain awake, thinking of what-ifs and might-have-beens, torturing myself with hindsight and regrets. Daylight had brought no respite, only a grainy weariness.

And it had been in that frame of mind that I'd answered the call from DS Chaudry, asking me to help search for a missing teenager in Carlisle.

Now, sitting by the dying fire in the dark bedroom, it seemed as though all that had happened to someone else. There was still a sadness, but it was bittersweet. Rachel deserved her happiness, and I'd no right to begrudge it her. It had been over between us long before this.

It was time to move on.

I put the letter back in the envelope. For a moment I considered dropping it in the fire's embers, watching the paper curl and blacken. But if there was no need for me to keep the letter, there was no need to destroy it either.

Tucking it away in my holdall, I put fresh water down for Max and got myself ready for bed.

I wanted to make an early start.

Chapter 26

A pale dawn was only just breaking when I left Hillside House next morning. Nisha was upset at having to stay behind again, but she'd reluctantly agreed. We'd no way of knowing what the weather would be later, and the situation was difficult enough without her and Kiran being caught out in another blizzard.

So, after promising her I'd be back as soon as I could with an update, I left the two of them with Max and set off to check on Jon. The heavy white overcast of the day before had given way to high, tattered streamers of cloud, and even as early as it was, the air didn't feel as cold as the day before. The snow had a thin, brittle crust where it had frozen overnight, but it was already starting to thaw. Every now and then the quiet would be broken with a whispering thump as a chunk slid off the laden branches.

I was still stiff and sore from the day before, but my muscles began to loosen as I walked. By the time I reached the cross-roads the sun was starting to break through, and the sweeping vista over the vale to the snow-covered mountains, the white still purpled with shadow, was stunning. Despite everything, I felt my spirits rise.

Perhaps the beautiful morning was a good omen.

I'd just passed the snow-covered gate at the bottom of the lane when I saw a figure coming towards me along the road. Even at a distance and bundled up in heavy clothes, the brightly coloured bobble hat made it easy to recognise Eddie.

'Morning,' he said, his breath steaming in the cold air. He hadn't shaved, and the dark circles under his eyes suggested he hadn't slept well. 'Wasn't expecting to see you this early.'

'I told Evie I'd come first thing. How's Jon?'

'Not great. Evie's been keeping an eye on him. She says he's feverish this morning.'

So much for good omens. 'Is he conscious?'

'On and off. I'm just off to sort out the snowplough, but . . . to be honest, I don't know if he's going to be fit enough to move even once the road's been cleared.'

'Is Evie OK about that?'

'She's not thrilled,' he said, morosely. 'Will you be staying at the bungalow for a bit? It's just, with the kids being home and everything, Evie's worried what'll happen if Jon takes a turn for the worse. She'd be relieved if you could hang around.'

If Jon deteriorated there'd be precious little I could do about it, but I didn't blame Evie for being worried. She hadn't asked to have an injured man turn up on their doorstep.

'I can stay for a while, but I'll have to get back to let Nisha know how he is. I need to collect some things Jon left at the army camp, as well.'

The worry lines on Eddie's forehead deepened. 'You're going back up to Foss Ghyll?'

'Yes, but I shouldn't be long,' I told him.

I didn't want to say why I was going. It wasn't that I didn't trust Eddie, but it was better not to broadcast that there was a shotgun lying around, unloaded or not. Even so, Jon's health would have to take priority. If he was in a bad way then the shotgun I'd hidden inside the rotting wooden cabinet would have to wait.

I hoped not, though. I had another reason for wanting to go back up there that had nothing to do with retrieving an abandoned firearm.

But Eddie didn't need to know about that either.

We parted ways after that. Eddie trudged off towards the village, looking as though he had the weight of the world on his shoulders, while I continued to the bungalow. The lopsided snowman in the front garden had lost an eye but his manic smile had survived the night.

That was the only smile I got, though.

If Evie was relieved to see me she hid it well when she let me in. She looked tired, worried and angry.

'You know where he is. Take your boots off this time,' she said, leaving me in the hallway as she went back into the kitchen. The racket from inside surged when she opened the door. 'Keep it DOWN, I won't tell you again!'

Jon didn't look good. His cheeks were flushed yet his face had a pallor, its bones prominent beneath the skin. He was propped slightly on one side with pillows to keep him off the wound. His eyes were closed, but opened sluggishly when I went in.

'Morning, Jon. How are you feeling?'

'Hurts . . .'

'I know. Do you mind if I take a quick look at you?'

I took it as permission when he didn't answer. Evie didn't have a thermometer, but I didn't need one to know he was running a temperature. His forehead was hot to the touch and his pulse was racing. I considered changing his dressing but decided against it. The wound didn't appear to be bleeding, and I didn't want to expose it to the air any more than I had to. It wasn't as though I could do much about it anyway.

'Do you know where you are?' I asked.

His eyes tracked round the room but it was hard to say if there was any recognition in them. 'Nisha and Kiran, are they OK . . .?'

'They're fine. How much of yesterday can you remember?'

He frowned, as though confronted by a complex puzzle. 'I remember getting shot . . . Snowing . . . I was cold.'

'You're safe now. Do you want some water? Anything to eat?'

But he was already drifting away again. There was nothing more I could do there, so I turned to go. Jon's voice came from behind me as I reached the door.

'Should have told me . . ..'

The words were slurred, and when I looked around I saw his eyes were bright and unfocused. 'Told you what, Jon?'

'All my fault . . .'

'What is?'

'Everything. They didn't leave . . .'

He was rambling. 'Do you mean Nisha and Kiran? They're still at home. There's no need to worry about them.'

But his eyes had closed again and I was talking to myself. I looked at him for a while longer, satisfied that his breathing was strong and regular, then quietly went out.

Evie came out of the kitchen as I closed the bedroom door behind me.

'Not doing so well, is he?'

I didn't think that needed an answer. 'Has he had anything to eat or drink?'

'Water and a bit of soup, that's all. He's nearly due for more paracetamols, for all the good they're doing.' Her chin came up. 'As soon as the road's clear I want him out of here.'

'He isn't fit to travel.'

'I don't care! Where's his wife anyway? She should be looking after him, not us.'

'She's got a baby. It's too cold and too far for her to walk over just yet.'

She gave a harsh laugh. 'That's convenient, isn't it? Leave all the shitty jobs for other people.'

'Her husband's been shot. I don't think she feels it's very convenient,' I said, pulling on and fastening my boots. 'I'll come back to check on him again this afternoon.'

I got as far as the front door before Evie spoke again.

'I didn't mean it, all right?'

I stopped and turned, my hand on the door handle. Evie looked on the point of tears, so taut she was ready to snap.

'I'm just . . . I'm *scared!* I know it's hard for his wife but *Christ*, of all the people to have to stay here! Especially now! If my dad finds out . . .'

I took a breath. 'I'll try and think of something.'

'Like what? Magic him to hospital?' She turned her head away, shaking her head. 'Oh, don't take any notice. It's not your fault. I know you're doing your best.'

It didn't feel that way as I went back down the drive. Evie's words played in my head as I retraced my steps along the road. Jon wasn't fit to be moved in anything except an ambulance. Even if we managed to get him back to Hillside House, he'd still need urgent medical attention. Waiting for the snow to thaw so someone might try to reach Edendale and report the washed-out road was no longer an option.

Jon couldn't last that long.

I knew then what I had to do, although it was too late to attempt it today. If I was going to have any chance of succeeding I'd need as much daylight as I could get. Even then it might not be enough, but I didn't have a choice. Not unless I was prepared to let Jon die.

First thing in the morning I'd set out across the fells to fetch help.

There was no sign of the snowplough on the way back to Hillside House. Even though I knew it was too soon for Eddie to have walked all the way out to the plantation yard, and he'd probably need someone to help him to fit the plough blade to a truck, I still found myself hoping I might be surprised. But the morning was still and silent, except for the drip of melting snow and calling of crows and magpies.

Nisha seemed worn down and more edgy than ever when I got back. 'How long do you think it'll take to clear the road?' she asked, after I'd updated her on her husband's condition.

'I don't know, Eddie didn't say. I don't think you should go over there on your own, though, even when it's been cleared.'

The weather might have improved, but with Maud's killer still roaming loose it wasn't safe for her and Kiran to be out alone on that lonely stretch of road.

'I won't be on my own. I can take Max.'

I looked at where the young labrador was lolling on a rug in the kitchen, grinning good-naturedly and beating his tail on the floor while Kiran laughed and pulled on his ears.

'I don't think Max'll make much of a guard dog,' I said, trying to make light of it.

It backfired. Nisha whipped round on me.

'I'm not made of fucking glass!' she flashed. 'How come it's OK for you to go and not me? What are you going to do if this nutjob has a go at *you*?'

'I don't know,' I admitted, knowing it was her fear and worry talking. 'But I've not got a baby with me.'

Nisha screwed up her face. 'Sorry, I shouldn't take it out on you. It's just . . . this is driving me *mad!*'

'The road should have been cleared by the time I get back. If you wait till then I'll go over there with you.'

Nisha gave a strained smile, only slightly mollified. 'Thanks. Just try not to be too long, won't you? I don't think I can stand another day like yesterday.'

I stayed only long enough to make a flask of coffee, then headed back out. I felt a weary sense of déjà vu as I climbed over the stile and started up the hiking trail, following the same tracks Jon and I had made yesterday. Yet at least this time there were some positives. The sun was still struggling to break through the cloud cover and it was noticeably warmer. There was a clammy dampness in the air as the snow melted, turning to mush underfoot, while the buried marker posts for the hiking trail were visible again, poking through the snow like angular stumps.

If I'd just been going to collect Jon's shotgun from the cabin I'd have stayed on the hiking trail all the way up to the glade at Foss Ghyll. But there was something I wanted to do first, so instead I followed the same route I'd taken the day before, cutting up the steeper slope that came out by the plantation logging track. The climb was no easier than I remembered, and when I emerged onto the no man's land between the old woods and the plantation I had to stop to recover. While I rested I checked my phone for a signal. Predictably there wasn't one, and the email and text to DS Chaudry still hadn't been sent. Adding salt to the wounds, the phone's battery was also running dangerously low. With everything else that had happened I hadn't had an opportunity to recharge it in my car. Not that the phone was much use anyway, I thought, putting it away before carrying on.

After cutting across the strip of scrubland separating the woods from the spruce plantation, I started up the logging trail where I'd followed Jon the previous day. Our tracks had been partially covered over by the blizzard, and were beginning to lose their definition now as the snow thawed. No other tracks had joined them, and I let myself relax a little when I saw that.

So far, at least, no one else had been up here.

When I reached the point on the logging track where Jon had fallen after being shot with the crossbow, I retraced our steps into the plantation. The thin covering of snow was thawing even faster under the canopy of branches, but there was still enough of a trail left to follow. Now I knew roughly which way I was going I was able to make better time than before. The spruce plantation was as dark and oppressive as ever, but by now I was growing used to it. There was a sense of familiarity about the towering press of straight trunks and the heavy spruce scent. And while the trees themselves seemed near-identical, I was beginning to recognise features in the plantation's topography. This would be how Jon, and probably Drew Beddoes as well, could navigate the timber maze without getting lost. When I came to the disturbed snow and needles where Jon had pulled out the crossbow bolt, I pressed on even faster, knowing I was getting close. Not long after that I heard the rippling chunter of flowing water.

Fed by the melting snow, the stream was in full spate. In places it had overflowed its banks, but I was relieved to see it hadn't reached the area I was interested in. This was where Jon's tracks had veered away from the waterside, leading to a lopsided spruce that grew on a shoulder-high bank overhanging the stream. The snow around it was trampled down, and I'd assumed that Jon must have fallen there, floundering about before managing to regain his feet and stumble on. I'd been too preoccupied with finding him to give it much thought, but now I'd come to realise there might be another explanation.

He'd been looking for something.

The leaning spruce looked taller than its neighbours, precari-ously balanced on top of the eroded bank. Clambering down, I went to where the snow was most heavily disturbed. The bank here was four or five feet high, undercut by past floodwaters to expose the tangled roots that had somehow kept it anchored. They were still clogged with snow, but it was already beginning to turn translucent, melting away drip by drip.

I reached out with a gloved hand to clear it.

Beneath was a lattice of moss-covered tree roots, fronting the eroded bank like the bars of a cage. The soil between them had been washed away, leaving a hollow black space underneath the tree. A rich, damp smell of loam came from it as I cleared away more snow. All I could see were more roots, snaking around each other as they clung to what little soil remained.

I'd wasted my time.

Disappointed, I began to stand up. As I did, the light and shadows changed, and like abstract shapes resolving into a hidden face in a picture, I suddenly saw it.

Nestled among the tree roots was a human skull.

Chapter 27

At first glance it could have been a rock or stone embedded in the soil. Now I'd seen it, though, I couldn't believe I'd missed it in the first place. Camouflaged among the tree roots, I could see there were more bones protruding from the eroded soil of the bank. Curved ribs, the smooth line of a humerus, a chain of pebble-like vertebrae. The skeletal remains were lying face down but with the skull tilted back, so it appeared to be staring out. The hips and legs were still buried but the torso had partly emerged from the mud, as though it was trying to drag itself from under the leaning tree.

Yet, wreathed in shadows and mottled with lichen and moss, the skeleton was perfectly concealed. It had weathered to the same texture and muddy brown hue as the tree roots that encased it. Its curves echoed their form and shape, blending in with them so well it could have been like this for years. Hidden in plain sight, unless you knew what to look for.

Or were wearing night-vision goggles.

I hadn't believed Nisha when she'd told me Jon had found the body weeks ago, long before the storm brought down the spruce above Foss Ghyll. She'd been telling the truth, though. Perhaps the infra-red of the goggles he used in his nocturnal deer hunts had cancelled out the natural camouflage of lichen, moss and weathering, allowing him to see the skull among the exposed tree roots. Either way, Jon really had found human remains, weeks before I did.

Just not the same ones.

Christ . . . No wonder he'd reacted so badly when I'd taken him to the other burial site. Until then he'd have thought we'd both stumbled across the same body, that the leaning spruce tree he'd seen must have blown down in the storm. And it would have been only natural for him to assume that the remains he'd discovered belonged to the missing Jed Beddoes, his father's supposed victim.

But two men had gone missing twenty-six years ago, not just one. And while a single body seemed to confirm the accepted narrative of those events, the discovery of a second upended everything. Like everyone else, Jon had always believed his father had fled justice after murdering his rival, abandoning his wife and son in the process. Now he was confronted with a possibility he'd never even considered.

That his father might be another victim.

That was why Jon had gone out into the snow the previous morning. He'd seen that someone had destroyed one victim's remains with a chainsaw. Drunk and emotionally battered, he'd wanted to make sure that the other skeleton was still intact. It was a bad idea, but understandable given what he now suspected.

That one of them belonged to his father.

I considered the skull that gazed out through the tree roots. Once I'd realised that the skeletal remains I'd found at Foss Ghyll were too old and too big to belong to Jed Beddoes, I'd begun to think about the other person who'd gone missing at the same time. They belonged to a man the same sort of age as Owen Reese when he disappeared, and probably a similar build. Although Jed Beddoes' small stature had proved that genes weren't always predictable, I felt reasonably confident that Jon would have inherited his large frame from his father.

The ID would need to be confirmed, but that could be done with DNA from the surviving bones, as well as dental records from the mandible I'd salvaged. But for now my working hypothesis was that the skeleton that had been destroyed belonged to Owen Reese.

The question now was who this other victim might be?

Slipping the rucksack from my shoulders, I set it down and took out my phone to photograph the remains. This time I didn't even get the low battery warning: the screen remained dead. I swore, wishing I still had my old digital camera. Not so long ago it had been an essential part of my kit, but as technology moved on I'd begun relying on my phone instead. The photographs were a better quality, and it was more convenient.

Until it didn't work.

It meant I'd have to rely on more old-school methods. Taking a pen and notepad from my jacket pocket, I made a rough sketch of the skeleton's position and began making notes. Rags of old cobwebs clung to the skeleton and roots alike, curled with the husks of long-dead spiders, but there was no adipocere that I could see. I'd have expected the pale, crumbly by-product of underground decomposition – also known as 'grave wax' – to be present in soil as moist as this, so its absence was an indication that the skeleton must have been exposed to air for a considerable time. So too was the pitted and rough appearance of the visible bones, as well as the mottling of fungal growth and furring of moss. Jon might have only found this body a few weeks ago, but it had been exposed in the eroded stream bank for much longer than that.

Years, probably.

Like the other skeletal remains, the skull of these also displayed typically male characteristics, with a slanting forehead and pronounced brow ridges. Angular eye orbits again hinted at a white ancestry, and I could see that the wisdom teeth had erupted, which meant this had been someone in their late teens or older. Though probably not too much older, given the general lack of wear and tear. That pointed to this being a young adult, probably under thirty. It was hard to get an accurate idea of stature from such a limited view, but I didn't think this had been a tall person. The long limb bones – the humerus, radius and ulna of the arm, and the femur, tibia and fibula of the leg – are reasonably accurate indicators of stature. Although there are exceptions, tall individuals usually have long arms and legs, but as far as I could tell that wasn't the case here. Only the left arm was visible, almost its full length embedded in the mud of the eroded bank. But what I could see suggested this individual had been average height at most.

253

None of which was conclusive. It was a rule of thumb at best, and without any means of taking measurements I was relying on a purely visual estimate.

Even so, everything I could see told me this could be Jed Beddoes.

For all I knew he could still have been killed by Owen Reese, who'd then been murdered himself. Perhaps by one of the Beddoes, wanting revenge. But there was another possibility as well. That Owen Reese was innocent, and both he and Jed Beddoes had by killed by someone else.

I flinched as a lump of melting snow landed on my shoulder with a wet *smack*. I glanced around, half-expecting to see someone in the trees behind me. But there was no one there. Except for the remains of a man who'd died two decades before, I was alone in the spruce plantation.

I took one last look at the skeleton, emerging from under the leaning tree like a broken jack-in-a-box. Then, putting away my notepad, I set off to retrieve Jon's shotgun from the log cabin.

The steady drip of melting snow accompanied me as I followed the stream through the plantation, heading back to the glade at Foss Ghyll. Shafts of light broke through the canopy overhead, slanting through the pillared trunks like sunbeams through a cathedral window. The weather was improving but that didn't lighten the thoughts that prowled around my mind. Unless Jon miraculously improved, next morning I was going to have to set off cross-country to fetch help. I only needed to get to a road, or a farmhouse with a working phone, but I was under no illusions how hard that would be. Maud and Jon had both warned against trying to cross the fells, and that was even before it had snowed. In these conditions I didn't know if it was possible.

But I had to try.

As I neared the glade, I focused on planning what I'd need to take with me. I'd have to borrow Jon's rucksack again, as well as the Thermos flask. It would be a trade-off between taking enough food and drink to see me through and not tiring myself out by carrying too much weight. I'd need some way of navigating, as well. An Ordnance Survey map might be too much to hope for, but I might be able to get hold of something more detailed than my road atlas. A compass, too, now the app on my phone wasn't working. It would be worth asking Eddie if he could help supply me with what I needed.

I'd take any help I could get.

By the time I reached the glade, the morning had been transformed. The winter sunlight cast sharp-edged shadows, blue-black against the dazzling whiteness. Already, I could see the difference the thaw had made. The tracks Jon and I had left the day before were beginning to shrink and lose definition, while at the far side of the glade the oaks and beeches of the old woods were stark and black again, no longer bowed down by the snow's weight.

After the grey misery of recent days, it felt like a promise of better things. The thought buoyed me as I crossed the glade, heading for the rhododendron thicket and derelict log cabins where Jon had taken shelter. Meltwater from the thawing snow dripped from the sagging roofs in fluid silver chains, a reminder that it wouldn't be long before they were engulfed by the sprawling rhododendrons again. Already the bushes were re-emerging from the snow that had flattened them, evergreen leaves glistening as they shrugged off the snow.

I was a few yards away from the thicket's outermost edge when a far-off noise carried to me in the quiet. Faint, but jarringly out of place in this setting.

The throaty chug of a diesel engine.

Eddie had been as good as his word, I thought, relieved. It had to be the snowplough, clearing the road at the bottom of the lane. Yet something about that didn't seem right. The road was too far for the sound to carry all the way up here. I stopped to listen. The engine noise was growing louder. Nearer.

With a shock I realised it wasn't coming from the far-off road, it was coming from the lane.

Coming up *here*.

The engine seemed to be straining, and over its growl I could make out the crackle of snapping branches. A crunch of gears interrupted its rhythm, unsettling me for a reason I couldn't

255

identify. Then the memory came back of standing on the roadside by the collapsed culvert, hearing the approaching lorry grind its gears as it laboured up the steep gradient. I told myself I was being paranoid, that the snowplough had probably finished clearing the roads in the village, and was just . . .

The thought petered out.

The straining engine was becoming much louder. I glanced back towards the spruce trees, briefly entertaining the idea of making for the safety of the plantation. But it was too far away, and something told me I didn't want to be caught out in the open when the snowplough got here. I looked around the glade, suddenly desperate to get out of sight. The huge rhododendron thicket stood between me and the woods, cutting off any escape that way. The bushes would provide some cover, though, so with the snowplough's exhaust fumes now tainting the clean air, I ran over and ducked behind them.

Clumps of melting snow dropped onto me as I crouched at the edge of the green-leafed rhododendrons. Even partially flattened by snow, the sprawling thicket was twice my height. The dense branches blocked my view of the lane, but the snowplough sounded almost at its top. A moment later the engine tone changed as it idled, then stopped.

Silence settled over the hollow.

The metallic slam of a truck door came from the far side of the rhododendrons. I tried to see through the branches, but I couldn't make out the snowplough or who had climbed out. There was a hawking cough, then a rumbling voice came from the other side of the bushes.

'Fuck me . . .' Hooley muttered.

I swore, silently. *Jesus, Eddie . . .* He'd said Maud usually got one of the crew to drive the snowplough, but it had stupidly never occurred to me that he might ask Hooley. It should have. Suspended or not, the big man was used to driving heavy vehicles, so he'd be the natural choice to operate the snowplough. I tried to tell myself there might be a reason why he'd brought it all this way up an overgrown lane, but I couldn't think of one.

Nothing good, anyway.

The crump of footsteps in the snow started up, heading towards me. I looked around for a better place to hide. There was nowhere else to go. The rhododendrons shielding me from Hooley boxed me in as well. If I moved away from them he'd see me, and I'd make too much noise if I tried to push further into the thicket or reach the log cabins. He'd be bound to hear.

But I couldn't stay where I was. He was getting closer, and in a few more seconds I'd be in full view. *Come on, decide!*

The crunch of footsteps stopped.

I hardly dare breathe. From a few yards away I heard Hooley clearing his throat and hawk again. He was close enough to hear how laboured his breathing was.

'Jesus Christ . . .' he wheezed.

Slowly, I moved until I could see more of him. Through the dripping branches I glimpsed the grubby yellow of a high-vis jacket, no more than twenty metres away. The burly figure was stooped over, hands braced on his meaty thighs as he drew in hoarse, painful breaths. Even the short walk from the top of the lane had winded him. Perhaps I could make it to better cover after all, I thought. Then I noticed something by his feet. It was red and bulky, and a shock ran through me when I realised what it was.

Sitting on the snow next to Hooley was a chainsaw.

Chapter 28

Any lingering hope that Hooley had an innocent reason for being there died when I saw what he'd brought with him. It was the same scuffed red as the chainsaws in the plantation yard's tool room, and I didn't doubt it was the one that was missing from there. Or that its teeth would be clogged with bone and blood.

I watched through the branches as he cleared his throat and spat into the snow, cursing myself for not seeing this coming. Eddie probably thought he was doing the right thing, getting the snowplough out as quickly as possible as well as giving Hooley a chance to redeem himself after the crash.

The bigger question was why was Hooley here?

The only reason I could think of was the skeleton under the leaning spruce. Hooley – and any doubts I'd had about his guilt were fast vanishing – had destroyed the remains of one victim already. It wasn't such a stretch to think he'd want to do the same to the other. I didn't know why he'd waited so long, since the bones I'd just seen had obviously been exposed for some time. But none of that mattered.

He wouldn't have brought the chainsaw unless he intended to use it.

Grunting, he stooped down, and I heard the slosh of petrol as he picked up the chainsaw. He looked around, rubbing his unshaven chin as he tried to decide what to do. I'd told Eddie I needed to collect something Jon had left at Foss Ghyll. But I hadn't said where, and it didn't seem to occur to Hooley that I might have arrived first.

I silently urged him to move away. He was badly out of condition, out of breath just walking a short distance in the snow. With enough of a lead I could make a break for it. Head for the spruce plantation, or even the hiking trail through the woods. He couldn't come after me in the snowplough then, and with his bulk I couldn't see him chasing after me very far on foot.

I watched as he started walking away from me, his breathing hoarse as he plodded through the snow. After he'd gone a few steps the rhododendron branches obscured my view, but I could still hear the heavy tramp of his boots in the snow. *That's right, keep going . . .*

The footsteps stopped.

I held my breath, hoping they'd resume. They didn't. Careful not to make a noise, I shifted position until I could see him again through the branches. He was motionless, staring off across the glade. I breathed a little easier when I saw that, relieved he wasn't looking in my direction. Then I realised what he'd seen.

My tracks, running across the snow-covered glade from the spruce plantation. Pointing towards me like an accusing finger.

Oh, Christ . . . They were clearly freshly made, not yet starting to thaw like the ones from the day before. Hooley was frowning as he stared at them, and for a heartbeat I thought he might not realise what they meant.

Then he turned in my direction.

I stayed perfectly still behind the rhododendron's evergreen foliage, scared any sudden movement would give me away. Hooley was still frowning, as though undecided even now.

Then, as though he'd worked out some intricate puzzle, his whiskered jowls creased in a grin.

'You there, Dr Hunter?'

His words hung in the damp air. I didn't answer, resisting the urge to duck or pull back.

'Eddie sent me to get you,' he went on, the wolfish grin still in place. 'He wanted you to know Reese has taken a turn.'

For a second or two I wanted to believe him. Jon's condition *could* have worsened. Perhaps Eddie really had sent Hooley to find me, and I was making a fool of myself. Then reality blew the fantasy to tatters.

He didn't need a chainsaw to deliver a message.

'He's in a bad way,' he went on, when I didn't respond. 'They don't think he'll last much longer.'

I remained silent. Hooley stood for a few moments, the same look of contrived innocence on his face as when he'd told me there was a hotel in the village. Then he scowled.

'Look, stop pissing about. I know you're here, you might as well come out.'

He sounded annoyed. I looked around, desperately searching for a way of escape. But Hooley was between me and the spruce plantation, and the bank of choking rhododendrons blocked off the woods as effectively as a barrier. I could try to get past Hooley, hope he was too slow and unfit to catch me. But he'd be waiting for that, and I'd have forty or fifty yards of snow-covered glade to cross before I reached the plantation treeline. If I fell . . .

Hooley had tired of waiting. 'Fuck it,' he said, striding forward.

The chainsaw roared to life.

The noise was deafening. I turned to run and gasped as something grabbed and pulled me back. For an instant I thought Hooley had caught me. Frantic, I wrenched free, tearing my rucksack from the rhododendron branch that had snagged it. But even those seconds had cost me. Hooley was only yards away now, kicking up flurries of snow as he lumbered towards me, the chainsaw snarling in front of him. I shot a last agonised glance towards the promised safety of the treeline, knowing I'd never make it, and took the only option left.

I threw myself into the rhododendron thicket.

Branches snapped and cracked as I forced my way through them. They whipped at me, scratching my exposed skin while their meaty leaves slapped against my face. I pushed blindly into the thicket, with no idea of what was ahead or where I was going. At my back I heard the chainsaw rise in pitch as Hooley began slashing at the rhododendrons, carving his way in after me. An image of Maud's body flashed into my mind as I crashed deeper into the bushes. When my rucksack snagged

261

again I fought against it in a frenzy. *Come ON, you bastard!* But this time it was caught fast. Stabbed and lacerated by the branches, I began wrestling out of the straps, expecting at any second to feel the white-hot bite of the chainsaw. I'd got one arm free before a thought penetrated my panic.

Hooley had been right behind me. He should have caught me by now.

So why hadn't he?

I risked a backward glance through the branches, ready to run again.

There was no one there.

My heart was pounding as I gasped for breath, not daring to trust the reprieve. I could still hear the chainsaw but now it was coming from further away. From outside the thicket, I realised. Its snarl had diminished to an idling growl.

Over it, I could make out Hooley's oaths.

'*Fucker* . . .*!* Jesus *wept,* that's bastard great!'

Now I was no longer fighting against it, the rucksack slid free without protest as I slowly turned round. Interlocking branches crowded in from every angle, extending high above my head. Most of the leaf cover was on the rhododendron's outer branches, making the interior of the bushes shadowed and dark. It was like being in a cave. From what I could see I'd managed to come about twenty feet into the thicket, leaving a ragged tunnel of splintered branches and torn leaves behind me. Through it I caught glimpses of Hooley's yellow high-vis jacket as he moved around outside.

'You listening in there?' he shouted.

I didn't answer, my chest rising and falling as I sucked in breaths.

'Look, I'm not coming to fucking get you, all right?' Hooley called. 'I've cut my face open on a bastard branch, so congratu-fuckinglations! You win. All I want is your phone, OK? Give me that and we'll call it quits.'

My phone? I struggled to understand, and then suddenly I did. It wasn't my phone Hooley was interested in.

It was what was on it.

I'd been wrong. He wasn't here to destroy the second set of remains. He'd come looking for me. Eddie must have let slip that I was coming up here, and that was all the invitation Hooley needed. For whatever the reason, it was clear now that he'd killed Owen Reese, and likely Jed Beddoes as well. And for twenty-six years he'd literally got away with murder, because everyone believed Jon's father was guilty of the crime.

But that fiction would collapse if it became known that the remains in the tree roots belonged to Owen Reese. That was why Hooley had destroyed them, in the futile hope that would protect his secret. And when Maud had walked in as he was taking the chainsaw, he'd panicked and killed her. That escalation might not have been intended, but it meant Hooley was committed now. He was intent on destroying anything that might identify the remains and expose his guilt.

Including the photographic evidence on my phone.

It was possible he'd seen me taking photographs when he came up to Foss Ghyll with Alun Beddoes, after the remains had been destroyed. But even if not he'd have heard from Drew that I'd been taking shots of the intact skeleton the day before that. He might not know exactly what they showed or how incriminating they were, but he wouldn't want to take the chance. So here he was, leaving a trail of carnage in another botched attempt to cover his tracks. Never mind that DNA testing would still identify the bone shards as belonging to Owen Reese, or that Hooley had left his boot prints all over the crime scene. I doubted that had even occurred to him. He was like a psychotic child, covering its eyes in the hope it wouldn't be seen. He'd got away with two murders that way for over twenty years.

He probably thought he could get away with two more.

I felt something wet trickling down my face. Blood, I realised, when I touched it, and now I became aware of all the other cuts and scratches I'd got from blundering through the bushes. I ignored them, trying to calm down and think what to do. If I'd thought Hooley would let me go I'd have thrown the phone out there and then. Destroying it wouldn't do him any good,

263

not when the photographs were backed up on my laptop back at Hillside House.

But Hooley was going to kill me no matter what. The knowledge tightened the knot in my stomach. It also shored up my resolve.

If he wanted my phone he'd have to work for it.

'It won't do you any good,' I called. 'I've already sent the photos to the police.'

'Yeah, fuck off, no you haven't. Phone lines were down before you took them, you haven't sent them anywhere. Come on, just throw it out and I'll let you go.' There was a pause. 'Honest.'

It would have been laughable if it wasn't so serious. I wiped the blood from my face, not bothering to answer.

'Oh, for *fuck's* sake, just give me the bastard phone!' Hooley yelled, exasperated. 'Don't make me have to come in there again, I'm fucking warning you! Bring it out or I'll come and get it!'

Trying to ignore the shaking in my muscles, I looked around the tangle of gnarled rhododendron branches for some means of escape. It was no use trying to force my way out through the bushes. All Hooley would have to do was follow the noise I'd make and then wait outside for me to emerge. For a moment or two I felt a surge of hope when I remembered Jon's shotgun, still hidden in the derelict log cabin. It wasn't loaded but Hooley didn't know that. If I could get to it and bluff him . . .

The brief hope snuffed out. I couldn't see far through the interlocking branches surrounding me, but the cabin was nowhere in sight. I'd lost my bearings during my panicked flight, so I didn't even know which direction it was in. I could be anywhere in the massive evergreen thicket.

I fought for calm as the reality of my situation sank in. If I couldn't escape from the thicket then I'd have to stay where I was. Hooley couldn't just leave me in here. Sooner or later he'd have to come and get me, and when he did I'd have a chance to get away. If I could make it out of the thicket I might have enough of a lead to reach the safety of the woods or spruce plantation. After that, if I could make it to the village and raise the alarm . . .

If, if, if . . .

A sense of hopelessness filled me. I could fantasise as much as I liked, it didn't alter the fact that Hooley would slash his way through to me with the chainsaw long before I could force my way out.

But any plan was better than nothing. Closing my mind to what might happen in the next few minutes, I shrugged out of the rucksack straps. It was a dead weight and had already snagged on one branch: I didn't want to risk that happening again. I was going to leave it behind but then changed my mind. If I held it in front of me it would protect my face and eyes while I forced my way through the branches. It would be something to fend off Hooley with as well, if it came to that.

Though not for long.

'Last chance!' he called from outside.

I waited, wiping the blood from my face again.

'Fuck this,' he spat. 'I warned you.'

The chainsaw's grumble rose to a howl. I shrank from the sound, everything in me crying out to get away. But I had to know Hooley had committed himself. Only when I saw his big silhouette blocking out the light and heard the shriek of the chainsaw biting into wood did I start to run.

Except running was impossible. Even with the rucksack thrust in front of me, breaking through the branches was like wading through mud, a nightmare chase in slow motion. My plan seemed ludicrous as branches tore at me and the chainsaw's shriek filled the air. I'd no idea how close Hooley was, no idea of where I was going, and without the rucksack my back felt horribly naked. I thought I could feel the spatter of wood chips on my shoulders as I bludgeoned at the branches in front of me. Every thought was subsumed into a wild urge to escape, and when the ground began to slide away beneath me I'd no idea what was happening. I floundered as I found myself sinking into the earth, my feet suddenly without traction. I tried to scramble free, clutching at branches until, with an ear-splitting *CRACK*, the ground under me gave way. There was a weightless moment as I plunged into darkness, choked by a cascade of dirt and shattered branches.

Then something slammed into me and everything stopped.

Chapter 29

I couldn't breathe.

That was the first thing I was aware of, a sense of suffocation. I fought against it, heaving in air and a mouthful of soil and bark. Weakly, I tried to spit it out and pain racked through me. I hurt all over. I lay in pitch blackness, cold and wet, with no idea of where I was. Memory returned in fragments. I remembered falling, the ground vanishing beneath my feet. Crashing my way through branches, chased by . . . by . . .

Oh, Jesus . . .!

A fresh surge of pain hammered me when I tried to move, but that was nothing compared to the sudden sense of panic. Christ, where was Hooley? He'd been right behind me, the chainsaw snarling and spitting shards of wood at my back. It was too dark to see anything, but the silence was complete. Everything was still. I couldn't hear the chainsaw and there was no sign of Hooley. So where was he?

Where was *I*?

I was lying at an angle rather than flat, on a sloping, uneven surface. I remembered falling, but I couldn't think how that could have happened. Had a sinkhole or pit of some sort opened under me? There was a dank, musty smell, a sweetness of vegetal rot and something else. But in the blackness there was no way of seeing my surroundings or gauging how far I'd fallen.

Tentatively, I tried to move. Small pieces of dirt and debris pattered down onto me. My head was sore and there were aches all over my body, but nothing felt broken or dislocated.

I hadn't fallen very far, then. There was something restricting my legs. I reached down and felt rough cloth. A sheet of some kind, tough and stiff. I tried to pull it away but it resisted. It seemed to be trapped.

I kicked and pushed it off until my legs were free, then lay back and waited for the throbbing in my head to subside. I put my hand to it, feeling cuts from the branches but nothing more serious. I didn't feel sick or dizzy, or any other indication that I might be concussed, which was a good sign. The fall had stunned and winded me, not knocked me out completely.

Something was digging into my side. I started to reach for it when the darkness was split by a bright shaft of a light. I froze. It was a torch beam, coming from a few metres above me. As it moved around its light fell through a crosshatched silhouette of leafy branches over my head, creating a broken strobe effect as it shone through them. I lay perfectly still as their shadows played across me, knowing who it had to be. As though to prove it, a muttering came from above.

'*Fuck!* Fucking great!'

I flinched as the torch beam hit my face, waiting for Hooley's cry of discovery. But it didn't come. The light passed from my closed eyelids. I opened them carefully and saw the beam had moved away. It was only then I realised I'd been holding my breath. I let it out slowly. *God . . .*

The tangle of branches was screening me, I realised. Hooley couldn't see through them.

'You down there?' he called as the torch beam roved. His voice echoed hollowly. 'Can you hear me?'

I didn't answer. The torch continued to search, stirring the shadows as it ranged around.

'I was just messing about earlier. Let me know where you are and I'll pull you up.'

Hooley's offer would have been unconvincing even if he hadn't just chased me with a chainsaw.

'I can see you,' he said, and my heart seemed to miss a beat. But the torch beam was nowhere near me, continuing to probe around as he spoke. 'You might as well say something.'

I half-closed my eyes again, stiffening as the beam of light came towards my face. But it passed by without touching me. For a few seconds it stabbed around at random, accompanied by Hooley's adenoidal breathing. Then it stopped.

'Fuck it,' he muttered, and the torch beam went out.

Blackness descended again, deeper than ever. From above I heard branches snapping as Hooley forced his way back through the thicket. The noise grew fainter until finally there was silence.

Even then I didn't move. I lay there listening, not quite believing it wasn't a trick. Only when several minutes had passed did I accept that Hooley really was gone. He was too clumsy and impatient to creep back without making a sound.

I shifted, wincing but still trying to be quiet. More aches announced themselves as I sat up, broken branches and clods of dirt sliding from me. *Christ.* What the hell had I fallen into? The blackness was total, but from what I'd managed to glimpse in the light from Hooley's torch it didn't look like a sinkhole or anything natural. An underground cistern or tank, perhaps? It had seemed too big for that, but whatever it was it didn't matter.

I needed to get out.

First, though, I needed to see. My phone's flashlight was useless without a charge, but there had been a torch in the rucksack. I'd been holding that in front of me when I fell. If it had ended up down here with me . . .

I started to grope around in the dark. The surface under me was some kind of rough timber board, propped up at an angle against a hard, uneven wall. The board felt rotten, as though it might break if I moved too quickly. Feeling for its edge, I reached down and snatched back my gloved hand as it sank into something soft and rustling.

Dirt, fleshy leaves and broken branches.

Moving slowly in the darkness, I swung my legs over the edge and felt my boot nudge something.

The rucksack.

I dragged it nearer, fumbling uselessly at the zip before I gave up and took off my gloves. The air was frigid and clammy on the bare skin of my hand as I felt for the rucksack's zip. Taking the cold metal cylinder of the torch from the rucksack, I offered up a silent prayer that it hadn't been broken and switched it on.

A dazzling beam of light sprang to life in the darkness.

Yes! Pulling my glove back on, I shone the torch around. Motes of dust and fibres swirled in its beam. *Christ, what is this place?* I was at the bottom of a deep chamber, but my view was restricted by a swathe of filthy canvas that hung down from above, like the flap of a collapsed tent. I couldn't see beyond it, but when I pointed the torch upwards I saw it was part of a huge tarpaulin that formed the ceiling of the chamber I'd fallen into. It was several metres above me, supported by an untidy latticework of criss-crossed planks, battens and boards through which the rotting canvas bulged like a dirty cloud.

The torchlight showed the gap where I'd fallen through, bringing down the swag of tarpaulin along with splintered rhododendron branches, timbers and soil. I'd been lucky. They'd broken my fall and saved me from serious injury, while the bushes that now leaned precariously into the gap had hidden me from Hooley's view.

I didn't feel lucky, though. As I shone the torch around my surroundings, confusion joined the pain and shock.

What the hell is this place?

The dangling tarpaulin restricted my view, but from what I could see it looked like I'd fallen into some kind of large pit. Moving the torch further along, I saw that the rotting board underneath me was leaning against a slate face, sheer and rough-hewn. It butted up against a high expanse of badly spalled concrete. A man-made wall, I realised, with rusted steel reinforcing rods showing through where the concrete had fallen away. I felt a tug of recognition, but for a second or two I couldn't think why. Then it came to me.

This must be the other side of the buttressed concrete wall I'd seen from the lane.

It had been so overgrown by rhododendrons I hadn't been able to tell what it was. I still couldn't. What I'd taken to be a retaining wall or part of an old army bunker seemed to be forming one side of the pit I was standing in. A rusted metal drainage grate was set into it, low down at its base, Shining the torch higher I saw the mouth of a pipe jutting out close to the wall's top. It looked like a water inlet, but that didn't make any sense unless . . .

Ah, Christ . . .

I remembered Nisha saying that the original owner of Hillside House had planned to turn Foss Ghyll into a mountain spa, with swimming and cold-water treatments. He'd gone bankrupt, but evidently not before building some of the spa facilities as well as the log cabins. The concrete wall had been built to cap off the open side of an old slate quarry pit, effectively damming it. The inlet at the top must have been fed by the stream at Foss Ghyll, so the pit could be flooded and used for swimming. Diving as well, because it was certainly deep enough.

And I'd fallen into it.

At least there wasn't any water still in it, though that wasn't much consolation. I swore, cursing whoever had thought covering a quarry pit with timbers and a tarpaulin would be a good idea. Overrun by the rhododendron thicket, it was completely invisible from outside. The invasive bushes had even managed to grow on *top* of the tarpaulin, I saw now, their roots probing down through the rotting canvas like strands of dirty brown lightning.

But I was too busy wondering how I was going to get out to worry about anything else. Moving stiffly, I gingerly pushed myself to my feet, grimacing as new hurts announced themselves. My breath swirled in the torch beam as I shone the torch around. It didn't look good. The concrete wall and slate sides of the quarry were too high and sheer to climb, at least as far as I could see. The tarpaulin hung down across it like a curtain, blocking my view of the rest of the pit. Hoping there'd be a way out behind it, I went to move the filthy canvas aside. It was heavier than I'd thought, stiff and clogged with dirt. I tried to heave it away again, more firmly this time, and felt it shift.

Suddenly, an avalanche of earth was raining down onto me.

I ducked, covering my head, terrified the entire tarpaulin was coming down, timbers and all. But after what seemed an age the cascade of soil and debris petered out. Heart thudding,

I straightened. *Christ* . . . The tarpaulin was still in place above me, but the mess of sagging cloth and planks looked ready to give way. God knew how many years it had been here, silently rotting away inside the rhododendron thicket. I'd been lucky not to drag the whole thing down already.

I daren't risk disturbing it again.

But I had to see the rest of the pit, because there was no way out where I was. I shone my torch along the edges of the tarpaulin, hoping to find a way past. Off to one side, my torch fell on the blackness of a gap underneath it, big enough to crawl through. Lowering myself onto my hands and knees, I eased through to the other side, making sure I was well clear of the tarpaulin before I climbed to my feet.

As soon as I stood up I knew there was something else in there.

Whether it was a change in air pressure or smell, or some other subconscious sense, I couldn't say. But I could feel a presence, a subliminal impression of something large and looming in the shadows. I shone the torch at it, telling myself it was simply an atavistic fear of darkness, that the pit would be empty here as well. Then the light fell on what was there, and I took an involuntary step backwards.

Lying at the bottom of the quarry pit was the wreckage of a VW Camper.

Chapter 30

The wreckage took up almost half of the quarry pit. The old Camper had crashed down front first, crumpling its whole front end and coming to rest with its rear canted up against the slate wall of the quarry pit. The windscreen and most of the windows had shattered, but the distinctive orange and cream paintwork was still recognisable under the thick layer of grime. So was the iconic chrome VW badge, rusted and bent between the shattered headlights.

The sight was a shock, yet I knew straight away what I was looking at. I'd been told that Megan, the so-called hippy who Jed Beddoes and Jon's father had fought over, had driven a VW Camper. She and her daughter, Willow, had stayed in it up at Foss Ghyll, at least until they'd found themselves no longer welcome in Edendale. And then they'd left, reportedly waking half the village as they drove the Camper through it in the dead of night.

Or so everyone thought.

My breath steamed in the torchlight as I stared at the wrecked VW. If this was the same van – and the chances of it being a different one were too remote to seriously consider – then someone had driven it back up here without anyone knowing. It had to have been after the police had carried out their search for the missing Jed Beddoes or the van would have been found, even down here. Sometime after that, then, and probably late at night. The same way it had departed.

Though more quietly this time.

I still hadn't moved. I didn't want to look inside the Camper, but I knew I had to. Glass crunched under my boots, the noise jarringly loud as I crossed the few yards to the van. It was resting on its wheelrims, only tatters of rubber left of the perished tyres. The inside of the van was dark, and the shadows leapt and jerked when I shone my torch through the broken windscreen. The driver's and passenger seats were empty except for dirt and shards of glass. Shining my torch past them, I saw a chaotic jumble of scattered clothes, crockery and saucepans strewn over a grimy table and rotting bench seats. The rusted remains of a portable gas heater had tumbled against the dashboard, but I didn't see anything else. There were narrow bunks under the roof but they were empty too.

I was turning away when the torch beam passed over an untidy heap of clothing, half-hidden behind the front seats.

I shone the light directly onto it.

The two skeletons lay crumpled behind the seats as though flung there. Strands of hair still clung to the smooth domes of two skulls, while rags of rotting sweaters and jeans were tented out over bare bones. Neither were large but from my limited view I could see that one was considerably smaller than the other, while the larger of the two had an obviously gracile bone structure. Even if I hadn't known the story behind them I'd have said they were an adult female and young or pre-adolescent child.

No wonder the police hadn't been able to trace Megan and Willow.

I couldn't begin to guess what their bodies were doing in this dank hole, if it was more of Hooley's handiwork or something else. But now I had another reason to get out of this place. Whatever had happened to them, the mother and daughter had been down here long enough.

And so had I.

Letting darkness reclaim the campervan's grim secrets, I shone the torch onto the rest of the quarry pit. The slate walls were just as high and unclimbable here as well, quarried slate slabs rising five or six metres to where it had been capped off with the timber and tarpaulin ceiling. Too high to reach even if I stood on top of the VW Camper, I saw, aiming the torch above it to the pit's edge.

But as I moved the torch beam away it flitted over something angular, a geometric shape at the uppermost corner of the pit. I swung the beam over to it and felt a surge of hope.

Fixed to the side of the pit was a swimming pool ladder.

It wasn't very big, no more than four or five feet in length. Long enough for swimmers to pull themselves out but well beyond my reach. Unless I could find something to stand on, and there was nothing like that in the pit. The boards and planks that had fallen in with me were too small and rotten anyway. There was only one thing I could use.

I shone the torch back to the VW Camper.

I might – might – be able to stretch up and grab hold of the ladder if I climbed onto its roof, but I still found myself hesitating. Not so much because I'd be clambering all over a crime scene, although there was that. It felt disrespectful to the mother and daughter whose bodies lay inside the van. A desecration, almost. Yet there was no alternative if I wanted to get out.

It wouldn't bring them justice if I died down here as well.

The campervan was resting with its back end wedged against the wall, tilted upwards at about a thirty-degree angle. That would give me welcome extra height, but it made it more difficult to climb onto. After testing to make sure it was stable, I stepped up onto what was left of a rear wheel and tried to push myself up. I needed both hands, so I tucked the torch into the sleeve of my jacket, leaving its head poking out while I tried again. The torch beam threw crazy shadows on the sides of the pit as I scrabbled for purchase on the cold and gritty metal. But at last, panting, I managed to heave myself up onto the roof.

The van creaked and protested as I slowly stood upright. When it didn't shift after a few seconds, I shuffled to where the back end leaned against the slate wall of the pit. The torch was still stuffed down my jacket sleeve, which was cumbersome but better than dropping it if I lost my balance and had to grab for something. Pointing its beam upwards, I considered the swimming ladder. It was coated with dirt and grime but didn't appear to be too rusted. A pool ladder would probably be stainless steel rather than chrome plate, so at least it shouldn't have corroded. The lowest rung was still several feet away, though, above me and off to one side.

It looked a long way to reach.

Taking a breath, I eased to the edge of the campervan's curved roof and stretched out my hand. Now my gloved fingers were only inches from the steel rungs, but I was still too far away. I swore, resting my forehead against the unyielding side of the pit.

OK, you can do this.

Flattening myself against the quarry wall for support, I began to lean towards the ladder, my jacket whispering across the slate. It was cold and gritty against my cheek. My breaths blew puffs of fine dust from its surface, scratching my eyes and tickling my nose. *Jesus, don't sneeze.* The thought brought a bubble of hysterical laughter that I had to choke back. At full stretch, my fingertips brushed the edge of the diving ladder, agonisingly short. *Come on, it's right there. All you have to do is reach for it.* I leaned a little further, felt myself on the edge of overbalancing. *God, no, don't—*

My hand closed on a steel rung.

Relief made me weak. Keeping hold of the ladder, I allowed myself a few seconds to recover. Now came the hard part.

I'd have to step off the top of the van, trusting the ladder to take my weight while I pulled myself up the rungs.

Raising my head, I looked above me to where the top of the ladder was engulfed by the bulging tarpaulin. The rotten canvas sagged heavily over the steel frame, with no gap between them. Even if I managed to pull myself up the ladder far enough to get my feet onto the lowest rung, I'd still have to crawl underneath the tarpaulin to drag myself over the edge. If it became dislodged and fell into the pit it would take me down with it.

But I didn't have any choice. *Come on, then.* I took deep breaths, snorting against the tickle of slate dust. Then, still gripping the rung tightly with one hand, I lunged with my free arm to grab hold of the ladder with that as well.

With a grating squeal, it pulled out of the wall.

No! There was a second of gut-swooping vertigo as I began to topple backwards. The torch beam swung crazily, slashing through the darkness, then something checked the ladder's fall. My feet scrabbled for the top of the Camper as I fought to regain my balance. Letting go of the ladder, I flattened myself against the rough slate wall, scraping my cheek as I slid to my knees onto the campervan's roof. There was a metallic groan of protest as the van shifted.

Gradually, the movement stopped.

From above me, the ladder swung gently back and forth with a regular, metronomic creak: *high-low, high-low.* In the light from the torch, I saw it was dangling by a single bolt. Its other fixings had pulled out of the wall, leaving the ladder swinging like a lopsided pendulum.

Jesus . . . Relief at the narrow escape was already dissipating, replaced by the knowledge that my only chance of getting out of the pit had gone. The ladder had almost stopped swinging but now hung down at an angle, further out of reach than ever. Even if by some miracle I could stretch to it, it wouldn't take my weight. The top of the quarry pit might as well be a mile away.

There was no point in staying on the van's roof any longer. I might as well climb down. Listlessly, I straightened from the quarry wall and without thinking lowered my arms. Straight away I felt the torch tucked into my sleeve start to slip. *No!* I tried to grab it as it slid out, but my gloved fingers only knocked it further away. I watched, horrified, as its beam cartwheeled through the blackness.

Then, with an echoing clatter, it hit the ground and went out.

I lost track of how long I spent in the dark. My watch's luminous hands said it was still only early afternoon. It felt later than that, and when I checked again later I realised the hands hadn't moved. It must have been broken when I fell, but it didn't really matter.

I wasn't going anywhere.

I'd managed to climb down from the Camper's roof without incident. Even in complete darkness it was easy enough. I felt for handholds, then lowered myself down where I thought the wheel arch would be. My jacket snagged on something as I slid down, tearing the tough fabric.

That didn't matter either.

I could have stayed by the campervan. There was no way out on the other side of the draped tarpaulin either, and the skeletons of the woman and child held no fear for me. Sadness, yes, but I felt comfortable in their company. They were the physical remnants of two individuals who had died years ago, that was all. Now they were completing the slow transition back to the inorganic minerals that had formed them. Ashes to ashes, dust to dust. The process was as natural as it was inevitable, the end of the journey made by all living things.

Including me.

Even if Hooley didn't come back – and by now it was obvious he didn't have to – I wouldn't survive very long in that freezing temperature. There was no warmth or comfort at the bottom of the stone pit, and even my thick clothing and boots were no protection against the penetrating cold. The slate walls seemed to gather and hoard it, so that it radiated from them.

Like a tomb.

That was the reason I went back to the side of the pit where I'd fallen in. If I was going to die down there I'd rather it be with the thought of open sky above me, not rotting boards and filthy canvas. And it was better to keep moving. If I wanted to stay alive even a short time longer I couldn't afford to stay still. My body's core temperature was already dropping, and I'd lose heat even faster if I was inactive.

So, arms outstretched, I'd edged blindly across the pit's uneven floor towards where I knew the tarpaulin was hanging down. I'd found the torch almost straight away, inadvertently kicking it with my boot. I heard it skitter away across the rocky ground, following the sound and groping with my gloved hands until they felt the cold metal cylinder. I'd hoped I might be able to get it working again, but pressing the on/off switch produced no results, and the LED bulbs fell away in pieces when I touched them.

Even in the dark, it wasn't difficult to find the hanging folds of tarpaulin. I felt for the gap carefully, not wanting to dislodge any more of the stiff canvas. Once I'd found it I crouched down and crawled underneath, keeping as low as I could until I could stand without snagging myself on it.

I must have got turned around somehow, because the rucksack wasn't where I'd thought it would be. It took me a while to find it, and I felt a small flicker of satisfaction as I reached inside. I'd packed a Thermos of coffee that morning, and while it wouldn't ultimately make any difference, just the promise of a hot drink felt like luxury in that cold sepulchre.

When I lifted it out and heard the soft chinking sound my heart sank. The Thermos was ancient, its vacuum chamber made of glass rather than steel. Broken glass, now.

I put it down again without bothering to open it.

There was nothing to do after that. The darkness was so deep it hurt my eyes. No light came from above me, not even from the opening I'd made when I'd fallen. Without my watch I'd no way of knowing if it was night outside, or if the remaining daylight couldn't filter all the way down here. To keep myself warm I paced backwards and forwards, one hand outstretched to touch the slate wall so I didn't become disorientated and blunder into the tarpaulin. When I bored of that I tried running on the spot or doing knee bends, rubbing my arms briskly to try and encourage circulation.

It was a trade-off, though. The more effort I put into keeping warm, the faster I used up what reserves I had left. And no matter what I did, eventually I was going to succumb to the cold. All I was doing was postponing it.

But it was better than giving up.

I'd become aware my attention was wandering. The cold sapped my strength and dulled my senses, and the dark was hypnotic. More than once I jerked back to myself, realising I'd wandered away from the pit wall without noticing. The fourth or fifth time it happened, I stopped pacing, bleakly wondering if perhaps I shouldn't just sit down and rest. Wrap my arms around myself for warmth and just . . . let it happen.

I wasn't ready for that yet, though. Reaching out my hands, I began edging back over to where I thought the pit wall should be.

From somewhere in the darkness, I heard a *crack*.

I couldn't tell where the noise came from. I stood still, thinking I must have trodden on something. Then I heard it again, and this time I knew I hadn't made it myself.

It was coming from above me.

I stayed where I was, not daring to move. The sounds grew louder, distinguishable now as the snap of breaking branches.

Hooley was coming back.

The realisation brought a rush of panic. I'd thought he'd given up, decided he might as well just leave me to die down here. I looked around, instinctively searching for a place to hide. But the blackness surrounding me was impenetrable. The noise of Hooley's approach was already much closer, and now I could see a glimmer above me as a bright light revealed the opening I'd made when I'd fallen through the tarpaulin. The next second a dazzling torch beam split the darkness as it stabbed into the pit. Anger, fear and impotence churned in me as I stood rooted to the spot, knowing there was no place to run or hide. A moment later a voice echoed down.

'Dr Hunter?'

I didn't answer. The voice wasn't the gruff bellow I'd been expecting. Familiar, but not Hooley's.

'Dr Hunter, you down there?'

The torch beam probed through the silhouetted rhododendron branches before fixing on me. I flinched from the sudden brightness, still not able to believe it was who I thought.

'Who's that?' I called, shielding my eyes.

'Sorry.' The light moved out of my face. 'It's Eddie. Eddie Drummond?'

He turned the torch around and shone it on himself. His round face peered down anxiously from the edge of the pit. *Oh, Thank Christ . . .*

'You all right, Dr Hunter?'

I am now. I found my voice. 'How did you find me?'

'Jon took a turn for the worse, and when you didn't come back like you said, I thought I'd better see where you were.'

He sounded so apologetic it was all I could do not to laugh. 'I-I didn't know whereabouts you were, but you said you were coming up here. And then I saw all the tracks in the snow so I . . . I followed them.'

Relief made me weak. 'Can you get me out?'

He didn't answer. He'd moved the torch so it was shining behind me, onto where the tarpaulin hid the rest of the pit.

'Eddie, did you hear me?' I called up.

'I-I'm just thinking . . . There's a tow rope in my car. Hang on.'

The light disappeared, plunging me into darkness. I felt a sudden pang at being left alone again. *Car?* I couldn't see how Eddie would have been able to drive up here, and if he had to go all the way home again for the rope I'd have a long wait for him to get back. Then I remembered that Hooley had brought the snowplough up the lane. That would have cleared the undergrowth from it as well as the snow.

It would be ironic if he'd done me a favour.

Eddie was back sooner than I'd expected, but I was still relieved when he appeared at the top of the pit again.

'Here, tie this round you.'

He threw one end of a rope down. It snagged on one of the rhododendron branches protruding into the gap, and it took him a few goes to flick it loose. His aim was better the second time, and the rope made it all the way down.

Doubts began to form as I looped it around me. It was blue nylon, no thicker than my finger. It could probably take my weight, but I hadn't climbed a rope in years. And if I fell I wasn't sure Eddie would be able to take the strain.

'Do you think you need to get help?' I called.

'Uh . . . No, I-I should be all right.' He tried to sound confident, but I could hear the undertone of worry. 'I've fastened the other end of the rope around a tree. That'll hold it, and I'll take the slack as you pull yourself up.'

I wanted to ask if he was sure, that I didn't know if I *could* pull myself up. But the longer I stayed down there the harder it would be. And I'd no idea where Hooley was. If he came back. . .

'Did you tell Hooley where I was going?' I asked, fumbling as I tried to tie the rope around my chest. My hands were unsteady, clumsy from the cold.

'Uh . . . I-I might have said to him earlier, when he took the snowplough out. Sorry, shouldn't I have said anything?'

'It doesn't matter.'

This wasn't the time to go into it. I needed to get out, but my numb fingers wouldn't co-operate as I struggled to fasten the rope.

'You want to tie that off in a double-hitch so it doesn't come undone.' Eddie called down, holding the torch beam onto me so I could see what I was doing. 'No, the other end. That's it.'

I finished tying the rope, cinching it tight to make sure it wouldn't come loose.

'I'm ready,' I told him.

'All right. You climb and I'll pull you up.'

Looking up the shadowy slate face to its edge, where Eddie was peering down with the torch, I felt my doubts grow. It looked a long way away, and I hadn't given much thought as to *how* I'd climb out. Did I try to shimmy up the rope, or brace my boots against the wall? Suddenly, the whole idea seemed like madness.

'You ready?' Eddie called.

No. 'Yes.'

He disappeared, taking the torch with him. He must have set it on the ground nearby because some light still spilt over the edge, enough for me to see where I was climbing. A moment later I felt the rope draw taut. Reaching up to grip it with both hands, I began to climb, pulling myself up the rope while I tried to push with my feet against the wall. It was even harder than I'd expected. The rope tightened uncomfortably around my chest as it took my weight. I'd managed to go two or three metres when one of my boots slipped and suddenly I was falling.

For a heartbeat I was weightless, then I jerked to a stop as the rope broke my fall. It constricted my chest, forcing the breath from me. I clutched at the rough nylon as my feet scrabbled against the slate face.

'You . . . you all right, Dr Hunter?' Eddie panted, his voice hoarse.

I closed my eyes, gasping as I braced my boots against the wall again.

'Just slipped . . .'

Taking a painful breath, I began to climb again.

Inch by inch, the top of the pit came closer. My arms and shoulders quivered and burnt with the strain, but then my head was above the edge, followed by my shoulders. I dragged myself over the lip, clawing at the ground until my legs were clear before allowing myself to collapse.

Face down, I sucked in breaths scented by wet, loamy earth. Rolling onto my back, I looked up through the canopy of rhododendron leaves at the bright glimmers of sky, letting icy drips from the thawing snow patter down onto me. I'd never seen or felt anything more glorious.

'Thank you . . .' I panted, fumbling at the knotted rope with clumsy fingers. They throbbed painfully, but through the discomfort and blood pulsing in my ears a new sound registered. I looked up to see Eddie's face twisted in misery.

He was crying.

'Eddie, what's—?'

My words faltered as I saw there was someone standing behind him. The other end of the rope that was tied around my chest dangled from the big hands.

'You're heavier than you look,' Hooley grinned.

Chapter 31

I stared at him, too stunned to speak.

'Cat got your tongue?' Hooley's grin was savage. 'I just saved your life. Aren't you going to thank me?'

He was standing in the ragged tunnel hacked through the rhododendron thicket. Chopped branches, leaves and sawdust lay everywhere, and one of his cheeks was gashed open, the wound clotted with dried blood. He hadn't been lying about that, but he'd played me for a fool in every other way.

He wasn't the only one.

Eddie wouldn't meet my eyes. He'd stopped crying but stood with his head bowed, his tear-blotched face etched with self-loathing.

The euphoria I'd felt moments before had turned to ash. I started to push myself up, but Hooley yanked on the rope, jerking me to my knees in the dirt.

'I didn't tell you to get up.'

I started to speak but then I saw the red chainsaw on the ground next to Hooley, and the words died in my throat. His grin widened when he saw where I was looking.

'Play nice and I won't have to use it.'

I found my voice. 'What do you want?'

'What, you deaf? I told you, I want your phone. Soon as you give it me we can all go home.'

The lie was so obvious it wasn't worth acknowledging. 'Deleting the photographs won't do you any good. There's too much other evidence.'

'Yeah, like what? Bits of chopped-up bone? What good's that going to do 'em?' He tapped the side of his head with a finger. 'I'm not fucking stupid, I've thought it through.'

No! No, you haven't! Nothing Hooley had done, or was about to do, would stop the truth from coming out, but the man was too blinkered, too smugly deluded, to see it. Anger and exasperation drowned out my fear.

'You've thought it *through*?' I almost yelled. 'What about Maud? Did you think *that* through as well?'

I saw Eddie flinch at her name, but I'd no time for him. Hooley's grin soured but he tried to shrug it off.

'What about her? I'd got waterproofs and gloves on. Nobody's going to know it was me.'

'She'd just *suspended* you! Don't you think the police are going to find *out*?'

'So what?' He seemed genuinely baffled. 'She walked in when I was putting the chainsaw back, that's why I offed her. It had fuck all to do with being suspended. Old Maud would've probably let me off with another warning, same as before.'

'It's still a *motive!* You're going to be the first person the police want to question, do you seriously believe you're going to fool them? This isn't like twenty-six years ago! They're going to be focusing on *you* this time!'

'Yeah?' He laughed, looking at Eddie as though inviting him to share the joke. 'Like I'm going to believe whatever bollocks this wanker tells me.'

Oh, for God's sake . . . I turned to Eddie as well. He'd said nothing since I'd climbed out of the pit, but his face was a mask of guilt and shame. Whatever was going on between him and Hooley, I couldn't believe he was a willing party.

'Tell him, Eddie. You know killing me isn't going to do any good.'

Hooley smirked. 'Go on, Eddie, tell me.'

Eddie's eyes were haunted. 'He's right, Vic. Maybe you should—'

'What? Tell the police everything? That what you want?' Hooley glared at him, daring him to argue, then gave a nod. 'Thought not.'

286

'Listen—' I began, but my words were cut off as Hooley gave the rope another jerk, pulling me off balance.

'Last chance. Give me your phone or I'll cut your fucking legs off and take it anyway.'

The jaundiced eyes burnt with the promise of violence. He was going to kill me whatever I did, but I couldn't see any way out. The only way through the thicket was past Hooley, and even if I didn't have the rope tied round my chest I was in no shape to try that. I barely had enough strength to stand, let alone run or fight.

'It won't do you any good without the code,' I stalled.

'Big deal, I'll break the fucker.'

'If you do you won't know what else is on it.'

I was bluffing. There was nothing on my phone that could incriminate him except the photographs, but Hooley didn't know that. His eyes narrowed.

'What's that supposed to mean?'

'Tell me what happened to Jed Beddoes and Owen Reese first.'

Hooley gave an incredulous laugh. 'You're a cheeky fucker, aren't you?'

'Tell me what happened and I'll give you the code,' I said, desperate to keep him talking. 'I know you killed them—'

'You know fuck all!'

'—but I don't know why. Or what the campervan's doing down there.' I motioned behind me to the quarry pit. 'I saw the bodies in it. Did you kill Megan and Willow as well?'

'Fuck this,' Hooley said, and reached for the chainsaw.

'For Christ's sake, Vic, just tell him!' Eddie burst out. 'What difference does it make?'

Hooley glared at him, then back at me. I held my breath, trying to show a confidence I didn't feel.

'Fuck it,' he said. 'Yeah, I killed Reese. I didn't kill Jed, though. That was nothing to do with me, was it Eddie?'

He was grinning, beginning to enjoy himself. Eddie hung his head, saying nothing. I was starting to realise there was more going on here than I'd thought.

'Start with Owen Reese,' I said. 'Why did you kill him?'

'He had it coming. Stuck-up cunt.' Hooley's grin had vanished, replaced by an ugly scowl. 'Thought he was hard, smacking Jed around in front of half the pub. I could've taken him, no problem. Fucker just got lucky.'

I tried to make sense of that. 'What are you talking about?'

'Owen had a fight with Jed, outside The Perseverance,' Eddie said, his chin coming up with something like defiance. 'Over a woman. Vic tried to jump him, so Owen decked him as well—'

'Fuck off, Eddie! I slipped,' Hooley snarled. 'I didn't see you trying to do anything, either! You just stood there like a wet fart!'

It was beginning to come together now. They were talking about the fight first Maud and then Nisha had told me about, when Owen Reese had confronted Jed over Megan. Maud had said something about one of Jed's friends trying to intervene and being knocked down as well.

Now I knew who.

'*That's* why you killed Owen Reese?' I said, unable to keep the contempt from my voice. 'Because you lost a *fight* with him?'

'I didn't fucking lose it! Bastard got lucky!' Hooley's face had darkened, his big fist bunching on the rope I still had tied around me. 'Twat deserved everything he had coming to him. Poncing round, acting like his shit didn't stink! Didn't stop him fucking that hippy bitch did it? Or killing her and her kid!'

Whatever I'd expected, it wasn't that. '*Owen Reese* killed them?'

'Didn't know that, did you?' Hooley grinned, his good humour returning. 'I'd gone out early hunting rabbits and saw him up near the ghyll, standing by this big hole he'd dug. I didn't know what it was for, not then. There were no bodies in it or anything. He was just stood there, crying like a baby. He'd got a spade next to him and there was a mattock lying a few feet away. You know what one of them is?'

I didn't bother to nod, knowing where this was going. A mattock was a heavy digging tool, like a cross between a pick and a blunt-bladed axe. Hooley's eyes had a sadistic glitter as he continued.

'I mean, he was practically asking for it. Everybody already thought he'd topped Jed, so I thought gift horse and mouth,

288

and all that. He was making so much noise he never heard me go up behind him. I picked up the mattock and whacked him in the head with it. Boom, down he goes, straight in the hole! Silly fucker dug his own grave!'

He gave a wheezing laugh.

'I filled it in and thought that was it, job's a good 'un. Then I came down here and saw the van with them inside.' He jerked his head towards the pit behind me. 'It was parked on top then, not down there. Jesus, talk about fucking *stink*. That was why the bastard was digging the hole, Mr-respectable-fucking-family-man was going to bury them. I thought about leaving it where it was, but the cops'd only just finished looking for Jed. I didn't want those bastards sniffing round again if anybody found it, so I rolled it into the pit and then fetched Eddie to help me cover it up. That tarpaulin you fell through? That was his idea. He's good at covering things up. Aren't you, Eddie? My little helper.'

Hooley's smirk was sadistic. Eddie stared down at his feet, his shoulders slumped as though the weight of the world was on them. I was more certain than ever that Hooley had some hold over him. Whatever it was, it had to be something bad. Bad enough for Eddie to help him cover up three murders.

'Owen Reese didn't kill Jed Beddoes, did he?' I asked.

Eddie wouldn't look up, but Hooley's sly grin grew broader.

'Fuck, no, that wasn't him. Was it, Eddie?'

The look on Eddie's face was awful to see. 'Come on, Vic, there's no need to—'

'"*Come on, Vic*,"' Hooley mocked. 'Go on, tell him who killed Jed, Eddie. You were the one wanting to tell him, so tell him.'

'Please, Vic—'

'*Fucking tell him!*'

For an instant the look Eddie gave him was murderous, then the brief rebellion died. Eddie seemed to slump, looking down as he spoke.

'It was his dad.'

I thought at first I must have misheard. 'Wynn Beddoes killed his own *son*?'

'That's right. Evie's old man,' Hooley said, gleefully. 'I was in the gym with them when it kicked off. Wynn had a *fit* when he heard Reese had beaten the shit out of Jed. Said it made him look bad, told Jed he was ashamed of him, all that stuff. The old man was getting on even then, but he was still hard as nails. Jed gave him a bit of lip back, so his dad clouted him across his face. Only a slap but it sounded like a fucking gun going off! So then Jed, the stupid fucker, loses his rag and pops his old man one! I don't think he could believe he'd done it, because he just stood there, like *oh shit*. Next thing, Wynn just *hits* him! Not a slap this time, I mean a proper full-on punch. *Bam!*'

Still holding the rope, Hooley smacked his own fist into his open palm, eyes shining as he relived it.

'Fuck me, I've never seen anybody hit so hard! It was like Jed's lights had been switched off. He goes down backwards, like a plank, and bang! Cracks his head on a steel dumbbell! Blood everywhere, you could see straight off he was a goner. His old man just lost it. Starts wailing, crying, he was in a right state.' Hooley puffed himself up, as though proud of the memory. 'So I told him I'd sort it. And we did. Didn't we, Eddie?'

Eddie said nothing, his expression one of shame and misery. Hooley's sneer broadened as he looked at him.

'Evie doesn't know about that, though, does she? What do you reckon she'd say if she found out her old man killed her big brother and then Eddie helped get rid of his body?'

Eddie was ashen. 'Jesus, Vic . . .'

'What? You're the one who wanted to tell fuckface here. Happy now?' He turned to me, any pretence of a smile gone. 'Right, so now you know. Let's have your phone.'

I tried to think of something else I could say, some way to head off what was coming, but couldn't. With an almost out of body sense of unreality, I took my phone from my jacket pocket.

'Unlock it first,' Hooley said.

'I can't.'

'Don't piss me about—'

'I *can't*. It's dead, it ran out of charge.'

The yellow eyes glared at me. 'Go and get it, Eddie.'

'Vic, I don't—'

'Just fucking get it!'

Eddie came over, broken branches snagging on his jacket in the narrow space. He still couldn't look at me.

'I'm sorry,' he muttered when I gave him the phone.

So was I.

Hooley snatched the phone from Eddie. He scowled at the screen, stabbing at it uselessly.

'I told you, it's dead,' I said.

'Think you're fucking clever, don't you?' He lowered the phone. 'You said there was other stuff on it, not just photos. What?'

'You'll have to find that out yourself.'

Hooley stared at me for a second or two, then shook his head. 'Naw, that's bollocks. Fuck it.'

He threw down the phone down and stamped on it. There was a crunch of breaking glass and plastic. He stamped on it again, grinding the heel into it until the phone's casing was in shards. With a grunt he bent down and picked the sim card out of the broken circuitry.

Holding it up for me to see, he snapped it in his thick fingers.

I kept my face impassive, taking a grim satisfaction in the thought of the copied photographs on my laptop. Hooley's next words shattered it.

'What about back-ups?'

I tried to hide my shock. 'There aren't any. You said yourself the internet was down.'

'You must have another way to back shit up. One of those memory sticks or some other bollocks.'

'I don't.'

'Don't fucking lie.'

'I'm not. I wasn't expecting to get stuck here. Or for some idiot to knock out the phones and internet.'

Hooley's small eyes considered me. I stared back, trying to hide my tension and praying he'd swallow the half-truth. A crafty smile split the stubbled jowls.

'Lying bastard. That first night in The Persey, I saw you with—'

He broke off, cocking his head to listen. A moment later I heard it as well, a soft whickering noise. I felt disbelief, still not allowing myself to hope. But the sound grew louder until it was obvious to all of us what it was.

The rotors of a helicopter.

Eddie broke the frozen silence. 'Vic, is that—?'

Hooley was already hurrying from the thicket, branches cracking and snapping as he crashed through them. He still had hold of the rope, and I was almost dragged from my feet as it snapped taut. I tried to pull against him, but it was like trying to stop a runaway truck. I almost fell over the abandoned chainsaw as I was hauled after him, barging Eddie out of the way as he looked on in shock.

Raising my arms to protect my face, I stumbled through the gauntlet of broken branches and into what remained of the daylight. Hooley had stopped as well, the rope now dangling limply from his hand as he scanned the sky. The sound of the helicopter echoed from the surrounding mountains. It was impossible to pinpoint but the air thrummed with the echoing chop of its rotors.

Then I saw it, angling across the mountainside perhaps a half mile away. It was flying low, its livery standing out against the white snow.

The dark blue and yellow of a police helicopter.

'HERE!' I shouted, waving my arms. 'OVER HERE!'

'*Shuddup!*' Hooley snarled, yanking on the rope.

I stumbled but kept on my feet, ignoring him as I waved and shouted at the helicopter. It was too far away to see me, let alone hear, but I didn't care.

'HERE!' I yelled, exultantly.

'*Shut the FUCK UP!*' Hooley bellowed, and now I could hear the panic in his voice. I staggered as he wrenched at the rope again, but his heart wasn't in it. He couldn't tear his eyes from the helicopter, and when it banked to double back he abruptly dropped the rope and ran.

Breathless, I watched him go. No longer a threat, just a big, overweight man floundering through the snow. He disappeared behind the rhododendron thicket towards the lane, and a few seconds later the snowplough's diesel engine coughed to life. It quickly receded, and as though co-ordinated the helicopter chose that moment to leave as well.

I watched until it was no longer in sight, feeling a pang of loss as the sound of its rotors faded to silence.

I knew it would be back, though. Somehow, miraculously, the police must have found out that the village was cut off. The helicopter hadn't made any attempt to land, so it was probably a reconnaissance flight. The low cloud would have prevented satellite imagery being used to assess the situation on the ground, and given the conditions a suitable landing site would need to be identified before emergency teams were flown in.

I realised I was shivering, and not just from the cold. Now the immediate threat was over, all the aches and discomfort I'd shut my mind to were making themselves felt. Every muscle ached, my hip was throbbing from where I must have banged it, and my ribs hurt when I breathed, bruised from either the fall or the rope tied around my chest. Or both.

I began plucking at the knot, trying to work some feeling back into my numb fingers, and only then remembered Eddie.

In all the drama I'd somehow forgotten him. He'd emerged from the rhododendron thicket, but he didn't have the chainsaw with him, and he was making no attempt to escape. Standing in the snow he looked small and defeated, like an ageing schoolboy in a too-big parka.

Neither of us said anything. Then Eddie gestured at the rope. 'Here, let me—'

'Stay there!' I raised a warning hand as he started forward.

He stopped. 'I wasn't . . . I'm not going to do anything. I'm done. With all of it.'

I looked at him, still wary. I didn't get any sense of threat from him, only sadness and shame.

That didn't mean I was letting him anywhere near me.

293

'I can manage,' I said, pulling off my gloves. 'Where's Hooley going?'

'I don't know.'

'Do you want him to hurt anyone else?' I asked. 'You can't cover for him anymore. If you know where he's gone you need to tell me.'

'I *don't*, I swear!' He sounded close to tears again. 'On Evie and the kids' lives!'

Bizarrely, I found myself believing him. 'Will he go after Jon?' I asked, picking at the knot. The rope was wet and my weight had pulled it taut as iron.

'Jon Reese?' Eddie seemed surprised. 'Why should he?'

'He murdered Jon's father, didn't he?'

'There's no reason for Vic to go after him, though. Anyway, he wouldn't do anything while Jon is staying with us. Not with Evie and the kids there.'

I didn't share his confidence. But I couldn't believe Eddie would be so blasé if he thought his family was in any danger. He frowned, watching me struggle with the knot.

'You should let me—'

'No!' It came out more violently than I'd intended. 'I said stay where you are.'

Eddie actually looked hurt. 'I don't blame you for not wanting to trust me, but . . . Look at you. You can barely stand up.'

He had a point. I'd made no headway on the rope. My fingers were raw and bleeding, and my hands felt like blocks of ice.

Reluctantly, I let them drop. 'If you try anything . . .'

'I won't,' he said, hurrying forwards.

He seemed pathetically relieved to help. I watched him warily, but even after what had happened I still didn't feel in any danger.

'If Hooley's not going after Reese then where would he go?' I asked, as he began to unravel the knot.

'I don't *know*, honestly. Vic doesn't tell me what he's going to do. He doesn't know himself half the time. He's probably just going to hole up somewhere.'

I hoped he was right, but somehow I couldn't believe it. A kernel of disquiet had begun to form in my chest. Hooley couldn't get far, not with the village snowbound and cut off. He'd already smashed my phone, so as far as he knew there wasn't any reason to—

All the fatigue, my aches and pains, everything vanished as it came to me. Hooley had been about to say something before he'd heard the police helicopter. Something about the first time I'd gone into The Perseverance, and I knew now what it was. I'd been complacent about him smashing my phone, thinking he didn't know about the copies of the crime scene photographs on my laptop. But I'd forgotten he'd seen me with it in the pub the night I'd become lost. Christ, he'd even ridiculed me over it.

'What's this for? Bit of secretarial work?'

And now he'd remembered. He couldn't be sure I'd backed up the crime scene photographs onto it, but he wouldn't take the chance. Even though destroying them wouldn't help, that wouldn't stop him. Hooley hadn't thought through anything he'd done so far, and with the police on the way he'd be panicking more than ever. And even he would be able to guess where the laptop was now. I snatched the rope from Eddie's hands as he finished untying the knot.

'The hotel,' I said, fear for Nisha and Kiran wiping out everything else. 'Hooley's gone to Hillside House.'

Chapter 32

The fastest way back to Hillside House was down the hiking trail through the woods. Hooley would make much better time in the snowplough but it was a longer route, and he wouldn't have cleared the narrow and winding stretch of road that ran from the crossroads to the hotel. That would still be blocked with snow, and difficult to negotiate in a heavy truck, snowplough or not. It would slow Hooley up, though not for long.

I had to hope it would be long enough.

'Go home and wait for the police,' I told Eddie, and set off across the snow in a clumsy run.

'Wait . . .!' he called after me.

I kept on going. Even though the snow had begun to melt it was still deep enough to make running difficult, and I was already near-exhausted. I hurt all over and my legs felt weak and unsteady. I was labouring after only a few yards but I didn't slow.

If anything happened to Nisha and Kiran because of me . . .

Slogging through the snow, I didn't realise Eddie had come after me until I heard the crunch of his boots behind me.

'You need to go home,' I rasped, my breathing already ragged as he caught up.

'I'm coming with you.'

'No, you're—'

'I'm *done* with it, all right?' There was a determination I'd not heard before in his voice. 'I never wanted any of this! It's gone on too long already, I don't . . . I don't want anyone else getting hurt.'

It sounded sincere but the memory of how he'd helped Hooley was too fresh. By now we'd reached the top of the hiking trail. I hadn't come up this section with Jon, so the snow on the steeply wooded hillside was still untouched. But it was thawing fast, and the edges of the railway timber steps were already showing through. That at least meant we could see where the trail was, although the melting snow made the ground treacherously muddy. And the tree-lined slope looked dauntingly steep as it dropped away in front of me.

'It's a bit late for that,' I said, beginning to descend the rough steps. 'You've caused enough—'

I broke off as I slipped, snow cascading down onto me as I clutched onto a tree to keep myself from falling.

'Steady,' Eddie panted, grabbing hold of my arm. 'You're going to break your neck like that.'

I pulled my arm free, trying to disregard my protesting muscles. 'Go home, Eddie.'

I started down the steps again. He followed me.

'You need my help,' he said stubbornly. 'You can't tackle Vic on your own, not in the state you're in.'

I ignored him, focusing on not falling again on the steep hiking trail. But his words struck home. Even if I managed to make it back to Hillside House in time, I would still need to stop Hooley somehow. He'd left the chainsaw at Foss Ghyll, but he was still a big man and used to violence.

'Please!' Eddie persisted, still following. 'You said yourself, it's over. Look, I don't blame you for not trusting me, but it's all going to come out now anyway. I know it won't make up for what I've done but at least let me help stop Vic hurting anyone else!'

I didn't answer, grabbing hold of a low branch to help me negotiate a rugged stretch of slope. I knew I'd be a fool to trust Eddie. His contrition could be an act, an attempt to show himself in a better light now his and Hooley's crimes were about to come out.

Yet I found myself believing him. Not because his shame and remorse seemed real, although they did. But because he sounded *relieved*. As though a weight he'd been under for years had finally been lifted.

'You go first,' I said, moving to one side so he could pass me. I could use his help, and I couldn't stop him following me anyway.

Still, I felt easier having him where I could see him.

'It wasn't like Vic said,' he blurted, breath misting as he made his way down the snowy trail in front of me. 'I didn't want to help him. He didn't give me a choice.'

'There's always a choice,' I said, worry and fatigue making me harsh.

'I know, you're right, but . . . sometimes you make the wrong one, and then you're stuck. You can't take it back.'

As much as I wanted to know what had happened, I didn't want Eddie rehearsing his excuses on me. 'You should wait and tell it to the police.'

'I will, but . . . I just want someone to *know*, all right? I-I don't know what's going to happen, and if things go bad I don't . . .' He drew a shaky breath. 'I don't want Evie to think it was how Vic says.'

It was a valid point. We'd reached the section of trail that Jon and I had used before branching off. The trampled snow was thawing even more quickly, making the trail easier to see. Before much longer we'd be back at Hillside House, so this might be the only opportunity to find out the truth about what had happened.

Curiosity won out. 'So why did you help him?'

Eddie took a moment or two to answer, as though the words still didn't want to come.

'Vic turned up at my door one night, not long after Jed had the fight with Owen Reese. He said he was doing a favour for Evie's dad and wanted me to help him. He wouldn't say what it was, just that I should go with him. I didn't even know where we were going, but he drove us out to the yard and told me to open the gates. I'd only just been promoted and I didn't want to get into trouble, but Vic got mad when I asked why. He said he only wanted to go up into the plantation, and did I want him to tell Evie's dad that I wouldn't help?'

Ahead of me on the trail Eddie paused, as though expecting me to comment. When I didn't, he continued.

'He . . . he drove us up one of the logging tracks and parked in the plantation. I swear to God, I'd no idea what was going on. I thought Wynn might have killed one of his dogs or something and wanted us to bury it. But then Vic opened the car boot and . . . and he'd got *Jed* in there! He was lying on bin liners, and his head was covered in blood. Vic told me the same as he told you, that Wynn had hit him. Killed him with one punch. I felt sick, I-I didn't know what to *do!* I wanted to call the police, but Vic asked if I really wanted to be the one to send Evie's dad to prison for killing her brother? He said . . . he said he was doing me a *favour* letting me help, because Evie's dad would owe both of us. As if that mattered.'

'But you still helped him.'

I couldn't keep the accusation from my voice. I saw Eddie bow his head, then he nodded.

'Vic was going to bury him where the spruces were already fully grown. But I knew they'd be felled in a few years, and we'd have to dig through their roots to bury him. There was an area that had just been planted with spruce whips – you know, saplings? – so I thought there was less chance of the grave being found there. It'd be decades before they were felled, and if we planted one on top no one'd ever think there was a grave under it. Not once it'd grown.' He hesitated, as though embarrassed. 'It seemed more respectful, as well. Like a marker.'

I didn't think Evie would appreciate the gesture. 'I don't—'

'There's more,' he said. 'When we went to get Jed out of the boot he . . . he opened his eyes and started gasping. For a second I thought, Oh, thank God, he's still alive, it's going to be all right! But then . . . then Vic put his hands over Jed's face, covering his mouth and nose, and started pressing down. Hard, putting all his weight on it. I shouted at him to-to *stop* but he wouldn't and then . . . then Jed went still again. I-I said Jesus, Vic, what have you *done*, but he just shrugged. Said he was just tidying things up for Evie's dad. And then . . . then he came over and wiped his hands on me. All the blood, on my *face*, my

300

clothes! And he *grinned* and goes, there you go, he's on you as well. Now you've got to help. Oh, fuck . . .!'

I felt a strange mix of pity and disgust as Eddie broke off, his shoulders heaving. I gave him a few seconds before I spoke.

'Did Beddoes ever say anything to you about it himself?'

'Not a word.' Eddie cleared his throat, fighting to steady his voice. 'I had to help Vic clean the gym afterwards, with the blood and everything. Wynn was there but he seemed out of it. Like he didn't know what was going on. It wasn't long after that he had his first stroke. He was in hospital for weeks, and when he came out it was like he couldn't remember what had happened. He acted like he really thought Owen Reese had done something to Jed.'

Shock could have contributed to Beddoes' stroke, and his impaired memory might be the result of neurological damage from that. But his amnesia seemed suspiciously selective.

'Could he have been putting it on?' I asked, breathless as we picked our way down a steeper stretch of slope.

Eddie seemed to think about it before he answered. 'I don't think so. And if he was, he ended up believing it himself. He goes berserk if anyone so much as mentions Owen Reese. You saw that yourself in the pub.'

I hadn't forgotten. 'What about the rest of it? Was Hooley telling the truth about Jon's father?'

'I think so. He was pleased with himself because he got a spruce whip from the plantation and planted that on the grave, same as we had with Jed. But I had nothing to do with it,' Eddie said quickly, glancing back at me. 'Or that poor woman and her little girl. I didn't feel so bad about Owen Reese getting the blame for Jed when I found out about that. First I knew about it was when Vic turned up wanting me to help him after he'd rolled the campervan into the quarry pit. He should have just left well alone. The police already thought Owen Reese had done a runner, and they'd searched up by the old army camp for Jed. They wouldn't have bothered searching round there again, so it wasn't as though they'd have found either of the graves. And at least the woman and her daughter could have had a decent burial. But Vic panicked, same as he's doing now. Left his fingerprints and God knows what else all over the van and then wanted me to bail him out.'

An aggrieved note had crept into Eddie's voice, but I was thinking about the pathetic remains in the wrecked VW Camper. Jon's father might be innocent of Jed Beddoes' death, but he was guilty of something worse. For whatever reason, jealousy or something else, he hadn't just murdered the woman he'd been sleeping with, he'd taken the life of her daughter as well.

Jon's father was a child killer.

'Weren't you worried the van would be found anyway?' I asked.

'I was worried about *everything!* But the quarry pit was too big to fill in without an excavator, and the tarpaulin was the only thing I could think of to cover it. I hoped if anyone saw it they'd think it was to keep people from falling in, but I was a nervous wreck. To start with I kept going back up there to check the tarpaulin, make sure it hadn't blown off or anything, but it hadn't and after a bit I stopped. I suppose the van would have been found eventually, but we got lucky with the rhododendrons spreading round it like that. When I went up again there a couple of years later, I wouldn't have guessed the pit was there if I hadn't known.'

Tell me about it.

The hiking trail was starting to level out. It wouldn't be long before we were back at Hillside House and I speeded up, sick with worry for Nisha and Kiran. Eddie misread my silence.

'I-I know what you're thinking,' he stammered breathlessly, keeping pace with me. 'I'm a weak piece of shit, I know I am. But how could I say anything after that? How could I tell Evie? She's got no time for Vic, she can't understand why I put up with him. Jesus, the times I've thought I couldn't stand it anymore, that I'd have to say *something*. But I never had the nerve, and then we had the kids and . . . I-I just *couldn't!*'

'You're going to have to say something now,' I said.

'I know.' He sounded empty. 'I just . . . I just want to be the one to tell Evie. That's all.'

There was no time for more questions. Ahead of us in the fading light I saw we'd come to the stile leading to Hillside House. Neither of us spoke as we approached it. Eddie climbed over first. He stopped on the other side, chest rising and falling as he looked up and down the long driveway we'd emerged onto.

'It's not been cleared. We must've beaten Vic here.'

By then I'd climbed over the stile and seen the thick snow still on the drive for myself. *Thank God . . .* The winter twilight was peaceful and quiet, unbroken by even a faint growl of a diesel engine. Yet even through my relief there was a growing disquiet. Hooley should have been here by now. Even if he'd had to clear the road up from the crossroads, he should have beaten us to Hillside House in the snowplough. I told myself I might be wrong about him going after my laptop, that he might be trying to hole up somewhere as Eddie had said. But that didn't ring true, and even as I tried to convince myself I saw new tracks beside the ones I'd left on the driveway earlier.

'Somebody's been along here,' Eddie said, worriedly.

For a bad moment I thought Hooley might have abandoned the snowplough and come the rest of the way on foot. But the impressions in the snow were too small to be his, and they were heading away from the hotel. Running next to them was a line of smaller tracks made by a dog's paws, and when I saw those I realised Nisha had grown tired of waiting. She'd taken Kiran and Max and gone to see her husband.

Along the same road as Hooley.

Chapter 33

Dusk was falling as Eddie and I hurried after Nisha. The hedge-rows on either side of the winding road blocked our view of what lay ahead, and at each curve or bend I found myself tensing for what we might find. But the thawing snow showed only Nisha and Max's tracks, hers straight, the labrador's more meandering where he'd veered off to investigate some new scent.

'These could be from hours ago,' Eddie had said, hurrying after me as I'd set off up the driveway. 'She could've left long before Vic came back. She's probably with Evie by now.'

I hoped he was right, but I saved my breath for the walk through the snow.

The hedgerows prevented us from seeing the crossroads until we were almost on top of it. Nisha's tracks turned off here, taking the road to Evie and Eddie's bungalow. Both that road and the one that led into the village had been cleared, the snow shoved into dirty white banks on either side where the plough blade had passed.

'Looks like you were right. He's gone back to the village,' I said, feeling some of the urgency leaving me.

Though only until I saw Eddie's face.

'That's where he cleared the road earlier,' he said, and his voice held a new tension. 'The plough's only been down there once. He's not come back this way.'

Now he'd pointed it out, I saw what he meant. The snow-plough's tyres had left heavy cross-hatched impressions in the scraped and flattened snow on the road. But there was only one set. If Hooley had taken the snowplough back to the village there should have been another set as well, overwriting them.

Wherever he'd gone, Hooley hadn't come this far.

Eddie began walking even faster. 'Vic wouldn't go to ours, there's no reason to. It's not like Jon Reese knows anything. And Evie and the kids are there.'

He sounded as though he hoped repeating it might make it true. The thin smear of snow left by the plough was starting to freeze over, crisping and cracking underfoot as we followed the road to Evie and Eddie's. My tracks from before had been erased by the snowplough but Nisha's were clearly visible, accompanied by neater holes made by the labrador's paws as Max had trotted alongside.

That meant they'd come along here after the road had been cleared, but there was still nothing to suggest Hooley had been back this way after he'd gone tearing off down the lane from Foss Ghyll in the snowplough. It didn't make any sense.

Until we saw why.

The snowplough was overturned at the bottom of the lane. It lay on its side, a grubby old truck with its V-shaped plough blade buried in the hedgerow opposite. It was easy to see what had happened. Hooley had come down the lane too fast and lost control when he tried to make the turn. The steel-barred gate had been torn off, and the snowplough lay in a mess of splintered bushes, churned earth and muddy snow. Its windscreen was crazed, as though someone's head had hit it, and the driver's door stood open. A weaving line of footprints led away from the truck.

Heading towards Evie and Eddie's bungalow.

'Oh, no . . .' Eddie said, his voice hushed. 'Oh, no.'

He broke into a run.

Finding a second wind from somewhere, I set off after him. I was hobbling, my bruised hip throbbing mercilessly, but I'd have had no hope of catching Eddie anyway. He was running like a man possessed, kicking through the snow on the uncleared road to his home, but he knew as well as I did that Hooley had too big a lead.

No matter how fast we ran we were already too late.

One small relief was that Nisha's tracks continued past the overturned snowplough. She must have come this way before Hooley crashed, though only just. There was a patch of more disturbed snow where she seemed to have stopped and turned. Probably when she'd heard the snowplough coming down the lane behind her. Her tracks even started back towards it, before she'd turned and headed for the bungalow again. But now her tracks were more ragged, while Max's pawprints were more widely spaced.

They'd been running.

My chest and throat were burning as I struggled to keep up with Eddie. The bungalow's low roofline was visible ahead of us now, the dim lights showing in its windows glowing in the twilight. The sound of a dog barking carried across the snow.

Then it cut off.

As we approached the bungalow I saw that the front door was hanging open, broken on its hinges. Eddie pounded up the driveway ahead of me and vanished into the house.

'*Evie! EVIE!*'

Over the blood pumping in my ears I could hear shouting and a dog's frantic barks as I went inside. The hallway was empty, the only light coming from a knocked-over hurricane lantern.

In its dirty orange glow I saw the blood.

It was spattered on the wall, pooled in dark gouts on the floor. On the floor, a trail of bloodied bedding led towards the bedroom Jon had been in. The door of that stood open as well, enough for me to see the bed was empty. A commotion was coming from the kitchen at the far end, loud voices and hysterical crying. I started towards it and had to lean against the wall, knocking some of the framed photographs askew as a wave of dizziness swept over me. *Don't pass out now! Get it together!*

I staggered down the hallway and into the kitchen. The sudden noise and colours were overwhelming. Eddie stood in the centre of the room, tears streaming down his contorted face. His two youngest children clung to him, crying and all talking at once. Evie was hugging their sobbing older daughter with one arm.

307

Her face was like stone, bone-white but for a livid bruise on one cheek and blood smeared from a swollen lip.

There was no sign of anyone else.

'Is everyone all right?' I gasped.

Evie's look was scathing, but she gave a stiff nod.

'Nisha and Kiran . . . ?'

'They're in the lounge. Her husband got knocked about a bit but he's OK.' A shrug. 'No worse, anyway.'

It was slowly registering that no one here was badly hurt, that the blood spilt wasn't any of theirs.

'Where's Hooley?' I asked.

'Gone.' Still hugging her daughter, Evie motioned with her head towards the back door. 'Out there.'

The back door was closed, but I saw now that blood spatters led across the vinyl flooring to it. Bloodied handprints were smeared around the door handle, as though someone had groped at it before wrenching it open. I looked back at Evie. A spasm of emotion creased her face, but her chin came up in defiance.

'I shot him.'

I tried to make sense of that. I couldn't see any gun, and there was no smell of gunpowder. But then, as though drawn to it, my eyes went to what was on the kitchen table.

Lying among the scattered plates and mugs was Drew's pistol crossbow.

My breath swirled in the light from the hurricane lantern as I closed the back door behind me. I stood for a few seconds in the freezing darkness, holding up the lantern to survey the snow-covered back garden. It wasn't hard to see which way Hooley had gone. An unsteady furrow showed where he'd blundered through the snow, dappling it with bloody spatters.

It led into the spruce plantation.

The tall trees reared up behind the bungalow, a wall of deeper shadow looming over the garden. I tramped across the snow and stopped at their edge. Beyond the lantern's glow was an impenetrable blackness. It wasn't the thought of going after Hooley on my own that made me hesitate. He was badly injured and had lost too much blood to pose any threat. But I was aching and exhausted, and the idea of going into that dark and silent forest filled me with a primitive dread.

It had been bad enough in daylight.

I'd been to look in on Nisha and Jon before coming outside. The three of them had been huddled in the lounge. Jon was on the sofa, sleeping but with a feverish flush to his cheeks. He had a new graze on the side of his head, nasty but not serious. Nisha sat on an armchair next to him. She had Kiran on her lap and Max lay by her feet as though protecting them.

'I couldn't wait any longer,' she'd said quietly, her voice on the verge of breaking. 'I waited as long as I could, but the light started to drop and you still hadn't come back. I couldn't just stay there.'

While I'd checked Jon over Nisha told me how, frantic with worry, she'd bundled up Kiran and set off with Max to Evie's and Eddie's. She'd only just gone past the lane when the snow-plough had come tearing down, going too fast to stop. It had overturned, crashing into the hedgerow as it tried to make the turn, and as Nisha had started back to help she'd seen Hooley crawl out.

'When I saw it was him, I don't know why, I-I just *knew*,' she'd said, her hands clenched tight. 'I just turned and ran.'

It was as well she had. She'd heard Hooley shout. Then, like a hound pursuing a fleeing rabbit, he'd set off after her.

Floundering with Kiran through the snow on the uncleared stretch of road, she'd made it to Evie and Eddie's bungalow and banged on the door with Hooley close behind. Opening it, Evie had taken one look outside and let her in. She'd managed to slam and lock the door, but it had burst open when Hooley had thrown himself against it.

'He'd got blood all over his face and he was bellowing like a *madman!*' Nisha's voice was unsteady. 'Evie tried to stop him coming in, and he just *hit* her! It was awful! The dogs were barking, the kids were screaming and crying, and all the time Hooley was yelling, "W*here is it? Where is it?*"'

My laptop, I realised. Panicked by the police helicopter and dazed, probably concussed from the crash, I doubted he even knew what he was doing anymore. Any rational thought had been swept away by the blind need to destroy the photographs. And in that chaos of violence and noise, Jon had stumbled out of his bedroom and tried to stop him.

'I thought Hooley was going to kill him,' Nisha said, a tremor in her voice. 'Jon could barely stand up, and then Hooley suddenly *screamed* and grabbed his stomach. There was so much blood! I didn't know what had happened, until I saw Evie standing there with a crossbow.'

Not long after that Eddie and I had arrived. And now here I was, standing in the cold night, preparing to look for the injured man who'd tried to kill me. I'd put it off long enough. Holding the lantern in front of me, I went into the plantation.

The tall spruce trees closed ranks around me. Even though the lighter covering of snow under the canopy had thawed, the light from the lantern showed which way Hooley had gone. He'd left a scuffed trail through the dead covering of spruce needles, dark smears of blood showing where he'd clutched at tree trunks for support.

I'd gone a short way in when I saw gleaming eyes ahead of me in the dark. A moment later Beddoes' young lurcher trotted out from the shadows. It greeted me like an old friend, dark patches glistening wetly on its muzzle. When I tried to usher the dog back home it pranced away, bounding ahead of me into the trees.

Hooley wasn't much further. He was slumped at the base of a spruce tree, lying with his back against the trunk and his hands clasped to his stomach. In the lamplight the blood that soaked his lower body looked black against the grubby yellow of the high-vis jacket. His face was shockingly pale beneath the dirty stubble, his lips tinged blue from either cold or blood loss. I thought he was dead, but his eyes flickered open when I knelt next to him.

'Bitch shot me . . .'

'Don't talk. Lie still, let me take a look.'

It wasn't good. The crossbow bolt had punched through the high-vis jacket, burying itself in his stomach up to the quarrel. The short stub rose and fell with his breathing like a buoy on a bloodstained ocean. I could smell Hooley's rank odour: alcohol, sour sweat and blood. And the heavier stink of faecal matter where the bolt had pierced his intestines.

'Hurts . . .' Hooley said.

The lurcher appeared beside us out of the darkness, tongue lolling. I pushed it away as it tried to nuzzle at Hooley.

''S all right,' Hooley slurred, extending an unsteady hand for the dog to lick. 'He came to find me . . . Keeping me warm . . .'

The dog wasn't there out of affection, the blood glistening on its muzzle testified to that. But I let Hooley cling to the illusion as I took hold of its collar, trying to decide what to do. Any attempt to move him would only make things worse. It wasn't like Jon's injury, where the puncture was in the meat of a large muscle. As bad as that was, a stomach wound like this was something else. Years before I'd survived a stabbing myself, but it had been a close thing and I'd been hospitalised straight away. Hooley's injury looked worse, and his panicked flight from the house would have caused more internal damage. This was far beyond any first aid I could provide. He needed emergency surgery, and I wasn't sure a wound like this would be survivable even then.

Out here, in freezing conditions . . .

'I'm going to go back for some blankets,' I told him, beginning to get up. If nothing else, I could at least try to make him more comfortable.

'No . . .' he moaned, his face puckering.

'I won't be long—'

His clutched at my sleeve. 'No! Don't leave me on my own . . .'

I had to resist the impulse to pull away. This was the same man who'd brutally murdered Maud and Owen Reese, who only a few hours before had tried to kill me with a chainsaw. But whatever Hooley had done, whether this was the justice he deserved or not, he was suffering now. I lived with enough regrets already without adding to them with an act of petty spite.

I knelt beside him again. Hooley's eyes were squeezed shut, tears leaking from them as he groped for my hand. His was icy, calloused and sticky with blood. I hesitated, then held it.

A short time later I saw the glow from a lantern approaching through the trees. Its ghostly white glow uplit Eddie's face, turning it into a shadowed Halloween mask as he stood by Hooley's feet, staring down without expression.

'He's dead, then?'

I nodded, setting down the cold hand and climbing stiffly to my feet. Light-headed from standing up, I swayed as I looked down at the dead man. All Hooley's violence and bluster was gone. Whoever and whatever he'd been, nothing of it remained here.

Only the carnage he'd left behind.

There was nothing else I could do out there, and I needed to get back to Jon. Too drained to talk, I started off back to the house with Eddie. He had hold of the lurcher, which had come trotting back happily when he'd called it.

'How long do you think it'll take the police to get here?' he asked, as we made our way back through the spruce trees.

I'd been wondering that myself. The helicopter would have confirmed the washed-out road, and by now the police would have realised the phone lines were down as well. But they didn't know about the remains, or the deaths, or that there was a medical emergency. As far as they were concerned this was still only a cut-off village, and probably not the only one after the storm and snow.

Urgent, but not life or death.

'A few hours. Morning, perhaps,' I said. 'Have you talked to Evie yet?'

He gave a short nod, his expression bleak.

'What she did, it was self-defence,' he blurted, as though it had been building up in him. 'She didn't have any choice. She was protecting Reese's family as well as her and the kids.'

'I'm sure that'll be taken into account.'

There would have to be an investigation, but I couldn't imagine Evie being charged.

There was no sign of her when we reached the bungalow, but that wasn't surprising. Leaving Eddie to try and make peace with his family, I went into the lounge.

Jon was still lying on the sofa but he was awake now, sitting propped up. He still looked terrible but at least he was conscious. Nisha had gone to sit on the sofa beside him, with Kiran sleeping on her lap. She'd been crying, and from the way she glanced at Jon I had the impression I'd walked in on something.

'Did you find Hooley?' she asked, keeping her voice low so as not to wake her son.

Exhaustion made me blunt. 'He's dead.'

Nisha looked winded. 'If I'd not come here. . .'

'If you'd not come here Hooley might have caught you and Kiran. I'm glad the bastard's dead.' Jon's voice was slow and weak. His face was flushed but although his eyes shone with fever there was a clarity in them as he looked at me. 'Did he kill my dad?'

There was no point in lying. Jon already knew there were two bodies buried in the spruce plantation, not one. Even if he didn't know which was which, he'd have worked out that one of them must be his father's.

'He admitted it, yes.'

Jon closed his eyes, turning his head away. 'What about Maud and Jed Beddoes? Did he kill them as well?'

'That's for the police to decide.' I didn't want to get into how Beddoes' youngest son had died, not in Evie and Eddie's house. 'You need to get some sleep.'

'He's right,' Nisha told him worriedly, reaching to squeeze his hand. 'It can wait till later—'

'No, it can't. It's waited too long already.' Jon's chest rose and fell. 'There's something you need to tell the police. In case I can't.'

'Jon, don't,' Nisha said, urgently.

He ignored her. 'The woman and girl who my dad and Jed fought about . . . they never left the village. They . . . they died.'

I tried not to react but the memory of the wrecked VW Camper in that dank pit was still too fresh. Some of what I was feeling must have shown. A frown crossed Jon's face.

313

'You already knew, didn't you . . . ?'

Even if information like that wasn't better coming from the police, telling Nisha and Jon about it was the last thing I felt like then. But I wouldn't be doing Jon any kindness by refusing to confirm it, and I was too tired to beat about the bush.

'I . . . found their bodies,' I said, trying to pick my words through the fatigue. 'They're at Foss Ghyll, but—'

'They were *there*? All this time? Oh, fuck. . .'

'Look, you need to rest,' I told him. 'Whatever your dad did, it can wait until—'

'*He didn't do anything!*'

Jon tried to sit up, but it was too much for him. He groped for Nisha's hand as he sank back, tears running down his cheeks. When he spoke, his voice was a whisper.

'My dad didn't kill them. I did.'

Chapter 34

Jon had just turned nine when the cream and orange VW Camper came to Edendale. The summer holiday was approaching and the long days were hot and dry. The boy spent most of them on his own, out on the mountains behind the hotel. There weren't many other boys his age in the village. He had some friends at school but that was five miles away, and none of them lived in Edendale.

Jon didn't mind. He'd always been content with his own company, and there was more than enough to keep him occupied. When he wasn't helping his father with the slow renovation of Hillside House, he would hike up the fell through the woods, clambering around the old slate quarry workings or building deadwood dams in the stream. Occasionally, if he was lucky, he'd see a deer. He'd creep towards it, trying to get as close as he could before, with a twitch of its ears, the animal would startle and bolt away.

But his favourite place was the old army training camp at Foss Ghyll. He would spend hours exploring the decaying log cabins and fighting imaginary battles among the overgrown brick fortifications. It was like having his personal ghost town to explore. He knew that his parents wanted to develop it, make the cabins habitable and refill the empty swimming pit, so grown-ups could pay to come here and play much as he was doing now.

But from what he'd overheard from his parents, among talk of banks and loans he didn't understand, that was a long way off. In the meantime, young Jon had Foss Ghyll to himself. The only other person who went there sometimes was his father, either taking measurements or working on one of the abandoned cabins. But that wasn't often. He was too busy trying to repair the hotel, and Jon's mother never even set foot up there. Foss Ghyll was his own private kingdom, abandoned and secret.

Until the afternoon the campervan came.

Jon was stunned when he saw it parked outside the cabin. It felt like a violation, an upturning of the natural order for someone else to be in this place. The van had an awning, under which a woman was cooking on a gas camping stove. She wore a loose top and faded jeans, her hair braided and beads and bracelets chinking around her neck and wrists. Music played from a radio, further shattering the tranquillity of the spot. Shocked immobile, Jon didn't even realise he was standing in plain view until the woman looked up and smiled.

Hey, you must be Jon, she'd said.

Her name was Megan, she told him. His dad was letting them use the campsite for a while. Still dazed by the news, he was distracted by someone climbing down from the campervan. A girl, a few years older than him, slim and pretty.

This is my daughter Willow, the woman told him. Blushing, Jon stammered out a hello. The girl smiled at him.

From that point on, Jon didn't mind sharing the campsite.

For the rest of the school holidays he went to see them most days. Megan didn't seem to mind, even seemed pleased to have him there. She found it funny – sweet – that he followed Willow around, colouring up whenever the girl spoke to him. Megan was an artist who used natural pigments for her paintings and created jewellery from pieces of wood and pebbles. Both she and Willow were vegetarians. They took Jon out foraging, showing him which plants, berries and fungi were edible or medicinal, and which should be avoided. In return he showed off his knowledge of the mountain and woods, taking them to his favourite spots. One of them, a rocky knoll of ground with a far-reaching view over the ravine, became their favourite as well.

I could stay here forever, Megan said.

Jon wasn't unaware of the undercurrents that followed the pair's arrival. Even before then his mother and father had been going through a rough patch. They argued frequently, generally about money. That was one reason Jon spent so much time outside by himself.

But the arguments rose to a new pitch after Megan and Willow set up camp on the mountain. Even though he tried to close his ears to it, he couldn't avoid noticing, or hearing Megan's name in the raised voices. A change was evident in the village, too. There were sniping comments, some veiled, others less so. One afternoon, he was on his way back from visiting the store for his mother when there was a burst of cruel laughter from across the street. Jed Beddoes, still in his tracksuit from the gym, was standing outside the pub with a jowly, heavy-set man with pig-like eyes, pints in hands. They were smirking as they looked over at Jon.

'Tell your dad to give her one for me!' the heavy-set man called, and they both laughed again.

It was Jon's first encounter with Vic Hooley.

The weather broke on the same day as the school holidays ended. Within days it was as though summer had never happened. The temperature plummeted while driving winds and rain, more like November than September, lashed the mountain. Jon rarely visited the campsite anymore, not only because of the foul weather but because the atmosphere up there was nearly as bad as at home. Without the summer sun, Megan and Willow seemed bereft. They'd come down with colds and rarely ventured far from the van. Cloistered in the cramped warmth of the camper, with a hissing stove to keep out the chill, Megan was distracted, while Willow seemed taciturn and morose.

By now Jon wished they'd never come to Edendale in the first place. He just wanted them to go, so everything could return to how it was before. Young as he was, even he could see they were unhappy as well, yet still they showed no sign of leaving.

Then came the fight between Jon's father and Jed Beddoes. Afterwards, his parents had their worst argument ever. Standing outside, he'd listened to the angry slamming and shouts coming from the kitchen. For God's sake, they're destroying this family, his mother yelled at his father. Just tell them to go! Who are you going to put first, us or them?

Unable to bear hearing any more, Jon ran off without hearing his father's answer.

The rain was pouring from grey skies when he reached the campsite. The campervan was battened down against the weather, its awning folded away and windows fogged with condensation. It seemed to take a long time before anyone answered his knock, but at last the door was slid back. A fug of humid warmth rolled out from inside as Megan gave him a wan smile.

I've brought you these, he said, holding out a carrier bag. Jumbled inside were things he'd foraged on his way there. Blackberries and beechnuts, bunches of sorrel and dandelion leaves, and a selection of wild mushrooms. Saucer-like field mushrooms, ceps and gold-coloured chanterelles; all edible fungi that Megan had taught him about over the summer.

Hidden among them were some she'd warned him to avoid.

Jon stared down at his hands, as though he could still see his gift to Megan and Willow in them.

'I just thought it'd make them ill. Give them an upset stomach or something, I never thought . . .'

He shut his eyes, tears running down his cheeks. I took a deep breath, absorbing what I'd heard. Many poisonous fungi were difficult to distinguish from harmless varieties. Not all were deadly, but some contained powerful toxins that could prove fatal without quick medical intervention, and sometimes even with it.

'Did you tell your parents?' I asked.

Jon couldn't look at me. 'Not straight away. I was too scared. But I blurted it out to them next day. God, the *look* my dad gave me . . . He didn't say anything, just ran out. He was gone ages, but then I heard the door go. I went into the kitchen, and he was sitting there, *crying*. I'd never seen my dad cry before, not even when his grandparents died. My mum was white. She didn't say a word, but my dad tried to pull himself together. He told me everything was all right, that he was just upset because

318

he'd run over a deer. He said Megan and Willow were fine, they hadn't eaten the mushrooms. But they'd decided to leave, and I could still get into trouble for it, so I was banned from going up to the old army camp in future. And he made me promise not to tell anyone what I'd done. Ever.'

A spasm of self-contempt contorted his features.

'Jesus, I can't believe I fucking *believed* him! I mean, crying because he'd run over a *deer*? He used to go hunting, I'd seen him skin and gut them!'

'You were just a kid, Jon,' Nisha said quietly, so as not to wake Kiran who was snuggled against her, asleep again. 'And you weren't the only one who thought they'd left. Half the village saw the campervan leave. Everybody thought they'd gone.'

'Was that your dad?' I asked him.

Jon gave a nod, wiping a hand clumsily across his eyes. 'I only found out just before my mum died. She told me Megan and Willow were already dead when he got to the campervan. He waited till it was dark then drove it through the village so people would think they'd packed up and left, then hid it in an abandoned barn a few miles away. It was only supposed to be for a day or two, while he could think what to do. But then Jed Beddoes went missing so my dad daren't go back for it, not while all the attention was on him. My mum said he hardly ate or slept for days. Clammed up, wouldn't talk to her. She started to wonder if he really *had* done something to Jed. Then one night after the police had finished searching, she woke up as my dad was getting ready to fetch the van. He said not to worry, he'd worked out what to do and he was going to sort everything. And that was the last time she saw him.'

Jon sagged back into the cushions, exhausted. He licked dry lips.

'Can I have some water . . .?'

'Here, let me,' I said as Nisha started to reach for the plastic child's mug on the coffee table, awkward because of Kiran.

I held it while Jon drank, thinking about what he'd said. I'd guessed that Owen Reese had been driving the Camper that had been seen leaving the village one night, the dazzle of its headlights preventing witnesses from seeing who was behind the wheel. But I'd assumed he would have doubled back to Foss Ghyll with the bodies relatively quickly. If he'd hidden the campervan and then been forced to wait before going back for it, the bodies would have been in an advanced state of decomposition after even a few days, bloated and seething with maggots.

In the campervan's close confines the stench would have been indescribable.

Yet Jon's father had still driven all the way back to Foss Ghyll with his silent passengers. That seemed an unnecessary risk when there were plenty of equally remote places for a grave on the surrounding moors and fells.

So why had he taken it?

Jon finished drinking and laid his head back onto the cushion. 'Do you want to rest?' I asked, setting the mug down.

But Jon wasn't listening. 'All this time, I blamed my dad. I thought he'd just abandoned us. Fucked off and left us to face what *he'd* done. The police were convinced he'd killed Jed and then done a runner. Everyone was, including me. No one in the village would talk to us, kids at school were saying my dad was a murderer. Christ, I *hated* him! My mum didn't want to believe it, but in the end even she did. And now it turns out he didn't do any of it, he was just trying to protect me. And Hooley, fucking *Hooley* . . .' He stared at me, his eyes glinting with fever. 'You sure he's dead?'

'I'm sure.'

He closed his eyes again. I thought he'd talked himself out, but then he carried on.

'Christ, I couldn't wait to get away from this place . . . I could never understand why my mum didn't just sell up and leave. It was obvious she hated it. I thought she was just being stubborn, holding on to it because of my dad. But she couldn't leave when she didn't know where my dad had buried Megan and Willow. She knew it would be somewhere on our land, and she didn't want to risk them being found. That's the only reason she told me, because if not she knew I'd sell the whole

320

fucking place as soon as she'd died.' Jon's face screwed up in pain. 'Jesus, Foss Ghyll . . . I should have known. Megan and Willow loved it up there . . .'

There it was again. There was still something missing here, one last piece that would provide context for everything else that had happened.

'He was taking a risk driving them back there,' I said, choosing my words carefully. 'Do you know why your dad would have done that?'

Jon opened his eyes and glared at me. 'He wasn't sleeping with her, if that's what you're thinking. Everybody got that wrong, including me. Megan . . .'

'It's all right, Jon,' Nisha cut in when he broke off. 'You don't have to do this now.'

'Yes, I do.' He groped for her hand, gripping it tightly before going on. 'Megan was my dad's sister.'

'His *sister*?' I echoed, stupidly.

'Half-sister, really.' Jon gave a listless shrug. 'Same mother, different fathers. My dad didn't even know she existed until she showed up out of the blue. Their mother had died a couple of years before and Megan didn't have any other family, so she felt it was time to introduce Willow to her uncle. No one else knew who she was, not even me. My dad always thought my grandma met his father after she ran off to London, but she told Megan she'd been raped by a local man when she was sixteen. She was too ashamed to tell anyone, so when she found out she was pregnant she ran away. That's why she never got in touch with my dad or wanted Megan to come here. She was scared what Wynn Beddoes might do.'

It took a moment for what he'd said to sink in. I stared at him. 'Wynn Beddoes is your *grandfather*?'

'Why do you think I grew the beard?' Jon gave a crooked smile. 'Families, eh?'

Christ, I thought, stunned. Yet even through my shock I realised the signs had been there all along. One reason I'd thought the skeleton in the spruce tree's roots belonged to Jed Beddoes was because its size and stature was similar to Wynn Beddoes'.

I'd taken that as a potential genetic inheritance, passed from father to son. And so it was.

Just not the son I'd thought.

That same resemblance was in front of me now, evident in the muscular build and strong facial bones of the man lying on the sofa.

'Megan said Beddoes persuaded my grandmother to meet him one night,' Jon went on, still holding Nisha's hand. 'He was the cock of the village back then. In his twenties, an up-and-coming boxer, good-looking, lots of girls hanging round. A real catch. My grandmother had to sneak out to meet him. He'd got some wine with him, and she wasn't used to drinking so . . . yeah. Afterwards Beddoes called her a whore and threatened to tell everyone she'd been begging for it and then wanted paying afterwards. Told her it'd be his word against hers, and who would they believe?'

Weak as he was, Jon's expression was murderous.

'After my dad was born in London, my grandmother couldn't cope. She was only a kid herself, so she came back and left my dad with her parents. She went back to London and got pregnant with Megan a couple of years later. Megan never knew who her own father was, because her mother was sleeping around by then, drinking and doing drugs. By the sound of it, Megan must have had a rough time. She started hanging around bands in her teens and had a fling with a guitarist or bass player, or something. He took off not long after she had Willow, though, and Megan didn't like being dependent on anyone after that. She got the Camper and home-schooled Willow so they could travel round. And they ended up here.'

Jon was starting to flag, his voice slurred and drowsy as whatever adrenaline had been fuelling him burnt off.

'When my dad found out about Beddoes he wanted to confront him, but my mum talked him out of it. She said he'd only be causing trouble, for us as well as Megan and Willow. Wasn't like there was any proof, and my mum was terrified what'd happen if my dad went to see him. Beddoes was still a hard bastard back then, and my dad had a temper as well. But then Jed started

322

spreading lies about Megan. Claiming she was sleeping with him, selling him drugs and stuff. My mum said that was bollocks because Megan didn't even drink after what she'd seen happen to her own mother, and she wouldn't have any time for a dickhead like Jed Beddoes anyway. But it was the final straw for my dad. He went to warn Jed off and . . . yeah. Things went to shit.'

So that was why Jon's father had fought with Jed Beddoes, publicly humiliating him – and Hooley, for good measure – and threatening Jed in front of eyewitnesses. Not because he was a jealous rival, but because he was protecting his sister.

Go near her again and I'll fucking kill you.

And with those few words, the tragedy that was still playing out had been set in motion.

'Does Wynn Beddoes know you're his grandson?' I asked.

'Who knows? My mum thought he might, but . . . what was she going to say? He wasn't going to admit it, was he?'

No, I thought, remembering the old man's uncompromising belligerence; no, he wasn't. A familial DNA test could confirm if Wynn Beddoes was Jon's grandfather, but that could only be done with his consent. I couldn't see Beddoes agreeing to that. And even then it would only prove their genetic relationship, not that he'd raped Jon's grandmother.

Jon was visibly tiring now. He needed to sleep, but there was one more thing I needed to ask.

'Did you ever go back to the army camp afterwards?'

If he had, he could hardly have missed the tarpaulin Eddie and Hooley used to conceal what was in the quarry pit at its edge. There was a haunted look in Jon's eyes as he answered.

'Would you?' He turned down his mouth, as though too exhausted to shrug. 'I went back once, a few years later, but the cabins had all been overgrown. It didn't look the same. Yesterday was the first time I'd been back since. Funny how you remember . . .'

He was slurring now, his eyelids drooping. It was time to end the conversation, but before I could Jon's face creased in a puzzled frown, as though something had only now occurred to him.

'You said Megan and Willow were at Foss Ghyll . . . How'd you find their graves in the snow . . . ?'

I hesitated. Jon didn't need to hear that his father had been killed by Hooley before he could bury them, not right now. He'd learn the truth soon enough, but those details were better left till he was stronger.

And not in Evie and Eddie's house.

'You need to rest,' I said, getting to my feet. 'We can—'

I broke off as Max suddenly sat upright, ears cocked and alert. A moment later I heard it myself.

The heavy chop of an approaching helicopter.

'That's the police,' I said, and ran from the room.

I fumbled my boots back on and grabbed my coat, still struggling into it as I rushed outside. Stepping out into the cold night was a shock after the bungalow's warmth, but I barely noticed. Relief washed away my aches and fatigue as I hurried back along the icy road. The police were back much sooner than I'd expected. I could already see lights where the helicopter had put down near the village, an eerie white nimbus in the dark.

Soon, though, my injuries began to reassert themselves. By the time I'd reached the crossroads I was limping heavily, favouring my bruised hip. It wasn't helped when I slipped on the black ice that had formed as the cleared road re-froze, wrenching my side even more.

But not long after that I saw the helicopter itself. It had landed in a field on the outskirts of the village, on the side I was approaching from. It was much bigger than a standard force helicopter, and as I drew nearer I saw it was a large RAF transport. Police officers in bulky high-vis jackets were unloading lighting and equipment when I reached the field. A small crowd of people from the village had beaten me there, drawn by the noise and lights. Their questions were being fielded by two PCs who were also keeping them back from the helicopter. I thought I might have to shout to make myself heard, but then one of a group of officers poring over a map looked over. She seemed to recognise me, and after speaking to the rest of the group she peeled off and came over.

324

She was a solidly built woman in her forties. I saw her take in my coat, scuffed and filthy from my fall into the quarry pit, but she made no comment as she led me past the crush of people.

'Dr Hunter?' she said, giving me a tight smile. 'Recognised you from your photograph. I'm DS Chaudry. Good to finally meet you.'

It took a second or two for her name and voice to register. Chaudry was the detective sergeant who'd I'd been liaising with about the search operation in Carlisle. The last thing I'd heard from her was when she'd texted to say the operation had been cancelled, and in my tired state I couldn't grasp how she could be in Edendale now, standing in a field with an RAF helicopter behind her.

'Are you OK, Dr Hunter?' she asked, frowning.

I tried to shake off my confusion. 'Yes, I'm just . . . I wasn't expecting to see you here.'

'Yeah, sorry about that. I tried to let you know we were coming, but I couldn't get hold of you with the comms down. I'm surprised your email managed to get through.'

'My email?'

'The one you sent earlier?' She was looking at me warily, now. 'You said there'd been a fatality, and you'd also found human remains? Please don't tell me it was a hoax.'

I'd completely forgotten about the email I'd tried to send. The last time I'd looked it was still sitting in my outbox. I'd assumed it had failed along with the text, and then things had happened too quickly to give it any more thought. But at some point – before my phone had run out of charge and then been smashed by Hooley – I must have passed through the same pocket of reception as before. Or perhaps a different one. It didn't matter, and I didn't care.

The police were here.

'It's not a hoax,' I told her, trying to collect my thoughts. 'We need an air ambulance for an adult male with a serious crossbow injury to the upper thigh. He's in a bad way. And there's been another fatality.'

'Another? Shit—'

'There are more human remains, as well,' I added, barely hearing her. 'Three of them, all skeletonised, although . . .'

I trailed off as I lost the thought, swaying on my feet. The other officers nearby had all stopped talking to stare at me. Chaudry was looking at me oddly.

'Let's get you sitting down,' she said, leading me towards the helicopter. 'Then you better tell me what the hell's going on.'

Chapter 35

It took over two weeks for a temporary bridge to be erected, connecting Edendale to the outside world once more. Even split into smaller sections, transporting the ungainly structure along the narrow mountain road was a tricky process. Once on site it had to be painstakingly assembled on the steep and uneven terrain, where one miscalculation could send the whole thing tumbling down the fell. Finally, though, the bridge was coaxed into place. Power and phone lines had already been restored by then, and now people were able to come and go to the village without a helicopter, some semblance of normality returned. But only a semblance.

It would be a long time before Edendale returned to normal.

On the night the police came, an air ambulance had arrived within the hour to take Jon to hospital. He'd been accompanied by Nisha and Kiran, and as I'd watched them go it had felt like a weight had been lifted from me. I'd turned down the offer of being checked out at the hospital as well. My injuries were painful but not serious, and if I left there was a good chance another forensic anthropologist would be brought in to work on the investigation. I didn't want that. The decision would ultimately be up to the SIO, but after all that happened I wanted to see things through myself.

Besides, someone had to look after Max.

It was too dangerous to show the police where I'd found the remains in the dark, so I spent the next few hours answering questions and giving my statement. I'd kept myself awake with hot coffee and sandwiches, but by the time I made my way back along the ice-smeared road to the hotel with Max and two PCs, I was nearly asleep on my feet. Nisha had given me the keys before she'd left with Jon, so I could use my room while they were away.

'Help yourself to whatever's there,' she'd told me, anxiously watching the paramedics tending to Jon. 'There's food in the pantry and plenty of firewood, so just make yourself at home.'

That would be easier said than done. In the dead of night, unlit and unlovely, Hillside House looked more like the setting for a horror film than ever. The PCs eyed it warily as we made our way down the snow-covered drive.

'This is where you've been staying?' one of them said. 'Jesus Christ.'

Wait till you see inside. Letting us into the darkened extension, I fetched the laptop from my room. Its battery still had enough power left to copy the crime scene photographs Hooley had tried so hard to destroy and transfer them to a police tablet. I thought I'd be relieved to finally hand them over, but I was too tired to feel anything. Once the PCs had gone, I fed Max, then dragged myself past the glittering eyes of the stuffed animals and up to my room.

I barely remember climbing into bed.

Sleep, food and anti-inflammatories didn't quite work miracles, but after a cold shower and breakfast, I at least felt able to function again. By then Max and I were no longer on our own. Since there was no way for police trailers or vehicles to be brought in without road access, Nisha had given permission for the hotel to be used as a makeshift incident room. While I'd slept an emergency generator and temporary satellite communications had been set up, along with chairs, desks and all the paraphernalia of a major police inquiry. The foyer was bustling when I came downstairs, voices echoing from the wood panelling and parquet floor.

For a short time, Hillside House had come back to life.

The transformation wasn't restricted to the hotel. A critical incident had been declared, and the sky over the village thrummed as RAF helicopters brought in civil engineers and technicians along with more police teams and equipment. The plantation yard, Evie and Eddie's bungalow and the section of spruce plantation behind it were cordoned off while SOCO teams carried out searches and recovered Maud's and Hooley's bodies. The crimes came as a shock to most people in the village, who'd gone to bed believing the worst problem facing their small community was a collapsed road. Instead, Edendale had woken to find itself at the centre of a homicide inquiry with multiple victims.

And suspects.

Eddie had surrendered himself to the police voluntarily. He'd confessed everything, cutting a forlorn figure as he was arrested and led away. I heard later from DS Chaudry that Evie had herded their children into another room when their father was taken from the house. Only she was there to see him go, standing in the kitchen with her arms folded, her feelings hidden behind a stony face.

In that much, at least, she was her father's daughter.

No charges were brought against her over Hooley's death. It was a clear case of self-defence, backed up by Nisha's witness statement. Evie had been offered counselling but had brusquely refused. Why do I need that, she'd asked. He's dead, isn't he?

No one grieved over Hooley, but his death left unanswered questions. It meant the police had to rely on Eddie's testimony as to what had happened, because Wynn Beddoes wasn't talking. The old man had met every attempt to question him with an intransigent silence. His age and frailty meant he wasn't fit to be taken into custody, so the police interviews had been carried out at The Perseverance. Unlike Eddie, there had been no confession, no expressions of remorse from him. The old man had refused even to confirm his name, his lantern jaw clamped shut as though to prevent any words escaping.

'He doesn't say a word. Just sits there jutting his chin out and glaring at you,' Chaudry complained over a paper cup of coffee from the police canteen set up at Hillside House. 'He's been checked out physically and we've heard him speaking, so we know he can. He just clams up when we start to question him. Not just us, either. He blanked his own daughter when she tried to get him to tell her what he'd done. A PC had to intervene when she lost it and started screaming at him, but the old man just sat there. We can't tell if he's just being bloody-minded or if there's some sort of cognitive issue going on. We're getting social services out to do an assessment, but my feeling is we're not going to get much out of him.'

Somehow that didn't surprise me. Still, Eddie had claimed that his father-in-law's apparent amnesia was genuine, and that might be true. People had been known to block out traumatic memories, and Beddoes was ninety, in poor health and with a history of strokes. He could well have some neurological damage, and at his age dementia couldn't be ruled out either.

Yet I had my doubts. Whatever guilt or remorse Beddoes might feel, I couldn't imagine him admitting to it, even to himself. That would have been a sign of weakness. And, after twenty-six years of silence, so would a confession.

Nobody told a Beddoes what to do.

As I'd hoped, I was asked to stay on to help recover the remains of the victims. Or four of them, at least. Brutal as Maud's murder was, it didn't require a forensic anthropologist to help with either identification or establishing the cause of death.

But the older crime scenes were a different matter. The Senior Investigation Officer, a balding Detective Superintendent called Buckley, didn't regard my being a witness as an obstacle, since police officers regularly appeared as witnesses on cases they'd worked on. As far as he was concerned it made no sense to bring in another forensic anthropologist when I was already on site and familiar with the crime scenes.

Too familiar, in some cases.

I'd chosen to stay in Edendale for the duration of the recovery work. It was more convenient than being shuttled to and from Carlisle every day, at least until the bodies had been taken to the mortuary. With Nisha and Kiran still staying in a B&B near the hospital to be close to Jon, the echoing corridors of Hillside

House would have made bleak lodgings if I'd been there on my own. But with the old hotel doubling as the major incident room, it was far from empty. As a bonus, it meant there was no shortage of volunteers to look after Max while I was out at the crime scenes, an arrangement the young labrador and his police babysitters all seemed happy about.

That first morning I'd taken Chaudry and teams of police and SOCOs up the fell to where I'd found the bodies. The thaw that had started the day before was continuing, and the musical drip of melting snow provided a constant backdrop as we went up the hiking trail and into the spruce plantation, first to where Owen Reese's fragmented skeleton was still covered over with snow, and then to where Jed Beddoes' remains were partially exposed in the eroded stream bank under the leaning spruce.

Lastly, I'd taken them to the old army camp at Foss Ghyll. The snow around the sprawling rhododendron thicket was churned and littered with leaves, scraps of bark and splintered branches scattered around the tunnel Hooley had slashed into the bushes. I led the way into the cave-like interior, the others following behind in single file as meltwater splashed onto us from the branches. In my mind I'd gone yards into the centre of the thicket, but we seemed to have gone hardly any distance before we came to the clearer area Hooley had hacked out by the quarry pit. The rotten tarpaulin sagged down into the hole where I'd fallen through, a six-foot-long black gash, like a toothless maw in the muddy ground.

Lying to one side, where Hooley had abandoned it, was the red chainsaw.

Until then I'd been too focused on bringing the police here to give any thought to how coming back might affect me. I'd been vaguely aware of feeling a building pressure of tension, but I'd tried to ignore it. Now it rose up and overwhelmed me. Suddenly I could feel the branches clawing at me again as I ran for my life, hear the deafening snarl of the chainsaw as Hooley slashed his way after me. I stopped dead, feeling as though the air had been sucked out of my lungs.

'You all right, Dr Hunter?' Chaudry asked.

The moment passed. I took a breath. Nodded.

'Fine.'

Jon had confessed everything to the police as soon as he was stable enough to make a statement. No decision had been taken on whether to press charges over the deaths of his aunt and cousin, but it looked unlikely. For one thing Jon had only been nine at the time and hadn't even realised they were dead. All he had to go on was what he'd heard from his mother, twenty-six years later, and even she hadn't seen the bodies herself. She'd only been relating what she'd been told by her husband.

'We can't build a case around a childhood memory and what amounts to hearsay from more than two decades ago,' Chaudry had said. 'Reese can't even remember what the mushrooms he's supposed to have given them looked like, let alone tell us what type they were. We've only got his word for it that they *were* poisonous, and even if they were there's no guarantee anyone ate them. Megan was supposed to be an experienced forager, so would she really have fed herself and her daughter mushrooms picked by a nine-year-old without checking what they were?'

It was a fair question. Establishing what had killed Megan and Willow wasn't going to be easy, but it was pointless speculating until we could examine their remains. Before that could happen the rhododendron thicket would have to be cleared from around the quarry pit, and the heavy tarpaulin carefully removed. Then, once the pit was open, a way to access it and safely recover the bodies in the wrecked campervan would have to be devised.

That would take time. So would recovering Owen Reese's pulverised bones, which were still buried under several inches of snow. The recovery couldn't start until that had melted and the SOCOs could see what they were dealing with. There had been talk of bringing in industrial gas heaters to speed up the process, but that was dismissed as impractical. As well as the difficulty of transporting heavy and cumbersome heaters up to the inaccessible spruce plantation – not to mention the fire risk, even in winter – such a rapid defrosting could potentially damage the bones even more. With the daytime temperatures higher now anyway, it was decided to wait and let the snow thaw naturally.

In the meantime, attention turned to Jed Beddoes' remains.

The spruce tree that had grown on top of the grave had to be felled first, as carefully as possible so as not to disturb the bones underneath. Then the skeleton had to be freed from its cage of roots. The ones growing through it were left in place to preserve the skeleton's integrity, each of them painstakingly sawn through further back so the entire thing could be lifted out intact and transported to the mortuary, roots and all.

The forensic pathologist, a cadaverously thin man called Lee, seemed delighted by the bizarre find. 'I have to say, this is a first for me,' he said as we watched the remains being cut free. 'Have you ever seen anything like this before?'

I thought about the grotesquerie of Owen Reese's skeleton before it had been destroyed, suspended scarecrow-like above my head. Lee would have seen the photogrammetry model I'd made of that from my photographs, but as striking as the 3D image was, it wasn't the same as seeing the real thing.

'Not often,' I said.

It was difficult to draw many conclusions with the skeleton still dirt-clogged and deformed by the roots that had grown through it. A post-mortem would have to be carried out and a formal identification made back at the mortuary, which I'd be helping Lee with. After that I'd be able to clean the skeleton of any remaining shreds of soft tissue prior to carrying out a thorough examination myself. But there was little doubt as to who this was, or how he'd died. Rotting leather training shoes were found in the grave, still with the disarticulated bones of the feet in them, while the skeleton was clothed in disintegrating rags of a sweat top and bottoms.

The sort of thing someone might wear for a gym workout.

Even more conclusive were the injuries. The left-hand side of the mandible – the lower jawbone – was dislocated and had several fractures along its length. The dislocation didn't appear to have caused any damage to the joint, which suggested the bone had still been 'wet' at the time, rather than dry and brittle.

Nor was there was any indication that the bone had begun to knit back together. The evidence all pointed to the injuries being perimortem, sustained close to or at the time of death. So were the fractures lines visible on the occipital – the triangular section of bone that forms the lower rear part of the skull.

That supported Hooley's account of Jed falling backwards and cracking his head on a barbell after being hit by his enraged father. Either of those injuries on their own could have been enough to kill him outright, as Hooley had claimed. Single punch killings were more common than many people thought, and a blow powerful enough to dislocate and shatter the jaw could easily have caused a fatal brain injury, even without the additional blunt trauma to the back of the skull.

But Jed Beddoes had sustained another injury as well, one that suggested a different version of events. The hyoid is a small, horseshoe-shaped bone that sits at the front of the neck under the mandible. Free-floating, meaning it connects to ligaments and cartilage rather than other bones, it's a fallacy that it always breaks in cases of strangulation. In fact it withstands pressure well, often surviving even in hangings or ligature deaths. So an intact hyoid doesn't necessarily rule out that someone was strangled.

A broken hyoid, however, is a strong indication that they were.

Jed Beddoes hyoid bone had snapped clean through in its body, or thickest part, as well as one of the 'horns' that formed one side of the horseshoe. It would have taken a considerable amount of pressure to do that, and while the damage could have been post-mortem, there was another explanation.

Hooley's brutal *coup de grace*.

According to Eddie, Hooley had smothered Jed Beddoes when the supposedly dead man had started to revive, pressing down with both hands on his nose and mouth and putting his full weight behind it. They were big hands, and that was a lot of weight.

Enough to have snapped the hyoid bone situated just under the jawbone as Jed struggled.

There was no way of proving that's what had happened, just as there was no way of proving the broken jawbone had been caused by a single punch from Wynn Beddoes. Hooley was dead and Beddoes wasn't talking, so there was only what Hooley had told me and Eddie's own account to go on. He could be lying, but if so it was hard to see what he hoped to gain. And his story fit the facts, explaining how Jed Beddoes' hyoid had been broken. There was no way Eddie could have known about that.

On the day his youngest son's body was recovered, Wynn Beddoes' condition suddenly deteriorated. He was taken by air ambulance to hospital, coincidentally the same one that housed the mortuary where Jed's remains were transported. How much of this Beddoes himself was aware no one was sure, because he was no longer speaking at all by then. He survived three more days, silent and uncommunicative to the end. None of his family visited him, even though they were offered seats on one of the regular police helicopter flights from the village.

When Chaudry told me he'd died, meekly and without fuss, she'd shaken her head in disgust.

'Can't help but think he's got off lightly,' she said. 'All the grief that man caused, and he gets to slip away in a hospital bed without even being charged. Where's the justice in that?'

I'd no answer. But for a man like Wynn Beddoes, who'd lived his entire life dominating those around him, dying alone and rejected by his family and community was a justice of sorts.

It would have to be enough.

Epilogue

Nearly a month after the winter storm blew me into Edendale, spring had transformed the village. The snow was long gone except for where it lingered on the blunt tops of the surrounding fells. Branches that had been bare and black were now bursting with buds and blossom, their colours vibrant in the bright sunlight.

My tyres bumped across the temporary bridge as I drove over where the culvert used to be. The lorry and flatbed trailer Hooley had crashed had been removed from the fell, but some of the timbers were still scattered on the slope below, too big and impractical to move. The gates of the spruce plantation were open when I drove past, the business of logging and timber finally resuming now the police cordon had been removed. I'd heard that a new manager had been brought in, and the vacant posts of bookkeeper and driver had also been filled.

It had been a good time for the job market in Edendale, if nothing else.

I'd spent the last ten days in Carlisle, staying at a modern hotel that had hot water, light and central heating, without a stuffed animal in sight. It was close to the mortuary where the remains of Megan and Willow Summers, Owen Reese and Jed Beddoes had been taken. Maud and Hooley's bodies were there as well, but I'd declined Professor Lee's invitation to be present at their post-mortems. There was no need for me to be there, and I'd no wish to observe as a forensic tourist.

I'd enough work to do of my own.

Helped by two mortuary assistants, I'd disarticulated the skeletal remains of the victims individually, soaking them in mild detergent baths overnight to clean and degrease the bones before reassembling them on gleaming steel mortuary tables. There were no surprises with the body recovered from beneath the leaning spruce tree. DNA testing and dental records identified it as belonging to Jed Beddoes, and while it wasn't possible to establish a cause of death purely from the bone trauma, the fractures to his jawbone and rear of the skull, and damage to the hyoid, all supported Eddie's account of how he'd died.

That still left the question of who was responsible for his death. His father, who'd punched him hard enough to shatter his jaw and cause him to fall and crack his skull? Or Hooley, who in his eagerness to ingratiate himself with Wynn Beddoes had snuffed out any chance of his injured son's survival? There was no way of knowing, but I found myself regretting that neither of them were still alive.

They both deserved to stand trial for what they'd done.

Owen Reese's reassembly proved more challenging. Once the snow had melted, SOCOs had spent days going over the muddy ground around the base of the fallen spruce, painstakingly searching for fragments of bone. Precious little remained intact after Hooley's assault with the chainsaw. The damage was comparable to the aftermath of a plane crash and needed much the same approach.

Reassembling the shattered pieces of skeleton was a grim jigsaw puzzle, made even harder because some of the fragments were so small that identifying them was virtually impossible. Still, together with the 3D photogrammetry model and photographs, it was possible to establish an accurate picture of the skeleton before Hooley had taken a chainsaw to it. Additional pieces of broken cranium had been found buried in the crater left by the fallen spruce's roots, and combined with the larger sections that had survived the chainsaw attack, these had allowed me to partially reassemble the skull. Enough, at least, to confirm how Owen Reese had died.

Hooley had told me he'd hit Jon's father from behind with a mattock, but he'd omitted some details. The shape of the wound showed the murder weapon had been a pick-mattock, double-ended with one side bladed and the other spiked like a pick-axe.

It had been the pick end that had killed Owen Reese.

The overhand blow had punched a large, jagged hole through the right parietal bone at the upper rear of the skull, allowing the tree's roots to penetrate the braincase and force their slow way out through the eye orbits. The mattock's pick would have pushed some bone fragments inside, but it had pulled others outwards as it was withdrawn. Held in place initially by the soft tissues, as they decomposed the broken fragments had become detached, falling outside the skull and remaining in the crater when the spruce blew down. The irony was that these had escaped Hooley's follow-up attack with the chainsaw, allowing me to reconstruct enough of the cranium to see the extent of the terrible wound.

Owen Reese would never have known what hit him.

A positive identification had been made by comparing the teeth of the mandible I'd rescued from the lurcher to Owen's old dental records. That was confirmed by familial DNA testing that showed the remains belonged to Jon Reese's biological father. Further tests had supported Jon's claim about his father's parentage, establishing beyond any reasonable doubt that Owen Reese was Wynn Beddoes' illegitimate son.

'That's going to ruffle a few feathers,' Chaudry commented. 'Can't see the Beddoes inviting Jon Reese round for a family Christmas dinner, somehow.'

Neither could I.

While there were still unanswered questions surrounding both Jed Beddoes' and Owen Reese's deaths, at least there was no doubt over *how* they'd died. The same couldn't be said for Megan and Willow. Once the rhododendron thicket had been cut back and the tarpaulin removed, the quarry pit and what it had hidden were exposed for the first time in twenty-six years. It seemed smaller and more mundane than I remembered, robbed of its menace in the daylight. A scaffolding tower had been erected for access, and after the wrecked campervan had been made secure, SOCOs had carefully removed the bundles of bone and cloth from inside.

The mother's and daughter's skeletal remains showed no signs of any trauma that might explain their deaths. Although that was far from conclusive – not all violence leaves its mark on bone – it was in keeping with Jon's claim that they'd been poisoned.

The problem was there was no evidence of that either. Even if the mushrooms Jon had given them were poisonous, and even if Megan and Willow had eaten them – which there was no way of knowing – after all this time there wouldn't be any trace of them left. Heavy metals such as lead can leave traces in bone but even that takes prolonged exposure. A natural, fast-acting toxin like Jon was talking about might have been detectable in the soft tissues but they had long since rotted away. It wouldn't have been absorbed into the bones.

And bones were all that we had left.

It meant there was no way to say conclusively how mother and daughter had died. That didn't mean the nine-year-old Jon *wasn't* responsible for their deaths. His mother and father had evidently believed he was, and now so did he. I couldn't entirely rule it out either, but there was another possibility.

One that Jon had unknowingly revealed himself.

There had been a noticeable change since I'd last been in Edendale. During the complicated body recoveries the huge police operation had practically taken over the village. I'd become used to seeing police vehicles, as well as the inevitable microphones and TV cameras once the bridge was in place. Now they'd all moved on, leaving behind a dazed community struggling to come to terms with what had happened. Still, as I drove along the main street I saw that the village store was open and people were going about their lives, just as they always had. Having finally yielded up its secrets – most of them, anyway – Edendale seemed to be doing its best to forget them again.

Although that would be harder for some than others. The doors of The Perseverance were closed, but as I drew level they opened

340

and Alun came out. He looked gaunter than I remembered, the strong bones of his face more prominent under the skin. He glanced at my car as I approached, and for a moment I could have been looking at his father. Then he turned away without expression, leaving me unsure if he'd recognised me or not.

I drove by without stopping.

The hedgerows on the road to the hotel were bursting with fresh green buds, their banks dappled with bluebells and yellow primroses. I had my window down and their scent filled the car, smelling like the essence of spring. As I drove up to Hillside House I saw the cheerful yellow flowers weren't the only sign that change was on its way.

Stuck into the ground by one of the crumbling gateposts was an estate agent's *For Sale* sign.

The towering rhododendrons lining the driveway were beginning to flower; pink, red and mauve blooms starting to burst from their buds. Seeing the dense, fleshy-leaved shrubs I felt a momentary tension, a fading echo of snapping branches, but the sunlight soon dispelled it. A few seconds later the driveway curved and I saw the hotel.

The dark granite of Hillside House seemed impervious to the new season. Its turreted walls looked angular and brutal against the backdrop of green peaks, no more inviting in the sunshine than at night in the driving rain.

Or perhaps that was just me. I parked in the same place as before and started along the path that led around the side of hotel. As I reached the back Max suddenly came bounding round the corner, almost bowling me over. I bent down to fuss him as he jumped up, whimpering and wagging his tail furiously.

'Hey, Max. Where've you come from?'

Maud didn't have any immediate family, and since her will hadn't made any provision for her pet the labrador's future was uncertain. I hadn't been able to take him with me to Carlisle so Nisha had offered to look after him until a new owner could be found.

I'd decided that might as well be me.

341

I'd grown fond of the young labrador while I'd been looking after him. It would mean making changes to fit him in with my work, but that was no bad thing. There was a park near my flat where I could take him for walks, and he could travel with me at least some of the time.

The more I thought about it, the more I liked the idea.

Nisha was in the garden, plucking new weeds from a freshly turned vegetable plot. She straightened, smiling when she saw me.

'I wondered why Max took off.' She straightened, pulling off a pair of gardening gloves. She looked better than the last time I'd seen her, her face less worn by strain. 'Jon won't be long. He's just taken Kiran out for a walk.'

'His leg's not bothering him too much, then?'

'Not really. He keeps doing his physio and goes for regular walks. Not too far yet, but he tries to do a bit more each day.' She looked at her watch. 'They shouldn't be long now. I'll stick the kettle on, if you fancy a coffee?'

'Thanks, I would.'

Max ran ahead of us, breaking off to investigate some scent in the garden when we went into the kitchen. A vase of wildflowers on the windowsill, and another on the table, added splashes of spring colour, brightening the dark room. Screensavers lit both computer monitors in the corner, one showing a tropical beach, the other the glowing lights of a night-time cityscape.

'I'm taking a morning off,' Nisha said, seeing me looking. 'The last couple of weeks have been full-on with work. Turns out disasters are good publicity.'

Her tone was wry, but she couldn't quite keep the smile from her face.

'I saw the "For Sale" sign when I came in,' I said, taking a seat as Nisha filled the kettle.

'Yeah, we decided to take the plunge. The estate agent warned us not to expect miracles, but if someone offers half even what they're asking we'll snatch their hands off.' Her expression was unclouded as she set the kettle onto the range hob. 'We might as well. There's no reason not to sell now.'

342

No, there wasn't. Not now the family skeletons had been brought out to air.

'Did you hear that the police aren't pressing charges against Jon?' Nisha asked, as though following the same train of thought.

'I did.' Chaudry had told me. 'That must be a relief.'

A trace of a shadow crossed her face. 'It is, yeah. Jon's still conflicted about it, though. I think part of him feels he shouldn't get off scot-free. But at least the media are finally leaving us alone. We haven't had anyone offering to buy his story for a few days now.'

'Did he consider it?' I could understand why he wouldn't, but in their situation the money must have been hard to resist.

'No, he wouldn't even speak to them. I'd be a liar if I said I wasn't tempted. Some of them were offering a *lot* of money. But Jon's still trying to come to terms with what happened. And what he did.' A heaviness seemed to come over her. 'It's a lot to contend with. For all of us.'

That was one of the reasons I was there. But I wanted to wait until Jon was back before broaching it.

'Have you seen anything of Evie?' I asked, changing the subject.

'Well, she's talking to us now, which is something. That's more than Alun's doing, but he doesn't talk much to anybody so that's no loss. Jon's met Evie a couple of times, but it's still awkward. Suddenly finding out they're related, and how Eddie helped Hooley cover everything up. There's a lot to unpick.'

There was. Not least because Evie was Jon's aunt. It would be nice to think there might be some sort of rapprochement between the two families, but that might be too much to expect.

'Has she mentioned Eddie?'

'Not to us. From what we've heard she's been to visit him, though. And she's taking their kids to see him soon, so perhaps she's coming round. He's going to be away for years, so I suppose they're going to have to work something out.' Nisha gave me a sideways glance. 'Jon's not pressing charges against Drew.'

That wasn't too big a surprise. The two were cousins, after all. 'Did Evie or Alun ask him not to?'

'No, but things are difficult enough for them as it is without another family member going to prison. Like Jon said, Drew's just a kid. If he gets a criminal record for assault it'll be with him for the rest of his life, and Jon doesn't want to be responsible for that. He might get his wrists slapped, community service or something, but it's being treated as a joke gone wrong.'

Some joke. 'I hope Drew appreciates it.'

Nisha gave a snort as she set the cup of coffee in front of me. 'I wouldn't go that far. But it was his crossbow that Evie shot Hooley with, and if not for that . . . Anyway, he's got a second chance, so it's up to him if he uses it.'

We both looked round as the door opened. Jon came in, carrying Kiran. He looked well, or better, at least. He'd still not regained the weight he'd lost, but there was a healthy colour to his face.

'Deer have been in the orchard again—' He broke off when he saw me. 'David. Nisha said you were coming.'

Shutting the door behind him, he set Kiran down on the floor. His son grinned gummily, hauling himself up by my leg before tottering across the floor towards Max. He sat down with a bump and gave the labrador a hefty pat, delighted with his new trick. The dog thumped its tail happily.

'How long has he been walking?' I asked, smiling.

'Just started.' A rare grin spread across Jon's face. 'We're learning together.'

'Nisha said your leg wasn't giving you too many problems.'

'It's getting there,' he said as he crossed the kitchen to the sink. He was still favouring his injured leg, but the limp was barely noticeable. 'So, have you finished in Carlisle?'

He couldn't bring himself to say *at the mortuary*. I saw the tension he tried to hide as he filled a glass with water from the tap.

'For now, anyway. I'm on my way back to London, so I wanted to drop by before I left.'

I'd have to appear at the coroner's inquest that would be held to investigate the flurry of violent deaths the village had seen, both old and new, but that wouldn't be for months. That was part of the reason I was there.

344

Jon came to sit down at the table. Both he and Nisha were trying to hide their nervousness.

'When you phoned you said there was something you wanted to talk about?' he said.

'I do, but this isn't official.' I hadn't cleared it with Chaudry or her SIO. Technically, I might be crossing a line. But if so it was a small one, and sometimes it's better to take the step regardless. 'There are a few questions I'd like to ask you about Megan and Willow.'

'I've already told the police everything I know. What's the point in going over it again?'

'Like I said, this isn't anything official. Please, just humour me.'

The tension was more evident in them both now. Jon sat stiffly, and Nisha remained standing, her hands tightly clenched as though she'd forgotten how to move.

'What do you want to know?' Jon asked, after a moment.

'You said that they had colds before they died. Is that right?'

He was frowning, trying to see where this was going. 'As far as I can remember. Why? Is it important?'

'Can you tell me anything more about their symptoms?'

'Christ, it's nearly thirty years ago! I was only nine, what do you expect me to remember?'

'Anything you can. It might be important.'

I thought he was going to baulk, but Nisha came over to stand beside him. She squeezed his shoulder.

'It can't hurt, Jon.'

He sighed. 'For what it's worth, I can remember they didn't look so good, and Megan saying they'd got a cold or flu or something. She joked that I shouldn't get too close, but that's about it. I'd got other things on my mind around then, I didn't take much notice.'

'Can you remember when this was?'

'God, I don't . . .' He stopped himself and gave a shrug. 'They were laid up in the Camper when I went to see them the day before. And then when . . . when I went there that last time, they seemed worse. But they were probably upset as well, what with all the shit that was going on. Look, is there a point to this?'

345

'Bear with me. You said they were spending a lot of time in their van?'

'That's right, the weather broke a few days before. The rain didn't let up and it turned really cold. I remember the weather being as shitty as I felt.'

'How did they keep warm?'

I remembered what he'd told me before, but I wanted him to go through it again now. He threw out his hands, growing exasperated.

'Jesus, I don't know. Extra sweaters and blankets, I expect. They'd got a portable gas heater, so they used to keep that going. Are you going to tell me why you're asking all this?'

I already knew about the gas heater. I'd noticed it jammed against the dashboard when I'd first shone my torch into the wreckage of the VW Camper. I'd not given it a thought at the time – I hadn't heard Jon's confession then, and I'd been more worried about finding a way out of the quarry pit. It was only later, during the recovery of Megan's and Willow's bodies, that its potential significance had occurred to me.

Nisha got it before Jon did. Her eyes widened as her hand went to her mouth. 'Oh my God . . .'

'*What*?' Jon demanded, exasperated. 'Jesus, will someone *talk* to me!'

'There's no way to be sure how Megan and Willow died,' I told him. 'Yes, it could have been from eating poisonous mushrooms. Depending on what type they are, symptoms can start relatively quickly. But they aren't usually fatal straight away, and Megan and Willow were dead when your father found them next morning. That's very quick. And you said they were ill before then, before they'd even eaten anything.'

'OK, so they had cold or flu. Maybe that made them more susceptible.'

'Perhaps. But the flu-like symptoms you've described fit early signs of carbon monoxide poisoning.'

Jon stared at me. 'Are you serious?'

'It can build up in any enclosed space where there's a gas heater or stove. Even a tent. There weren't carbon monoxide alarms

346

back then, and if the Camper's doors and windows were closed because of the bad weather there wouldn't have been much ventilation. It's odourless so Megan and Willow wouldn't have known it was building up. They'd just have felt progressively more tired and unwell, until eventually they lost consciousness.'

'No, but I mean . . .' Jon shook his head, trying to unscramble his thoughts. 'Wouldn't my dad have noticed when he found them?'

'Not necessarily. He'd gone up there thinking they'd eaten poison mushrooms, so when he found them dead he'd have assumed that was why. He wouldn't have been able to smell it, and the carbon monoxide would disperse once he opened the van door. If the heater had been left running constantly the gas cylinder could have run empty by then anyway. He might not have realised the heater had even been left on.'

Once he'd seen there was nothing he could do, Owen Reese would have been unlikely to linger in the van in any event. Apart from the shock of finding his sister and niece, their bodies would have already started to decompose after being inside the warm van for almost a day. Add to that vomiting being one symptom of carbon monoxide poisoning, and the likelihood that they would have voided their bowels, and Jon's father would have been too overwhelmed to notice details.

No wonder he'd needed time to think before deciding what to do with their bodies.

'That's . . .' Jon struggled to find words. 'Are you saying I *didn't* poison them? It wasn't the mushrooms?'

'I'm saying we don't know. There'll have to be an inquest, and the coroner might reach a different decision once all the evidence has been heard. But my guess is the verdict will still be inconclusive.'

He looked winded. 'So I'm never going to know if it was my fault.'

'Not for certain, no. But from what you've said I know which I think is more likely.'

When it came down to it there were few real certainties, in life or death. Jon would always have to live with the possible consequences of his actions. I couldn't help him with that.

But sometimes even a small hope can lighten the load.

I didn't stay long after that. Jon and Nisha were best left to process it on their own. Jon still looked troubled, but less so than before, and Nisha's eyes were brimming as she gave him a hug before busying herself making fresh coffee.

There was just one more thing to discuss.

'I've been thinking about Max,' I said. 'I don't think Maud would like to see him going to a dogs' shelter until he's rehomed. It's been good of you to look after him all this time, but—'

'Oh, don't worry about that.' Nisha waved off what I was going to say. 'I know we said it couldn't be for long, but . . . Well, everything was a bit up in the air back then. We've enjoyed having him and Kiran loves him to bits. It'll be nice for him to grow up with a dog in the house, so we'd like to keep him. I mean, we haven't spoken to Maud's solicitor or anything yet, but do you think that'll be all right?'

I looked down at Max. He was lying on the floor while Kiran sat beside him, using him as a backrest. The labrador saw me looking at him and thumped his tail, happily.

'I think that's a great idea,' I said.

Acknowledgements

A lot of research goes into a David Hunter novel that never makes it into print, and without the help of real-life experts it would take me even longer to write them. Thank you to Tim Thomson, Professor of Anthropology at Maynooth University; forensic ecologist Professor Patricia Wiltshire, whose books *Traces* and *The Natural History of Crime* provide fascinating insights into real-life cases; and Tony Cook OBE, Head of Operations at the UK's National Crime Agency.

Thanks are also due to my agent Gordon Wise and colleagues at Curtis Brown; my UK editors Sam Eades and Louisa Cusworth and the team at Orion; my German editors Ulrike Beck, Friederike Ney and all at Rowohlt, and to Ben Steiner for the read-through.

Lastly, thank you to my wife Hilary, for reading more drafts of *The Bone Garden* than anyone should have to.

Simon Beckett

Credits

Orion Fiction would like to thank everyone at Orion who worked on the publication of *The Bone Garden*.

Editor
Sam Eades
Leodora Darlington

Copy-editor
Alex Davis

Proofreader
Francine Brody

Editorial Management
Anshuman Yadav
Snigdha Koirala
Jane Hughes
Charlie Panayiotou
Lucy Bilton
Patrice Nelson

Audio
Paul Stark
Louise Richardson
Georgina Cutler-Ross

Contracts
Rachel Monte
Ellie Bowker
Tabitha Gresty

Design
Charlotte Abrams-Simpson
Nick Shah
Deborah Francois
Helen Ewing

Photo Shoots & Image Research
Natalie Dawkins

Finance
Nick Gibson
Jasdip Nandra
Sue Baker
Tom Costello

Inventory
Jo Jacobs
Dan Stevens

Production
Ruth Sharvell
Katie Horrocks

Marketing
Hennah Sandhu

Publicity
Sian Baldwin

Sales
Dave Murphy
Victoria Laws
Esther Waters
Group Sales teams across
Digital, Field, International and
Non-Trade

Operations
Group Sales Operations team

Rights
Rebecca Folland
Tara Hiatt
Ben Fowler
Maddie Stephens
Ruth Blakemore
Marie Henckel

If you loved *The Bone Garden*, find out where the story began in *The Chemistry of Death*!

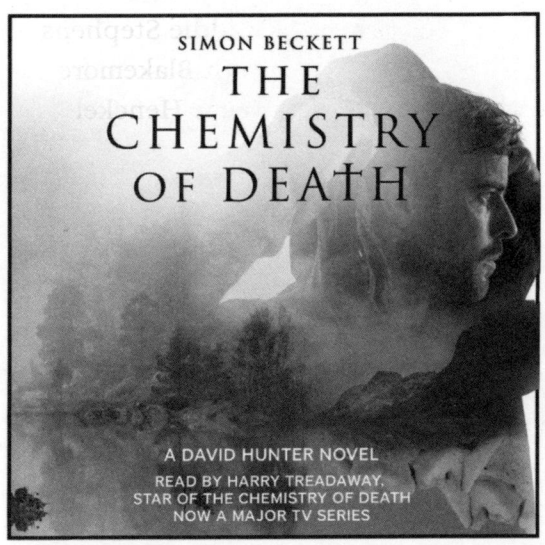

Dr David Hunter hoped he might at last have put the past behind him. But then they found what was left of Sally Palmer and no one, not even Hunter is safe from suspicion . . .

The thrilling audiobook, read by Harry Treadway, is out now!

Gone but never forgotten . . .

LOST

'A terrific thriller
from our finest
crime writer'
PETER JAMES

**SIMON
BECKETT**

THE *MULTIMILLION COPY* BESTSELLER

A MISSING CHILD

Ten years ago, the disappearance of firearms police officer
Jonah Colley's young son almost destroyed him.

A GRUESOME DISCOVERY

A plea for help from an old friend leads Jonah to Slaughter
Quay, and the discovery of four bodies. Brutally attacked and
left for dead, he is the only survivor.

A SEARCH FOR THE TRUTH

Under suspicion himself, he uncovers a network of secrets
and lies about the people he thought he knew - forcing him
to question what really happened all those years ago...

Dr David Hunter returns for his biggest case yet
in *Whispers of the Dead*.

A serial killer is at work, and the death toll is rising.
Can Dr David Hunter find the killer before they strike again?

The heart-stopping audiobook, read by Harry Treadway,
is out now!

Don't miss *Written in Bone*, the second thrilling adventure
featuring forensic anthropologist Dr David Hunter!

An isolated community. A killer on the loose. A murder
disguised as an accident. Dr David Hunter is in a race against
time to discover the culprit before the death toll rises . . .

The gripping audiobook, read by Harry Treadway,
is out now!

RAISING READERS
Books Build Bright Futures

Dear Reader,

We'd love your attention for one more page to tell you about the crisis in children's reading, and what we can all do.

Studies have shown that reading for fun is the **single biggest predictor of a child's future life chances** – more than family circumstance, parents' educational background or income. It improves academic results, mental health, wealth, communication skills, ambition and happiness.[1]

The number of children reading for fun is in rapid decline. Young people have a lot of competition for their time. In 2024, 1 in 10 children and young people in the UK aged 5 to 18 did not own a single book at home.[2]

Hachette works extensively with schools, libraries and literacy charities, but here are some ways we can all raise more readers:

- Reading to children for just 10 minutes a day makes a difference
- Don't give up if children aren't regular readers – there will be books for them!
- Visit bookshops and libraries to get recommendations
- Encourage them to listen to audiobooks
- Support school libraries
- Give books as gifts

There's a lot more information about how to encourage children to read on our website: **www.RaisingReaders.co.uk**

Thank you for reading.

hachette
UK

[1] OECD, '21st-Century Readers: Developing Literacy Skills in a Digital World', 2021, https://www.oecd.org/en/publications/21st-century-readers_a83d84cb-en.html

[2] National Literacy Trust, 'Book Ownership in 2024', November 2024, https://literacytrust.org.uk/research-services/research-reports/book-ownership-in-2024